Make time for friends. Make time for

DEBBIE MACOMBER

EDAR COVE
6 Lighthouse Road
04 Rosewood Lane
11 Pelican Court
44 Cranberry Point
50 Harbor Street
6 Rainier Drive
74 Seaside Avenue
Sandpiper Way
2 Pacific Boulevard
022 Evergreen Place
105 Yakima Street
Merry Little Christmas
featuring
225 Christmas Tree Lane
nd *5-B Poppy Lane*)

LOSSOM STREET
he Shop on Blossom Street
Good Yarn
usannah's Garden
previously published as
ld Boyfriends)
ack on Blossom Street
previously published as
Wednesdays at Four)
Twenty Wishes
Summer on Blossom Street
Hannah's List
A Turn in the Road

Thursdays at Eight

Christmas in Seattle
Falling for Christmas
A Mother's Gift
Angels at Christmas
A Mother's Wish
Be My Valentine
Happy Mother' s Day
On a Snowy Night
Home for Christmas
Summer in Orchard Valley
Summer Wedding Bells
Summer Brides
This Matter of Marriage
The Perfect Match

THE MANNINGS
The Manning Sisters
The Manning Brides
The Manning Grooms

THE DAKOTAS
Dakota Born
Dakota Home
Always Dakota
The Farmer Takes a Wife
(Exclusive short story)

The Perfect Match

DEBBIE MACOMBER

HARLEQUIN® MIRA®

Published in Great Britain 2015
by Harlequin MIRA, an imprint of Harlequin (UK) Limited,
Eton House, 18-24 Paradise Road,
Richmond, Surrey, TW9 1SR

ISBN 978-1-848-45375-3

59-0215

Harlequin (UK) Limited's policy is to use papers that are natural, renewable and recyclable products and made from wood grown in sustainable forests. The logging and manufacturing processes conform to the legal environmental regulations of the country of origin.

Printed and bound by
CPI Group (UK) Ltd, Croydon, CR0 4YY

CONTENTS

FIRST COMES MARRIAGE 9

YOURS AND MINE 179

First Comes Marriage

To Anna and Anton Adler,
Russian immigrants and
my loving grandparents.
Thank you for the wonderful heritage
you gave me.

One

"You must be Zachary Thomas," Janine said breathlessly as she whirled into the office. "Sorry I'm late, but I got hung up in traffic on Fourth Avenue. I didn't realize they'd torn up the whole street." Still a little winded, she unfastened her coat, tossed it over the back of the visitor's chair and threw herself down, facing the large executive desk.

The man on the other side blinked twice as though he didn't know quite what to think.

"I'm Janine Hartman." She drew in a deep breath. "Gramps said if he wasn't back from his appointment, I should introduce myself."

"Yes," Zachary said after a moment of strained silence. "But he didn't tell me you'd be wearing—"

"Oh, the bandanna dress," Janine said, smoothing one hand over her lap. The dress had been constructed of red and blue bandannas; it featured a knee-length zigzag hemline and closely hugged her hips. "It was a gift. And since I'm meeting the girl who made it later, I thought I should wear it."

"And the necklace?"

Janine toyed with the colored Christmas-tree lights strung between large beads on a bootlace that dangled from her neck. "It's a bit outrageous, isn't it? That was a gift, too. I think it's kind of cute, don't you? Pamela is so clever."

"Pamela?"

"A teenager from the Friendship Club."

"I…see," Zach said.

"I do volunteer work there and the two of us hit it off as soon as we met. Pam's mother doesn't live in the area and she's at that awkward age and needs a friend. For some reason she took a liking to me, which was fine because I think she's wonderful."

"I see," he said again.

Janine doubted he did.

"The necklace is *different* I'll grant you," Zach was saying—which wasn't admitting to much. His dark eyes narrowed as he studied it.

Now that she'd met Zachary Thomas, Janine could understand why her grandfather was so impressed with him—if appearances were anything to judge by. In his well-tailored suit, he was the very picture of a high-powered executive, crisp, formal and in control. He was younger than she'd assumed, possibly in his early thirties, but it was difficult to tell. His facial features were attractive enough, but he wasn't strikingly handsome. Still, she found herself fascinated by the strength of character she saw in the uneven planes of his face. His dark hair was cut military short. His jaw was strong, his cheekbones high and his mouth full. That was the way she'd describe him physically, but there was apparently much more to this man than met the eye. At least, her grandfather was convinced of it.

Several months earlier Anton Hartman had merged his well-established business-supply firm with the fast-expanding company owned by Zachary Thomas. Together the two men had quickly dominated the market.

For weeks now, Gramps had wanted Janine to meet Zachary. His name had popped up in every conversation, no matter what they were discussing. To say her grandfather thought highly of his partner was an understatement.

"Gramps has spoken…well of you," she said next.

A hint of a smile—just the merest suggestion—touched his mouth, giving her the impression that he didn't smile often. "Your grandfather has one of the keenest business minds in the country."

"He's incredible, isn't he?"

Zachary's nod betrayed no hesitation.

There was a polite knock on the door and a tall middle-aged woman wearing a navy-blue pin-striped suit stepped into the room. "Mr. Hartman phoned," she announced primly. "He's been delayed and asked that you meet him at the restaurant."

Zach's lean dark face tightened briefly before he cast Janine an uneasy glance. "Did he say when he was going to get there?"

"I'm sorry, Mr. Thomas, but he didn't."

Janine looked at her watch. She was supposed to meet Pam at three. If they were delayed much longer, she'd be late.

She scowled at Zach's apparent reluctance to entertain her in Gramp's absence. "Maybe it would be best if we rescheduled for another day," she offered brightly. She wasn't any happier about the prospect of waiting in a restaurant, just the two of them, than he was. "Gramps is held up, I'm meeting Pam, and you're obviously a busy man."

An uncomfortable silence followed her remark. "Is it your habit not to show up when your grandfather's expecting you?" he asked sharply.

Janine bristled. "Of course not." She swallowed the words to defend herself. Her suggestion hadn't been unreasonable and he had no right to insinuate that she was inconsiderate and rude.

"Then I feel we should meet your grandfather at the restaurant as he requested," he finished stiffly.

"By all means," she said, forcing a smile. She stood and reached for her coat, watching Zach from the corner of her eye. He didn't like her. That realization had a peculiar effect on Janine. She felt disappointed and a little sad. Zach hadn't said much, and actually there hadn't been time for a real conversation, but she'd sensed his attitude almost from the first. He thought of her as spoiled and frivolous, probably because he knew she didn't hold a responsible job and loved to travel. Part of her longed to explain that there were good reasons she'd chosen the lifestyle she had. But from the looks he was sending her, it would be a waste of breath.

Besides, it was more important to maintain the peace, however strained, for Gramps's sake. She'd have enjoyed getting to know Zach, perhaps even becoming friends, but that didn't seem likely.

That morning, before Gramps had left the house, he'd been as excited as a little boy about their luncheon date. He'd come down the stairs whistling when he'd joined her for breakfast, his blue eyes sparkling. When she'd refused the use of the limousine, he'd spent the next fifteen minutes giving her detailed directions, as though she'd never driven in downtown Seattle.

Almost as an afterthought, he'd mentioned that he had

a morning meeting with an important client. If he hadn't returned by the time she arrived, she was to go directly to Zach's office, introduce herself and wait for him there.

Shrugging into a raincoat, Zachary moved toward the door. "Are you ready?"

She nodded, burying her hands in her pockets.

Thankfully the restaurant her grandfather had chosen was close by. Without further discussion, they began to walk the few short blocks, although Janine had trouble matching her stride with Zach's much longer one.

Struggling to keep up with him, Janine studied Zachary Thomas, trying to determine exactly what disturbed her about the man. His height was a good example. He wasn't tall—under six feet, she guessed—and since she was almost five-eight there wasn't more than a few inches' difference between them. Why, then, did he make her feel much shorter?

He must have sensed her scrutiny because he turned and glared at her. Janine gave him a feeble smile, and felt the color rise in her cheeks. Zach's dismissive glance did nothing to boost her ego. She wasn't vain, but Janine knew she was attractive. Over the years, plenty of men had told her so, including Brian, the man who'd broken her heart. But she could have warts on her nose for all the notice Zachary Thomas gave her.

If he found the bandanna dress disconcerting, he was probably put off by her hairstyle as well. She wore it short, neatly trimmed in the back with extra-long bangs slanted across her forehead. For years Janine had kept her hair shoulder-length, parted in the middle. One afternoon a few weeks earlier, for no particular reason, she'd decided to have it cut. She was in the mood for something radical and the style she now sported seemed more appropriate to the pages of a fashion magazine. Pam had been crazy about the change, insisting she looked "phenomenal." Janine wasn't convinced. Her one comfort was that, given time, her hair would grow back.

Janine suspected Zach had characterized her as flamboyant, if not downright flashy. She, in turn, would describe him as austere and disciplined, perhaps solitary. Her grandfather saw all that, she knew, and a good deal more.

"Mr. Hartman is waiting for you," the maître d' informed them when they entered the plush waterfront restaurant. He led them across the thick carpet to a high semicircular booth upholstered in blue velvet.

"Janine, Zach." Anton Hartman smiled broadly as they approached. The years had been kind to her grandfather. His bearing was still straight and confident, although his hair had grown completely white. His deep blue eyes, only a little faded, were filled with warmth and wisdom. "I apologize for the inconvenience."

"It wasn't any problem," Zach answered for both of them before Janine could respond—as if he'd expected her to complain!

Ignoring him, Janine removed her coat and kissed her grandfather's leathery cheek.

"Janine," he began, then gasped. "Where did you get that…dress?"

"Do you like it?" She threw out her arms and whirled around once to give him the full effect. "I know it's a bit unconventional, but I didn't think you'd mind."

Gramps's gaze flickered to Zach, then back to her. "On anyone else it would be scandalous, but on you, my dear, it's a work of art."

"Honestly, Gramps," she said, laughing softly. "You never

could lie very well." She slid into the booth next to her grandfather, forcing him into the center, between her and Zach. Gramps looked a bit disgruntled, but after her turbulent first encounter with Zach, she preferred to keep her distance. For that matter, he didn't seem all that eager to be close to her, either.

She glanced at him and noted, almost smugly, that he was already studying the menu. No doubt he found ordinary conversation a waste of time. Janine picked up her own menu. She was famished. At breakfast she'd only had time for coffee and a single piece of toast, and she had every intention of making up for it now.

When the waiter came to take their order, Janine asked for the seafood entrée and soup *and* salad. She'd decide about dessert later, she said. Once he'd left, Gramps leaned toward Zach. "Janine never has to worry about her weight." He made this sound as if it was a subject of profound and personal interest to them both. "Her grandmother was the same way. How my Anna could eat, and she never gained an ounce. Janine's just like her."

"Gramps," Janine whispered under her breath. "I'm sure Zach couldn't care less how much I weigh."

"Nonsense," Gramps said, gently patting her hand. "I hope you two had the chance to introduce yourselves."

"Oh, yes," Janine returned automatically.

"Your granddaughter is everything you claimed," Zachary said, but the inflection in his voice implied something completely different to Janine than it did to her grandfather. She guessed that to Anton, he seemed courteous and complimentary. But he was telling Janine he'd found her to be the spoiled darling he'd long suspected. He didn't openly dislike her, but he wasn't too impressed with her, either.

Unfortunately, that was probably due to more than just the dress and the lightbulb necklace.

Janine watched for her grandfather's reaction to Zach's words and she knew she was right when his gaze warmed and he nodded, obviously pleased by his partner's assessment. Zachary Thomas was clever, Janine had to grant him that much.

"How did the meeting with Anderson go?" Zach asked.

For a moment her grandfather stared at him blankly. "Oh, Anderson… Fine, fine. Everything went just as I'd hoped." Then he cleared his throat and carefully spread the linen napkin across his lap. "As you both know," he said, "I've been wanting the two of you to meet for some time now. Janine is the joy of my life. She's kept me young and brought me much happiness over the years. I fear that, without her, I would have turned into a bitter old man."

His look was so full of tenderness that Janine had to lower her eyes and swallow back a rush of tears. Gramps had been her salvation, too. He'd taken her in after the sudden deaths of her parents, raised her with a gentle hand and loved her enough to allow her to be herself. It must've been difficult for him to have a six-year-old girl unexpectedly thrust into his life, but he'd never complained.

"My only son died far too young," Anton said slowly, painfully.

"I'm sorry," Zachary murmured.

The genuine compassion Janine heard in his voice surprised her. And it definitely pleased her. Zach's respect and affection for her grandfather won her immediate approval—even if the man didn't seem likely to ever feel anything so positive toward *her*.

"For many years I mourned the loss of my son and his

wife," Anton continued, his voice gaining strength. "I've worked all my life, built an empire that stretches across these fifty states, and in the process have become a wealthy man."

Janine studied her grandfather closely. He was rarely this serious. He wasn't one to list his accomplishments, and she wondered at his strange mood.

"When Zach brought his business into the area, I saw in him a rare gift, one that comes along seldom in this life. It's said that there are men who make things happen, those who watch things happen and those who wonder what happened. Zachary is a man who makes things happen. In many ways, the two of us are alike. That's one of the primary reasons I decided to approach him with a proposal to merge our companies."

"I'm honored that you should think so, sir."

"Sir," Anton repeated softly and chuckled. He raised his hand, motioning for the waiter. "You haven't called me that in six months, and there's no reason to start again now."

The waiter returned with a bottle of expensive champagne. Soon glasses were poured and set before them.

"Now," Anton continued, "as I said earlier, I have the two people I love most in this world together with me for the first time, and I don't mind telling you, it feels good." He raised his glass. "To happiness."

"Happiness," Janine echoed, sipping her champagne.

Her eyes met Zach's above the crystal flute and she saw a glint of admiration. If she were dining on it, she'd starve—to quote a favorite expression of her grandfather's—but it was just enough for her to know that he'd think more kindly of her because of her love for Anton.

Her grandfather chuckled and whispered something in his native tongue, a German dialect from the old country.

Over the years she'd picked up a smattering of the language, but when she'd repeated a few phrases to a college German professor, he'd barely recognized the words. Gramps paused and his smile lingered on Janine, then went to Zach. Whatever Gramps was muttering appeared to please him. His blue eyes fairly twinkled with delight.

"And now," he said, setting his glass aside, "I have an important announcement to make."

He turned to Janine and his face softened with affection. "I feel as though I've been an impossible burden to you, child, what with running this company." He shook his head. "Never in all my dreams did I expect to accumulate so much in a single lifetime. I've stayed in the business far longer than I should. It's time for me to retire and do a little traveling."

"It's past time," Janine said. For years, she'd been urging her grandfather to lessen his heavy work schedule. He'd often spoken of revisiting his birthplace and the surrounding countries. He talked at length of cousins and friends he'd left behind in the small German settlement. It was located in what was now part of Russia.

"This is where Zachary comes into the picture," Anton explained. "I know myself all too well. Full retirement would be impossible for me. If I stopped working, I'd shrivel up and die. That's just the way I am," he said simply.

Neither Janine nor Zachary disputed his words.

"I'll never be able to keep my fingers out of the business, yet I want to enjoy my travels. I couldn't do that if I was fretting about what was going on at the office." He paused as if he expected one of them to contradict him. "I believe I've come upon a solution. As of this afternoon, Zachary, I'm handing the reins to you. You will assume my position as chairman of the board. I realize this is sooner than we discussed, but the time is right and I hope you'll agree."

"But, Anton—"

"Gramps—"

Anton held up his hand. "I've thought about this long and hard," he said confidently. "I find Zach's honesty unquestionable, his loyalty certain and his intelligence keen. He's shrewd, perceptive and insightful. I can think of no better man, and there's no better time."

Janine noticed that Zach seemed uncomfortable with the praise. "Thank you," was all he said.

"A share of this company will belong to you someday, Janine," Anton said next. "Do you have any objections to this appointment?"

She opened her mouth, but nothing came out. Of course she approved. What else could she do? "Whatever you decide is fine with me."

Anton turned his attention to the other man. "Zachary, do you accept?"

Although their acquaintance had been brief, Janine knew instinctively that it took a lot to fluster this man. But her grandfather had managed to do so.

Zachary continued to stare at him as though he couldn't quite believe what he was hearing. But when he spoke, his voice was well modulated, revealing little emotion. "I'm honored."

"For the next few months, we'll be working closely together, much as we have in the past, but with a difference. No longer will I be showing you the ropes. I'll be handing them to you."

The first course of their lunch arrived, and after that, the conversation flowed smoothly. Her grandfather made sure of it. He was jubilant and entertaining, witty and charming. It would have been impossible not to be affected by his good humor.

When they'd finished the meal, Zachary looked at his watch. "I'm sorry to leave so soon, but I have an appointment."

Janine took a last sip of her coffee. "I should be leaving, too." She reached for her purse and coat, then slid out of the booth, waiting for her grandfather to join her.

"If neither of you objects, I'm going to linger over my coffee," Anton said, nodding toward his steaming cup.

"Of course." Janine leaned over to kiss him goodbye.

Zachary walked out to the street with her. Before he left, he shook her hand. "It's been a pleasure, Ms. Hartman."

"You're sure?" she teased, unable to stop herself.

"Yes." His eyes held hers and he smiled. She walked away feeling oddly excited about their meeting. Zach wasn't an easy person to know, but she suspected he was everything her grandfather claimed and more.

Gramps's mood remained cheerful when he got home later that evening. Janine was in the library sipping herbal tea with her feet tucked under her as she watched the local news.

Sitting in the wingback leather chair next to her, Gramps crossed his legs and chose one of his Havana cigars. Janine shook her head affectionately as he lit it; she loved her grandfather dearly and wished he'd stop smoking, though she no longer bothered to express that wish. He was the kind of man who did exactly as he chose, got exactly what he wanted. He was obviously pleased with the way their luncheon had gone, and she wondered briefly if Zach had said anything about her afterward. Somehow she doubted it.

"Well," he said after a moment, "What do you think of Zachary Thomas?" He blew a steady stream of smoke at the ceiling while he awaited her answer.

All afternoon, Janine had prepared herself for his question. Several complicated answers had presented themselves, clever replies that would sidestep her true feelings, but she used none of them now. Her grandfather expected the truth, and it was her duty to give it to him.

"I'm not sure. He's a very…reserved man, isn't he?"

Anton chuckled. "Yes, he is, but I've never known you to walk away from a challenge. The boy's a little rough around the edges, but on the inside, he's pure gold."

Janine hadn't thought of Zach in those terms—a challenge. Frankly, she doubted there'd be much reason for her to have any future contact with him. Gramps and Zach would be working closely together, but she had almost nothing to do with the business.

"I've earned his trust, but it took time," Gramps was saying now.

"I'm glad you've decided to retire," she said absently, half listening to the weather report.

"Zachary will change," her grandfather added.

He had her full attention now. "Gramps," she said patiently, holding in a laugh. "Why should he? He's achieved considerable financial success. Everything's looking good for him. What possible reason could there be for him to change?"

Anton stood and poured himself a liberal dose of brandy, swirling it slowly in the bottom of the snifter. "You're going to change him," he said after a thoughtful moment.

"Me?" Janine laughed outright. "*I'm* going to change Zachary Thomas?" she repeated in wide-eyed disbelief. That would be the day!

"Before you argue with me, and I can see that's what you're dying to do, I have a story I want to tell you. A rather sad one as it happens."

Janine picked up the remote control and snapped off the television. She'd often listened to her grandfather's parables. "So tell me."

"It's about a boy, born on the wrong side of the tracks to an alcoholic father and a weak mother. He never had much of a chance in life. His father was abusive enough for the state to remove the lad and his younger sister. He was barely eight and subjected to a long series of foster homes, but he refused to be separated from his sister. He'd promised her he'd always take care of her.

"Once, there wasn't any alternative and the two were sent to separate homes. Beside himself with worry for his sister, the young boy ran away. The authorities were in a panic, but three days later, he turned up two hundred miles away at the home where they'd placed Beth Ann."

"He probably felt responsible for her."

"Yes. Which made matters much worse when she drowned in a swimming accident. He was twelve at the time."

"Oh, no." A pain squeezed Janine's heart at the agony the boy had suffered.

"He blamed himself, of course," Anton said softly.

"The poor kid."

"This lad never seemed to belong to anyone after that," Gramps said, staring into his brandy. "He never quite fit in, but that wasn't entirely his fault." He paused to take another puff of his cigar. "His mother died a month after his sister. They were the only ones who'd ever truly loved him. He lost contact with his father, which was probably for the best. So his family was gone and no one seemed to want this troubled, hurting boy."

"Did he turn into a juvenile delinquent?" It made sense to Janine that he would; she'd dealt with a number of troubled teenagers through her volunteer work and was familiar with the tragic patterns that so often evolved in cases like this.

"No, I can't say he did." Gramps dismissed her question with a shake of his head, more interested in continuing his tale than getting sidetracked by her questions. "He drifted through adolescence without an anchor and without ever being allowed to enjoy those formative years."

"Gramps—"

He raised his hand to stop her. "When he was eighteen, he joined the military. He did well, which isn't surprising, considering his intelligence and the fact that he had little regard for his own well-being. There was no one to mourn if he died. Because of his courage, he advanced quickly, volunteering for the riskiest assignments. He traveled all over the world to some of the most dangerous political hot spots. His duties were often top secret. There's no telling how far he might have gone had he chosen to remain in the armed services, but for some reason, he resigned. No one understood why. I suspect he wanted to start his life over. This was when he opened a business-supply company. Within a year, he had my attention. His methods were aggressive and creative. I couldn't help admiring the way he handled himself and the company. Within five years, he'd become one of my most serious rivals. I saw a strength in him that age had stolen from me. We met. We talked. As a result of these talks we joined forces."

"Obviously you're telling me about Zachary's life."

Anton grinned and slowly sipped his brandy. "You noticed his remoteness quickly. I thought knowing all this would help you. Zach's never had the security that a caring home and family provide. He's never really experienced love, except what he shared with his sister, Beth Ann. His life has been a long progression of painful experiences. By sheer force of will, he's managed to overcome every obstacle placed in his path. I realize Zachary Thomas isn't going to win any Mr. Personality contests, but by heaven, he's earned my respect."

Janine had rarely heard such emotion in her grandfather's voice. "Zach told you all this?"

Anton's laughter echoed through the room. "You're joking, aren't you? Zach has never spoken of his past to me. I doubt that he has to anyone."

"You had him investigated?"

Gramps puffed on his cigar before answering. "It was necessary, although I'd guessed early on that his life hadn't been a bed of roses."

"It's all very sad, isn't it?"

"You're going to be very good for him, my dear."

Janine blinked. "Me?"

"Yes, you. You're going to teach him to laugh and enjoy life. But most important, you're going to teach him about love."

She hesitated, uncertain of her grandfather's meaning. "I don't think I understand. I realize Zach and I will probably see each other now and then since he's assuming your responsibilities with the company, but I don't see how I could have any great impact on his life."

Gramps smiled, a slow lazy smile that curved the corners

of his mouth. "That's where you're wrong, my dear. You're going to play a very big role in Zach's life, and he in yours."

Janine was still confused. "Perhaps I missed something this afternoon. I thought you made Zach the chairman of the board."

"I did." A lazy swirl of smoke circled his head.

"I don't understand where I come into the picture."

"I don't suppose you do," he said softly. "You see, Janine, I've chosen Zachary to be your husband."

Two

For a stunned moment, Janine said nothing. "You're teasing, aren't you, Gramps?"

"No," he said, lighting a second cigar. He paused to stare at the glowing tip, his eyes filled with mischief—and with something else, less easily defined. "I'm serious."

"But..." Janine's thoughts were so jumbled she couldn't make sense of them herself, let alone convey her feelings to her grandfather.

"I've been giving the matter serious consideration for some time now. Zach's perfect for you and you're the ideal complement to him. You're going to have beautiful blond-haired children."

"But..." Janine discovered she was absolutely speechless. One minute she was listening to a touching story, and the next her grandfather was telling her about the husband he'd arranged for her—and even the color of her children's hair.

"Once you think about it," Gramps said confidently, "I'm sure you'll agree with me. Zach is a fine young man, and he'll make you an excellent husband."

"You…Zach talked…agreed?" The words stumbled over the end of her tongue.

"Do you mean have I suggested this arrangement to Zach?" Gramps asked. "Heavens, no. At least not yet." He chuckled as if he found the thought amusing. "Zach wouldn't appreciate my blatant interference in his personal affairs. With him, I'll need to be far more subtle. To be honest, I considered making this marriage part of my handing over the chairmanship, but after thinking it through, I changed my mind. Zach would never have agreed. There are other ways, I decided, better ways. But I don't want you to worry about it. That's between Zach and me."

"I…see." At this point, Janine wasn't sure *what* she saw, other than one determined old man caught between two worlds. In certain respects, the old ways continued to dominate his thinking, but his success in America allowed him to appreciate more modern outlooks.

Gramps inhaled deeply on his cigar, his blue eyes twinkling. "Now, I realize you probably find the idea of an arranged marriage slightly unorthodox, but you'll get used to it. I've made a fine choice for you, and I know you're smart enough to recognize that."

"Gramps, I don't think you fully understand what you're suggesting," she said, trying to gather her scattered wits, hoping she could explain the ridiculousness of this whole scheme without offending him.

"But I do, my child."

"In this country and in this age," she continued slowly, "men and women choose their own mates. We fall in love and then marry."

Gramps frowned. "Sadly, that doesn't work," he muttered.

"What do you mean, it doesn't work?" she cried, losing her patience. "It's been like this for years and years!"

"Look at the divorce rate. I read in the paper recently that almost fifty percent of all marriages in this country fail. In the old country, there was no divorce. Parents decided whom a son or daughter would marry, and their decision was accepted without question. First comes marriage, and then comes love."

"Gramps," Janine said softly, wanting to reason this out with him. Her grandfather was a logical man; surely, if she explained it properly, he'd understand. "Things are done differently now. First comes love, then comes marriage."

"What do you young people know about love?"

"A good deal, as it happens," she returned, lying smoothly. Her first venture into love had ended with a broken heart and a shattered ego, but she'd told Gramps little if anything about Brian.

"Pfft!" he spat. "What could you possibly know of love?"

"I realize," she said, thinking fast, "that your father arranged your marriage to Grandma, but that was years ago, and in America such customs don't exist. You and I live *here* now, in the land of the free. The land of opportunity."

Gramps gazed down into his brandy for a long moment, lost in thought. Janine doubted he'd even heard her.

"I'll never forget the first time I saw my Anna," he said in a faraway voice. "She was sixteen and her hair was long and blond and fell in braids to her waist. My father spoke to her father and while they were talking, Anna and I sat at opposite ends of the room, too shy to look at each other. I wondered if she thought I was handsome. To me, she was the most beautiful girl in the world. Even now, after all these years, I can remember how my heart beat with excitement when I saw her. I knew—"

"But, Gramps, that was nearly sixty years ago! Marriages aren't decided by families anymore. A man and a woman discover each other without a father introducing them. Maybe the old ways were better back then, but it's simply not like that now." Gramps continued to stare into his glass, lost in a world long since enveloped by the passage of time.

"The next day, Anna's parents visited our farm and again our two fathers spoke. I tried to pretend I wasn't concerned, determined to accept whatever our families decided. But when I saw our fathers shake hands and slap each other on the back, I knew Anna would soon be mine."

"You loved her before you were married, didn't you?" Janine asked softly, hoping to prove her point.

"No," he returned flatly, without hesitation. "How could I love her when I'd only seen her twice before the wedding? We hadn't said more than a handful of words to each other. Love wasn't necessary for us to find happiness. Love came later, after we arrived in America."

"Wasn't it unusual for a marriage to be arranged even then? It wasn't *that* long ago." There had to be some point for her to contend, Janine mused.

"Perhaps it was unusual in other parts of the world, but not in Vibiskgrad. We were a small farming community. Our world had been ravaged by war and hate. We clung to each other, holding on to our own traditions and rituals. Soon our lives became impossible and we were forced to flee our homes."

"As I said before, I can understand how an arranged marriage—back then—might be the best for everyone involved. But I can't see it working in this day and age. I'm sorry to disappoint you, Gramps, but I'm not willing to accept Zachary Thomas as my husband, and I'm sure he'd be equally unwilling to marry me."

Briefly Gramps's face tensed with a rare display of disappointment and indignation, then quickly relaxed. Janine had seldom questioned his authority and had never openly defied him.

"I suppose this is a shock to you, isn't it?" he said.

If it astonished *her,* she couldn't wait to hear what Zachary Thomas thought! They'd only met once, but he hadn't disguised his opinion of her. He wouldn't take kindly to Gramps's plan of an arranged marriage—especially to a woman he viewed as spoiled and overindulged.

"All I'm asking is that you consider this, Janine," Gramps said. "Promise me you'll at least do that. Don't reject marriage to Zach simply because you think it's old-fashioned."

"Oh, Gramps..." Janine hated to refuse him anything. "It isn't just me. What about Zach? What about *his* plans? What if he—"

Gramps dismissed her questions with an abrupt shrug. "How often do I ask something of you?" he persisted.

Now he was going to use guilt. "Not often," she agreed, frowning at him for using unfair tactics.

"Then consider Zach for your husband!" His eyes brightened. "The two of you will have such beautiful children. A grandfather knows these things."

"I promise I'll think about it." But it wouldn't do any good! However, discretion was a virtue Janine was nurturing, and there'd never been a better time to employ it than now.

Gramps didn't mention Zach Thomas or even hint at the subject of her marrying his business partner again until the following evening. They'd just sat down to dinner, prepared to sample Mrs. McCormick's delicious fare, when Gramps looked anxiously at Janine. "So?" he asked breathlessly.

From the moment he'd walked into the house that afternoon, Gramps's mood had been light and humorous. Grinning, he handed her the platter of thinly sliced marinated and grilled flank steak. It happened to be one of Janine's favorite meals. "So?" he repeated, smiling at her. "What did you decide?"

Janine helped herself to a crisp dinner roll, buttering it slowly as her thoughts chased each other in frantic circles. "Nothing."

His smile collapsed into a frown. "You promised me you'd consider marrying Zach. I gave you more time than Anna's father gave her."

"You have to know now?"

"Now!"

"But, Gramps, a simple yes or no isn't an appropriate response to something as complex as this. You're asking me to decide on a lifelong commitment in less than twenty-four hours." She was stalling for time, and Gramps had probably guessed as much. Frankly, she didn't know what to tell him. She couldn't, wouldn't, marry Zach—even if he was willing to marry her—but she hated disappointing her grandfather.

"What's so difficult? Either you marry him or not!"

"I don't understand why you've decided to match me up with Zach Thomas," she cried. "What's wrong with Peter?" She'd been dating the other man casually for the last few months. Her heart was too bruised after what had happened with Brian for her to date anyone seriously.

"You're in love with that whitewashed weakling?"

Janine signed loudly, regretting the fact that she'd introduced Peter into their conversation. "He's very nice."

"So is chocolate mousse!" Gramps muttered. "Peter Donahue would make you a terrible husband. I'm shocked you'd even think about marrying him."

"I hadn't actually thought about him in those terms," she said. Peter was witty and fun, but Gramps was right; they weren't suited as husband and wife.

"I thank the good Lord you've been given some sense."

Janine took a deep breath and finally asked a question that had been nagging at her all afternoon. "Did—did you arrange my father's marriage?"

Gramps lowered his eyes, but not before he could disguise the pain there. "No. He fell in love with Patrice while he was in college. I knew the match wasn't a good one, but Anna reminded me that this was America and young people fell in love by themselves. She convinced me they didn't need a father's guiding hand the way we did in the old country."

"Do you think he would've listened if you'd wanted to arrange a marriage?"

Her grandfather hesitated, and his hand tightened on his water glass. "I don't know, but I'd like to believe he would have."

"Instead he married my mother."

Neither spoke for a long moment. Janine remembered little of her parents, only bits and pieces of memory, mostly unconnected. What she did recall were terrible fights and accusations, a house filled with strife. She could remember hiding under her bed when the shouting started, pressing her hands to her ears. It was her father who used to find her, who comforted her. Always her father. Her memory included almost nothing of her mother. Even pictures didn't jar her recollection, although Janine had spent hour upon hour looking at photographs, hoping to remember *something.* But the woman who'd given birth to her had remained a stranger to her in life and in death.

"You're the only consolation I have from Steven's marriage," Anton said hoarsely. "At least I had you after Steven and Patrice died."

"Oh, Gramps. I love you so much and I hate to disappoint you, but I can't marry Zach and I can't see him agreeing to marry me."

Her grandfather was silent after that, apparently mulling over her words as he finished his dinner. "I suppose I seem like a feeble old man, still trying to live the old ways."

"Gramps, no, I don't think that at all."

He planted his elbows squarely on the table and linked his fingers, gazing at her. His brow was puckered in a contemplative frown. "Perhaps it would help if you told me what you want in a husband."

She hesitated, then glanced away, avoiding eye contact. Once she'd been so certain of what she wanted. "To be perfectly honest, I'm not sure. Romance, I suppose."

"Romance." Gramps rolled the word off his tongue as though he was tasting an expensive wine.

"Yes," she said with a nod of her head, gaining confidence.

"And what exactly is romance?"

"Well..." Now that she'd been called upon to define it, Janine couldn't quite put that magical feeling into words. "It's...it's an awareness that comes from the heart."

"The heart," her grandfather repeated, smacking his palm against his chest.

"Romance is the knowledge that a man would rather die than live his life without me," she said, warming to the subject.

"You want him to die?"

"No, just to be willing."

Gramps frowned. "I don't think I understand."

"Romance is forbidden trysts on lonely Scottish moors," she added, thinking of an historical romance she'd read as a teenager.

"There aren't any moors in the Seattle area."

"Don't distract me," she said, smiling, her thoughts gaining momentum. "Romance is desperate passion."

He snorted. "That sounds more like hormones to me."

"Gramps, please!"

"How can I understand when all you say is ridiculous things? You want romance. First you claim it's a feeling in the heart, then you say it's some kind of passion."

"It's more than that. It's walking hand in hand along the beach at twilight and gazing into each other's eyes. It's speaking of love without ever having to say the words." She paused, feeling a little foolish at getting so carried away. "I don't know if I can adequately describe it."

"That's because you haven't experienced it."

"Maybe not," she agreed reluctantly. "But I will someday."

"With Zach," he said with complete assurance and a wide grin.

Janine didn't bother to argue. Gramps was being obstinate and arguing with him was pointless. The only recourse she had was time itself. Soon enough he'd realize that neither she nor Zach was going to fall in with his scheme. Then, and only then, would he drop the subject.

A week passed and Gramps hadn't said another word about arranging a marriage between her and Zachary Thomas. It was a cold windy March evening and the rain was coming down in torrents. Janine loved nights like this and was curled up in her favorite chair with a mystery novel when the doorbell chimed. Gramps had gone out for the evening and she wasn't expecting anyone.

She turned on the porch light and looked out the peephole to discover Zach standing there, a briefcase in his hand. His shoulders were hunched against the pelting rain.

"Zach," she said in surprise, throwing open the door.

"Hello, Janine," he said politely, stepping inside. "Is your grandfather here?"

"No." She held the book against her chest, her heart pounding hard. "He went out."

Zach frowned, clearly confused. "He asked me to stop by. There were some business matters he wanted to discuss. Did he say when he'd be home?"

"No, but I'm sure if he asked you over, it'll be soon. Would you care to wait for him?"

"Please."

She took his raincoat, then led him into the library where she'd been reading. A fire was burning, and its warmth hugged the room. The three-story house, situated in Seattle's Mt. Baker district, was a typical turn-of-the-century home with high ceilings and spacious rooms. The third floor had once housed several servants. Charles was their only live-in help now, and his quarters had always been an apartment over the carriage house. He worked exclusively for Gramps, driving the limousine. Mrs. McCormick arrived early in the mornings and was responsible for housekeeping and meal preparation.

"Can I get you something to drink?" she asked, once he was comfortably seated.

"Coffee, if you have it."

"I made a fresh pot about twenty minutes ago."

Janine brought him a cup from the kitchen, then sat across from Zach, wondering what, if anything, she should say about Gramps and his idea of an arranged marriage.

She doubted that Gramps had broached the subject yet. Otherwise he wouldn't be sitting there so calmly sipping coffee. He'd be outraged and infuriated, and studying him now, she concluded that he wasn't even slightly ruffled. It was on the tip of her tongue to warn him about what was coming, but she decided against it. Better that he learn the same way she had.

Lacing her fingers together, she smiled, feeling awkward and a little gauche. "It's nice to see you again."

"You, too. I'll admit I'm a bit disappointed, though."

"You are?"

"On the drive over, I was trying to guess what you'd be wearing this time. A dress made from bread sacks? A blouse constructed out of men's socks?"

She muttered under her breath, annoyed by his teasing. He had the uncanny ability to make her feel fifteen all over again. So much for any possibility that they'd ever be compatible. And Gramps seemed to think he knew them both so well.

"I'll admit that an Irish cable-knit sweater and jeans are a pleasant surprise," he said.

A flicker of admiration sparked in his dark eyes, something that had been missing the first time they met.

In that instant, Janine knew.

She went stock-still, almost dizzy with the realization. Not only had Gramps approached Zach, but they'd apparently reached some sort of agreement. Otherwise Zach would never have been this friendly, this openly appreciative. Nor would he arrive unannounced when Gramps had specifically stated that he'd be gone for the evening.

They were obviously plotting against her. Well, she had no intention of putting up with it. None. If Zach and Gramps thought they could lure her into marriage, they had a real shock coming.

Squaring her shoulders, she slid to the edge of her chair. "So you gave in to the pressure," she said, shooting him a scalding look. Unable to stay seated, she jumped to her feet and started pacing, rubbing her palms together as she cornered her thoughts. "Gramps got to you, didn't he?"

"I beg your pardon?" Zach stared up at her, his eyes curious.

"And you agreed?" She threw up her hands and groaned, "I don't believe it, I simply don't believe it. I thought better of you than this."

"What don't you believe?"

"Of all the men I've met over the years, I would've sworn you were the type who'd refuse to be bought. I'm disappointed in you, Zach."

He remained calm and unperturbed, which infuriated her more than anything he could have said or done.

"I haven't got the slightest idea what you're talking about," was all he said.

"Oh, sure, play the innocent," she snapped. She was so incensed that she continued to pace. Standing still was impossible.

In response, Zach merely glanced at his watch and drank his coffee. "Does your grandfather know you suffer from these bouts of hysteria?"

"Funny, Zach, very funny."

He exhaled an exaggerated sigh. "All right, I'll take the

bait. What makes you think I've been bought? And what exactly am I getting in exchange?"

"Technically you're not getting anything, and I want that understood this very minute, because *I* refuse to be sold." Arms akimbo, she turned to glare down at him with the full force of her disdain. "What did he offer you? The entire company? Lots of money?"

Zach shrugged. "He's offered me nothing."

"Nothing," she repeated slowly, feeling unreasonably insulted. "He was just going to *give* me away." That was enough to deflate the billowing sails of her pride. Stunned, she sat down again. "I thought the bride's family was supposed to supply some kind of dowry. Gramps didn't even offer you money?"

"Dowry?" Zach repeated the word as if he'd never heard it before.

"Gramps's family received a cow and ten chickens from my grandmother's family," she said, as if that explained everything. "But apparently I'm not even worth a single hen."

Zach set his coffee aside and sat straight in his chair. "I think we'd better begin this conversation again. I'm afraid I lost you back there when you said something about cracking under pressure. Perhaps you should enlighten me about what I'm supposed to have done."

Janine just glared at him.

"Humor me."

"All right, if you insist. It's obvious that Gramps talked to you about the marriage."

"Marriage," he echoed in a shocked voice. His face went blank. "To whom?"

"Me, of course."

Zach flung himself out of the chair, bolting to his feet. "To you?"

"Don't look so horrified! My ego's taken about all it can for one evening. I'm not exactly the Wicked Witch of the West, you know. Some men would be more than happy to marry me." Not Brian, and certainly not Peter, but she felt it was important that Zach think she was sought after.

"Marriage between us is…would be impossible. It's completely out of the question. I don't ever plan to marry—I have no use for a wife or family."

"Tell that to Gramps."

"I have every intention of doing so." His face tightened and Janine guessed her grandfather was due for an earful when he got home. "What makes that crazy old man think he can order people's lives like this?" he asked angrily.

"His own marriage was arranged for him. Trust me, Zach, I argued until I was exhausted, but Gramps hasn't given up his old-country beliefs and he thinks the two of us—now this is really ridiculous—are perfect for each other."

"If you weren't serious, I'd find this highly amusing."

Janine noticed that he seemed rather pale. "I appear to have jumped to the wrong conclusion earlier. I apologize for that but, well, I thought…I assumed Gramps had spoken to you already and you'd agreed."

"Was that when you started mumbling about a cow and a few chickens?"

She nodded and her long bangs fell over her eyes. Absently she pushed them aside. "For a moment there, I thought Gramps was offering me to you gratis. I know it's silly, but I felt insulted by that."

For the first time since they'd entered into this conversation, Zach's face softened and he granted her a faint smile. "Your grandfather loves you, no question."

"I know." Feeling self-conscious, she threaded her fingers through her hair. "I've used every argument I could come up with. I explained the importance of romance and told him how vital it is for men and women to fall in love with the person of their choice. However, he refused to accept any of it."

"He wouldn't listen to you?"

"He listened," she replied, feeling defeated, "but he disputed everything I said. Gramps says the modern version of love and marriage is a complete failure. With the divorce rate what it is, I'm afraid I don't have much of an argument."

"That's true enough," Zach said, looking frustrated.

"I told him men and women fall in love and then decide to get married, but Gramps insists it's better if marriage comes first."

Zach rubbed a hand over his face. "Now that I think about it, your grandfather's been introducing you into every conversation, telling me how wonderful you are."

Janine gasped softly. "He's done the same to me about you. He started weeks before we even met."

Pressing his lips together, Zach nodded. "A lot of things are beginning to make sense."

"What should we do?" Janine wondered aloud. "It's perfectly obvious that we'll have to agree on a plan of action. I hate to disappoint Gramps, but I'm not willing to be married off like…like…" Words failed her.

"Especially to me."

Although his low words were devoid of emotion, Janine recognized the pain behind his statement. Knowing what she did about his past, the fact that he'd experienced only brief patches of love in his life and little or no approval tugged at her heart.

"I didn't mean it to sound like that," she insisted. "My grandfather wouldn't have chosen you if he didn't think you were pretty special. He prides himself on his ability to judge character, and he's always been impressed with you."

"Let's not kid ourselves, Janine," Zach returned, his voice hardening. "You're an uptown girl. We're totally unsuited."

"I agree with you there, but not for the reasons you assume. From the minute I stepped into your office, you made it clear that you thought of me as some kind of snob. I'm not, but I refuse to waste my breath arguing with you."

"Fine."

"Instead of hurling insults at each other," she suggested, crossing her arms in a show of indignation, "why don't we come up with a plan to deal with Gramps's preposterous idea?"

"That isn't necessary," he countered. "I want no part of it."

"And you think I do?"

Zach said nothing.

Janine expelled her breath loudly. "It seems to me the solution is for one of us to marry someone else. That would quickly put an end to this whole thing."

"I already told you I have no intention of marrying," he said emphatically. "You're the one who insinuated you had plenty of men hanging around just waiting for you to say 'I do.'"

"None that I'd consider marrying, for heaven's sake," she grumbled. "Besides, I'm not currently in love with anyone."

Zach laughed, if the sound that came from his throat could be called a laugh. "Then find a man who's current. If you fall in and out of love that easily, surely there's got to be at least one prospect on the horizon."

"There isn't. *You're* going to have to come up with someone! Why don't you go out there and sweep some sweet young thing off her feet," she muttered sarcastically.

"I'm not willing to sacrifice my life so you can get off scot-free." His words were low and furious.

"But it's perfectly all right for *me* to sabotage mine? That makes a lot of sense."

"Okay," he said after a tense moment. He paused, shaking his head. "That idea's obviously not going to work. I guess we'll have to come up with something better."

"Okay, then." Janine gestured toward him. "It's your turn."

He glared at her, seeming to dislike her even more. In all honesty, Janine wasn't too pleased with the way she was behaving, either. She'd been sarcastic and needlessly rude, but then, Zach had driven her to it. He could be the most unpleasant man.

Still, Janine was about to say something conciliatory when the sound of the front door opening distracted her. Her gaze flew to Zach and he nodded, reassuring her that he'd handle the situation.

They'd returned to their chairs and were seated by the time Gramps appeared in the library doorway.

"Zach, I'm sorry for the delay. I'm glad to see Janine entertained you." Her grandfather smiled brightly as if to tell her he approved and hoped she'd taken advantage of this hour alone with Zach.

"We did manage to have a stimulating conversation," Zach said, his eyes briefly meeting Janine's.

"Good. Good."

Zach stood and reached for his briefcase. "There were some figures you wanted to go over with me?"

"Yes." Looking satisfied with himself, Gramps led the way out of the room. Zach followed him, with a glance back at Janine that said he'd get in touch with her later.

Later turned out to be almost a week. She was puttering around outside, trimming back the rosebushes and deciding where to plant the geraniums this year, when Mrs. McCormick came to tell her she was wanted on the phone.

"Hello," Janine said cheerfully.

"We need to talk," Zach said without preamble.

"Why?" she demanded. If he was going to keep her hanging for six anxious days, then she wasn't going to give the impression that she was thrilled to hear from him.

"Your grandfather laid his cards on the table this afternoon. I thought you might be interested in hearing what he's offering me to take you off his hands."

Three

"All right," Janine said, bracing herself. "What's he offering you? Huge bonuses?"

"No," Zach said quickly.

"Cash? I want to know exactly how much."

"He didn't offer me money."

Janine frowned. "What then?"

"I think we should meet and talk about it."

If her grandfather had openly approached Zach with the arranged-marriage idea, Janine knew darn well that Gramps would've made it worth Zach's while. Despite his claims to the contrary, it wouldn't have surprised Janine to discover that the newly appointed chairman of the board of Hartman-Thomas Business Supply had taken the bait.

"You want us to meet?" she repeated in a faltering voice.

"There's a restaurant on University Way—Italian 642. Have you heard of it?"

"No, but I'll find it."

"Meet me there at seven." Zach paused, then added, "And

listen, it might not be a good idea to tell your grandfather that we're getting together. He might misunderstand."

"I won't say anything," she promised.

Zach hesitated once more. "We have a lot to discuss."

Janine's heartbeat accelerated, and she felt the perspiration break out on her forehead. "Zach," she began, "you haven't changed your mind, have you? I mean, you're not actually considering this ridiculous idea of his? You can't… We agreed, remember?" She swiped at her forehead with the back of her free hand as she waited for him to answer.

"There's nothing to worry about," he finally said.

Replacing the receiver, Janine had the sudden horrible sensation of being completely at her grandfather's mercy. He was an unshakably stubborn man who almost always got what he wanted. Faced with a mountain, Anton Hartman either climbed it, tunneled through it or forged a path around it; failing such active alternatives, he settled down in the foothills and waited for the mountain to dissolve. He claimed he won a majority of his battles by simply displaying patience. Janine called it not knowing when to pack up and go home.

She knew her grandfather's methods, but then so did Zach. She hoped Anton's candidate for her husband would at least be able to withstand a few bribes, however tempting. Apparently he did, because he'd told her she had nothing to worry about. On the other hand, he sounded downright eager to discuss the subject with her.

"He *says* he never wants to get married," she muttered aloud in an effort to reassure herself. Indeed, Zachary Thomas was the last man who'd be humming "The Wedding March"—especially when someone else was directing the band.

Janine was waiting in the library, coat draped over her arm, when her grandfather got home at six-thirty. He kissed her dutifully on the cheek and reached for the evening paper, scanning the headlines as he settled into his big leather chair.

"Zach called," she said without thinking. She hadn't intended to mention that to Gramps.

Anton nodded. "I thought he might. You meeting him for dinner?"

"Dinner? Zach and me?" she squeaked. "No, of course not! Why would you even think I'd agree to a dinner date with…him?" Darn, she'd nearly forgotten her promise to keep their meeting a secret. She detested lying to her grandfather, but there was no help for it.

"But you are dining out?"

"Yes." She couldn't very well deny that, dressed as she was and carrying her coat.

"Then you're seeing Peter Donahue again?"

"No. Not exactly," Janine said uncomfortably, "I'm meeting a…friend."

"I see." The corners of Gramps's mouth quirked into a knowing smile.

Janine could feel the telltale heat saturating her face. She was a terrible liar and always had been. Gramps knew as surely as if she'd spelled it out that she was meeting Zach. And when she told Zach she'd let it slip, he'd be furious with her, and rightly so.

"What did Zach want?"

"What makes you think he wanted anything?" Janine asked fervently. Her heart was thundering as she edged toward the door. The sooner she escaped, the better.

"You just said Zach phoned."

"Oh. Yes, he did, earlier, but it wasn't important. Something about…something." Brilliant! She rushed out of the house before Gramps could question her further. What a fool she was. She'd blurted out the very thing she'd wanted to keep secret.

By the time Janine located the Italian restaurant in the University district and found a parking place, she was ten minutes late.

Zach was sitting in a booth in the farthest corner of the room. He frowned when he saw her and glanced at his watch, just so she'd know she'd kept him waiting.

Ignoring his disgruntled look, Janine slid onto the polished wooden bench, removed her coat and casually announced, "Gramps knows."

Zach's frown deepened. "What are you talking about?"

"He knows I'm having dinner with you," she explained. "The minute he walked in the door, I told him you'd called—I just wasn't thinking—and when he asked why, I told him it had to do with *something*. I'm sure you'll be able to make up an excuse when he asks you later."

"I thought we agreed not to say anything about our meeting."

"I know," she said, feeling guiltier than ever. "But Gramps asked if I was going out with Peter and he just looked so smug when I told him I wasn't." At Zach's sudden movement, she burst out, "Well, what was I supposed to do?"

He grunted, which wasn't much of an answer.

"If I wasn't going out with Peter, I'd have to come up with another man on the spot, and although I'm clever, I don't think *that* fast." She was breathless with frustration when she'd finished.

"Who's Peter?"

"This guy I've been seeing off and on for the past few months."

"And you're in love with him?"

"No, I'm not." Doubtless Zach would suggest she simply marry Peter and put an end to all of this annoyance.

Zach reached abruptly for the menu. "Let's order, and while we're eating we can go over what we need to discuss."

"All right," Janine said, grateful to leave the topic of her blunder. Besides, seven was later than she normally dined, and she was famished.

The waitress appeared then, and even as she filled Janine's water glass, her appreciative gaze never strayed from Zach. Once more Janine was struck by the knowledge that although he wasn't handsome in the traditional sense, he seemed to generate a good deal of female interest.

"I'll have the clam spaghetti," Janine said loudly, eyeing the attractive waitress, who seemed to be forgetting why she was there. The woman was obviously far more interested in studying Zach than in taking their order.

"I'll have the same," Zach said, smiling briefly at the waitress as he handed her his menu. "Now, what were you saying?" he asked, returning his attention to Janine.

"As I recall, you were the one who insisted we meet. Just tell me what my grandfather said and be done with it." No doubt the offer had been generous; otherwise Zach wouldn't have suggested this dinner.

Zach's hand closed around the water glass. "Anton called me into his office to ask me a series of leading questions."

"Such as?"

Zach shrugged. "What I thought of you and—"

"How'd you answer him?"

Zach took a deep breath. "I said I found you attractive, energetic, witty, a bit eccentric—"

"A bandanna dress and a string of Christmas-tree lights doesn't make me eccentric," Janine said, her voice rising despite herself.

"If the Christmas-tree lights are draped around your neck it does."

They were attracting attention, and after a few curious stares, Zach leaned closer and said, "If you're going to argue with everything I say, we'll be here all night."

"I'm sure our waitress would enjoy that," Janine snapped, then immediately regretted it. She sounded downright *jealous*—which, of course, was ridiculous.

"What are you talking about?"

"Never mind."

"Shall we return to the conversation between your grandfather and me?"

"Please," she said, properly chastised.

"Anton spent quite a long time telling me about your volunteer work at the Friendship Club and your various other community activities."

"And I'll bet his report was so glowing, I rank right up there with Joan of Arc and Florence Nightingale."

Zach grinned. "Something like that, but then he added that although you were constantly busy, he felt your life lacked contentment and purpose."

Janine could see it coming, as clearly as if she were standing on a track and a freight train was heading toward her. "Let me guess. He probably said I needed something meaningful in my life—like a husband and children."

"Exactly." Zach nodded, his grin barely restrained. "In

his opinion, marriage is the only thing that will fulfill you as a woman."

Janine groaned and sagged against the back of her seat. It was worse than she thought. And to her chagrin, Zach actually seemed amused.

"You wouldn't look so smug if he said marriage was the only thing that would fulfill you as a *man,*" she muttered. "Honestly, Zach, do I look like I'm wasting away from lack of purpose?" She gestured dramatically with her hands. "I'm happy, I'm busy…in fact I'm completely delighted with my life." It wasn't until she'd finished that she realized she was clenching her teeth.

"Don't take it so personally."

Janine rolled her eyes, wondering what his reaction would be if he was on the receiving end of this discussion.

"In case you didn't know it, Anton's a terrible chauvinist," he remarked, still smiling. "An old-fashioned word, perhaps, for an old-fashioned man."

"That's true, but he *is* my grandfather," she said. "And he's so charming, it's easy to forgive him."

Zach picked up his wineglass and gazed at it thoughtfully. "What I can't figure out is why he's so keen on marrying you off now. Why not last year? Or next year?"

"Heavens, I don't know. I suppose he thinks it's time. My biological clock's ticking away and the noise is probably keeping him awake at night. By age twenty-four, most of the women from the old country had four or five children."

"He certainly seems intent on the idea of seeing you married soon."

"Tell me about it!" Janine cried. "I'd bet cold cash that when he brought up the subject he said you were the only suitable man he'd found for me."

"Anton also said you have a generous heart, and that he feared some fast-talker would show up one day and you'd fall for him."

"Really?" she asked weakly. Her heart stopped, then jolted to life again. Anton's scenario sounded exactly like her disastrous romance with Brian. She sighed deeply. "So then he told you he wants me to marry someone he respects, someone he loves like a son. A man of discretion and wisdom and honor. A man he trusts enough to merge companies with."

Zach arched his brows. "You know your grandfather well."

"I can just imagine what came next," Janine added scathingly and her stomach tensed at her grandfather's insidious cleverness. Zach wasn't someone who could be bought, at least not with offers of money or prestige. Instead, Gramps had used a far more subtle form of inducement. He'd addressed Zach's pride, complimented his achievements, flattered him. To hear Gramps tell it, Zachary Thomas was the only man alive capable of taking on the task of becoming Janine's husband.

"What did you tell him?" she asked, her voice low.

"I told him no way."

Janine blinked back surprise mingled with a fair amount of indignation. "Just like that? Couldn't you at least have mulled it over?" Zach was staring at her as though he thought someone should rush over and take her temperature. "Forget I said that," she mumbled, fussing with her napkin in order to avoid meeting his eyes.

"I didn't want to encourage him."

"That was wise." Janine picked up her water glass and downed half the contents.

"To your grandfather's credit, he seemed to accept my answer."

"Don't count on it," Janine warned.

"Don't worry, I know him, too. He isn't going to give up easily. That's the reason I suggested you and I meet to talk about this. If we keep in touch, we can anticipate Anton's strategy."

"Good idea."

Their salads arrived and Janine frowned when the waitress tossed Zach another suggestive glance. "So," she began in a conversational tone once the woman had left, "Gramps was smart enough not to offer you a large incentive if you went along with his scheme."

"I didn't say that."

She stabbed viciously at her salad. "I hadn't expected him to stoop that low. Exactly what tactics did he use?"

"He said something about family members having use of the limousine."

Janine's fork made a clanging sound as it hit the side of her salad bowl. "He offered you the limousine if you married me? That's all?"

"Not even that," Zach explained, not bothering to disguise his amusement, "only the *use* of it."

"Why…why, that's insulting." She crammed some salad into her mouth and chewed the crisp lettuce as though it were leather.

"I considered it a step above the cow and ten chickens you suggested the first time we discussed this."

"Where he came from, a cow and ten chickens were worth a lot more than you seem to realize," Janine exclaimed, and immediately regretted raising her voice, because half the patrons in the restaurant turned to stare. She smiled blandly at those around her, then slouched forward over her salad.

She reached for a bread stick, broke it in half and glared at it. "The use of the limo," she repeated, indignant.

"Don't look so upset." He grinned. "I might have accepted."

Zach was deriving far too much pleasure from this to suit her. "Your attitude isn't helping any," she said, frowning righteously.

"I apologize."

But he didn't act the least bit apologetic. When she'd first met Zach, Janine had assumed he was a man who rarely smiled, yet in the short time they'd spent together today, he'd practically been laughing outright.

The waitress brought their entrées, but when Janine took her first bite, she realized that even the pretense of eating was more than she could manage. She felt too wretched. Tears sprang to her eyes, which embarrassed her even more, although she struggled to hide them.

"What's wrong?" Zach surprised her by asking.

Eyes averted, Janine shook her head, while she attempted to swallow. "Gramps believes I'm a poor judge of character," she finally said. And she was. Brian had proved it to her, but Gramps didn't know about Brian. "I feel like a failure."

"He didn't mean any of it," Zach said gently.

"But couldn't he have come up with something a little more flattering?"

"He needed an excuse to marry you off, otherwise his suggestion would have sounded crazy." Zach hesitated. "You know, the more we discuss this, the more ludicrous the whole thing seems." He chuckled softly and leaned forward to set his elbows on the table. "Who would've believed he'd come up with the idea of the two of us marrying?"

"Thank you very much," Janine muttered. He sat there shredding her ego and apparently found the process just short of hilarious.

"Don't let it get to you. You're not interested in me as a husband, anyway."

"You're right about that—you're the last person I'd ever consider marrying," she lashed out, then regretted her reaction when she saw his face tighten.

"That's what I thought." He attacked his spaghetti as though the clams were scampering around his plate.

The tension between them mounted. When the waitress arrived to remove their plates, Janine had barely touched her meal. Zach hadn't eaten much, either.

After paying for their dinner, Zach walked her to her car, offering no further comment. As far as Janine was concerned, their meeting hadn't been at all productive. She felt certain that Zach was everything Gramps claimed—incisive, intelligent, intuitive. But that was at the office. As a potential husband and wife, they were completely ill-suited.

"Do you still want me to keep in touch?" she asked when she'd unlocked her car door. They stood awkwardly together in the street, and Janine realized they hardly knew what to say to each other.

"I suppose we should, since neither of us is interested in falling in with this plan of his," Zach said. "We need to set our differences aside and work together, otherwise we might unknowingly play into his hands."

"I won't be swayed and you won't, either." Janine found the thought oddly disappointing.

"If and when I do marry," Zach informed her, "which I sincerely doubt, I'll choose my own bride."

It went without saying that Janine was nothing like the woman he'd want to spend his life with.

"If and when *I* marry, I'll choose my own husband," she said, sounding equally firm. And it certainly wouldn't be a man her grandfather had chosen.

"I don't know if I like boys or not," thirteen-year-old Pam Hudson admitted over a cheeseburger and French fries. "They can be so dumb."

It'd been a week since Janine's dinner with Zach, and she was surprised that the teenager's assessment of the opposite sex should so closely match her own.

"I'm not even sure I like Charlie anymore," Pam said as she stirred her catsup with a French fry. Idly she smeared it around the edges of her plate in a haphazard pattern. "I used to be so crazy about him, remember?"

Janine smiled indulgently. "Every other word was Charlie this and Charlie that."

"He can be okay, though. Remember when he brought me that long-stemmed rose and left it on my porch?"

"I remember." Janine's mind flashed to the afternoon she'd met Zach. As they left the restaurant, he'd smiled at her. It wasn't much as smiles went, but for some reason, she couldn't seem to forget how he'd held her gaze, his dark eyes gentle, as he murmured polite nonsense. Funny how little things about this man tended to pop up in her mind at the strangest moments.

"But last week," Pam continued, "Charlie was playing basketball with the guys, and when I walked by, he pretended he didn't even know me."

"That hurt, didn't it?"

"Yeah, it did," Pam confessed. "And after I bought a T-shirt for him, too."

"Does he wear it?"

A gratified smile lit the girl's eyes. "All the time."

"By the way, I like how you're doing your hair."

Pam beamed. "I want it to look more like yours."

Actually, the style suited Pam far better than it did her, Janine thought. The sides were cut close to the head, but the long bangs flopped with a life of their own—at least on Janine they did. Lately she'd taken to pinning them back.

"How are things at home?" Janine asked, watching the girl carefully. Pam's father, Jerry Hudson, was divorced and had custody of his daughter. Pam's mother worked on the East Coast. With no family in the area, Jerry felt that his daughter needed a woman's influence. He'd contacted the Friendship Club about the same time Janine had applied to be a volunteer. Since Jerry worked odd hours as a short-order cook, she'd met him only once. He seemed a decent sort, working hard to make a good life for himself and his daughter.

Pam was a marvelous kid, Janine mused, and she possessed exceptional creative talent. Even before her father could afford to buy her a sewing machine, Pam had been designing and making clothes for her Barbie dolls. Janine's bandanna dress was one of the first projects she'd completed on her new machine. Pam had made several others since; they were popular with her friends, and she was ecstatic about the success of her ideas.

"I think I might forgive Charlie,"she went on to say, her

look contemplative. "I mean, he was with the guys and everything."

"It's not cool to let his friends know he's got a girlfriend, huh?"

"Yeah, I guess...."

Janine wasn't feeling nearly as forgiving toward Zach. He'd talked about their keeping in touch, but hadn't called her since. She didn't believe for an instant that Gramps had given up on his marriage campaign, but he'd apparently decided to let the matter rest. The pressure was off, yet Janine kept expecting some word from Zach. The least he could do was call, she grumbled to herself, although she made no attempt to analyze the reasons for her disappointment.

"Maybe Charlie isn't so bad, after all," Pam murmured, then added wisely, "This is an awkward age for boys, especially in their relationships with girls."

"Say," Janine teased, "who's supposed to be the adult here, anyway? That's my line."

"Oh, sorry,"

Smiling, Janine stole a French fry from Pam's plate and popped it into her mouth.

"So when are you leaving for Scotland?" Pam wanted to know.

"Next week."

"How long are you going to be gone?"

"Ten days." The trip was an unexpected gift from her grandfather. One night shortly after she'd met Zach for dinner, Gramps had handed her a packet with airline tickets and hotel reservations. When she'd asked why, his reply had been vague, even cryptic—something about her needing to get away. Since she'd always dreamed of visiting Scotland, she'd leapt at the chance.

It wasn't until she'd driven Pam home that Janine thought she should let Zach know she was going to be out of the country. It probably wasn't important, but he'd made such a point of saying they should keep in touch....

Janine planned her visit to the office carefully, making sure Gramps would be occupied elsewhere. Since she'd been shopping for her trip, she was carrying several department and clothing store bags. She was doing this for a reason. She wanted her visit to appear unplanned, as if in the course of a busy day, she'd suddenly remembered their agreement. She felt that dropping in would seem more spontaneous than simply calling.

"Hello," she said to Zach's efficient secretary, smiling cheerfully. "Is Mr. Thomas available? I'll only need a moment of his time."

The older woman clearly disapproved of this intrusion, but although she pursed her lips, she didn't verbalize her objection. She pushed the intercom button and Janine felt a tingle of awareness at the sound of Zach's strong masculine voice.

"This is a pleasant surprise," he said, standing as Janine breezed into the room.

She set her bags on the floor and with an exaggerated sigh, eased herself into the chair opposite his desk and crossed her legs. "I'm sorry to drop in unannounced," she said casually, "but I have some news."

"No problem." His gaze fell to the bags heaped on the floor. "Looks like you had a busy afternoon."

"I was shopping."

"So I see. Any special reason?"

"It's my trousseau." Melodramatically, she pressed the back of her hand against her forehcad. "I can't take the pressure anymore. I've come to tell you I told my grandfather to go ahead and arrange the wedding. Someday, somehow, we'll learn to love each other."

"This isn't amusing. Now what's so important that it can't—"

"Mr. Thomas," his secretary said crisply over the intercom, "Mr. Hartman is here to see you."

Janine's eyes widened in panic as her startled gaze flew to Zach, who looked equally alarmed. It would be the worst possible thing for Gramps to discover Janine alone with Zach in his office. She hated to think how he'd interpret that.

"Just a minute," Zach said, reading the hysteria in her eyes. She marveled at how composed he sounded. He pointed toward a closed door and ushered her into a small room—or a large closet—that was practically a home away from home. A bar, refrigerator, microwave, sink and other conveniences were neatly arranged inside. No sooner was the door slammed shut behind her than it was jerked open again and three large shopping bags were tossed in.

Janine felt utterly ridiculous. She kept as still as she could, afraid to turn on the light and almost afraid to breathe for fear of being discovered.

With her ear against the door, she tried to listen to the conversation, hoping to discover just how long Gramps intended to plant himself in Zach's office.

Unfortunately, she could barely hear a thing. She risked opening the door a crack; a quick glance revealed that both men were facing away from her. That explained why she couldn't understand their conversation.

It was then that Janine spotted her purse. Strangling a gasp, she eased the door shut and staggered away from it. She covered her mouth as she took deep breaths. When she found the courage to edge open the door and peek again, she saw that all her grandfather had to do was glance downward.

If he shuffled his feet, his shoe would catch on the strap and he'd drag it out of the office with him.

Zach turned away from the window, and for the first time Janine could hear and see him clearly.

"I'll take care of that right away," he said evenly. He was so calm, so composed, as though he often kept women hidden in his closet. He must have noticed Janine's purse because he frowned and his gaze flew accusingly toward her.

Well, for heaven's sake, she hadn't purposely left it there for Gramps to trip over! He wasn't even supposed to be in the building. That very morning, he'd told her he was lunching at the Athletic Club with his longtime friend, Burt Coleman. Whenever Gramps ate lunch with his cronies, he spent the afternoon playing pinochle. Apparently he'd changed his habits, just so her hair would turn prematurely gray.

Several tortured minutes passed before Zach escorted Gramps to the door. The instant it was shut, Janine stepped into the office, blinking against the brightness after her wait in the dark. "My purse," she said in a strangled voice. "Do you think he saw it?"

"It would be a miracle if he didn't. Of all the stupid things to do!"

"I didn't purposely leave it out here!"

"I'm not talking about that," Zach growled. "I'm referring to your coming here in the first place. Are you crazy? You couldn't have called?"

"I…had something to tell you and I was in the neighborhood." So much for her suave, sophisticated facade. Zach was right, of course; she *could* have told him just as easily by phone.

He looked furious. "For the life of me I can't think of a solitary thing that's so important you'd do anything this foolish. If your grandfather saw the two of us together, he'd immediately jump to the wrong conclusion. Until this afternoon, everything's been peaceful. Anton hasn't mentioned your name once and, frankly, I appreciated that."

His words stung. "I…I won't make the mistake of coming again—ever," she vowed, trying to sound dignified and aloof. She gathered her purse and her bags as quickly as possible and hurried out of the office, not caring who saw her leave, including Gramps.

"Janine, you never did say why you came." Zach had followed her to the elevator.

Janine stared at the light above the elevator that indicated the floor number, as though it was a message of the utmost importance. Her hold on the bags was precarious and something was dragging against her feet, but she couldn't have cared less. "I'm sorry to have imposed on your valuable time. Now that I think about it, it wasn't even important."

"Janine," he coaxed, apparently regretting his earlier outburst. "I shouldn't have yelled."

"Yes, I know," she said smoothly. The elevator opened and with as little ceremony as possible, she slipped inside. It wasn't until she was over the threshold that she realized her purse strap was tangled around her feet.

So much for a dignified exit.

Four

"The castle of Cawdor was built in the fifteenth century and to this day remains the seat of the earl of Cawdor," the guide intoned as Janine and several other sightseers toured the famous landmark. "In William Shakespeare's *Macbeth,* the castle plays an important role. Macbeth becomes the thane of Cawdor. . . ."

For the first few days of Janine's visit to Scotland, she'd been content to explore on her own. The tours, however, helped fill in the bits and pieces of history she might otherwise have missed.

The castle of Cawdor was in northeastern Scotland. The next day, she planned to rent a car and take a meandering route toward Edinburgh, the political heart of Scotland. From what she'd read, Edinburgh Castle was an ancient fortress, built on a huge rock, that dominated the city's skyline. Gramps had booked reservations for her at an inn on the outskirts of town.

The Bonnie Inn, with its red-tiled roof and black-trimmed gables, had all the charm she'd expected, and more. Janine's room offered more character than comfort, but she felt its welcome as if she were visiting an old friend. A vase filled with fresh flowers and dainty jars of bath salts awaited her.

Eager to explore, she strolled outside to investigate the extensive garden. There was a chill in the April air and she tucked her hands in her pockets, watching with amusement as the partridges fed on the lush green lawn.

"Janine?"

At the sound of her name, she turned, and to her astonishment discovered Zach standing not more than ten feet away. "What are you doing here?" she demanded.

"Me? I was about to ask you the same question."

"I'm on vacation. Gramps gave me the trip as a gift."

"I'm here on business," Zach explained, and his brow furrowed in a suspicious frown.

Janine was doing her own share of frowning. "This is all rather convenient, don't you think?"

Zach took immediate offense. "You don't believe I planned this, do you?"

"No," she agreed reluctantly.

Zach continued to stand there, stiff and wary. "I had absolutely nothing to do with this," he said.

"If you hadn't been so rude to me the last time we met," she felt obliged to inform him, with a righteous tilt to her chin, "you'd have known well in advance that Gramps was sending me here, and we could have avoided this unpleasant shock."

"If you hadn't been in such an all-fired hurry to leave my office, you'd have discovered I was traveling here myself."

"Oh, that's perfect! Go ahead and blame me for everything," she shrieked. "As I recall, you were furious at my being anywhere near your precious office."

"All right, I'll admit I might have handled the situation poorly," Zach said, and the muscles in his jaw hardened. "But as you'll also recall, I did apologize."

"Sure you did," she said, "after you'd trampled all over my ego. I've never felt like more of a fool in my life."

"You?" Zach shouted. "It may surprise you to know that I don't make a habit of hiding women in my office."

"Do you think I enjoyed being stuffed in that...closet like a bag of dirty laundry?"

"What was I supposed to do? Hide you under my desk?"

"It might've been better than a pitch-black closet."

"If you're so keen on casting blame, let me remind you I wasn't the one who left my purse in full view of your grandfather," Zach said. "I did everything but perform card tricks to draw his attention away from it."

"You make it sound like I'm at fault," Janine snapped.

"I'm not the one who popped in unexpectedly. If you had a job like everyone else—"

"If I had a job," she broke in, outraged. "You mean all the volunteer work I do doesn't count? Apparently the thirty hours a week I put in mean nothing. Sure, I've got a degree. Sure, I could probably have my pick of a dozen different jobs, but why take employment away from someone who really needs it when so many worthwhile organizations are hurting for volunteers?" She was breathless by the time she finished, and so angry she could feel the heat radiating from her face.

She refused to tolerate Zach's offensive insinuations any longer. From the moment they'd met, Zach had clearly viewed her as spoiled and frivolous, without a brain in her head. And it seemed that nothing had altered his opinion.

"Listen, I didn't mean—"

"It's obvious to me," she said bluntly, "that you and I are

never going to agree on anything." She was so furious she couldn't keep her anger in check. "The best thing for us to do is completely ignore each other. It's obvious that you don't want anything to do with me and, frankly, I feel the same way about you. So, good day, Mr. Thomas." With that she walked away, her head high and her pride intact.

For the very first time with this man, she'd been able to make a grand exit. It should have felt good. But it didn't.

An hour later, after Janine had taken the tourist bus into Edinburgh, she was still brooding over her latest encounter with Zachary Thomas. If there was any humor at all in this situation, it had to be the fact that her usually sage grandfather could possibly believe she and Zach were in any way suited.

Determined to put the man out of her mind, Janine wandered down Princes Street, which was packed with shoppers, troupes of actors giving impromptu performances and strolling musicians. Her mood couldn't help but be influenced by the festive flavor, and she soon found herself smiling despite the unpleasant confrontation with her grandfather's business partner.

Several of the men who passed her in the street were dressed in kilts, and Janine felt as if she'd stepped into another time, another world. The air swirled with bagpipe music. The city itself seemed gray and gloomy, a dull background for the colorful sights and sounds, the excitement of ages past.

It was as Janine walked out of a dress shop that she bumped into Zach a second time. He stopped, his eyes registering surprise and what looked to Janine like a hint of regret—as though confronting her twice in the same day was enough to try anyone's patience.

"I know what you're thinking," he said, pinning her with his dark intense gaze.

"And I'm equally confident that you don't." She held her packages close and edged against the shop window to avoid hindering other pedestrians on the crowded sidewalk.

"I came here to do some shopping," Zach said gruffly. "I wasn't following you."

"You can rest assured I wasn't following *you.*"

"Fine," he said.

"Fine," she repeated.

But neither of them moved for several nerve-racking seconds. Janine assumed Zach was going to say something else. Perhaps she secretly hoped he would. If they couldn't be friends, Janine would've preferred they remain allies. They should be uniting their forces instead of battling each other. Without a word, Zach gestured abruptly and wheeled around to join the stream of people hurrying down the sidewalk.

A half hour later, with more packages added to her collection, Janine strolled into a fabric store, wanting to purchase a sizable length of wool as a gift for Pam. She ran her fingertips along several thick bolts of material, marveling at the bold colors. The wool felt soft, but when she lifted a corner with her palm, she was surprised by how heavy it was.

"Each clan has its own tartan," the white-haired lady in the shop explained. Janine enjoyed listening to her voice, with its enthusiastic warmth and distinct Scottish burr. "Some of the best-known tartans come in three patterns that are to be worn for different occasions—everyday, dress and battle."

Intrigued, Janine watched as the congenial woman walked around the table to remove a blue-and-green plaid. Janine had alrcady seen that pattern several times. The shop owner said that tourists were often interested in this particular tartan, called Black Watch, because it was assigned to no particular clan. In choosing Black Watch, they weren't aligning themselves with any one clan, but showing total impartiality.

Pleased, Janine purchased several yards of the fabric.

Walking down the narrow street, she was shuffling her packages in her arms when she caught sight of Zach watching a troupe of musicians. She started to move away, then for no reason she could name, paused to study him. Her impression of him really hadn't changed since that first afternoon. She still thought Zach Thomas opinionated, unreasonable and…fine, she was willing to admit it, attractive. *Very* attractive, in a sort of rough-hewn way. He lacked the polish, the superficial sophistication of a man like Brian, but he had a vigor that seemed thoroughly masculine. He also had the uncanny ability to set her teeth on edge with a single look. No other man could irritate her so quickly.

The musicians began a lively song and Zach laughed unselfconsciously. His rich husky tenor was smooth and relaxed as it drifted across the street toward her. Janine knew she should've left then, but she couldn't. Despite everything, she was intrigued.

Zach must have felt her scrutiny because he suddenly turned and their eyes locked before Janine could look away. The color rose to her cheeks and for a long moment, neither moved. Neither smiled.

It was in Janine's mind to cross the street, swallow her pride and put an end to this pointless antagonism. During the past several weeks her pride had become familiar fare; serving it up once more shouldn't be all that difficult.

She was entertaining that thought when a bus drove past her belching a thick cloud of black smoke, momentarily blocking her view of Zach. When the bus had passed, Janine noticed that he'd returned his attention to the musicians.

Disheartened, she headed in the opposite direction. She hadn't gone more than a block when she heard him call her name.

She stopped and waited for him to join her. With an inquiring lift of one eyebrow, he reached for some of her packages. She nodded, repressing a shiver of excitement as his hand brushed hers. Shifting his burden, he slowed his steps to match Janine's. Then he spoke. "We need to talk."

"I don't see how we can. Every time you open your mouth you say something insulting and offensive."

Only a few minutes earlier, Janine had been hoping to put an end to this foolish antagonism, yet here she was provoking an argument, acting just as unreasonable as she accused him of being. She stopped midstep, disgusted with herself. "I shouldn't have said that. I don't know what it is about us, but we seem to have a hard time being civil to each other."

"It might be the shock of finding each other here."

"Which brings up another subject," Janine added fervently. "If Gramps was going to arrange for us to meet, why send us halfway around the world to do it?"

"I used to think I knew your grandfather," Zach murmured. "But lately, I'm beginning to wonder. I haven't got a clue why he chose Scotland."

"He came to me with the tickets, reminding me it'd been almost a year since I'd traveled anywhere," Janine said. "He told me it was high time I took a vacation, that I needed to get away for a while. And I bought it hook, line and sinker."

"You?" Zach cried, shaking his head, clearly troubled. "Your grandfather sent me here on a wild-goose chase. Yes, there were contacts to make, but this was a trip any of our junior executives could've handled. It wasn't until I arrived at the inn and found you booked there that I realized what he was up to."

"If we hadn't been so distracted trying to figure out who was to blame for that fiasco at your office, we might've been able to prevent this. At least, we'd have guessed what Gramps was doing."

"Exactly," Zach said. "Forewarned is forearmed. Obviously, we have to put aside our differences and stay in communication. That's the key. Communication."

"Absolutely," Janine agreed, with a nod of her head.

"But letting him throw us together like this is only going to lead to trouble."

What kind of trouble, he didn't say, but Janine could guess all too easily. "I agree with you."

"The less time we spend together, the better." He paused when he noticed that she was standing in front of the bus stop.

"If we allow Gramps to throw us together, it'll just encourage him," she said. "We've got to be very firm about this, before things get completely out of hand."

"You're right." Without asking, he took the rest of the packages from her arms, adding them to the bags and parcels he already carried. "I rented a car. I don't suppose you'd accept a ride back to the inn?"

"Please." Janine was grateful for the offer. They'd started off badly, each blaming the other, but fortunately their relationship was beginning to improve. That relieved her. She'd much rather have Zachary for a friend than an enemy.

They spoke very little on the twenty-mile ride back to the Bonnie Inn. After an initial exchange of what sights they'd seen and what they'd purchased, there didn't seem to be much to say. They remained awkward and a little uneasy with each other. And Janine was all too aware of how intimate the confines of the small rented car were. Her shoulder and her thigh were within scant inches of brushing against Zach, something she was determined to ignore.

The one time Janine chanced a look in his direction, she saw how intent his features were, as if he was driving a dangerous, twisting course instead of a straight, well-maintained road with light traffic. His mouth was compressed, bracketed by deep grooves, and his dark eyes had narrowed. He glanced away from the road long enough for their eyes to meet. Janine smiled and quickly looked down, embarrassed that he'd caught her studying him so closely. She wished she could sort out her feelings, analyze all her contradictory emotions in a logical manner. She was attracted to Zach, but not in the same way she'd been attracted to Brian. Although Zach infuriated her, she admired him. Respected him. But he didn't send her senses whirling mindlessly, as Brian had. Then again, she didn't think of him as a brother, either. Her only conclusion was that her feelings for Zach were more confusing than ever.

After thanking him for the ride and collecting her parcels, she left Zach in the lobby and tiredly climbed the stairs to her room. She soaked in a hot scented bath, then changed into a blue-and-gold plaid kilt she'd bought that afternoon. With it, she wore a thin white sweater under her navy-blue blazer. She tied a navy scarf at her neck, pleased with the effect. A little blush, a dab of eye shadow and she was finished, by now more than ready for something to eat.

Zach was waiting to be seated in the dining room when she came downstairs. He wore a thick hand-knit sweater over black dress slacks and made such a virile sight she found it difficult not to stare.

The hostess greeted them with a warm smile. "Dinner for two?"

Janine reacted first, flustered and a little embarrassed. "We're not together," she said. "This gentleman was here before me." Anything else would negate the agreement they'd made earlier.

Zach frowned as he followed the hostess to a table set against the wall, close to the massive stone fireplace. The hostess returned and directed Janine to a table against the same wall, so close to Zach that she could practically read the menu over his shoulder. She was reading her own menu when Zach spoke. "Don't you think we're both being a little silly?"

"Yes," she admitted. "But earlier today we agreed that being thrown together like this could lead to trouble."

"I honestly don't think it would hurt either of us to have dinner together, do you?"

"No...I don't think it would." They'd spend the entire meal talking across the tables to each other, anyway.

He stood up, grinning. "May I join you?"

"Please." She couldn't help responding with a smile.

He pulled out the other chair, his gaze appreciative. "Those colors look good on you."

"Thanks." She had to admit he looked good—darkly vibrant and masculine—himself. She was about to return his compliment when it dawned on her how senselessly they were challenging fate.

"It's happening already," she whispered, leaning toward him in order to avoid being overheard.

"What?" Zach glanced around as though he expected ghostly clansmen to emerge from behind the drapes.

"You're telling me how good I look in blue and I was about to tell you how nice *you* look and we're smiling at each other and forming a mutual admiration society. Next thing you know, we'll be married."

"That's ridiculous!"

"Sure, you say that now, but I can see a real problem here."

"Does this mean you want me to go back to my table and eat alone?"

"Of course not. I just think it would be best if we limited the compliments. All right?"

"I'll never say anything nice about you again."

Janine smiled. "Thank you."

"You might want to watch that, as well," he warned with a roguish grin. "If we're too formal and polite with each other, that could lead us straight to the jewelers. Before we know what's happening, we'll be choosing wedding bands."

Janine's lips quivered with a barely restrained smile. "I hadn't thought about that." They glanced at each other and before either could hold it in, they were laughing, attracting the attention of everyone in the dining room. As abruptly as they'd started, they stopped, burying their faces in the menus.

After they'd ordered, Janine shared her theory with Zach, a theory that had come to her on their drive back to the inn. "I think I know why Gramps arranged for us to meet in Scotland."

"I'm dying to hear this."

"Actually, I'm afraid I'm the one responsible." She heaved a sigh of remorse. Every part of her seemed aware of Zach, which was exactly what she didn't want. She sighed again.

"When Gramps first mentioned the idea of an arranged marriage, I tried to make him understand that love wasn't something one ordered like…like dinner from a menu. He genuinely didn't seem to grasp what I was saying and asked me what a woman needed to fall in love."

"And you told him a trip to Scotland?" Zach's eyes sparkled with the question.

"Of course not. I told him a woman needed romance."

Zach leaned forward. "I hate to appear dense, but I seem to have missed something."

Pretending to be annoyed with him, Janine explained, "Well, Gramps asked me to define romance…"

"I'd be interested in learning that myself." Zach wiped the edges of his mouth with his napkin. Janine suspected he did it to cover a growing need to smile.

"It isn't all that easy to explain, you know," Janine said. "And remember this was off the top of my head. I told Gramps romance was forbidden trysts on Scottish moors."

"With an enemy clan chieftain?"

"No, with the man I loved."

"What else did you tell him?"

"I don't remember exactly. I think I said something about a moonlight stroll on the beach, and…and desperate passion."

"I wonder how he'll arrange that?"

"I don't think I want to find out," Janine murmured. Considering how seriously Gramps had taken her impromptu definition, she almost dreaded the thought of what he might do next.

When they'd finished, their plates were removed by the attentive waiter and their coffee served. To complicate her feelings, she was actually a little sad their dinner was about to end.

They left the dining room, and Zach escorted her up the stairs. “Thank you for being willing to take a risk and share dinner with me,” he said, his voice deadpan. “I enjoyed it, despite the, uh, danger.”

“I did, too,” Janine said softly. More than she cared to admit. Against her better judgment, her mind spun with possible ways to delay their parting, but she decided against each one, not wanting to tempt fate any more than she already had.

Zach walked her to her room, pausing outside her door. Janine found herself searching for the right words. She longed to tell him she’d enjoyed spending the evening with him, talking and laughing together, but she didn’t know how to say it without sounding like a woman in love.

Zach appeared to be having the same problem. He raised one hand as though to touch her face, then apparently changed his mind, dropping his hand abruptly. She felt strangely disappointed.

“Good night,” he said curtly, stepping back.

“Good night,” she echoed, turning to walk into her room. She closed the door and leaned against it, feeling unsettled but at a loss to understand why.

After ten restless minutes she ventured out again. The country garden was well lit, and a paved pathway led to rocky cliffs that fell off sharply. Even from where she stood, Janine could hear the sea roaring below. She could smell its salty tang, mixed with the scent of heath. Thrusting her hands into her blazer pockets, Janine strolled along a narrow path into the garden. The night air was cool and she had no intention of walking far, not more than a few hundred feet.

She'd return in the morning when she planned to walk as far as the cliffs with their buffeting winds.

The moon was full and so large it seemed to take up the entire sky, sending streaks of silvery light across the horizon. With her arms wrapped aroung her middle, she gazed up at it, certain she'd never felt more peaceful or serene. She closed her eyes, savoring the luxurious silence of the moment.

Suddenly it was broken. "So we meet again," Zach said from behind her.

"This is getting ridiculous." Janine turned to him and smiled, her heart beating fast. "Meeting on the moors..."

"It isn't exactly a tryst," Zach said.

"Not technically."

They stood side by side, looking into the night sky, both of them silent. During their meal they'd talked nonstop, but now Janine felt tongue-tied and ill at ease. If they'd been worried about having dinner together, they were placing themselves at even greater risk here in the moonlight.

Janine knew it. Zach knew it. But neither suggested leaving.

"It's a beautiful night," Zach said at last, linking his hands behind his back.

"It is, isn't it?" Janine replied brightly, as if he'd introduced the most stimulating topic of her entire vacation.

"I don't think we should put any stock in this," he surprised her by saying next.

"In what?"

"In meeting here, as if we'd arranged a tryst. Of course you're a beautiful woman and it would be only natural if a man...any red-blooded man were to find himself charmed. I'd blame it on the moonlight, wouldn't you?"

"Oh, I agree completely. I mean, we've been thrust together in a very romantic setting and it would be normal to…find ourselves momentarily…attracted to each other. It doesn't mean anything, though."

Zach moved behind her. "You're right, of course." He hesitated, then murmured, "You should've worn a heavier jacket." Before she could assure him that she was perfectly comfortable, he ran his hands slowly down the length of her arms, as though to warm her. Unable to restrain herself, Janine sighed and leaned against him, soaking up his warmth and his strength.

"This presents a problem, doesn't it?" he whispered, his voice husky and close to her ear. "Isn't moonlight supposed to do something strange to people?"

"I…think it only affects werewolves."

He chuckled and his breath shot a series of incredible light-as-air sensations along her neck. Janine felt she was about to crumple at his feet. Then his chin brushed the side of her face and she sighed again.

His hands on her shoulders, Zach urged her around so that she faced him, but not for anything would Janine allow her gaze to meet his.

He didn't say a word.

She didn't, either.

Janine experienced one worry after another, afraid to voice any of them. Zach apparently felt the same way, because he didn't seem any more eager to explain things than she did. Or to stop them…

After a moment, Zach pressed his hands over her cheekbones. Leisurely, his thumbs stroked the line of her jaw, her chin. His eyes were dark, his expression unreadable. Janine's heart was churning over and over, dragging her emotions with it. She swallowed, then moistened her lips.

He seemed to find her mouth mesmerizing. Somewhere deep inside, she discovered the strength to warn him that her grandfather's plan was working. She opened her mouth to speak, but before she could utter a single word, Zach's arms came around her and drew her close against him. She felt his comforting warmth seep through her, smelled the faint muskiness of his skin. The sensations were unlike anything she'd ever known. Then he lowered his mouth to hers.

The immediate shock of pleasure was almost frightening. She couldn't keep from trembling.

He drew back slightly. "You're cold. You should've said something."

"No, that's not it." Even her voice was quivering.

"Then what is?"

In response she kissed him back. She hadn't meant to, but before she could stop herself, she slipped her arms around his neck and slanted her mouth over his.

Zach's shoulders were heaving when at last she pulled her mouth away and hid her face against his chest.

"What are we doing?" he whispered. He broke hastily away from her.

Janine was too stunned to react. In an effort to hide his effect on her, she rubbed her face as though struggling to wake up from a deep sleep.

"That shouldn't have happened," Zach said stiffly.

"You're telling me," she returned raggedly. "It certainly wasn't the smartest move we could've made."

Zach jerked his fingers roughly through his hair and frowned. "I don't know what came over me. Over us. We both know better."

"It's probably because we're both tired," Janine said soothingly, offering a convenient excuse. "When you stop to think about it, the whole thing's perfectly understandable. Gramps arranged for us to meet, hoping something like this would happen. Clearly the power of suggestion is stronger than either of us realized."

"Clearly." But he continued to frown.

"Oh, gee," Janine said glancing at her watch, unable to read the numbers in the dark. Her voice was high and wavering. "Will you look at the time? I can't believe it's so late. I really should be getting back inside."

"Janine, listen. I think we should talk about this."

"Sure, but not now." All she wanted was to escape and gather some perspective on what had happened. It had all started so innocently, almost a game, but quickly turned into something far more serious.

"All right, we'll discuss it in the morning." Zach didn't sound pleased. He walked through the garden with her, muttering under his breath. "Damn it!" he said, again shoving his fingers through his hair. "I knew I should never have come here."

"There's no need to be so angry. Blame the moonlight. It obviously disrupts the brain and interferes with wave patterns or something."

"Right," Zach said, his voice still gruff.

"Well, good night," Janine managed cheerfully when they reached the staircase.

"Good night." Zach's tone was equally nonchalant.

Once Janine was in her room, she threw herself on the bed and covered her eyes with one hand. *Oh, no,* she lamented silently. They'd crossed the line. Tempted fate. Spit in the eye of common sense.

They'd kissed.

Several minutes later, still shaking, Janine got up and undressed. She slid under the blankets and tried to find a relaxing position. But she didn't feel like sleeping. Tomorrow she'd have to make polite conversation with Zach and she didn't know if she could bear it. She was sure he'd feel just as uncomfortable with her. She'd seen how he could barely look at her when they entered the inn.

Tossing aside the blankets, Janine decided she had only one option. She'd leave Scotland, the sooner the better. Grabbing the phone, she called the airport, booked a seat on the earliest flight home and immediately set about packing her bags.

Not bothering to even try to sleep, she crept down the stairs a little before midnight and checked out.

"You're leaving sooner than you expected, aren't you, Miss Hartman?" the night manager asked after calling for a cab.

"Yes," she said.

"I hope everything was satisfactory?"

"It was wonderful." She pulled a folded piece of paper from her purse and placed it on the counter. "Would you see to it that Mr. Thomas receives this in the morning?"

"Of course." The young man tucked it in a small cubbyhole behind him.

Satisfied that Zach would know she was leaving and wouldn't be concerned by her hurried return to Seattle, she sat in a chair in the small lobby to wait for her cab.

About fifteen minutes later, Janine watched silently as the cabdriver stowed her luggage in the trunk. She paused before climbing in the backseat of the car and glanced one last time at the muted moonlit landscape, disappointed that she wouldn't have an opportunity to visit the cliffs.

The ride to the airport seemed to take an eternity. She felt a burning sense of regret at leaving Scotland. She'd fallen in love with the country during her short visit and hoped someday to return. Although the memory of her evening stroll through the garden would always bring with it a certain chagrin, she couldn't completely regret that time with Zach. In fact, she'd always remember the fleeting sense of contentment she'd felt in his arms.

Janine arrived at the airport long before her flight was scheduled to leave. She spent an hour drinking coffee and leafing through fashion magazines, several of which she took with her to give to Pam later.

A cup of coffee in one hand, she approached the airline counter with her passport in the other. The bag she had draped over her shoulder accidentally collided with the man standing next to her. An automatic apology formed on her lips, but before she could voice it, that same man turned to face her.

"Zach," she cried, nearly dropping her coffee in shock. "What are you doing here?"

Five

"You think this is intentional, don't you?" Zach demanded. "It's obvious *you're* the one running after me. You found the note I slipped under your door and—"

"I checked out just before midnight so I couldn't possibly have read your note," she said angrily. "And furthermore I left a message for you."

"I didn't get it."

"Then there's been a misunderstanding."

"To say the least," Zach muttered. "A misunderstanding..." His tone was doubtful, as if he suspected she'd purposely arranged to fly home with him. She launched into an indignant protest.

"Excuse me, please."

The interruption was from a uniformed airline employee who was leaning over the counter and waving in an effort to gain their attention.

"May I have your ticket and passport?" she asked Janine. "You're holding up the line."

"Of course. I'm sorry." The best thing to do, she decided, was to ignore Zach completely. Just because they were booked on the same flight didn't mean they had to have anything to do with each other. Evidently they'd both panicked after their encounter in the garden. He was as eager to escape as she was.

Okay, so she'd ignore him and he'd ignore her. She'd return to her life, and he'd return to his. From this point forward, they need never have contact with each other again. Then they'd both be satisfied.

The airline clerk punched something into her computer. "I can give you your seat assignment now," she remarked, concentrating on the screen.

Standing on tiptoe, Janine leaned toward the woman and lowered her voice to a whisper. "Could you make sure I'm as far from Mr. Thomas's seat as possible?"

"This flight is booked solid," the attendant said impaiently. "The only reason you and your…friend were able to get seats was because of a last-minute cancellation. I'll do the best I can, but I can't rearrange everyone's seat assignments just before the flight."

"I understand," Janine said, feeling foolish and petty. But the way her luck had been going, Zach would end up in the seat beside hers, believing she'd purposely arranged that, too.

They boarded the flight separately; in fact, Zach was one of the last passengers to step onto the plane.

By that time, Janine was settled in the second row of the first-class section, flipping through the in-flight magazine. Zach strolled past her, intent on the boarding pass clutched in his hand.

Pretending she hadn't seen him seemed the best tactic, and she turned to gaze out the window.

"It seems I'm sitting here," Zach announced brusquely, loading his carry-on luggage in the compartment above the seats.

Janine had to bite her tongue to keep from insisting she'd had nothing to do with that. She'd even tried to prevent it, but she doubted Zach would believe her.

"Before you claim otherwise, I want you to know I didn't arrange this," he said, sitting down beside her.

"I know that."

"You do?"

"Of course," Janine told him. "The fates are against us. I don't know how my grandfather arranged our meeting at the airport or the adjoining seats, any more than I know why I stumbled on you my first day at the Bonnie Inn. We might never have crossed paths. But somehow, some way, Gramps is responsible." That didn't sound entirely reasonable, but she thought it best not to mention their stroll in the moonlight.

"So you're not ready to unleash the full force of your anger on me?"

"I don't see how I can be upset with you—or the reverse. Neither of us asked for this."

"Exactly."

Janine yawned loudly and covered her mouth. "Excuse me. I didn't sleep last night and now it's catching up with me."

Her yawn was contagous and soon Zach's hand was warding off his own admission of drowsiness. The flight attendant came by with coffee, which both Zach and Janine declined.

"Frankly, I'd be more interested in a pillow," Janine said, yawning again. The attendant handed her one, as well as a blanket, then offered the same to Zach. He refused both, intending to work on some papers he'd withdrawn from his briefcase. The minute the plane was safely in the air, Janine laid her head back and closed her eyes. Almost immediately she felt herself drifting into a peaceful slumber.

She stirred twice in the long hours that followed, but both times a gentle voice soothed her back to sleep. Sighing, she snuggled into the warmth, feeling more comfortable than she had in weeks.

She began to dream and could see herself walking across the moors, wearing traditional Scottish dress, while bagpipes wailed in the background.

Then, on the crest of a hill, Zach appeared, dressed in a Black Watch kilt and tam-o'-shanter; a set of bagpipes was draped over his shoulder. Their eyes met and the music ceased. Then, out of nowhere, her grandfather appeared, standing halfway between the two of them, looking distinctly pleased. He cupped his hands over his mouth and shouted to Janine."Is this romance?"

"Yes," she shouted back.

"What else do you need?"

"Love."

"Love," Gramps repeated. He turned to Zach, apparently seeking some kind of assistance.

Zach started fiddling with his bagpipes, avoiding the question. He scowled as he concentrated on his task.

"Look at the pair of you," Gramps called. "You're perfect together. Zach, when are you going to wake up and realize what a wonderful girl my Janine is?"

"If I do get married, you can be sure I'll choose my own bride," Zach hollered.

"And I'd prefer to pick out my own husband!"

"You're falling in love with Zach!" Gramps declared, obviously elated.

"I—I—" Janine was so flustered she couldn't complete her thought, which only served to please her grandfather more.

"Look at her, boy," Gramps directed his attention to Zach

again. "See how lovely she is. And think of what beautiful children you'll have."

"Gramps! Enough about babies! I'm not marrying Zach!"

"Janine." Zach's voice echoed in her ear.

"Keep out of this," she cried. He was the last person she wanted to hear from.

"You're having a dream."

Her eyes fluttered open and she saw Zach's face close to her own, her head nestled against his chest. "Oh…" she mumbled, bolting upright. "Oh, dear…I am sorry. I didn't realize I was leaning on you."

"I hated to wake you, but you seemed to be having a nightmare."

She blinked and tried to focus on him, but it was difficult, and to complicate matters her eyes started to water. She wiped her face with one sleeve. Then, straightening, she removed the pillow from behind her back and folded the blanket, trying to disguise how badly her hands were trembling.

"You're worried about what happened after dinner last night, aren't you?"

Janine released a pent-up breath and smiled brightly as she lied. "Nothing really happened."

"In the garden, when we kissed. Listen," Zach said in a low voice, glancing quickly around to ensure that no one could overhear their conversation, "I think it's time we talked about last night."

"I… You're right, of course." She didn't feel up to this, but she supposed it was best dealt with before she had to face her grandfather.

"Egos aside."

"By all means," Janine agreed. She braced herself, not

knowing what to expect. Zach had made his views on the idea of an arranged marriage plain from the first; so had she. In fact, even her feelings about a marriage based on love weren't all that positive at the moment. Brian had taught her a valuable lesson, a painful lesson, one she wouldn't easily forget. She'd given him her heart and her trust, and he'd betrayed both. Falling in love had been the most shattering experience of her life, and she had no intention of repeating it anytime soon.

"I'd be a liar if I didn't admit how nice kissing you was," Zach said, "but I wish it had never happened. It created more problems than it solved."

Janine wasn't exactly flattered by his remark. Keeping egos out of this was harder than it sounded, she thought ruefully. Her expression must have revealed her thoughts because Zach elaborated. "Before I arrived in Scotland, we hardly knew each other. We met that first afternoon over lunch—with Anton—and talked a couple of times, but basically we were strangers."

"We had dinner one night," Janine reminded him, annoyed that he could so casually dismiss it.

"Right," he acknowledged. "Then we met at the Bonnie Inn and, bingo, we were having dinner together and walking in the moonlight, and before either of us knew how it happened, we were kissing."

Janine nodded, listening quietly.

"There are several factors we can take into account, but if we're going to place blame for that kiss, I'm the one at fault."

"You?"

"Me," he confirmed with a grimace. "Actually, I'm prepared to accept full responsibility. I doubt you were aware of what was going on. It didn't take me long to see how innocent you are, and—"

"Now just a minute," Janine snapped. Once again he was taking potshots at her dignity. "What do you mean by that?"

"It's obvious you haven't had a lot of sexual experience and—"

"In other words I'm so incredibly naive that I couldn't possibly be held accountable for a few kisses in the moonlight?"

"Something like that."

"Oh, brother," she muttered.

"There's no need to feel offended."

"I wasn't exactly raised in a convent, you know. And for your information, I've been kissed by more than one man."

"I'm sure you have. But we're getting sidetracked here—"

"I'm sorry you found me so inept. A man of your vast worldly experience must've been sorely disappointed by someone as unsophisticated as me, and—"

"Janine," he said firmly, stopping her. "You're putting words in my mouth. All I was saying is that we—*I*—let matters get out of hand and we can't blame your grandfather for what happened."

"I'm willing to accept my part in this. I can also see where this conversation is leading."

"Good," Zach said. It was clear that his composure was slipping. "Then you tell me."

"You think that because I enjoyed spending time with you and we shared this mildly romantic evening and—"

"*Mildly* romantic?"

"Yes, you did say egos aside, didn't you? I'm just being honest."

"Fine," he said, tight-lipped.

"You seem to think that because you have so much more

experience than I do, there's a real danger I'll be *swooning* at your feet." She drew out the word, enjoying her silliness, and batted her eyelashes furiously.

"Janine, you're behaving like a child," he informed her coldly.

"Of course I am. That's exactly what you seem to expect of me."

Zach's fingers tightened on the armrest. "You're purposely misconstruing everything I said."

"Whatever you're trying to say isn't necessary. You figure we had a borderline interest in each other and now we've crossed that border. Right? Well, I'm telling you that you needn't worry." She sucked in a deep breath and glared at him. "I'm right, aren't I? That's what you think, isn't it?"

"Something like that, yes."

Janine nodded grimly. "And *now* you think that since you held me in your arms and you lost your control long enough to kiss me, I'm suddenly going to start entertaining thoughts of the M word."

"The…M word?"

"Marriage."

"That's ridiculous," Zach said, jamming the airline magazine back into the seat pocket in front of him.

"Well?"

"All I mean is that the temptation might be there and we should both beware of it."

"Oh, honestly, Zach," she said sarcastically, "you overestimate yourself."

"Listen, I wasn't the one mumbling about babies."

"I was having a dream! That has absolutely nothing to do with what we're talking about now."

"Could've fooled me." He reached for the same magazine

he'd recently rejected and turned the pages hard enough to rip them in two. "I don't think this discussion is getting us anywhere."

Janine sighed. "You were right, though. We did need to clear the air."

Zach made a gruff indistinguishable reply.

"I'll try to keep out of your magnetic force field, but if I occasionally succumb to your overwhelming charm and forget myself, I can only beg your forgiveness."

"Enough, Janine."

He looked so annoyed with her that she couldn't help smiling. Zach Thomas was a man of such colossal ego it would serve him right if she pretended to faint every time he glanced in her direction. The image filled her mind with laughter.

Zach leaned his head back and closed his eyes, effectively concluding their conversation. Janine stared out the window at the first signs of sunrise, thinking about all kinds of things—except her chaotic feelings for the man beside her.

Some time later, the pilot announced that the plane was approaching Seattle-Tacoma International Airport. Home sounded good to Janine, although she fully intended to have a heart-to-heart talk with her grandfather about his matchmaking efforts.

Once they'd landed, she cleared customs quickly. She struggled with her two large pieces of luggage, pulling one by the handle and looping the long strap of her carry-on bag over her shoulder. Zach was still dealing with the customs agent when she maneuvered her way outside into the bright morning sunlight, joining the line of people waiting for cabs.

"Here," Zach said, from behind her, "I'll carry one of those for you." He'd managed to travel with only his briefcase and a garment bag, which was neatly folded and easily handled.

"Thank you," she said breathlessly.

"I thought we'd agreed to limit our expressions of gratitude toward each other," he grumbled, frowning as he lifted the suitcase.

"I apologize. It slipped my mind."

Zach continued to grumble. "What'd you pack in here, anyway? Bricks?"

"If you're going to complain, I'll carry it myself."

He muttered something she couldn't hear and shook his head. "Once we get a cab—"

"We?"

"We're going to confront your grandfather."

"Together? Now?" She was exhausted, mentally and physically. They both were.

"The sooner the better, don't you think?"

The problem was, Janine hadn't given much thought to what she was going to say. Yes, she intended to challenge Gramps but she'd planned to wait for the most opportune time. And she'd hoped to speak to him privately. "He might not even be home," she argued, "and if he is, I'm not sure now would really be best."

"I want this settled once and for all."

"So do I," she said vehemently. "But I think we should choose when and how we do this more carefully, don't you?"

"Perhaps..." His agreement seemed hesitant, even grudging. "All right, we'll do it your way."

"It isn't my way. It just makes sense to organize our thoughts first. Trust me, Zach, I want this cleared up as badly as you do."

His reply was little more than a grunt, but whether it was

a comment on the weight of her suitcase or her tactics in dealing with Anton, she didn't know.

"And furthermore," she said, making a sweeping motion with her arm, "we've got to stop doubting each other. Nobody's following anyone and neither of us is in any danger of falling in love just because we were foolish enough to kiss."

"Fine," Zach murmured. He set her suitcase down as a cab arrived and the driver jumped out.

"How is it that we always seem to agree and yet we constantly find ourselves at odds?" she asked.

"I wish I knew," he said, looking weary in body and spirit. The cabdriver opened the trunk, storing her suitcases neatly inside. Zach threw his garment bag on top.

"We might as well still share this taxi," he said, holding the door for her.

"But isn't the Mt. Baker district out of your way?"

"I do need to talk to your grandfather. There're some estimates I need to give him."

"But can't it wait until tomorrow? Honestly, Zach, you're exhausted. One day isn't going to make any difference. And like I said, Gramps might not even be at the house."

Zach rubbed his eyes, then glanced irritably in her direction. "Honestly, Janine," he mocked, "you sound like a wife."

Biting her tongue to keep back her angry retort, Janine crossed her arms and glared out the side window. Indignation seeped through her with every breath she drew. Of its own accord, her foot started an impatient tapping. She could hardly wait to part company with this rude, unreasonable man.

Apparently Zach didn't know when to quit, because he added, "Now you even act like one."

She slowly turned to him and in a saccharine voice inquired, "And what's that supposed to mean?"

"Look at you, for heaven's sake. First you start nagging me and then—"

"Nagging you!" she exploded. "Let's get one thing straight, Zachary Thomas. I do *not* nag."

Zach rolled his eyes, then turned his head to gaze out the window on his side.

"Sir, sir," Janine said, sliding forward in the seat. She politely tapped the driver on the shoulder.

The middle-aged man glanced at her. "What is it, lady?"

"Sir," she said, offering him her warmest, most sincere smile. "Tell me, do I look like the kind of woman who'd nag?"

"Ah… Look, lady, all I do is drive a cab. You can ask me where a street is and I can tell you. If you want to go uptown, I can take you uptown. But when it comes to answering personal-type questions, I prefer to mind my own business."

"Are you satisfied?" Zach asked in a low voice.

"No, I'm not." She crossed her arms again and stared straight ahead.

The cabdriver's eyes met hers in the rearview mirror, and Janine tried to smile, but when she caught a glimpse of herself, she realized her effort looked more like a grimace.

"Me and the missus been married for near twenty years now," the driver said suddenly, stopping at a red light just off the James Street exit. "Me and the missus managed to stay married through the good times and the bad ones. Can't say that about a lot of folks."

"I don't suppose your wife is the type who nags, though, is she?" Zach made the question sound more like a statement, sending Janine a look that rankled.

"Betsy does her fair share. If you ask me, nagging's just part of a woman's nature."

"That's absurd," Janine countered stiffly. She should've known better than to draw a complete stranger into the discussion, especially another male who was sure to take Zach's side.

"I'll tell you the real reason me and the missus stayed together all these years," the cabbie continued in a confiding tone. "We never go to bed mad. I know I look like an easygoing guy, but I've got a temper on me. Over the years, me and Betsy have had our share of fights, but we always kiss and make up."

Janine smiled and nodded, sorry she'd ever gotten involved in this conversation.

"Go on," the cabbie urged.

Janine's puzzled gaze briefly met Zach's.

"Go on and do what?" Zach wanted to know.

"Kiss and make up." The cabbie turned for a moment to smile at them and wink at Janine. "If my wife was as pretty as yours, mister, I wouldn't be hesitating."

Janine nearly swallowed her tongue. "We are *not* married."

"And have no intention whatsoever of marrying," Zach added quickly.

The driver chuckled. "That's what they all say. The harder they deny it, the more in love they are."

He turned off Broadway and a few minutes later pulled into the circular driveway that led to Janine's house. As the talkative cabbie leapt from the car and dashed for the trunk, Janine opened her door and climbed out.

Apparently, Zach had no intention of taking her advice, because he, too, got out of the cab. It was while they were tussling with the luggage that the front door opened and Mrs. McCormick hurried outside.

"Janine," she cried, her blue eyes lighting up with surprise. "What are you doing back so soon? We weren't expecting you for another two days."

"I missed your cooking so much, I couldn't bear to stay away any longer," Janine said, throwing her arms around the older woman in a warm hug. "Has Gramps been giving you any trouble?"

"Not a bit."

Zach paid the driver, who got back in his cab, but not before he'd winked at Janine again. "Remember what I told you," he yelled, speeding off.

"How much was the fare?" Janine asked, automatically opening her purse.

"I took care of it," Zach said, reaching for his garment bag and the heavier of Janine's two suitcases. He said it as though he expected an argument from her, but if that was the case, Janine didn't plan to give him one.

"Is Gramps home?" Janine curved her arm affectionately around the housekeeper's waist as she spoke.

"He went out early this morning, but he should be back soon."

"Good," Zach mumbled, following them into the house.

"I imagine you're both starved," Mrs. McCormick said, heading toward the kitchen. "Let me whip up something for you that'll make you both glad you're home."

Left alone with Zach, Janine wasn't sure what to say to him. They'd spent almost twenty-four hours in each other's company. They'd argued. They'd talked. They'd laughed. They'd kissed.

"Janine—"

"Zach—"

They spoke simultaneously, then exchanged nervous smiles.

"You first," Zach said, gesturing toward her.

"I…I just wanted to say thanks for everything. I'll be in touch," she said. "By phone," she assured him. "So you don't need to worry about me dropping by the office unannounced."

He grinned sheepishly. "Remember, communication is the key."

"I agree one hundred percent."

They stood facing each other in the foyer. "You wanted to say something?" she prompted after a moment.

"Yes." Zach exhaled sharply, then drew a hand along the side of his jaw. "What that cabbie said is true—even for us. I don't want us to part with any bad feelings. I shouldn't have said what I did back there, about nagging. You don't nag, and I had no right to say you did."

"I overreacted." The last thing she'd expected from Zach was an apology. His eyes, dark and tender, held hers, and without even realizing what she was doing, Janine took a step forward. Zach met her and she was about to slip into his arms when the sound of the front door opening drove them apart.

"Janine," Anton cried, delighted. "Zach. My, my, this is a pleasant surprise." He chuckled softly as he removed his coat. "Tell me, was your tryst on the moors as romantic as I hoped?"

Six

"Our best bet is to present a united front," Janine said to Zach four days later. They'd met at her house early in the afternoon to outline their strategy. Gramps was gone for the day, but by the time he returned, Zach and Janine planned to be ready to talk him out of this marriage idea. The sooner Anton understood that his ploy wasn't working, the better. Then they could both get on with their lives and forget this unfortunate episode.

"It's important that we stand up to him together," Janine said when Zach didn't comment. From the moment he'd arrived, he'd given her the impression that he'd rather not be doing this. Well, she wasn't overjoyed about plotting against her grandfather, either, but in this instance it was necessary. "If we don't, I'm afraid Gramps will continue to play us against each other."

"I'm here, aren't I?" Zach grumbled. He certainly wasn't in one of his more charming moods.

"Listen, if you're going to act like this—"

"Like what?" he demanded, standing up. He walked over

to the polished oak sideboard and poured himself a cup of coffee. When he'd finished, he ambled toward the fireplace and leaned against the mantel.

"Like you're doing me a big favor," Janine elaborated.

"You're the one who's left *me* dangling for three days. Do you realize what I've been forced to endure? Anton kept giving me these smug smiles, looking so pleased with himself and the way things worked out in Scotland. Yesterday he went so far as to mention the name of a good jeweler."

Before Janine could stop herself, she was on her feet, arms akimbo, glaring at Zach. "I thought you were going to call me! Weren't you the one who said communication is the key? Then it's as if you'd dropped off the face of the earth! And for your information, it hasn't exactly been a Sunday school picnic around here, either."

"It may surprise you to learn that I have other things on my mind besides dealing with you and your grandfather."

"Implying I don't have anything to do with *my* time?"

"No," he said slowly. "Damn it, Janine, we're arguing again."

She sighed regretfully. "I know. We've got to stop this squabbling. It's counterproductive."

Zach's nod was curt and she saw that he was frowning. "What bothers me most is the way your grandfather found us the other day. We were standing so close and you were staring up at me, practically begging me to kiss you."

"I most certainly was not," she denied, knowing Zach was right. Her cheeks grew pink. She *had* wanted him to kiss her, but she hated having to admit that she would've walked into his arms without a second's hesitation. She decided to blame that unexpected longing on the exhausting flight home.

Zach shook his head and set his coffee cup carefully on the mantel. He thrust both hands into his pockets, still slouching against the fireplace wall. "The problem is, I was ready to do it. If your grandfather hadn't walked in when he did, I would've kissed you."

"You would?" she asked softly, feeling almost light-headed at his words.

Zach straightened, and a nerve in his jaw pulsed, calling her attention to the strong chiseled lines of his face. "I'm only human," he said drly. "I'm as susceptible to a beautiful woman as the next man, especially when she all but asks me to take her in my arms."

That was too much. Janine pinched her lips together to keep from crying out in anger. Taking a moment to compose herself, she closed her eyes and drew in a deep breath. "Instead of blaming each other for something that *didn't* happen, could we please return to the subject at hand, which is my grandfather?"

"All right," Zach agreed. "I'm sorry. I shouldn't have said anything." He went to the leather wingback chair and sat down. Leaning forward, he rested his elbows on his knees. "What are you going to say to him?"

"Me? I thought...I'd hoped...you'd want to do the talking."

Zach shook his head. "Tact doesn't seem to be my strong point lately."

"Okay, okay, I'll do it, if that's what you really want." She gazed silently down at the richly patterned carpet, collecting her thoughts. "I think we should tell him how much we both love and respect him and that we realize his actions have been motivated by his concern for us both and his desire for our happiness. We might even go so far as to thank him—" She stopped abruptly when Zach gave a snort of laughter. "All right, if you think you can do better, you do the talking."

"If it was up to me, I'd just tell that meddling old fool to stay out of our lives."

"Your sensitivity is really heartwarming," she muttered. "At first, this whole thing was one big joke to you and you really enjoyed tormenting me."

"You're exaggerating."

"As I recall, you played that cow-and-ten-chickens business for all it was worth, but I notice you're singing a different tune now and frankly—"

The library door opened, interrupting her tirade. Her grandfather and his longtime friend, veterinarian Dr. Burt Coleman, walked into the room.

"Zach. Janine," Gramps said, grinning broadly.

"Gramps," Janine burst out, rushing to her feet. They weren't prepared for this, and Zach was being impossible, so she said the first thing that came to mind. Pointing at Zach, she cried, "I don't know how you could possibly expect me to marry that man. He's stubborn and rude and we're completely wrong for each other." She was trembling by the time she finished, and collapsed gracelessly into the nearest chair.

"In case you haven't figured it out yet, you're no angel yourself," Zach said, scowling at Janine.

"Children, please," Gramps implored, advancing into the library, hands held out in supplication. "What seems to be the problem?"

"I want this settled," Zach said forcefully. "I'm not about to be saddled with Janine for a wife."

"As if I want to be *your* wife? In your dreams, Zachary Thomas!"

"We realize you mean well," Zach added, his face looking pinched. He completely ignored Janine. "But neither of us appreciates your matchmaking efforts."

Gramps walked over to the leather chair recently occupied by Zach and sat down. He smiled weakly at each of them, his shoulders sagging. "I thought…I'd hoped you two would grow fond of each other."

"I'm sorry to disappoint you, Gramps, I really am," Janine said, feeling guilty. "But Zach and I don't even like each other. We can barely carry on a civil conversation. He's argumentative and unreasonable—"

"And she's illogical and stubborn."

"I don't think we need to trade insults to get our message across," Janine said. Her face was so hot, she felt as if her cheeks were on fire.

"There's no hope?" Anton asked quietly.

"None whatsoever," Zach said. "Janine will make some man a wonderful wife one day, but unfortunately, he won't be me."

Her grandfather slumped against the back of his chair. "You're sure?"

"Positive," Zach said, loudly enough to convince Mrs. McCormick who was working in the kitchen.

"I love you, Gramps," said Janine, "and I'd do almost anything you wanted, but I can't and won't marry Zach. We know you have our best interests at heart, but neither of us is romantically interested in the other."

Burt Coleman, who stood by the library doors, looked as if he'd rather be anyplace else. His discomfort at witnessing this family scene was obvious. "I think it'd be best if I came back another time," he murmured as he turned to leave.

"No," Anton said, gesturing his friend back. "Come in. You've met Zachary Thomas, haven't you?"

The two men nodded at each other, but Janine noticed how rigidly Zach held himself. This meeting with Gramps hadn't gone the way she'd planned. She'd wanted everything to be calm and rational, a discussion uncluttered by messy emotions. Instead they'd ended up practically attacking each other, and worse, Janine had been the one to throw the first punch.

Without asking, she walked over to the sideboard and poured Gramps and his friend a cup of coffee. Burt sat across from her grandfather, clearly ill at ease.

"I should be going," Zach said starkly. "Good to see you again, Dr. Coleman."

"You, too," Gramps's friend said, glancing briefly at Zach. His puzzled gaze quickly returned to Anton.

"I'll walk you to the front door," Janine offered, eager to make her own escape. She closed the library door behind her.

Both she and Zach paused in the entryway. Janine tried to smile, but Zach was studying her intently, and her heart clenched like a fist inside her chest. They'd done what they had to do; she should be experiencing relief that the confrontation she'd dreaded for days was finally over. Instead she felt a strange sadness, one she couldn't fully understand or explain.

"Do you think we convinced him?"

"I don't know," Zach answered, keeping his tone low. "Your grandfather's a difficult man to read. Maybe he'll never bring up the subject of our marrying again and we're home free. I'd like to believe that's the case. It's just as likely, though, that he'll give us a few days' peace while he regroups. I don't expect him to back off quite so easily."

"No, I don't suppose he will."

Zach looked at his watch. "I should be going," he said again.

Janine was reluctant to see him leave, but there was no reason to detain him. Her hand was on the doorknob when she suddenly hesitated and turned around. "I didn't mean what I said in there," she blurted in a frenzy of regret.

"You mean you do want us to get married?"

"No," she cried, aghast. "I'm talking about when I said you were stubborn and rude. That isn't really true, but I had to come up with some reason for finding you objectionable. I don't really believe it, though."

"It was the same with me. I don't think you're so intolerable, either. I was trusting that you knew it was all an act for your grandfather's sake."

"I did," she assured him, but her pride *had* been dented, although that wasn't anything new.

"The last four days have been difficult," Zach went on. "Not only was Anton gloating about Scotland, but like I told you, he's been giving me these amused looks and odd little smiles. A couple of times I heard him saying something in his native tongue—I'm afraid to guess what."

"Well, I know what he was saying, because he's been doing the same thing to me. He's talking about babies."

"Babies?" Zach echoed, his eyes startled.

"Ours in particular."

One corner of Zach's mouth lifted, as if he found the thought of them as parents amusing. Or unlikely.

"That was my reaction, too. Every time I've seen Gramps in the last few days, he's started talking about…well, you know."

Zach nodded. “I do know. The situation hasn’t been pleasant for either of us.”

“Setting Gramps straight was for the best.” But if that was the case, why did she feel this terrible letdown? “If he accepts us at our word—and he just might—then I guess this is goodbye.”

“Yes, I suppose it is,” Zach responded, but he made no effort to leave.

Janine was glad, because these few moments gave her the opportunity to memorize his features. She stored them for the future, when there’d be no reason for her to have anything but the most infrequent and perfunctory contact with Zach.

“Unless, of course, your grandfather continues to throw us together.”

“Of course,” Janine added quickly, hating the way her heart soared at the prospect. “Naturally, we’d have to confront him again. We can’t allow ourselves to be his pawns.”

Zach was about to say something else when the library door flew open and Burt Coleman hurried out, the urgency on his face unmistakable. “Janine, I think we should call a doctor for your grandfather.”

“What’s wrong?”

“I’m not sure. He’s very pale and he seems to be having trouble breathing. It might be his heart.”

With Zach following, Janine ran into the library, her own heart in jeopardy. Dr. Coleman was right—she’d never seen her grandfather look worse. His breath came noisily and his eyes were closed as he rested his head against the back of the chair. He looked old, far older than she could ever remember seeing him. She felt a sense of panic as she raced across the room to the desk where there was a phone.

"I'm fine," Gramps said hoarsely, opening his eyes and slowly straightening. He raised his hand in an effort to stop Janine. "There's no need for everyone to go into a tizzy just because an old man wants to rest his eyes for a few minutes." His smile was weak, his complexion still pale. "Now don't go calling any doctor. I was in last week for a checkup and I'm fit as a fiddle."

"You don't look so fit," Zach countered and Janine noticed that his face seemed almost as ashen as her grandfather's. Kneeling beside him, Zach grasped his wrist and began to check his pulse.

"I'm fine," Gramps insisted again.

"Are you in any pain?"

Gramps's gaze moved from Zach to Janine. "None," he answered, dismissing their concern with a shake of his head.

"Dr. Coleman?" Janine turned to her grandfather's long-time friend. "Should I phone his doctor?"

"What does Burt know about an old man and his heart?" Gramps objected. "Burt's expertise is with horses."

"Call the doctor. Having him checked over isn't going to hurt," Burt said after a moment.

"Fiddlesticks," Gramps roared. "I'm in perfect health."

"Good," Janine said brightly. "But I'll just let Dr. Madison reassure me." She punched out the phone number and had to speak loudly in order to be heard over her grandfather's protests. A couple of minutes later, she replaced the receiver and told Zach, "Dr. Madison says we can bring him in now."

"I'm not going to waste valuable time traipsing downtown. Burt and I were going to play a few hands of cribbage."

"We can play tomorrow," Dr. Coleman said gruffly. "You keep forgetting, Anton, we're both retiring."

"I've got things to do at the office."

"No, you don't," Zach said firmly. "You've got a doctor's appointment. Janine and I are going to escort you there and we're not going to listen to a single argument. Do you understand?"

Gramps's eyes narrowed as if he were preparing a loud rebuttal. But he apparently changed his mind, because he relaxed and nodded sluggishly, reluctantly. "All right, if it'll make you feel better. But I'm telling you right now, you're going to look like a fine pair of fools."

The next two hours felt like two years to Janine. While Dr. Madison examined Gramps, she and Zach paced the waiting room. Several patients came and went.

"What could be taking so long?" Janine asked, wringing her hands nervously. "Do you think we did the right thing bringing him here? I mean, should we have gone directly to the hospital emergency room instead?"

"I doubt he would have agreed to that," Zach said.

"Do you honestly believe I would've listened to him?" She sat on the edge of a chair, her hands clenched so tightly together her knuckles whitened. "It's ridiculous, but I've never thought of Gramps as old. He's always been so healthy, so alive. I've never once considered what would happen if he became ill."

"He's going to be fine, Janine."

"You saw him," she cried, struggling against the dread and horror that churned inside her.

Zach's hand clasped hers and the fears that had torn at her composure only seconds earlier seemed to abate with his touch. He lent her confidence and strength, and she was badly in need of both.

When the door leading to the doctor's office opened, they

leapt to their feet. Zach's hand tightened around hers before he released it.

"Dr. Madison can talk to you now," the nurse told them briskly. She led them to a compact office and explained that the doctor would be with them in a few minutes. Janine sat in one of the cushioned chairs and studied the framed diplomas on the walls.

Dr. Madison came into the room moments later. He paused to shake hands with Janine and then with Zach. "So far, my tests don't show anything we need to be too concerned about," he said, shuffling through the papers on his desk.

"What happened? Why was he so pale? Why was he gasping like that?" Janine demanded.

Dr. Madison frowned and folded his hands. "I'm really not sure. He claims he hadn't been doing any strenuous exercise."

"No, he was drinking coffee and talking to a friend."

Dr. Madison nodded. "Did he recently receive any negative news regarding his business?"

"No," Janine replied, glancing at Zach. "If anything, the business is doing better than ever. Gramps is getting ready to retire. I hate the thought of anything happening to him now."

"I don't know what to tell you," Dr. Madison said thoughtfully. "He should take it easy for the next couple of days, but there's nothing to worry about that I can find."

Janine sighed and closed her eyes. "Thank God."

"Your grandfather's getting dressed now," Dr. Madison said. He stood, signaling the end of their interview. "He'll join you in a few minutes."

"Thank you, Doctor," Zach said fervently.

Relief washed through Janine like a tidal wave. She got

up and smiled at Zach. It was a smile full of gratitude. A smile one might share with a good friend when something has gone unexpectedly right. The kind of smile a woman would share with her husband. The thought hit her full force and she quickly lowered her eyes to cover her reaction.

When Gramps joined them in the waiting room, he looked immeasurably better. His blue eyes were filled with indignation and his skin tone was a healthy pink. "I hope the two of you are satisfied," he said huskily, buttoning his coat. "Most of the afternoon was wasted with this nonsense."

"You were a hundred percent correct, Gramps," Janine said brightly. "You're as fit as a fiddle and we wasted valuable cribbage time dragging you down here."

"I should've been back at the office hours ago," Zach put in, sharing a smile with Janine.

"And whose fault is that?" Anton muttered. He brushed off his sleeves as though he'd been forced to pick himself up off the floor, thanks to them.

Once more Janine and Zach shared an intimate look. They both seemed to realize what they were doing at the same moment and abruptly glanced away.

Zach drove Gramps and Janine back to the house, Gramps protesting loudly all the while that they'd overreacted and ruined his afternoon. His first concern seemed to be rescheduling his cribbage game.

Afterward Janine walked Zach to his car. "Thanks for everything," she said, folding her arms to repress the sudden urge to hug him.

"If you're worried about anything, give me a call," Zach said as he opened the car door. He hesitated fractionally, then lifted his head and gazed directly into her eyes. "Goodbye, Janine."

She raised her hand in farewell as a sadness settled over her. "Goodbye, Zach," she said forcing a lightness into her voice. "Thanks again."

For the longest moment, he said nothing, although his eyes still held hers. Finally he repeated, "Call me if you need anything, all right?"

"I will."

But they both knew she wouldn't. It was best to end this now. Make a clean break.

Janine stood in the driveway until Zach's car was well out of sight. Only then did she return to the house.

"This is really good of you," Patty St. John whispered, handing the sleeping infant to Janine. "I don't know what I would've done if I'd had to drag Michael to the interview. I need this job so badly."

"I'm happy to help." Janine peered down at the sweet face of the sleeping six-month-old baby. "I apologize if it was inconvenient for you to bring Michael here, but I've been sticking close to the house for the past few days. My grandfather hasn't been feeling well."

"It wasn't any problem," Patty whispered, setting the diaper bag on the floor. She glanced around the house. "This place is really something. I didn't have any idea that you… well, you know, that you were so well off."

"This house belongs to my grandfather," Janine explained, gently rocking Michael in her arms. The warmth and tenderness she felt toward the baby was a revelation. She supposed it was understandable, though. Gramps had spent last week constantly telling her what remarkable babies she and Zach would have, and here she was with one in her arms. All the maternal instincts she didn't know she had came bubbling to the surface.

"I'll be back in about an hour," Patty said. She leaned over and kissed Michael's soft forehead. He didn't so much as stir.

Still carrying the baby, Janine walked to the door with her friend. "Good luck."

Patty gave a strained smile and crossed her fingers. "Thanks. Here's hoping."

No sooner had the door closed than Anton walked into the living room. He paused when he saw Janine rocking in the old chair that had once belonged to his wife. His face relaxed into a broad grin.

"Is that a baby you've got there?"

Janine smiled. "Nothing gets past you, does it, Gramps?"

He chuckled. "Who's he belong to?"

"Patty St. John. She's another volunteer at the Friendship Club. She quit her job when Michael was born, but now she'd like to find some part-time work."

"Are you volunteering to babysit for her?"

"Just for today," Janine explained. "Her regular sitter has the flu."

"I thought you were going out?" Gramps muttered with a slight frown. "You haven't left the house all week. Fact is, you're becoming a recluse."

"I've had other things to do," she returned, not raising her voice for fear of disturbing the baby.

"Right. The other things you had to do were keep an eye on your grandfather," he said. "You think I didn't notice? How long do you plan on being my shadow? You should be gadding about, doing the things you normally do, instead of worrying yourself sick over me. I'm fine, I tell you. When are you going to listen to me?"

"Dr. Madison said to watch you for a few days."

"It's been a week."

Janine was well aware of it. In fact, she was beginning to suffer from cabin fever. She'd hardly spoken to anyone all week. She hadn't heard from Zach, either. Not that she'd expected to. Perhaps Gramps had taken them at their word. Or else he was doing what Zach had suspected and simply regrouping for the next skirmish.

Michael stirred in her arms and she held him against her shoulder, rocking him back to sleep.

"I'm going to the office tomorrow," Gramps announced, eyeing her defiantly as though he anticipated a challenge.

"We'll see," she said, delaying the showdown.

Yawning, baby Michael raised his head and looked around. Gramps's weathered face broke into a tender smile. "All right," he agreed easily. "We'll see." He offered the little boy his finger and Michael gripped it firmly in his hand, then started to chew on it.

Janine laughed, enjoying her grandfather's reaction to the baby. After a couple of minutes, Michael grew tired of the game with Anton's finger and yawned again, arching his back. Janine decided it was time to check his diaper. She got up, reaching for the bag Patty had left.

"I'll be back in a minute," she told her grandfather.

She was halfway across the living room when Anton stopped her. "You look good with a baby in your arms. Natural."

Janine smiled. She didn't dare let him know it felt good, too.

While she was changing the baby, she heard the doorbell. Normally she would've answered it herself, but since she was busy, either Gramps or Mrs. McCormick would see to it.

Michael was happily investigating his toes and making cooing sounds as Janine pulled up his plastic pants. "You're going to have to be patient with me, kiddo," she told him, carefully untwisting the legs of his corduroy overalls and snapping them back in place. When she'd finished, she lifted him high above her head and laughed when Michael squealed delightedly. They were both smiling when she returned to the living room.

Gramps was sitting in the chair closest to the grand piano, and across from him sat Zach.

Janine's heart lurched as her eyes flew instantly to Zach's. "Hello, Zach," she said, striving to sound as nonchalant as possible, tucking Michael against her hip. She cast a suspicious glare at her grandfather, who smiled back, the picture of innocence.

"Zach brought some papers for me to sign," Gramps explained.

"I didn't mean to interrupt you," she apologized. Her eyes refused to leave Zach's. He smiled that slanted half-smile of his that wasn't really a smile at all. The one she'd always found so appealing. Something seemed to pass between them—a tenderness, a hunger.

"Janine's not interrupting anything, is she?" Gramps asked.

"No," Zach responded gruffly. He seemed to be taking in everything about her, from her worn jeans and oversize pink sweatshirt to the gurgling baby riding so casually on her hip.

Gramps cleared his throat. "If you'll excuse me a moment, I'll go get a pen," he said, leaving them alone together.

"How have you been?" Zach asked, his eyes riveted to her.

"Fine. Just fine."

"I see you haven't had any problems finding another admirer," he murmured, nodding at Michael.

Zach kept his tone light and teasing, and Janine followed his lead. "Michael St. John," she said, turning slightly to give Zach a better view of the baby, "meet Mr. Zachary Thomas."

"Hello," Zach said, holding up his palm. He seemed awkward around children. "I take it you're watching him for a friend."

"Yes, another volunteer. She's looking for a part-time job, but she's having a problem finding one with the right hours. She's at an interview."

"I see."

Janine sank down on the ottoman in front of Zach's chair and set Michael on her knee. She focused her attention on gently bouncing the baby. "Now that your life's back in order," she said playfully, glancing up at Zach, "have you discovered how much you miss me?"

He chuckled softly. "It's been how long since we last talked? Seven days? I'm telling you, Janine, I haven't had a single disagreement with anyone in all that time."

"That should make you happy."

"You're right. It should." He shook his head. "Unfortunately it doesn't. You know what, Janine? I was bored to death. So the answer is yes, I missed you."

Seven

Before Janine could respond, Gramps wandered back into the living room, pen in hand.

"So where are those papers you wanted me to sign?" he asked Zach.

With obvious reluctance, Zach tore his gaze from Janine's. He opened his briefcase and pulled out several papers. "Go ahead and read over these contracts."

"Do you need me to sign them or not?" her grandfather grumbled.

Once more Zach dragged his gaze away from Janine. "Please."

Muttering under his breath, Gramps took the documents to the small table, scanned them and quickly scrawled his name.

Janine knew she should leave; the two men probably had business to discuss. But she couldn't make herself stand up and walk away. Not when Zach had actually admitted that he'd missed her.

Gramps broke into her thoughts. "Janine, I—"

"I was just going," she said. She clambered to her feet, securing her hold on Michael.

But Gramps surprised her.

"I want you to stay," he declared. "I wanted to talk to you and Zach. Fact is, I owe you both an apology. Burt and I had a good long talk the other day and I told him how I'd tried to arrange a marriage between the two of you. He laughed and called me an old fool, said it was time I stepped out of the Dark Ages."

"Gramps," Janine began anxiously, unwilling to discuss the subject that had brought such contention, "Zach and I have already settled that issue. We understand why you did it and…and we've laid it to rest, so there's no need to apologize."

"I'm afraid there is," Gramps insisted. "Don't worry, Burt pointed out the error of my ways. Haven't got any new tricks up my sleeve." He rose to bring Zach the signed papers, then sat wearily in the chair across from them. He'd never looked so fragile, so old and beaten.

"Janine's a wonderful woman," Zach said unexpectedly. "I want you to know I realize that."

"She's got her faults," Gramps responded, pulling a cigar from his pocket, "but she's pretty enough to compensate."

"Thank you very much," Janine whispered sarcastically and was rewarded with a grin from Zach. Gramps didn't seem to hear her; if he had, he was ignoring her comment.

"I only want the best for my granddaughter, but when I approached her about marrying you, she made a big fuss. Fact is, it would've been easier to pluck a live chicken. She said she needed *romance*." Gramps pronounced the word as if it evoked instant amusement.

"There isn't a woman alive who doesn't need romance," she wailed, defending herself.

"I'm from the old country," Gramps continued. "Romance wasn't something I knew about from personal experience, and when I asked Janine to explain, she had some trouble defining it herself. Said it was a tryst on the moors and a bunch of other hogwash. That's the reason I sent you both to Scotland."

"We figured that out soon enough," Zach said dryly.

"As you'll recall," Janine found herself saying, "that definition was off the top of my head. Romance isn't easy to explain, especially to a man who scoffs at the entire idea."

Anton chuckled, moving the cigar to the side of his mouth. "It's unfortunate the two of you caught on to me so soon. I was looking forward to arranging the desperate passion part."

"Desperate passion?" Zach echoed.

"Yes. Janine said that was part of romance, too. I may be over seventy, but I know about passion. Oh, yes, Anna and I learned about that together." His blue eyes took on a faraway look and his lips curved in the gentlest of smiles. He glanced at Janine and his smile widened.

"I'm glad you find this so funny," Janine snapped.

Gramps dismissed her anger with a flick of his hand and turned to Zach. "I suppose you've discovered she's got something of a temper?"

"From the start!" Zach declared.

"It may come as a surprise to you, Zachary Thomas," Janine said, "but you're not exactly Mr. Perfect."

"No," Zach countered smoothly. "I suspect your grandfather was thinking more along the lines of Mr. Right."

"Oh, brother!"

"Now, children, I don't see that arguing will do any good. I've willingly accepted defeat. Trying to interest you in each other was an old man's way of setting his world right before he passes on."

The doorbell chimed and, grateful for an excuse to leave the room, Janine hurried to answer it. Patty St. John stood there, her face cheerless, her posture forlorn.

"I wasn't expecting you back so soon."

"They'd already hired someone," Patty said, walking into the foyer and automatically taking her son from Janine. She held the infant close, as if his small warm body might absorb her disappointment. "I spent the whole day psyching myself up for this interview and it was all for nothing. Ah, well, who wants to be a receptionist at a dental clinic, anyway?"

"I'm so sorry," Janine murmured.

"Was Michael any problem?"

"None at all," Janine told her, wishing she could think of something encouraging to say. "I'll get his things for you."

It took Janine only a minute to collect Michael's diaper bag, but when she returned to the entryway, she discovered Zach talking to Patty. Janine saw him hand her friend a business card and overheard him suggesting she report to the Human Resources department early the following week.

"Thanks again," Patty said enthusiastically. She lifted Michael's hand. "Say bye-bye," she coaxed the baby, then raised his arm and moved it for him.

Janine let her out, with Zach standing next to her. Gramps had gone into the library, and Zach glanced anxiously in that direction before lowering his voice to a whisper. "Can you meet me later?"

"When?"

"In an hour." He checked his watch, then mentioned the

number of a pier along the waterfront. Janine had just managed to clarify the location when Gramps came back.

Zach left the house soon afterward and Janine was able to invent an excuse half an hour later. Gramps was reading and didn't bother to look up from his mystery novel, although Janine thought she saw the hint of a smile, as if he knew full well what she was doing. She didn't linger to investigate. The last time she'd agreed to a clandestine meeting with Zach had been the night they'd met at the Italian restaurant, when she'd all but blurted out the arrangements to her grandfather.

Zach was waiting for her, grim-faced. He stood against the pier railing, the wind whipping his raincoat against his legs.

"I hope there's a good reason for this, because I don't think Gramps was fooled," Janine said when she joined him. "He'll figure out that I'm meeting you if I'm not back soon." She buried her hands in her pockets, turning away from the wind. The afternoon sky was gray, threatening rain.

"Am I interrupting anything important?"

"Not really." Janine wouldn't have minded listing several pressing engagements, but she'd canceled everything for the next two weeks, wanting to stay close to home in case her grandfather needed her.

Zach clasped his hands behind his back and started strolling down the pier, the wind ruffling his neatly trimmed hair. Janine followed. "I'm worried about Anton," he said suddenly, stopping and facing Janine.

"Why?" Perhaps there was something she didn't know about his health, something Dr. Madison hadn't told her.

"He doesn't look good."

"What do you mean?" Although she asked, she already

knew the answer. She'd felt the same thing during the past few days. Gramps was aging right before her eyes.

"I think you know."

"I do," she admitted reluctantly.

"Furthermore I'm worried about you."

"Me?" she asked, her voice rising. "Whatever for?"

"If, God forbid, anything should happen to Anton," Zach said, drawing in a ragged breath, "what will happen to you? You don't have any other family, do you?"

"No," she told him, her chest tightening at the thought. "But I'm not worried about it. There are several friends who are very close to the family, Burt Coleman for one, so I wouldn't be cast into the streets like an orphan. I'll have the house and more than enough money to live on. There's no need for you to be concerned. I'm not."

"I see." Zach frowned as he walked to the farthest end of the pier, seeming to fix his gaze on the snow-capped peaks of the Olympic mountains far in the distance.

Janine hurried to catch up with him. "Why do you ask?" she demanded.

"He's always said he was concerned about your not having any other family. But it wasn't until recently that I really understood his motivation in trying to arrange a marriage between us."

"Good, then you can explain it to me, because frankly, I'm at a loss. He admitted he was wrong, but I don't think he's given up on the idea. He'd do just about anything to see the two of us together."

"I *know* he hasn't given up on us."

"What did he do? Up the ante?"

Zach chuckled and his features relaxed into a smile as he met her eyes. "Nothing so explicit. He simply told me that he's getting on in years and hates the thought of you being left so alone when he dies."

"I'll adjust. I'm not a child," she said, although her heart filled with dread at the thought of life without her cantankerous, generous, good-hearted grandfather.

"I don't doubt you would." Zach hesitated, then resumed strolling, apparently taking it for granted that she'd continue to follow him.

"I have plenty of friends."

Zach nodded, although Janine wasn't certain he'd heard her. He stopped abruptly and turned to look at her. "What I'm about to say is going to shock you."

Janine stared up at him, not knowing what to expect.

"When you think about it, our getting married does make an odd kind of sense."

"What?" Janine couldn't believe he was saying this.

"From a practical point of view," he added quickly. "Since the business is in both our names, and we're both alone. I realize I'm not exactly Prince Charming…" Zach paused as if waiting for her to contradict him. When she didn't, he frowned but went on. "The problem has more to do with whether we can get along. I don't even know if we're capable of going an entire day without arguing."

"What are you suggesting?" Janine asked, wondering if she was reading more into this conversation than he intended.

"Nothing yet. I'm trying to be as open and as honest as I can." He gripped the railing with both hands and braced himself, as though expecting a fierce wind to uproot him.

"Are you saying that our getting married wouldn't be such a bad idea after all?" Janine ventured. Initially he'd made a joke of the whole thing. Then he'd seen it as an annoyance. Now he seemed to have changed his mind again.

"I…don't know yet. I'm mulling over my thoughts, which I'm willing to confess are hopelessly tangled at the moment."

"Mine aren't much better."

"Does this mean you'd consider the possibility?"

"I don't know, either." Janine had been so sure she was in love with Brian. She remembered how he'd done everything a romantic hero should do. He'd sent her flowers, said all the things a woman longs to hear—and then he'd casually broken her heart. When she thought about it now, she couldn't really imagine herself married to Brian. But Zach, who'd never made any romantic gestures, somehow seemed to fit almost naturally into her life. And yet…

As she pondered these contradictions, Zach started walking again. "I'm not the kind of husband you want," he was saying, "and not nearly as good as you deserve. I'd like to be the man of your dreams, but I'm not. Nor am I likely to change at this stage of my life." He paused, chancing a look in her direction. "What are you thinking?"

Janine sighed and concentrated as hard as she could, but her mind was filled with so many questions, so many doubts. "Would you mind kissing me?"

Shock widened his dark eyes. He glanced around, then scowled. "Now? Right here?"

"Yes."

"There are people everywhere. Is this really necessary?"

"Would I ask you to do it if it wasn't?"

As he searched her face, she moistened her lips and looked up at him, tilting her head slightly. Zach slipped one arm around her waist and drew her close. Her heart reacted immediately, leaping into a hard fast rhythm that made her feel breathless. He lifted her chin with his free hand and slowly lowered his mouth to hers.

The instant his lips grazed hers, Janine was flooded with a sensual languor. It was as if they'd returned to the moors of Scotland with the full moon overhead, pouring magic onto their small corner of earth. Everything around them faded. No longer did Janine hear the sound of water slapping against the wooden columns of the pier. The blustery day went calm.

She supported her hands on his chest, breathing erratically, when he stopped kissing her. Neither spoke. Janine wanted to, but none of her faculties seemed to be working. She parted her lips and Zach lowered his mouth to hers again. Only this time it was a full-fledged kiss, deep and probing. His hands slid up her back as his mouth abandoned hers to explore the sweep of her neck.

Several glorious moments passed before he shuddered, raised his head and drew back, although he continued to hold her. "Does that answer your question?"

"No," she answered, hating the way her voice trembled. "I'm afraid it only raised more."

"I know what you mean," Zach admitted, briefly closing his eyes. "This last week apart was an eye-opener for me. I thought I'd be glad to put this matter between your grandfather and us to rest. If you want the truth, I thought I'd be glad to be rid of you. I was convinced you felt the same way." He paused, waiting for a response.

"The days seemed so empty," she whispered.

His eyes burned into hers, and he nodded. "You were constantly on my mind, and I found myself wishing you were there to talk to." He groaned. "Heaven knows you deserve a different kind of husband than I could possibly be."

"What about you? I've heard you say a hundred times that when it comes to finding a wife, you'll choose your own."

He blinked, as though he didn't recognize his words. Then

he shrugged. "Once I got to know you, I realized you're not so bad."

"Thanks." So much for wine and roses and sweet nothings whispered in her ear. But then again, she'd had those things and they hadn't brought her happiness.

"Like I said—and I hate to admit it—our getting married makes sense. We seem to like each other well enough, and there's a certain…attraction." Zach was frowning a little as he spoke. "It would be a smart move for both of us from a financial viewpoint, as well." He took her by the shoulders and gazed into her eyes. "The question is, Janine, can I make you happy?"

Her heart melted at the way he said it, at the simplicity and sincerity of his words. "What about you?" she asked. "Will you be content being married to me?"

The apprehension in his face eased. "I think so. We'll be good for each other. This isn't any grand passion. But I'm fond of you and you're fond of me."

"Fond?" Janine repeated, breaking away.

"What's wrong with that?"

"I hate that word," Janine said through gritted teeth. "*Fond* sounds so…watered down. So weak. I'm not looking for a grand passion, as you put it, but I want a whole lot more than *fond*." She gestured dramatically with her hands. "A man is fond of his dog or a favorite place to eat, not his wife." She spoke so vehemently that she was starting to attract attention from other walkers. "Would it be too much for you to come up with another word?"

"Stop looking at me as if it were a matter of life and death," he said.

"It's important," she insisted.

Zach looked distinctly uncomfortable. "I run a business.

There are more than three hundred outlets in fifty states. I know the office-supply business inside out, but I'm not good with words. If you don't like the word *fond,* you choose another one."

"All right," she said thoughtfully, biting the corner of one lip. Her eyes brightened. "How about *cherish?*"

"Cherish." Zach repeated it as if he'd never heard the word before. "Okay, it's a deal. I'll cherish you."

"And I'll cherish you," she said emphatically, nodding with satisfaction.

They walked along the pier until they came to a seafood stand, where Zach bought them each a cup of steaming clam chowder. They found an unoccupied picnic table and sat down, side by side.

Occasionally they stopped eating to smile at each other. An oddly exciting sensation attacked Janine's stomach whenever that happened. Finally, finishing her soup, she licked the back of her white plastic spoon. She kept her eyes carefully lowered as she said, "I want to make sure I understand. Did we or did we not just agree to get married?"

Zach hesitated, his spoon halfway between his cup and his mouth as an odd look crossed his face. He swallowed once. "We decided to go through with it, both accepting that this isn't the traditional love match, but one based on practical and financial advantages."

Janine dropped her spoon in the plastic cup. "If that's the case, the wedding is off."

Zach threw back his head and stared into the sky. "*Now* what did I say that was so terrible?"

"Financial and practical advantages! You make it sound about as appealing as a dentist appointment. There's got to be more of a reason than that for us to get married."

Shrugging, Zach gestured helplessly with his hands. "I already told you I wasn't any good at this. Perhaps we'd do better if you explained why you're willing to marry me."

Before she could prevent it, a smile tugged at her mouth. "You won't like my reason any better than I like yours." She looked around to ensure that no one could overhear, then leaned toward him. "When we kissed a few minutes ago, the earth moved. I know it's a dreadful cliché—the worst—but that's exactly what I felt."

"The earth moved," Zach repeated deadpan."Well, we are in an earthquake zone."

Janine rolled her eyes. "It happened when we were in Scotland, too. I don't know what's going on between us or even if we're doing the right thing, but there's definitely… something. Something special."

She wasn't surprised when Zach scowled. "You mean to say you're willing to marry me because I'm good at kissing?"

"It makes more sense to me than that stuff about financial advantages."

"You were absolutely correct," he said evenly. "I don't like your reason. Is there anything else that makes the prospect appealing?"

Janine giggled. "You know," she reflected, "Gramps was right. We're going to be good for each other."

A flash of light warmed his eyes and his hand reached for hers. He entwined their fingers as their eyes met. "Yes, we are."

The wedding was arranged so fast that Janine barely had time to reconsider their decision. They applied for a license that same afternoon. When they returned to the house, Gramps shouted for joy, slapped Zach on the back and repeatedly hugged Janine, whispering that she'd made an old man very happy.

Janine was so busy, the days and nights soon blended together and she lost all track of time. There were so many things to do—fittings and organizing caterers and inviting guests—that for the next five days she didn't talk to Zach even once.

The day before the ceremony, the garden was bustling with activity. Mrs. McCormick was supervising the men who were assembling the wedding canopy and setting up tables and chairs.

Exhausted, Janine wandered outside and glanced up at the bold blue sky, praying the sunshine would hold for at least another day. The lawn was lush and green, and freshly mowed. The roses were in bloom, perfuming the air with their rich fragrance.

"Janine."

She recognized his voice immediately. She turned to discover Zach striding purposefullly toward her, and her heart reacted of its own accord. Janine felt as though they'd been apart for a year instead of just a few days. She wore jeans and an old university sweatshirt and wished she'd chosen something less casual. In contrast, Zach was strikingly formal, dressed in a handsome pin-striped suit and dark tie. She was willing to admit she didn't know him as well as she should—as well as a woman who was about to become his wife. His habits, his likes and dislikes, were a mystery to her, yet those details seemed minor. It was the inner Zach she was coming to understand. Everything she'd learned assured her she'd made the right decision.

"Hello," she called, walking toward him. She saw that he

looked as tired as she felt. Obviously he'd been busy, too, although the wedding preparations had been left to her.

They met halfway and stopped abruptly, gazing at each other. Zach didn't hug her or make any effort to touch her.

"How are you holding up?" he asked.

"Fine," she answered. "How about you?"

"I'll live." He glanced over at the activity near the rose garden and sighed. "Is there someplace we can talk privately?"

"Sure." Janine's heart leapt to her throat at his sober tone. "Is everything all right?"

He reassured her with a quick nod. "Of course."

"I don't think anyone's in the kitchen."

"Good." Hand at her elbow, he guided her toward the house. She pulled out a chair with trembling fingers and sat down at the oak table. As he lowered himself into a chair opposite her, she gripped the edge of the table. His eyes had never seemed darker. "Tomorrow's the day."

He said this as if he expected it to come as a shock to her. It didn't—but she understood what he was saying. Time was closing in on them, and if they wanted to back out, it would have to be now.

"Believe me, I know," she said, and her fingers tightened on the table. "Have you had a change of heart?"

"Have you?"

"No, but then again, I haven't had much time to think."

"I've done nothing *but* think about this wedding," Zach said, raking his hands through his hair.

"And?"

He shrugged. "We may both have been fools to agree to this."

"It all happened so fast," Janine said in a weak voice.

"One minute we agreed on the word *cherish,* and the next thing I remember, we were deciding we'd be good for each other."

"Don't forget the kissing part," he added. "As I recall, that had quite a bit to do with this decision."

"If you're having second thoughts, I'd rather you said so now than after the ceremony."

His eyes narrowed fleetingly before he shook his head. "No."

"You're sure?"

He answered her by leaning forward, slipping his hand behind her neck and kissing her soundly. Tenderly. When they broke apart, they were silent. Not talking, not wanting to.

Janine stared into his dark warm eyes and suddenly she could hardly breathe.

"This is going to be a real marriage," he said forcefully.

She nodded. "I certainly hope so, Mr. Thomas." And her voice was strong and clear.

Less than twenty-four hours later, Janine stood at Zach's side, prepared to pledge her life to his. She'd never felt more uncertain—or, at the same time, more confident—of anything she'd ever done.

Zach seemed to grasp what she was feeling. His eyes held hers as she repeated the words that would bind them.

When she'd finished, Zach slid his arm around her waist and drew her close. The pastor smiled down on them, then looked to the fifty or so family friends who'd gathered on Anton's lawn and said, "I present to you Mr. and Mrs. Zachary Thomas."

A burst of applause followed his words.

Before Janine fully realized what was happening, they

were mingling with their guests. One minute she was standing in front of the pastor, trembling but unafraid, and the next she was a wife.

"Janine, Janine!" Pam rushed to her side before anyone else could. "You look so gorgeous," she said softly, and bright tears shone in her eyes.

Janine hugged her young friend. "Thank you, sweetheart."

Pam gazed up at Zach and shook her head. "He sure is handsome."

"I think so, too."

Zach arched his brows, cocked his head toward her and murmured, "You never told me that."

"There's no need for you to be so smug."

"My children," Gramps said, rejoining them. He hugged Janine, and she saw that his eyes were as bright as Pam's. "You've never been more beautiful. I swear you look more like my Anna every year."

It was the highest compliment Gramps could have paid her. From the pictures Gramps kept of his wife, Janine knew her grandmother had been exceptionally beautiful.

"Thank you," she said, kissing his cheek.

"I have something for you." Pam thrust a neatly wrapped box into Janine's hands. "I made them myself," she announced proudly. "I think Zach will like them, too."

"Oh, Pam, you shouldn't have," Janine murmured. Sitting on a cushioned folding chair, she peeled away the paper and lifted the lid. The moment she did, her breath jammed in her throat. Inside were the sheerest white baby-doll pajamas Janine had ever seen. Her smile faltered as she glanced up to see half a dozen people staring at her.

Zach's hand, resting at the nape of Janine's neck, tightened as he spoke, though his voice was warm and amused. "You're right, Pam. I like them very much."

Eight

Janine sat next to Zach in the front seat of his car. Dressed in a pink suit and matching broad-brimmed hat, she clutched her small floral bouquet. Although the wedding had been arranged in seven short days, it had been a lovely affair.

Zach had taken care of planning the short honeymoon. All he could spare was three days, so instead of scheduling anything elaborate, he'd suggested they go to his summer place in Ocean Shores, a coastal town two and a half hours from Seattle by car. Janine had happily agreed.

"So you think I'm handsome?" Zach asked, keeping his eyes on the road. Neither of them had said much since they'd set off.

"I knew if I told you, it'd go straight to your head, and obviously I was right," she answered. Then, unable to hold back a wide yawn, she pressed one hand to her mouth.

"You're exhausted."

"Are you always this astute?"

"Testy, too."

"I don't mean to be," she apologized. She'd been up since

before five that morning and in fact, hadn't slept well all week. This wasn't exactly the ideal way to start a marriage. There was an added stress, too, that had to do with the honeymoon. Zach had made it understood that he intended their marriage to be real, but surely he didn't expect them to share a bed so soon. Or did he?

Every now and then as they drove, she glanced in his direction, wondering what, if anything, she should say. Even if she did decide to broach this delicate subject, she wasn't sure how.

"Go ahead and rest," Zach suggested. "I'll wake you when we arrive."

"It should be soon, shouldn't it?"

"Another fifteen minutes or so."

"Then I'll stay awake." Nervously, she twisted the small floral bouquet. Unwrapping Pam's gift had made her all the more apprehensive, but delaying the subject any longer was impossible.

"Zach…are we going to…you know…" she stammered, feeling like a naive schoolgirl.

"If you're referring to what I think you're referring to, the answer is no. So relax."

"No?" He didn't need to sound so casual about it, as if it hardly mattered one way or the other.

"Why do you ask, Janine? Are you having second thoughts about…that?"

"No. Just some reservations."

"Don't worry. When it happens, it happens. The last thing we need is that kind of pressure."

"You're right," she answered, relieved.

"We need some time to feel comfortable. There's no reason to rush into the physical aspect of our marriage, is there?"

"None whatsoever," she agreed quickly, perhaps too quickly, because when she looked at him again, Zach was frowning. Yet he seemed so willing to wait, as though their lovemaking was of minor importance. But as he'd said, this marriage wasn't one of grand passion. Well, *that* was certainly true.

Before another five minutes had passed, Zach left the highway and drove into the resort town of Ocean Shores. He didn't stop in the business district, but headed down a side street toward the beach. The sun was setting as he pulled into a driveway and turned off the engine.

Janine was too enthralled with the house to say a word.

The wind whipped at them ferociously when they climbed out of the car. Janine held on to her hair with one hand, still clutching the flowers, and to Zach with the other. The sun cast a pink and gold reflection over the rolling hills of sand.

"Home, sweet home," Zach said, nudging her toward the house.

The front door opened before they reached it and a trim middle-aged man stepped onto the porch to greet them. He was grinning broadly. "Hello, Zach. I trust you had a safe trip."

"We did."

"Everything's ready. The cupboards are stocked. The firewood's stacked by the side of the house, and dinner's prepared."

"Wonderful, Harry, thanks." Zach placed his hand on Janine's shoulder. "This is my wife, Janine," he said. "We were married this afternoon."

"Your wife?" Harry repeated, looking more than a little surprised. "Why, that's fantastic. Congratulations to you both."

"Thank you," Janine said politely.

"Harry Gleason looks after the place for me when I'm not around."

"Pleased to meet you, Harry."

"So Zach got himself a wife," Harry said, rubbing his jaw in apparent disbelief. "I couldn't be more—"

"Delighted," a frowning Zach supplied for him, ushering Janine toward the front door.

"Right," Harry said. "I couldn't be more delighted."

Janine tilted back her head to survey the sprawling single-story house.

"Go on inside," Zach said. "I'll get the luggage."

Janine started to protest, suddenly wanting him to follow the traditional wedding custom of carrying her over the threshold. She paused, and Zach gave her a puzzled look. "Is something wrong?"

"No." She had no real grounds for complaint. She wasn't even sure why it mattered. Swallowing her disappointment, she made her way into the house. She stopped just inside the front door and gazed with wide-eyed wonder at the immense living room with its three long sofas and several upholstered chairs. A brick fireplace took up an entire wall; another was dominated by a floor-to-ceiling window that looked over the ocean. Drawn to it, Janine watched powerful waves crash against the shore.

Zach followed her inside, carrying their luggage, barely taking time to appreciate the scene before him. "Harry's putting the car away," he said.

"This place is incredible," Janine breathed, gesturing around her. She placed the flowers on the coffee table, then trailed after Zach into a hallway, off which were four bedrooms and an equal number of baths. At the back of the house, she found an exercise room, an office and an ultra-modern kitchen where a pot of coq au vin was simmering.

In the formal dining room, the polished mahogany table was set for two. On the deck, designed to take advantage of the ocean view, she discovered a steaming hot tub, along with a bottle of French champagne on ice.

Zach returned as she wandered back into the kitchen and a strained silence fell between them. He was the first to speak. "I put your suitcases in the master bedroom," he said brusquely. "I'm in the one across the hall."

She nodded, not taking time to question her growing sense of disappointment. They'd agreed to delay their wedding night, hadn't they?

"Are you hungry?" he asked, walking to the stove and lifting the pot's lid, as she'd done earlier.

"Only a little. I was thinking about slipping into the hot tub, unless you want to eat first."

"Sure. The hot tub's fine. Whatever you want."

Janine unpacked and located her swimsuit, then changed into it quickly. The warm water sounded appealing. And maybe it would help her relax. Draping a beach towel over her arm, she hurried into the kitchen, but Zach was nowhere to be seen. Not waiting for him, she walked out to the deck and stepped gingerly into the hot tub. The water felt like a soothing liquid blanket and she slid down, letting it lap just under her breasts.

Zach sauntered onto the deck a minute later, still in his suit. He stopped short when he saw her. "I…didn't realize you'd be out so soon," he said, staring at her with undisguised appreciation. He inhaled sharply and occupied himself by uncorking the bottle of champagne, then pouring a liberal glass. When he'd gulped it down, he reached for a second one and filled it for Janine.

"You're coming in, aren't you?" she asked, when he handed her the crystal flute.

"No," he said abruptly. "I won't join you, after all. There were several things I wasn't able to finish at the office this week, and I thought I'd look over some papers. You go ahead and enjoy yourself."

He was going to *work* on their wedding night! But she didn't feel she had any right to comment or complain. She was determined to conceal her bitter disappointment.

"The water's wonderful," she said, as cheerfully as she could manage, hoping her words would convince him to join her.

Zach nodded, but his eyes now avoided Janine. "It looks... great." He strode to the end of the deck, ran his fingers through his hair, then twisted around to face her. He seemed about to say something, but evidently changed his mind.

Baffled by his odd behavior, Janine set aside her glass of champagne and stood up so abruptly that water sloshed over the edge of the tub. "You don't need to say it," she muttered, climbing out and grabbing her towel.

"Say what?"

"You warned me before the wedding, so I walked into this with my eyes wide open. Well, you needn't worry. I got the message the minute we arrived at the house."

"What message is that?"

"Never mind." Vigorously, she rubbed her arms with the towel.

"No," he said. "I want you to tell me."

Against her better judgment, she pointed a quaking finger at the front door. "You went out of your way to tell me how *fond* of me you were and how there wasn't going to be any grand passion. Great. Perfect. I agreed to those terms. That's all fine with me, but—"

"But what?"

Mutely, she shook her head.

He sighed. "Oh, great, we're fighting. I suppose you're going to ask for a divorce and make this the shortest marriage in Washington state history."

Janine paled. Divorce was such an ugly word, and it struck her as viciously as a slap. Despite her efforts, scalding tears spilled down her cheeks. With as much dignity as she could muster, which admittedly wasn't a lot, Janine went back inside the house, leaving a wet trail in her wake.

"Janine!" Zach shouted, following her into the kitchen. "Listen, Janine, I didn't intend to argue with you."

She turned abruptly. "This marriage doesn't mean anything to you, does it? You won't even interrupt your work long enough to…to act like a man who just got married."

With her head held high, she stared past him to a painting of yellow flowers on the dining room wall. When her tears blurred the flowers beyond recognition, she defiantly rubbed her eyes.

"I'm sorry," he whispered, reaching for her as if he needed to hold her. But then his arms fell to his sides. "I should've realized wedding traditions would be important to you. Like that carrying-you-over-the-threshold business. I'm sorry," he said again. "I completely forgot."

"It's not just that, it's everything. How many men bring a briefcase with them on their honeymoon? I feel like…like excess baggage in your life—and we haven't even been married for twenty-four hours."

Zach looked perplexed. "What does catching up on my reading have to do with any of this?"

His question only irritated her more. "You don't have the foggiest notion of how impossible you are, do you?"

He didn't answer right away, but seemed to be studying her, weighing his answer before he spoke. "I just thought I might have a chance to read over some papers," he said slowly. "Apparently that bothers you."

Janine placed her hands on her hips. "Yes, it bothers me."

Zach frowned. "Since we've agreed to delay the honeymoon part, what would you suggest we do for the next three days?"

"Couldn't we spend the time having fun? Becoming better acquainted?"

"I guess I do seem like a stranger to you," he said. "No wonder you're so nervous."

"I am *not* nervous. Just tired and trying hard not to say or do anything that'll make you think of me as a…a nag."

"A nag?" Zach repeated incredulously. "I don't think of you as anything but lovely. The truth is, I'm having one heck of a time keeping my eyes off you."

"You are?" The towel she was holding slipped unnoticed to the floor. "I thought you said you didn't know how to say anything romantic."

"That was romantic?"

"And very sweet. I was beginning to think you didn't find me…attractive."

Astonished, Zach stared at her. "You've got to be kidding!"

"I'm not."

"I can see that the next few days are going to be difficult," he said. "You'll just need to be patient with me, all right?"

"All right." She nodded, already feeling worlds better.

"How about if I dish up dinner while you're changing?"

"Thanks," she said, smiling.

By the time she got back to the kitchen, wearing gray slacks and a sweater that was the color of fresh cream, Zach had served their meal and poured the wine. He stood behind her chair, waiting politely.

"Before we sit down, there's something I need to do."

The last thing Janine expected was to be lifted in his strong arms. A gasp of surprise lodged in her throat as her startled gaze met his.

"What are you doing?"

"It's tradition to carry the bride over the threshold, isn't it?"

"Yes, but you're doing it all wrong! You're supposed to carry me from the outside in—not the other way around."

Zach shrugged, unconcerned. "There's nothing traditional about this marriage. Why start now?" He made a show of pretending his knees were buckling under her weight as he staggered through the living room.

"This is supposed to be serious," she chastised him, but no matter how hard she tried, she couldn't keep the laughter out of her voice.

With a great deal of feigned effort, he managed to open the front door and then ceremoniously step onto the porch. Slowly he released her, letting her feet drop first, holding her upper body close against his chest for a long moment. The humor left his eyes. "There," he said tenderly. "Am I forgetting anything?"

It wouldn't hurt to kiss me, Janine told him in her heart, but the words didn't make it to her lips. When Zach kissed her again, she wanted it to be *his* idea.

"Janine?"

"Everything's perfect. Thank you."

"Not quite," he muttered. He turned her to face him, then covered her mouth with his own. Janine trembled, slipping her arms around his neck and giving herself completely to the kiss. She quivered at the heat that began to warm her from the inside out. This kiss was better than any they'd ever shared, something she hadn't thought possible. And what that meant, she had no idea.

Zach pulled his mouth abruptly from hers, but his eyes remained closed. Almost visibly he composed himself, and when he broke away he seemed in control of his emotions once again. Janine sighed inwardly, unsure of what she'd expected.

The next two days flew past. They took long walks on the shore, collecting shells. They rented mopeds and raced along the beach. They launched kites into the sky and delighted in their colorful dipping and soaring. The day before they were scheduled to return to Seattle, Zach declared that he intended to cook dinner. With that announcement, he informed her he had to go into town to buy the necessary groceries. After the first night, he'd given Harry a week off, and Janine had been fixing simple meals for them.

"What are you serving?" she wanted to know when he pulled into the parking lot of the town's only grocery store. "Tell me so I can buy an appropriate wine."

"Wine," he muttered under his breath. "I don't normally serve wine with this dish."

She followed him in, but when he discovered her trailing down the aisle after him, he gripped her by the shoulders and directed her back outside. "I am an artist, and I insist upon working alone."

Janine had a difficult time not laughing outright.

"In order to make this dinner as perfect as possible, I must concentrate completely on the selection of ingredients. You, my dear wife," he said, pressing his index finger to the tip of her nose, "are too much of a distraction. A lovely one, but nevertheless a distraction."

Janine smiled, her heart singing. Zach wasn't free with his compliments, and she found herself prizing each one.

While Zach was busy in the grocery store, Janine wandered around town. She bought a lifelike ceramic sea gull, which she promptly named Chester, and a bag of saltwater taffy. Then on impulse, she purchased a bottle of sun lotion in case they decided to lie outside, tempting a tan.

When she returned to the car, Zach was already there, waiting for her. She was licking a double-decker chocolate ice-cream cone and feeling incredibly happy.

"Did the master chef find everything he needed?" she asked. Two brown paper bags were sitting on the floor and she restrained herself from peeking inside.

"Our meal tonight will be one you'll long remember, I promise you."

"I'm glad to hear it." Holding out her ice-cream cone, she asked. "Do you want a taste?"

"Please." He rejected the offer of the cone itself and instead bent forward and lowered his mouth to hers. As she gazed into his dark heavy-lidded eyes her heartbeat accelerated and she was filled with a sudden intense longing. Janine wasn't sure what was happening between them, but it felt, quite simply, right.

Although the kiss was fleeting, a shiver of awareness

twisted its way through her. Neither of them spoke or moved. He'd meant the kiss to be gentle and teasing, but it had quickly assumed another purpose. For a breathless second, the smile faded from his eyes. He continued to hold her, his breathing rapid.

After nearly two full days alone together, Janine found it amusing that when he finally chose to kiss her, he'd do it in a crowded parking lot.

"I don't remember chocolate being quite that rich," he murmured. He strove for a casual tone, but Janine wasn't fooled. He was as affected by their kiss as she was, and struggling just as hard to disguise it.

They were uncharacteristically quiet on the short drive back to the house. Until the kiss, they'd spent companionable days together, enjoying each other's company. Then, in the space of no more than a few seconds, all that had changed.

"Am I banished from the kitchen?" Janine asked once they were inside the house, forcing an airy note into her voice.

"Not entirely," Zach surprised her by saying. "I'll need you later to wash the dishes."

Janine laughed and pulled her suntan lotion out of her bag. While Zach puttered around inside, she put on her swimsuit, then dragged the lounge chair into the sun to soak up the last of the afternoon's rays.

Zach soon joined her, carrying a tall glass of iced tea. "You look like you could use this."

"Thanks. If I'd known how handy you were in the kitchen, I'd have let you take over long before now."

He set the glass down beside her and headed back to the kitchen. "You'd be amazed by the list of my talents," he threw over his shoulder.

Kissing was certainly one of them, she thought. The sample he'd given her earlier had created a sharp need for more. If she was a sophisticated, experienced kind of woman, she wouldn't have any problem finding her way back into his arms. It would all appear so effortless and casual. He'd kiss her, and she'd kiss him, and then… They'd truly be husband and wife.

Lying on her back with her eyes closed, Janine imagined how wonderful it would be if Zach were to take her in his arms and make love to her….

She awoke from her doze with a start. She hurried inside to change, and as soon as she was ready, Zach announced that dinner was about to be served. He'd set the patio table so they could eat on the deck.

"Do you need any help?" she asked, trying to peek inside the kitchen.

"None. Sit down before everything cools." He pointed to the chair and waited until she was comfortable.

"I only have a spoon," she said, after unfolding the napkin on her lap. He must have made a mistake.

"A spoon is all you need," he shouted to her from the kitchen.

Playfully she asked, "You went to all this trouble for soup?"

"Wait and see. I'll be there in a minute."

He sounded so serious, Janine had to smile. She was running through a list of words to praise his efforts—"deliciously unique," "refreshingly different"—when Zach walked onto the deck, carrying a tin can with a pair of tongs.

"Good grief, what's that?" she asked in dismay.

"Dinner," he said. "The only real cooking I ever did was while I belonged to the Boy Scouts."

As though he was presenting lobster bisque, he set the

steaming can in front of her. Janine leaned forward, almost afraid to examine its contents.

"Barbecued beans. With sliced hot dogs," he said proudly.

"And to think I doubted you."

Her reservations vanished, however, the moment she tasted his specialty. The beans were actually quite appetizing. He surprised her, too, by bringing out dessert, a concoction consisting of graham crackers covered with melted chocolate and marshmallows. He'd warmed them in the oven and served them on a cookie sheet.

Janine ate four of what Zach called "s'mores." He explained that once they'd been tasted, everyone asked for "some more."

"I don't know how you've managed to stay single all these years," she teased, forgetting for the moment that they were married. "If the news about your talent in the kitchen got out, women would be knocking at your door."

Zach chuckled, looking extraordinarily pleased with himself.

An unexpected thought entered Janine's mind, filling her with curiosity. She was astonished that she'd never asked Zach about other women in his life. It would be naive to assume there hadn't been any. She'd had her relationship with Brian; surely there were women in Zach's past.

She waited until later that night when they were sipping wine and listening to classical music in front of the fireplace. Zach seemed relaxed, sitting with one knee raised and the other leg stretched out. Janine lay on her stomach, staring into the fire.

"Have you ever been in love?" She was trying for a casual tone.

Zach didn't answer her right away. "Would you be jealous if I said I had?"

"No." She sounded more confident than she felt.

"I didn't think so. What about you?"

She took her time answering, too. She'd thought she was in love with Brian. It wasn't until later, after the pain of Brian's rejection had eased, that she realized she'd been in love with the *idea* of being in love.

"No," she said, completely honest in her response. What she felt for Zach, whom she was only beginning to know, was already a thousand times stronger than what she'd ever felt for any other man. She didn't know how to explain it, so she avoided thc issuc by rcminding him, "I asked you first."

"I'm a married man. Naturally I'm in love."

"You're fond of me, remember?"

"I thought you detested that word."

"I do. Now stop tiptoeing around the subject. Have you ever *really* been in love—I mean head over heels in love? You don't need to go into any details—a simple yes or no will suffice."

"A desperate-passion kind of love?"

"Yes," she told him impatiently. "Don't make fun of me and please don't give me a list of all the women you've been *fond* of."

He grew so quiet and so intense that her smile began to fade. She pulled herself into a sitting position and looped her arms around her bent knees.

Zach stared at her. As she watched the harsh pain move into his eyes, Janine felt her chest tighten.

"Yes," he answered in a hoarse whisper. "I've been in love."

Nine

"Her name was Marie."

"Marie," Janine repeated the name as though she'd never heard it before.

"We met in Europe when I was on assignment with the armed forces. She spoke five languages fluently and helped me learn my way around two of them in the time we worked together."

"She was in the military with you?"

"I was army, she worked for the secret service. We were thrown together for a top-secret project that was only supposed to last a few days and instead dragged on for weeks."

"This was when you fell in love with her?" The ache inside her chest wouldn't go away. Her heart felt weighed down with the pain.

"We both were aware that the assignment was a dangerous one, and our working closely together was essential." He paused, sighing deeply. "To make a long story short, I fell in love with her. But she didn't love me."

"Then what?"

"I wanted her to leave the secret service and marry me. She wasn't interested. If you insist on knowing the details, I'll give them to you."

"No."

Zach took a sip of his wine. "I left the army soon after that. I didn't have the heart for it anymore. Unlike Marie—her work, with all its risks, was her whole life. She was the bravest and most dedicated woman I've ever known. Although it was painful at the time, she was right to turn down my proposal. Marriage and a family would have bored her within a year. It *was* painful, don't misunderstand me. I loved her more than I thought possible."

They both were silent for a moment, then Janine asked, "What did you do once you left the army?"

"Over the years, I'd managed to put aside some money, make a few investments. Once I was on my own, I decided to go into business for myself. I read everything I could get my hands on about the business-supply field and modeled the way I dealt with my clients and accounts after your grandfather's enterprise. Within five years, I was his major competitor. We met at a conference last year, and decided that instead of competing with each other, we'd join forces. And as they say, the rest is history."

"Was she pretty?" Even as she asked the question, Janine knew it was ridiculous. What difference would it make if his Marie was a former Miss America or had a face like a gorilla? None. Zach had loved Marie. Loved her as he'd probably never love again. Loved her more than he'd thought possible. By comparison, what he felt for her, Janine, was indeed only fondness.

"She was blond and, yes, she was beautiful."

Janine made a feeble attempt at a smile. "Somehow I knew that."

Zach shook himself lightly as if dragging himself back to the present and away from the powerful lure of the past. "You don't need to worry. It was a long time ago."

"I wasn't worried," Janine muttered. She got to her feet and collected their wineglasses. "I'm a little tired. If you don't mind, I'll go to bed now."

Zach was still staring into the fire and Janine doubted he'd even heard her. She didn't need a crystal ball to know he was thinking of the beautiful Marie.

No more than ten minutes after she'd turned off her bedroom light, Janine heard Zach move down the hallway to his room. For a moment she thought he'd hesitated in front of her door, but Janine convinced herself that was just wishful thinking.

From the second Zach had told her about the one great love of his life, Janine had felt as if a lump were building inside her. A huge lump of disillusionment that seemed to be located somewhere between her heart and her stomach. With every breath she took, it grew larger. But why should she care about Marie? Zach had never confessed to any deep feeling for *her.* He hadn't cheated Janine out of anything that was her right.

An hour later, she lay on her side, wide awake, her hands pressed to her stomach. She didn't mind that Zach had loved another woman so deeply, but what did hurt was that he could never love her with the same intensity. Marrying her, he'd claimed, made practical and financial sense. He was *fond* of her.

Like a romantic idiot, Janine had been frolicking through their short marriage, confident that they'd soon be in love with each other and live happily ever after with their two-point-five children in their perfect little home with the white picket fence.

Zach had loved Marie, who'd dedicated herself to her country.

The most patriotic thing Janine had ever done was cast her vote at election time. She didn't think she should include the two occasions she'd made coffee at Red Cross meetings.

Marie was a linguist. After two years of high-school French, Janine wasn't bad at conjugating verbs, but got hopelessly lost in real conversations.

"I had to ask," she groaned to herself. She was almost certain that Zach would never have mentioned Marie if she hadn't forced the subject. How blissful her ignorance had been. How comfortable.

She could never be the great love of his life and would always remain in the background. Far in the background…

When Janine heard Zach moving around the house a few hours later, she rolled over and glanced at the clock, assuming it was the middle of the night. Then she noticed it was midmorning; they'd planned to be on the road before now. Tossing aside the blankets, she stumbled out of bed and reached blindly for her robe. But she wasn't paying attention. She collided with the wall and gave a shout of pain. She cupped her hand over her nose and closed her eyes. Tears rolled slowly down her cheeks.

"Janine." Zach pounded on the door. "Are you all right?"

"No," she cried, still holding her nose. She looked in the mirror and lowered her hand. Just as she'd suspected, her nose was bleeding.

"Can I come in?" Zach asked next.

"No…go away." She hurried to the adjoining bathroom, tilting back her head and clamping both hands over her nose.

"You sound funny. I'm coming in."

"No," she hollered again. "Go away." She groped for a washcloth. The tears rained down now, more from humiliation than pain.

"I'm coming in," Zach shouted, his voice distinctly irritated.

Before Janine could protest, the bedroom door flew open and Zach stalked inside. He stopped in the bathroom doorway. "What happened?"

Pressing the cold cloth over the lower half of her face with one hand, Janine gestured violently with the other, demanding that he leave.

"Let me look at that," he said, obviously determined to deal with her bloody nose, as well as her anger. He pushed gently against her shoulders, lowering her onto the edge of the tub, and carefully removed the cloth.

"What did you do? Meet up with a prizefighter?"

"Don't you dare make fun of me!" The tears ran down her cheeks again and plummeted on her silk collar.

It took only a minute or so to control the bleeding. Zach seemed to know exactly what to do. Janine no longer had any desire to fight, and she allowed him to do what he wanted.

Zach wiped the tears from her cheeks. "Do you want me to kiss it and make it better?"

Without waiting for an answer, Zach brought his mouth to hers. Janine felt herself go completely and utterly still. Her heart started to explode and before she realized what she was doing, she'd linked her arms around his neck and was clinging to him helplessly. Zach kissed her forehead and her eyes. His thumbs brushed the remaining tears from her cheeks. Then he nuzzled her neck. Trembling, she immersed herself in his tenderness. No matter what had happened in the past, Zach was hers for this minute, this day.

He lifted Janine to her feet and seemed to be leading her toward the bed. She might have been tempted to let him if she hadn't learned about his love for Marie. Knowing she'd always place a remote second in his affections was a crippling blow to her pride—and her heart. It would take time and effort to accept that she could never be the woman who evoked an all-consuming passion in him.

With that thought in mind, she pushed him away, needing to put some distance between them before it was too late.

Accepting Janine's decision, Zach dropped his arms and moved to lean against the doorjamb, as if he needed its support to remain upright.

Janine couldn't look at him, couldn't speak. She began fumbling with her clothes.

"I'll give you a few minutes to dress while I begin loading the car," Zach said a moment later, sounding oddly unlike himself.

Janine nodded miserably. There was nothing she could say. Nothing she could do. He'd wanted to make love to her, and she'd turned him away.

While he packed the car, Janine dressed. She met him fifteen minutes later, her suitcase in hand. She was determined to act cool toward him. But not too cool. Friendly, she decided, but not excessively so.

"I'm ready," she announced, with her most cheerful smile.

Zach locked the house, and they were on their way. Pretending there was nothing out of the ordinary, Janine chatted amicably during the drive home. If Zach noticed anything amiss, he didn't comment. For his part, he seemed as hesitant as she was to talk about what had happened. They seemed to be of one mind about the morning's incident. The whole thing was best forgotten.

Only once did Zach refer to it. He asked her if her nose was causing her any pain, but she quickly assured him she was fine. She flashed a smile bright enough to blind him and immediately changed the subject.

The Seattle sky was gray and drizzling rain when they pulled into the parking garage at the downtown condominium owned by Zach. Silently, she helped him unload the car. They were both unusually quiet as they rode the elevator to the tenth floor.

Zach paused outside his door and eyed her skeptically. "Am I obliged to haul you over the threshold again, or is once enough?"

"Once is enough."

"Good." He grinned and unlocked the door, then pushed it open for her to precede him. Curious, she quickened her pace as she walked inside. The living room was a warm mixture of leather and wood, and its wide window offered a breathtaking view of the Seattle skyline.

"It's lovely."

He nodded, seeming pleased at her reaction. "If you prefer, we can move. I suppose now that we're married, we should think about purchasing a house."

"Why?" she inquired innocently.

"I'm hoping we'll have children someday. Whenever you're ready, that is. There's no pressure, Janine."

"I…know that." She looked past him at the panoramic view, and wrapped her arms around herself, her heart speeding up at his words.

Walking to his desk, Zach listened to his voice mail messages; apparently there were a lot.

While he did that, Janine wandered from room to room, eager to see her new home. In the hallway, she noted that Zach had diplomatically left her luggage on the carpet between the two bedrooms. His was in the master. In his own way, he was telling her that where she slept would be her decision. If she wished to become his wife in the fullest sense, all she had to do was place her suitcase in the master bedroom. Nothing more needed to be said.

It didn't take Janine long to decide. She pulled her suitcase toward the guest room. When she looked up, Zach was standing in the hall, studying her, his expression aggrieved.

"Unless you need me for anything, I'm going to the office," he said gruffly.

"See you tonight."

His gaze moved past her and rested briefly on the bed in the guest room. He cocked one eyebrow questioningly, as though to give her the opportunity to reconsider. "Are you sure you'd rather sleep in here?" he asked.

"I'm sure."

Zach raked his fingers through his hair. "I was afraid of that."

A minute later, he was gone.

Zach didn't come home for dinner that night. Janine had been in the bathroom when the phone rang; Zach had left her a message saying he'd be late. So she ate by herself in front of the television, feeling abandoned and unloved. She was just putting the dishes in the dishwasher when he came home.

"Sorry I'm late."

"That's okay," she lied, never having felt more alone.

Zach glanced through the mail on his desk, although Janine was sure he'd looked at it earlier. "You got the message I wouldn't be home for dinner?"

"Yes. Did you want anything to eat? I could fix you something."

"I ate earlier. Thanks, anyway."

They watched an hour's worth of television and then decided to go to bed.

Janine changed into her pajamas—the same no-nonsense type she'd been wearing all week, since she couldn't bring herself to wear the baby-dolls Pam had given her—and had just finished washing her face. She was coming out of the bathroom, her toothbrush between her teeth, when she nearly collided with Zach in the hallway. She'd forgotten her slippers and was going to her bedroom to retrieve them. They'd already said their good-nights, and Janine hadn't expected to see him again until morning. She wasn't prepared for this encounter, and the air between them crackled with tension.

She had to force herself not to throw her toothbrush aside. Not to tell him that she longed for him to love her with the same passion he'd felt for Marie.

His hands reached out to steady her, and when she didn't immediately move away, he ran the tips of his fingers down her thick brown hair, edging her bangs to the side of her face so he could gaze into her eyes.

Janine lowered her head. "Esh-coo me," she managed, but it was difficult to speak with a toothbrush poking out of her mouth.

"Pardon?"

Janine hurried back to the bathroom and rinsed out her

mouth. Turning, she braced her hands on the sink. "I said excuse me for bumping into you."

"Will you be comfortable in the guest room?"

"Yes, I'll be fine."

He held a blanket in his arms. "I thought you might need this."

"Thanks," she said as smoothly as possible, coming out of the bathroom to take the blanket from him. She wanted to be swept off her feet. She wanted love. She wanted passion.

He was offering a warm blanket.

"I…phoned Gramps," she said, looking for a way to delay their parting and cursing herself for her weakness.

"I intended to call him myself, but got sidetracked."

"He sounded good. Dr. Coleman and a couple of his other friends were at the house and the four of them were playing pinochle."

"I'm glad to hear he's enjoying his semi-retirement."

"I am, too."

A short silence followed.

"Good night, Janine," Zach said after a moment. He glanced, frowning, into the guest room.

"Good night," she said awkwardly.

Janine was sure neither of them slept a wink that night. They were across the hall from each other, but might as well have been on opposite sides of the state, so great was the emotional distance between them.

In the morning, Zach's alarm rang at seven, but Janine was already awake. She threw back her covers, dressed and had coffee waiting when he entered the kitchen.

Zach seemed surprised to see her. "Thanks," he murmured as she handed him a cup. "That's a very…wifely thing to do."

"What? Make coffee?"

"Get up to see your husband off to work."

"I happened to be awake and figured I should get out of bed and do something useful."

He opened the refrigerator, took out the orange juice and poured himself a glass. "I see." He replaced the carton and leaned against the counter. "You did agree that our marriage would be a real one."

"Yes, I did," she said somewhat defensively. But that agreement had been before she'd learned about the one great love of his life. Zach had warned her their marriage would be advantageous for a variety of reasons, the least of which was love. At the time, Janine had agreed, convinced their relationship would find a storybook ending nonetheless—convinced that one day they'd realize they were in love. Now she understood that would never happen. And she didn't know if she could stand it.

"Janine," Zach said, distracting her, "what's wrong?"

"What could possibly be wrong?"

"Obviously something's bothering you. You look like you've lost your best friend."

"You should've told me," she burst out, running from the kitchen.

"Told you what?" Zach shouted, following her down the hall.

Furious, she hurried into her room and sat on the end of the bed, her hands in tight fists at her sides.

"What are you talking about?" he demanded, blocking the doorway.

"About…this woman you loved."

"Marie? What about her? What's she got to do with you and me?"

"You loved her more than…more than you thought possible. She was brave and wonderful, and I'm none of those things. I don't deal with pain very well and…I'd like to be patriotic but all I do is vote and all I know in French are verbs."

"What's any of that got to do with you and me?" Zach repeated hoarsely, then threw his hands in the air. "What's it got to do with *anything?*"

Knowing she'd never be able to explain, Janine shook her head, sending her bangs fanning out in several directions. "All you are is *fond* of me."

"Correction," Zach said as he stepped into the bedroom. "I *cherish* you."

"It isn't enough," she said, feeling miserable and wretched and unworthy.

"What do you mean, it isn't enough? According to you the only reason you married me was that I was a good kisser, so you can't fault me for *my* reasons."

"I don't, it's just that you…you never told me about loving someone else. Not only that, you *admired* her—she was a hero. All you feel for me is fondness. Well, I don't want your fondness, Zachary Thomas!" She leapt to her feet, trying to collect her scattered thoughts. "If you cared for me, you would've told me about Marie before. Not mentioning her was a form of dishonesty. You were completely…unfair."

"And you weren't?" Zach's expression darkened and he buried his hands in his pockets. "You didn't say one word to me about Brian."

Janine was so shocked she sank back onto the bed. Zach still glared at her, challenging her to contradict him. Slowly gathering her composure, she stood, her eyes narrowing as she studied her husband. "Who told you about Brian?"

"Your grandfather."

"How did he know? I never said a word to him about Brian. Not one solitary word."

"But obviously he knew."

"Obviously." Janine had never felt more like weeping. "I suppose he told you Brian lied to me and claimed to love me when all the while he was seeing someone else." Another, more troubling thought entered her mind. "I…bet Gramps told you that to make you feel sorry for me, sorry enough to marry me."

"Janine, no."

She hid her face in both hands, humiliation burning her cheeks. It was all so much worse than she'd imagined. "You felt sorry for me, didn't you?"

Zach paced the length of the bedroom. "I'm not going to lie to you, although I suspect it would be better if I did. Your grandfather didn't mention that you'd fallen in love with Brian until after the day we took him to the doctor."

"He waited until we got to know each other a little," Janine whispered, staggered by the realization that her grandfather had known about Brian all along.

"By then I'd discovered I liked you."

"The word *like* is possibly even worse than *fond*," she muttered.

"Just hear me out, would you?"

"All right," she sighed, fearing that nothing he said now mattered, anyway. Her pride had suffered another major blow. The one love of his life had been this marvelous patriot, while Janine had fallen for a weak-willed womanizer.

"It isn't as bad as it seems," Zach tried to assure her.

"I can just imagine what Gramps told you."

"All he said was that he was afraid you'd never learn

to trust your own judgment again. For quite a while now, he's watched you avoid any hint of a relationship. It was as though you'd retreated from men and were content just to lick your wounds."

"That's not true! I was seeing Peter Donahue on a regular basis."

"Safe dates with safe men. There was never any likelihood that you'd fall in love with Peter, and you knew it. It was the only reason you went out with him."

"Is…is what happened with Brian why Gramps decided to play matchmaker?"

"I suspect that was part of it. Also his concern for your future. But I don't fully understand his intentions even now. I don't think it matters, though. He wanted you to be happy and secure. Anton knew I'd never purposely hurt you. And in his eyes, the two of us were perfect for each other." Zach sat down next to her and reached for her hand, lacing her fingers with his own. "*Does* it matter? We're married now."

She looked away from him and swallowed hard. "I…may not be blond and gorgeous or brave, but I deserve a husband who'll love me. You and Gramps both failed to take that into account. I don't want your pity, Zach."

"Good, because I don't pity you. You're my wife, and frankly, I'm happy about it. We can have a good life if you'll put this nonsense behind you."

"You'd never have chosen me on your own. I knew what you thought of me from the moment we met. You assumed I was a rich spoiled woman who'd never had anything real to worry about. I bet you thought I'd consider a broken nail a major disaster."

"All right, I'll admit I had the wrong impression, but that was before," Zach insisted.

"Before what?"

"Before I got to know you."

Janine's shoulders heaved with barely suppressed emotion. "As I recall, the reason you were willing to marry me was because I wasn't so bad. And let's not forget the financial benefits," she added sarcastically.

Zach's sigh was filled with frustration. "I told you I wasn't ever going to say the stuff you women like to hear. I don't know a thing about romance. But I care about you, Janine, I honestly care. Isn't that enough?"

"I need more than that," she said miserably. It was the promise of their future, the promise of learning about love together, that had intrigued her.

Zach frowned. "You told me even before we were married that you didn't need romantic words. You were content before I mentioned Marie. Why should my telling you change anything?"

She saw that Zach was losing his patience with her. She stared down at the thick carpet. "I really wish I could explain, but it does make a difference. I'm sorry, Zach, I really am."

A lifetime seemed to pass before he spoke again. "So am I," he whispered before turning away. A moment later the front door opened and almost immediately closed again. Zach had left.

"What did you expect?" she wailed, covering her face with both hands. "Did you think he was going to fall at your knees and declare his undying love?" The picture of the proud and mighty Zach Thomas playing the role of besotted husband was actually comical. If he'd done that for any woman, it would've been the brave and beautiful Marie. Not Janine.

* * *

After that disastrous morning, their relationship grew more strained than ever. Zach went to work early every day and returned late, usually past dinnertime. Janine never questioned where he was or who he was with, although she had to bite her tongue to keep from asking.

Zach proved to be a model housemate, if not a husband—cordial, courteous and remote. For her part, she threw herself into her volunteer work at the Friendship Club, spending hours each week with the children. She did her best to hide her unhappiness from her grandfather, although that was difficult.

"You look pale," he told her when she joined him for lunch one afternoon, several days after her return from Ocean Shores. "Are you losing weight?"

"I wish," she said, attempting to make a joke of it. They sat in the dining room, with Mrs. McCormick wandering in and out, casting Janine concerned glances. Janine resisted the urge to leap up and do aerobic exercises to demonstrate that she was in perfect health.

"You can't afford to get much thinner," Gramps said, eyeing her solemnly. He placed a dinner roll on the side of her plate and plunked the butter dish down in front of her.

"I'm not losing weight," she told him, spreading butter on the roll in order to please him.

"I took that sea gull you gave me into the office," Gramps said as he continued to study her. "Zach asked me where I got it. When I told him, he didn't say anything, but I could tell he wasn't pleased. Do you want it back?"

"No, of course not." Janine dropped her gaze. She'd never intended for Gramps to take Chester into the office. On impulse, she'd given him the ceramic bird, reluctant to have it around the condominium to remind her of those first glorious days with Zach.

"I wish I knew what was wrong with you two," Gramps blurted out in an uncharacteristic display of frustration. He tossed his napkin onto his dinner plate. "You should be happy! Instead, the pair of you look like you're recovering from a bad bout of flu. Zach's working so many hours it's a wonder he doesn't fall over from sheer exhaustion."

Janine carefully tore her roll into pieces. She toyed with the idea of bringing up the subject of Brian, but in the end, she didn't.

"So you say you're fine, and there's nothing wrong between you and Zach," Gramps said sarcastically. "Funny, that's exactly what he said when I asked him. Except he also told me to mind my own business—not quite in those words, but I got the message. The thing is, he looks as pathetic as you do. I can't understand it—you're perfect for each other!"

Gramps reached into his pocket for a cigar. "I'll be seeing Zach this afternoon and I intend to give that boy a piece of my mind. By all rights, you should be a happy bride." He tapped one end of the cigar against the table.

"We'll be fine, Gramps. Please stay out of it."

For a long moment, he said nothing; he only stared at the cigar between his fingers. "You're sure you don't want me to talk some sense into the boy?" he finally asked.

The mental picture of him trying to do so brought a quivering smile to her lips. "I'm sure," she said, then glanced at her watch. Pam would be waiting for her. "But since you're seeing Zach, would you please let him know I'll probably be late for dinner? He...should go ahead and eat without me."

"Do you do this often?" His question was an accusation.

"No," she replied, shaking her head. "This is the first

time. Pam needs my help with a school project and I don't know when we'll be finished."

Gramps glowered as he lit his cigar, puffing mightily before he spoke. "I'll tell him."

As it turned out, Janine spent longer with Pam than she'd expected. The homework assignment wasn't difficult, but Pam begged Janine to stay with her. Pam's father was working late and the girl seemed to need Janine more than ever. They made dinner together, then ate in the kitchen while Pam chatted about her friends and life in general.

It was almost nine by the time Janine pulled into the parking garage. The first thing she noticed was Zach's car. The atmosphere had been so falsely courteous between them that she dreaded each encounter, however brief. Since that first morning, Zach hadn't made any effort to talk about her role in his life. Janine wasn't looking for a long flowery declaration of love. Just a word or two more profound than *fond* or *like* to let her know she was important to him.

Drawing a deep breath, she headed for the condominium.

She'd just unlocked the door when Zach stormed into the room like a Minnesota blizzard. "Where the hell have you been?" he demanded.

Janine was so shocked by his fierce anger that she said nothing.

"I demand to know exactly where you were!"

She removed her sweater, hanging it carefully in the entry closet, along with her purse. Zach scowled at her silence, fists clenched at his sides. "Do you have any idea of the time? Did it even cross your mind that I might've been concerned about you? Your cell phone was off and you didn't return any calls."

"I'm sorry." Janine turned to face him. "But you knew where I was," she said calmly.

"All Anton said was that you'd be late. Not where you were going or who you were with. So naturally I was worried."

"I'm sorry. Next time I'll tell you myself." Janine yawned; the day had been exhausting. "If you don't mind, I think I'll go to bed now. Unless there's anything else you'd like to know?"

He glared at her, then shook his head. Wheeling around abruptly, he walked away.

Hours later, Janine was awakened by a gruff sobbing sound coming from the other room. It took her a moment to realize it was Zach. Was he having a nightmare?

Folding back the covers, she got out of bed and hurried into his room. The cries of anguish grew louder. In the light from the hallway, she could see him thrashing about, the bedding in disarray.

"Zach," she cried, rushing to his side. She sat on the edge of the bed and placed her hands gently on his shoulders. "Wake up. You're having a dream. Just a dream. It's okay. . . ."

Zach's eyes slowly opened. "Janine." He ground out her name as though in torment and reached for her, hauling her into his arms with such force that he left her breathless. "Janine," he said, his voice so husky she could barely understand him. "I thought I'd lost you."

Ten

"Zach, I'm fine," Janine whispered. Emotion clogged her throat at the hungry way his eyes roamed her face. He seemed to have difficulty believing, even now, that she was unhurt.

"It was so real," he continued, his chest heaving. He hid his face as if to block out the vivid images the dream had induced. Making room in the large bed, he pulled her down beside him. His hands stroked her hair as he released several jagged breaths. "We were at the ocean," he told her, "and although I'd warned you against it, you decided to swim. A huge wave knocked you off your feet and you were drowning. Heaven help me, I tried, but I couldn't get to you fast enough." He shut his eyes briefly. "You kept calling out to me and I couldn't find you. I just couldn't get to you fast enough."

"Zach," she whispered, her mouth so close to his that their breath mingled, "I'm right here. It was only a dream. It wasn't real."

He nodded, but his eyes still seemed troubled, refusing to

leave her face. Then ever so slowly, as though he expected her to object, he moved his mouth even closer to hers. "I couldn't bear to lose you. I'd rather die myself."

Helpless to deny him anything, Janine turned her face to receive his kiss.

His hands tangled in her thick dark hair, effectively holding her captive, while his mouth seized hers in a kiss that sent her senses swirling. Nothing mattered except his touch. Overcome for a moment by the fierce tenderness she felt in him, Janine eagerly fed his need.

"Janine, oh, my dear sweet Janine. I couldn't bear to lose you."

"I'm here…I'm here." Melting against him, she molded her body to the unyielding contours of his, offering her lips and her heart to his loving possession. Again and again, he kissed her. Janine slid her hands up his chest and twined them around his neck. This was what she'd longed for from the first, the knowledge that he needed her, and she gloried in the sensation.

With a groan, he reluctantly pulled his mouth from hers. He held her firmly to his chest, his breathing harsh and rapid. Peace combined with a delirious sense of happiness, and Janine released a deep sigh. Pressing her ear to his chest, she listened, content, to the heavy pounding of his heart.

"Did I frighten you?" he asked after a minute.

"No," she whispered.

He resumed stroking her hair as she nestled more securely in his arms. Zach had made her feel wondrous, exciting things every time he kissed her, but the way he held and touched her now went far beyond those kisses. She'd experienced a bonding with Zach, a true joining of spirits that had been missing until now. He had told her he'd cherish her, but she hadn't believed it until this moment. Tears clouded her eyes and she struggled to restrain them.

For a long while neither of them spoke. But Janine didn't need words. Her eyes were closed as she savored this precious time.

When Zach did speak, his voice was little more than a hoarse whisper. "I had a sister who drowned. Her name was Beth Ann. I'd promised I'd always be there for her—but I failed her. I couldn't bear to lose you, too."

Janine tightened her hold, knowing how difficult it must be for him to speak of his sister.

"I never forgave myself." His body tensed and his fingers dug roughly into her shoulder. "Losing Beth Ann still haunts me. She wouldn't have drowned if I'd been with her. She—"

Lifting her head slightly, Janine's misty gaze met his. "It wasn't your fault. How could it have been?"

"But I was responsible for her," he returned harshly.

Janine suspected that Zach had rarely, if ever, shared his sorrow or his guilt over his sister's death with anyone. A low groan worked its way through him and he squeezed his eyes tightly shut. "For years, I've drummed out the memories of Beth Ann's death. The nightmare was so real, only this time it wasn't her—it was you."

"But I'm safe and sound. See?" She pressed her hands to both sides of his face, smiling down on him.

He sighed and smiled back, a little uncertainly. "I'm all right now. I shouldn't have burdened you with this."

"It wasn't a burden."

His arms tightened around her, and he inhaled deeply as if absorbing her scent. "Stay with me?"

She nodded, grateful that he needed her.

Within minutes, Janine felt herself drifting into drowsiness. From Zach's relaxed, even breathing, she knew he was already asleep.

When Janine next stirred, she was lying on her side, and Zach was cuddling her spoon fashion, his arm about her waist. At some point during the night, she'd slipped under the covers, but she had no recollection of doing so. A small satisfied smile touched the edges of her mouth. She rolled carefully onto her back so as not to disturb Zach, and wondered what she should do. When Zach woke and found her in bed with him, she was afraid he might regret what had happened, regret asking her to stay. He might feel embarrassed that he'd told her about his sister's death and the guilt he still felt.

Closing her eyes, Janine debated with herself. If she left his bed and returned to her own room, he might think she was rejecting him, shocked by his heart-wrenching account of Beth Ann's death.

"Janine?" He whispered her name, his voice husky with sleep.

Her eyes flew open. "I…we fell asleep. What time is it?"

"Early. The alarm won't go off for another couple of hours."

She nodded, hoping to disguise any hint of disappointment in her voice. He didn't want her with him, she was sure of it. He was embarrassed to find her still in his bed. "I'll leave now if you want."

"No."

The single word was filled with such longing that Janine thought she'd misunderstood him. She tipped her head back to meet his gaze. The light from the hall allowed her to see the passion smoldering in his dark eyes. Turning onto her side, Janine lovingly traced the lines of his face.

"I'm sorry about the way I behaved over...Marie," she whispered. "I was jealous and I knew I was being ridiculous, but I couldn't help myself."

The corners of his eyes crinkled with his smile. "I'll forgive you if you're willing to overlook the way I behaved when you got home last night."

She answered him with a light kiss, and he hugged her to him. Janine surrendered to the sheer pleasure of being in Zach's arms, savoring the rush of warm sensations that sprang to life inside her.

"I don't know how to say all the words you deserve to hear, but I know one thing, Janine. I love you. It happened without my even being aware of it. One day I woke up and realized how important you'd become to me. It wasn't the grand passion you wanted, and I'm sorry for that. The love I feel for you is the quiet steady kind. It's buried deep in my heart, but trust me, it's there. You're the most important person in my life."

"Oh, Zach, I love you so much."

"You love me?"

"I have for weeks, even before we were married. That's what bothered me so much when I learned about Marie. I wanted you to love *me* with the same intensity that you felt for her...that I feel for you."

"It isn't like that. It never was. Marie was as brave as she was beautiful, but what we shared was never meant to last. And she was smart enough to understand that. I fell in love with her, but she was too much of a professional to involve her heart. She was the kind of person who thrives on excitement and danger. It wasn't until you and I met that I realized if I were ever to marry, it would be to someone like you."

"Someone like me?"

He kissed her briefly. “A woman who’s warm and gentle and caring. Someone unselfish and—” he hesitated “—desirable.”

Her throat tightened with emotion, and it was all she could do to meet his gaze. Zach found her desirable. He wanted to make love to her. He didn’t need to say it; the message was there for her to read in his eyes. It wasn’t the desperate passion she’d once craved, but his love, his need to have her in his life, was far more potent than any action he could have taken, any words he could have said.

“Love me, Zach,” she whispered simply.

Zach’s mouth touched hers with a sweet desperate ardor. If she had any lingering doubts they vanished like mist in the sun as his lips took hers, twisting her into tight knots of desire.

His arms locked around her and he rolled onto his back, pulling her with him. His hands outlined her face as though he half expected her to stop him.

“Make me your wife,” she said, bending forward to brush her moist mouth over his.

Zach groaned, and then he did the strangest, most wonderful thing. He laughed. The robust sound echoed across the room and was so infectious that it made Janine laugh, too.

“My sweet Janine,” he said. “You’ve changed my life.” And then he kissed her again, leaving her with no doubts at all.

For a long time afterward, their happiness could be heard in their sighs and gasps and whispered words of love….

The buzzing sound refused to go away. Janine moaned softly and flung out her hand, hoping to find the source of the distraction. But before she could locate it, the noise ceased abruptly.

"Good morning, wife," Zach whispered.

Her eyes remained closed as she smiled leisurely. "Good morning, husband." Rolling onto her back, she held her arms open to him. "I had the most marvelous dream last night."

Zach chuckled softly. "That wasn't any dream."

"But it must've been," she said, slipping her arms around his neck and smiling lazily. "Nothing could be that incredible in real life."

"I didn't think so, either, but you proved me wrong." He kissed her tenderly, and then so thoroughly that by the time he lifted his head, Janine was breathless.

Slowly, almost against her will, her eyes drifted open. His were dark with desire. "You'll be late for work," she warned him.

His smile was sensuous. "Who cares?"

"Not me," she murmured. And with a small cry of pleasure, she willingly gave herself to her husband.

Zach was already an hour late for the office when he dragged himself out of bed and headed for the shower. Wearing her husband's pajama top, Janine wandered into the kitchen and prepared a pot of coffee. She leaned against the counter and smiled into space, hardly aware of the passage of time.

A few minutes later—or perhaps it was longer—Zach stepped behind her and slid his arms around her waist, nuzzling her neck.

"Zach," she protested, but not too strenuously. She closed her eyes and cradled her arms over his, leaning back against his solid strength. "You're already late."

"I know," he murmured. "If I didn't have an important meeting this morning, I'd skip work altogether."

Turning in his arms, Janine tilted back her head to gaze into his eyes. "You'll be home for dinner?"

"Keep looking at me like that and I'll be home for lunch."

Janine smiled. "It's almost that time now."

"I know," he growled, reluctantly pulling away from her. "We'll go out to dinner tonight," he said, kissing her again. His mouth was hot on her own, feverish with demand and passion and need. He raised his head, but his eyes remained shut. "Then we'll come home and celebrate."

Janine sighed. Married life was beginning to agree with her.

At precisely five, Zach was back. He stood by the door, loosening his tie, when Janine appeared. A smile traveled to his mouth as their eyes met. Neither moved. They stared at each other as if they'd spent years apart instead of a few short hours.

Janine was feeling distinctly light-headed. "Hi," she managed to say, shocked that her voice sounded more like a hoarse whisper than the cheery greeting she'd intended. "How'd the meeting go?"

"Bad."

"Bad?"

He nodded slowly and stepped forward, placing his briefcase on the desk. "I was supposed to be listening to an important financial report, but unfortunately all I could do was wonder how much longer the thing would take so I could get home to my wife."

"Oh." That wasn't the most intelligent bit of conversation she'd ever delivered, but just looking at Zach was enough to wipe out all her normal thought processes.

"It got to be almost embarrassing." His look was intimate and loving as he advanced two more steps toward her. "In the middle of it, I started smiling, and then I embarrassed myself further by laughing outright."

"Laughing? Something was funny?"

"I was thinking about your definition of romance. The tryst on the moors was supplied by your grandfather. The walk along the beach, hand in hand, was supplied by me after the wedding. But the desperate passion, my dear sweet wife, was something we found together."

Her eyes filled with tears.

"I love you."

They moved toward each other then, but stopped abruptly when the doorbell chimed. Zach's questioning eyes met hers. Janine shrugged, not knowing who it could possibly be.

The second Zach answered the door, Anton flew into the room, looking more determined than Janine had ever seen him.

"All right, you two, sit down," he ordered, waving them in the direction of the sofa.

"Gramps?"

"Anton?"

Janine glanced at Zach, but he looked as mystified as she did. So she just shrugged and complied with her grandfather's demand. Zach sat down next to her.

Gramps paced the carpet directly in front of them. "Janine and I had lunch the other day," he said, speaking to Zach. "Two things became clear to me then. First and foremost, she's crazy in love with you, but I doubt she's told you that."

"Gramps—" Janine began, but her grandfather silenced her with a single look.

"The next thing I realized is that she's unhappy. Terribly unhappy. Being in love is difficult enough but—"

"Anton," Zach broke in, "if you'd—"

Gramps cut him off with the same laser-eyed look he'd sent Janine.

"Don't interrupt me, boy. I'm on a roll and I'm not about to stop now. If I noticed Janine was a little melancholy at lunch, it was nothing compared to what I've been noticing about you." Suddenly he ceased his pacing and planted himself squarely in front of Zach. "All week I've been hearing complaints and rumors about you. Folks in the office claim you're there all hours of the day and night, working until you're ready to drop." He paused. "I know you, Zach, probably better than anyone else does. You're in love with my granddaughter, and it's got you all tangled up inside."

"Gramps—"

"Shh." He dismissed Janine with a shake of his head. "Now, I may be an old man, but I'm not stupid. Maybe the way I went about bringing the two of you together wasn't the smartest, or the most conventional, but by golly it worked." He hesitated long enough to smile proudly. "In the beginning I had my doubts. Janine put up a bit of a fuss."

"I believe you said something about how it's easier to pluck a live chicken," Zach inserted, slanting a secret smile at Janine.

"True enough. I never knew that girl had so much spunk. But the fact is, Zachary, as you'll recall, you weren't all that keen on the idea yourself. You both think because I'm an old man, I don't see things. But I do. You were two lonely people, filling up your lives with unimportant relationships, avoiding love, avoiding life. I care about you. Too much to sit back and do nothing."

"It worked out," Janine said, wanting to reassure him.

"At first I thought it had. I arranged the trip to Scotland and it looked like everything was falling neatly into place, like in one of those old movies. I couldn't have been more pleased when you announced that you were going to get married. It was sooner than I'd expected, but I assumed that meant things were progressing nicely. Apparently I was wrong. Now I'm worried."

"You don't need to be."

"That's not the way I see it," Gramps said with a fierce glare. "Tell him you love him, Janine. Look Zach in the eye and put aside that silly pride of yours. He needs to know it. He needs to hear it. I told you from the first that he wasn't going to be an easy man to know, and that you'd have to be patient with him. What I didn't count on was that damnable pride of yours."

"You want me to tell Zach I love him? Here? Now?"

"Yes!"

Janine turned to her husband and, feeling a little self-conscious, lowered her eyes.

"Tell him," Gramps barked.

"I love you, Zach," she said softly. "I really do."

Gramps gave a loud satisfied sigh. "Good, good. Okay, Zach, it's your turn."

"My turn?"

"Tell Janine what you feel and don't go all arrogant on me."

Zach reached for Janine's hand. He lifted her palm to his mouth and brushed his lips against it. "I love you," he whispered.

"Add something else," Gramps instructed, gesturing toward him. "Something like…you'd be a lost and lonely soul without her. Women are impressed by that sort of thing. Damn foolishness, I know, but necessary."

"I'd be a lost and lonely soul without you," Zach repeated, then looked back at Janine's grandfather. "How'd I do?"

"Better than most. Is there anything else you'd like him to say, Janine?"

She gave an expressive sigh. "I don't think so."

"Good. Now I want the two of you to kiss."

"Here? In front of you?"

"Yes," Gramps insisted.

Janine slipped into Zach's arms. The smile he shared with her was so devastating that she felt her heart race with anticipation. Her eyes fluttered closed as his mouth settled on hers, thrilling her with promises for all the years to come.

Gently, provocatively, Zach moved his mouth over hers, ending his kiss far too soon to suit Janine. From the shudder that coursed through him, Janine knew it was too soon for him, too. Reluctantly they drew apart. Zach gazed into her eyes, and Janine responded with a soft smile.

"Excellent, excellent."

Janine had all but forgotten her grandfather's presence. When she turned away from Zach, she discovered Gramps sitting across from them, his hands on the arms of the leather chair. He looked exceedingly proud of himself. "Are you two going to be all right now?"

"Yes, sir," Zach answered for them both, his eyes hazy with desire as he smiled at Janine. She could feel herself blushing, and knew her eyes were foggy with the same longing.

"Good!" Gramps declared, nodding once for emphasis. A slow grin overtook his mouth. "I knew all the two of you needed was a little assistance from me." He inhaled deeply.

"Since you're getting along so well, maybe now would be the time to bring up the subject of children."

"Anton," Zach said, rising to his feet. He strode across the room and opened the door. "If you don't mind, I'll take care of that myself."

"Soon?" Gramps wanted to know.

Zach's eyes met Janine's. "Soon," he promised.

* * * * *

Yours and Mine

For Simone Hartman,
the sixteen-year-old German girl who came to live with
us to learn about America. Instead, she taught us about love,
friendship, Wiener schnitzel and fun...German style.
We love you, Simone!

One

"Mom, I forgot to tell you, I need two dozen cupcakes for tomorrow morning."

Joanna Parsons reluctantly opened her eyes and lifted her head from the soft feather pillow, squinting at the illuminated dial of her clock radio. "Kristen, it's after eleven."

"I know, Mom, I'm sorry. But I've *got* to bring cupcakes."

"No, you don't," Joanna said hopefully. "There's a package of Oreos on the top shelf of the cupboard. You can take those."

"Oreos! You've been hiding Oreos from me again! Just what kind of mother are you?"

"I was saving them for an emergency—like this."

"It won't work." Crossing her arms over her still-flat chest, eleven-year-old Kristen sat on the edge of the mattress and heaved a loud, discouraged sigh.

"Why not?"

"It's got to be cupcakes, home-baked chocolate ones."

"That's unfortunate, since you seem to have forgotten to mention the fact earlier. And now it's about four hours too late for baking anything. Including chocolate cupcakes." Joanna tried to be fair with Kristen, but being a single parent wasn't easy.

"Mom, I know I forgot," Kristen cried, her young voice rising in panic, "but I've got to bring cupcakes to class tomorrow. It's important! Really important!"

"Convince me." Joanna used the phrase often. She didn't want to seem unyielding and hard-nosed. After all, she'd probably forgotten a few important things in her thirty-odd years, too.

"It's Mrs. Eagleton's last day as our teacher—remember I told you her husband got transferred and she's moving to Denver? Everyone in the whole class hates to see her go, so we're throwing a party."

"Who's *we?*"

"Nicole and me," Kristen answered quickly. "Nicole's bringing the napkins, cups and punch, and I'm supposed to bring homemade cupcakes. Chocolate cupcakes. Mom, I've just got to. Nicole would never forgive me if I did something stupid like bring store-bought cookies for a teacher as wonderful as Mrs. Eagleton."

Kristen had met Nicole almost five months before at the beginning of the school year, and the two girls had been as thick as gnats in August from that time on. "Shouldn't the room mother be organizing this party?" That made sense to Joanna; surely there was an adult who would be willing to help.

"We don't have one this year. Everyone's mother is either too busy or working."

Joanna sighed. Oh, great, she was going to end up baking cupcakes until the wee hours of the morning. "All right," she muttered, giving in to her daughter's pleading. Mrs. Eagleton *was* a wonderful teacher, and Joanna was as sorry as Kristen to see her leave.

"We just couldn't let Mrs. Eagleton move to Denver without doing something really nice for her," Kristen pressed.

Although Joanna agreed, she felt that Oreos or Fig Newtons should be considered special enough, since it was already after eleven. But Kristen obviously had her heart set on home-baked cupcakes.

"Mom?"

Even in the muted light, Joanna recognized the plea in her daughter's dark brown eyes. She looked so much like Davey that a twinge of anguish worked its way through Joanna's heart. They'd been divorced six years now, but the pain of that failure had yet to fade. Sometimes, at odd moments like these, she still recalled how good it had felt to be in his arms and how much she'd once loved him. Mostly, though, Joanna remembered how naive she'd been to trust him so completely. But she'd come a long way in the six years since her divorce. She'd gained a new measure of independence and self-respect, forging a career for herself at Columbia Basin Savings and Loan. And now she was close to achieving her goal of becoming the first female senior loan officer.

"All right, honey." Joanna sighed, dragging her thoughts back to her daughter. "I'll bake the cupcakes. Only next time, please let me know before we go to bed, okay?"

Kristen's shoulders slumped in relief. "I owe you one, Mom."

Joanna resisted the urge to remind her daughter that the score was a lot higher than one. Tossing aside the thick warm blankets, she climbed out of bed and reached for her long robe.

Kristen, flannel housecoat flying behind her like a flag

unfurling, raced toward the kitchen, eager to do what she could to help. "I'll turn on the oven and get everything ready," she called.

"All right," Joanna said with a yawn as she sent her foot searching under the bed for her slippers. She was mentally scanning the contents of her cupboards, wondering if she had a chocolate cake mix. Somehow she doubted it.

"Trouble, Mom," Kristen announced when Joanna entered the well-lit kitchen. The eleven-year-old stood on a chair in front of the open cupboards above the refrigerator, an Oreo between her teeth. Looking only mildly guilty, she ate the cookie whole, then shook her head. "We don't have cake mix."

"I was afraid of that."

"I guess we'll have to bake them from scratch," Kristen suggested, reaching for another Oreo.

"Not this late, we won't. I'll drive to the store." There was an Albertson's that stayed open twenty-four hours less than a mile away.

Kristen jumped down from the chair. The pockets of her bathrobe were stuffed full of cookies, but her attempt to conceal them failed. Joanna pointed toward the cookie jar, and dutifully Kristen emptied her pockets.

When Kristen had finished, Joanna yawned again and ambled back into her bedroom.

"Mom, if you're going to the store, I suppose I should go with you."

"No, honey, I'm just going to run in and out. You stay here."

"Okay," Kristen agreed quickly.

The kid wasn't stupid, Joanna thought wryly. Winters in eastern Washington were often merciless, and temperatures in Spokane had been well below freezing all week. To be honest, she wasn't exactly thrilled about braving the elements herself. She pulled on her calf-high boots over two pairs of heavy woolen socks. Because the socks were so thick, Joanna could only zip the boots up to her ankles.

"Mom," Kristen said, following her mother into the bedroom, a thoughtful expression on her face. "Have you ever thought of getting married again?"

Surprised, Joanna looked up and studied her daughter. The question had come from out of nowhere, but her answer was ready. "Never." The first time around had been enough. Not that she was one of the walking wounded, at least she didn't think of herself that way. Instead, her divorce had made her smart, had matured her. Never again would she look to a man for happiness; Joanna was determined to build her own. But the unexpectedness of Kristen's question caught her off guard. Was Kristen telling her something? Perhaps her daughter felt she was missing out because there were only the two of them. "What makes you ask?"

The mattress dipped as she sat beside Joanna. "I'm not exactly sure," she confessed. "But you could remarry, you know. You've still got a halfway decent figure."

Joanna grinned. "Thanks…I think."

"I mean, it's not like you're really old and ugly."

"Coming from you, that's high praise indeed, considering that I'm over thirty."

"I'm sure if you wanted to, you could find another man. Not like Daddy, but someone better."

It hurt Joanna to hear her daughter say things like that about Davey, but she couldn't disguise from Kristen how selfish and hollow her father was. Nor could she hide Davey's roving eye when it came to the opposite sex. Kristen spent one month every summer with him in Seattle and saw for herself the type of man Davey was.

After she'd finished struggling with her boots, Joanna clumped into the entryway and opened the hall cupboard.

"Mom!" Kristen cried, her eyes round with dismay.

"What?"

"You can't go out looking like that!" Her daughter was pointing at her, as though aghast at the sight.

"Like what?" Innocently Joanna glanced down at the dress-length blue wool coat she'd slipped on over her rose-patterned flannel pajamas. Okay, so the bottoms showed, but only a little. And she was willing to admit that the boots would look better zipped up, but she was more concerned with comfort than fashion. If the way she looked didn't bother her, then it certainly shouldn't bother Kristen. Her daughter had obviously forgotten why Joanna was venturing outside in the first place.

"Someone might see you."

"Don't worry, I have no intention of taking off my coat." She'd park close to the front door of the store, run inside, head for aisle three, grab a cake mix and be back at the car in four minutes flat. Joanna didn't exactly feel like donning tights for the event.

"You might meet someone," Kristen persisted.

"So?" Joanna stifled a yawn.

"But your hair… Don't you think you should curl it?"

"Kristen, listen. The only people who are going to be in the grocery store are insomniacs and winos and maybe a couple of pregnant women." It was highly unlikely she'd run into anyone from the bank.

"But what if you got in an accident? The policeman would think you're some kind of weirdo."

Joanna yawned a second time. "Honey, anyone who would consider making cupcakes in the middle of the night has a mental problem as it is. I'll fit right in with everyone else, so quit worrying."

"Oh, all right," Kristen finally agreed.

Draping her bag strap over her shoulder, Joanna opened the front door and shivered as the arctic wind of late January wrapped itself around her. Damn, it was cold. The grass was so white with frost that she wondered, at first, if it had snowed. To ward off the chill, she wound Kristen's purple striped scarf around her neck to cover her ears and mouth and tied it loosely under her chin.

The heater in her ten-year-old Ford didn't have a chance to do anything but spew out frigid air as she huddled over the steering wheel for the few minutes it took to drive to the grocery store. According to her plan, she parked as close to the store as possible, turned off the engine and dashed inside.

Just as she'd predicted, the place was nearly deserted, except for a couple of clerks working near the front, arranging displays. Joanna didn't give them more than a fleeting glance as she headed toward the aisle where baking goods were shelved.

She was reaching for the first chocolate cake mix to come into sight when she heard footsteps behind her.

"Mrs. Parsons! Hello!" The shrill excited voice seemed to ring like a Chinese gong throughout the store.

Joanna hunched down as far as she could and cast a furtive glance over her shoulder. Dear Lord, Kristen had been right. She was actually going to bump into someone who knew her.

"It's me—Nicole. You remember me, don't you?"

Joanna attempted a smile as she turned to face her daughter's best friend. "Hi, there," she said weakly, and raised her right hand to wave, her wrist limp. "It's good to see you again." So she was lying. Anyone with a sense of decency would have pretended not to recognize her and casually looked the other way. Not Nicole. It seemed as though all the world's eleven-year-olds were plotting against her tonight. One chocolate cake mix; that was all she wanted. That and maybe a small tub of ready-made frosting. Then she could return home, get those cupcakes baked and climb back into bed where most sane people were at this very moment.

"You look different," Nicole murmured thoughtfully, her eyes widening as she studied Joanna.

Well, that was one way of putting it.

"When I first saw you, I thought you were a bag lady."

Loosening the scarf that obscured the lower half of her face, Joanna managed a grin.

"What are you doing here this late?" the girl wanted to know next, following Joanna as she edged her way to the checkout stand.

"Kristen forgot to tell me about the cupcakes."

Nicole's cheerful laugh resounded through the store like a yell echoing in an empty sports stadium. "I was watching Johnny Carson with my dad when I remembered I hadn't bought the juice and stuff for the party. Dad's waiting for me in the car right now."

Nicole's father allowed her to stay up that late on a school night? Joanna did her utmost to hide her disdain. From what Kristen had told her, she knew Nicole's parents were also divorced and her father had custody of Nicole. The poor kid probably didn't know what the word discipline meant. No doubt her father was one of those weak-willed liberal parents so involved in their own careers that they didn't have any time left for their children. Imagine a parent letting an eleven-year-old wander around a grocery store at this time of night! The mere thought was enough to send chills of parental outrage racing up and down Joanna's backbone. She placed her arm around Nicole's shoulders as if to protect her from life's harsher realities. The poor sweet kid.

The abrupt whoosh of the automatic door was followed by the sound of someone striding impatiently into the store. Joanna glanced up to discover a tall man, wearing a well-cut dark coat, glaring in their direction.

"Nicole, what's taking so long?"

"Dad," the girl said happily, "this is Mrs. Parsons—Kristen's mom."

Nicole's father approached, obviously reluctant to acknowledge the introduction, his face remote and unsmiling.

Automatically Joanna straightened, her shoulders stiffening with the action. Nicole's father was exactly as she'd pictured him just a few moments earlier. Polished, worldly, and too darn handsome for his own good. Just like Davey. This was exactly the type of man she went out of her way to avoid. She'd been burned once, and no relationship was worth what she'd endured. This brief encounter with Nicole's father told Joanna all she needed to know.

"Tanner Lund," he announced crisply, holding out his hand.

"Joanna Parsons," Joanna said, and gave him hers for a brisk cold shake. She couldn't take her hand away fast enough.

His eyes narrowed as they studied her, and the look he gave her was as disapproving as the one she offered him. Slowly his gaze dropped to the unzipped boots flapping at her ankles and the worn edges of the pajamas visible below her wool coat.

"I think it's time we met, don't you?" Joanna didn't bother to disguise her disapproval of the man's attitude toward child-rearing. She'd had Nicole over after school several times, but on the one occasion Kristen had visited her friend, the child was staying with a babysitter.

A hint of a smile appeared on his face, but it didn't reach his eyes. "Our meeting is long overdue, I agree."

He seemed to be suggesting that he'd made a mistake in allowing his daughter to have anything to do with someone who dressed the way she did.

Joanna's gaze shifted to Nicole. "Isn't it late for you to be up on a school night?"

"Where's Kristen?" he countered, glancing around the store.

"At home," Joanna answered, swallowing the words that said home was exactly where an eleven-year-old child belonged on a school night—or any other night for that matter.

"Isn't she a bit young to be left alone while you run to a store?"

"N-not in the least."

Tanner frowned and his eyes narrowed even more. His disapproving gaze demanded to know what kind of mother left a child alone in the house at this time of night.

Joanna answered him with a scornful look of her own.

"It's a pleasure to meet you, Mr. Lund," she said coolly, knowing her eyes relayed a conflicting message.

"The pleasure's mine."

Joanna was all the more aware of her disheveled appearance. Uncombed and uncurled, her auburn hair hung limply to her shoulders. Her dark eyes were nice enough, she knew, fringed in long curling lashes. She considered them her best asset, and purposely glared at Tanner, hoping her eyes were as cold as the blast from her car heater had been.

Tanner placed his hands on his daughter's shoulders and drew her protectively to his side. Joanna was infuriated by the action. If Nicole needed shielding, it was from an irresponsible father!

Okay, she reasoned, so her attire was a bit outlandish. But that couldn't be helped; she was on a mission that by rights should win her a nomination for the mother-of-the-year award. The way Tanner Lund had implied that *she* was the irresponsible parent was something Joanna found downright insulting.

"Well," Joanna said brightly, "I have to go. Nice to see you again, Nicole." She swept two boxes of cake mix into her arms and grabbed what she hoped was some frosting.

"You, too, Mrs. Parsons," the girl answered, smiling up at her.

"Mr. Lund."

"Mrs. Parsons."

The two nodded politely at each other, and, clutching her packages, Joanna walked regally to the checkout stand. She made her purchase and started back toward the car. The next time Kristen invited Nicole over, Joanna mused on the short drive home, she intended to spend lots of extra time with the girls. Now she knew how badly Nicole needed someone to nurture her, to give her the firm but loving guidance every child deserved.

The poor darling.

Two

Joanna expertly lowered the pressure foot of her sewing machine over the bunched red material, then used both hands to push the fabric slowly under the bobbing needle. Straight pins, tightly clenched between her lips, protruded from her mouth. Her concentration was intense.

"Mom." A breathless Kristen bounded into the room.

Joanna intercepted her daughter with one upraised hand until she finished stitching the seam.

Kristen stalked around the kitchen table several times, like a shark circling its kill. "Mom, hurry, this is really important."

"Wlutt?" Joanna asked, her teeth still clamped on the pins.

"Can Nicole spend the night?"

Joanna blinked. This wasn't the weekend, and Kristen knew the rules; she had permission to invite friends over only on Friday and Saturday nights. Joanna removed the pins from her mouth before she answered. "It's Wednesday."

"I know what day it is." Kristen rolled her eyes toward the ceiling and slapped the heel of her hand against her forehead.

Allowing his daughter to stay over at a friend's house on a school night was exactly the kind of irresponsible parenting Joanna expected from Tanner Lund. Her estimation of the man was dropping steadily, though that hardly seemed possible. Earlier in the afternoon, Joanna had learned that Nicole didn't even plan to tell her father she and Kristen were going to be performing in the school talent show. The man revealed absolutely no interest in his daughter's activities. Joanna felt so bad about Tanner Lund's attitude that she'd volunteered to sew a second costume so Nicole would have something special to wear for this important event. And now it seemed that Tanner was in the habit of farming out his daughter on school nights, as well.

"Mom, hurry and decide. Nicole's on the phone."

"Honey, there's school tomorrow."

Kristen gave her another scornful look.

"The two of you will stay up until midnight chattering, and then in the morning class will be a disaster. The answer is no!"

Kristen's eager face fell. "I promise we won't talk. Just this once, Mom. Oh, please!" She folded her hands prayerfully, and her big brown eyes pleaded with Joanna. "How many times do I ask you for something?"

Joanna stared incredulously at her daughter. The list was endless.

"All right, forget I asked that. But this is important, Mom, real important—for Nicole's sake."

Every request was argued as urgent. But knowing what she did about the other little girl's home life made refusing all the more difficult. "I'm sorry, Kristen, but not on a school night."

Head drooping, Kristen shuffled toward the phone. "Now

Nicole will have to spend the night with Mrs. Wagner, and she hates that."

"Who's Mrs. Wagner?"

Kristen turned to face her mother and released a sigh intended to evoke sympathy. "Her babysitter."

"Her father makes her spend the night at a babysitter's?"

"Yes. He has a business meeting with Becky."

Joanna stiffened and felt a sudden chill. "Becky?"

"His business partner."

I'll just bet! Joanna's eyes narrowed with outrage. Tanner Lund was a lowlife, kicking his own daughter out into the cold so he could bring a woman over. The man disgusted her.

"Mrs. Wagner is real old and she makes Nicole eat health food. She has a black-and-white TV, and the only programs she'll let Nicole watch are nature shows. Wouldn't you hate that?"

Joanna's mind was spinning. Any child would detest being cast from her own bed and thrust upon the not always tender mercies of a baby-sitter. "How often does Nicole have to spend the night with Mrs. Wagner?"

"Lots."

Joanna could well believe it. "How often is 'lots'?"

"At least twice a month. Sometimes even more often than that."

That poor neglected child. Joanna's heart constricted at the thought of sweet Nicole being ruthlessly handed over to a woman who served soybean burgers.

"Can she, Mom? Oh, please?" Again Kristen folded her hands, pleading with her mother to reconsider.

"All right," Joanna conceded, "but just this once."

Kristen ran across the room and hurled her arms around

Joanna's neck, squeezing for all she was worth. "You're the greatest mother in the whole world."

Joanna snorted softly. "I've got to be in the top ten percent, anyway," she said, remembering the cupcakes.

"Absolutely not," Tanner said forcefully as he laid a neatly pressed shirt in his open suitcase. "Nicole, I won't hear of it."

"But, Dad, Kristen is my very best friend."

"Believe me, sweetheart, I'm pleased you've found a soul mate, but when I'm gone on these business trips I need to know you're being well taken care of." And supervised, he added mentally. What he knew about Kristen's mother wasn't encouraging. The woman was a scatterbrain who left her young daughter unattended while she raided the supermarket for nighttime goodies—and then had the nerve to chastise him because Nicole was up a little late. In addition to being a busybody, Joanna Parsons dressed like a fruitcake.

"Dad, you don't understand what it's like for me at Mrs. Wagner's."

Undaunted, Tanner continued packing his suitcase. He wasn't any happier about leaving Nicole than she was, but he didn't have any choice. As a relatively new half owner of Spokane Aluminum, he was required to do a certain amount of traveling. More these first few months than would be necessary later. His business trips were essential, since they familiarized him with the clients and their needs. He would have to absorb this information as quickly as possible in order to determine if the plant was going to achieve his and John Becky's five-year goal. In a few weeks, he expected to hire an assistant who would assume some of this responsibility, but for now the task fell into his hands.

Nicole slumped onto the edge of the bed. "The last time

I spent the night at Mrs. Wagner's she served baked beef heart for dinner."

Involuntarily Tanner cringed.

"And, Dad, she made me watch a special on television that was all about fungus."

Tanner gritted his teeth. So the old lady was a bit eccentric, but she looked after Nicole competently, and that was all that mattered.

"Do you know what Kristen's having for dinner?"

Tanner didn't care to guess. It was probably something like strawberry ice cream and caramel-flavored popcorn. "No, and I don't want to know."

"It isn't sweet-and-sour calf liver, I can tell you that."

Tanner's stomach turned at the thought of liver in any kind of sauce. "Nicole, the subject is closed. You're spending the night with Mrs. Wagner."

"It's spaghetti and meatballs and three-bean salad and milk and French bread, that's what. And Mrs. Parsons said I could help Kristen roll the meatballs—but that's all right, I'll call and tell her that you don't want me to spend the night at a home where I won't be properly looked after."

"Nicole—"

"Dad, don't worry about it, I understand."

Tanner sincerely doubted that. He placed the last of his clothes inside the suitcase and closed the lid.

"At least I'm *trying* to understand why you'd send me to someplace like Mrs. Wagner's when my very best friend *invited* me to spend the night with her."

Tanner could feel himself weakening. It was only one night and Kristen's weird mother wasn't likely to be a dangerous influence on Nicole in that short a time.

"Spaghetti and meatballs," Nicole muttered under her breath. "My all-time favorite food."

Now that was news to Tanner. He'd thought pizza held that honor. He'd never known his daughter to turn down pizza at any time of the day or night.

"And they have a twenty-inch color television set."

Tanner hesitated.

"With remote control."

Would wonders never cease? "Will Kristen's mother be there the entire night?" he asked.

"Of course."

His daughter was looking at him as though he'd asked if Mrs. Parsons were related to E.T. "Where will you sleep?"

"Kristen has a double bed." Nicole's eyes brightened. "And we've already promised Mrs. Parsons that we'll go straight to bed at nine o'clock and hardly talk."

It was during times such as this that Tanner felt the full weight of parenting descend upon his shoulders. Common sense told him Nicole would be better off with Mrs. Wagner, but he understood her complaints about the older woman as well. "All right, Nicole, you can stay at Kristen's."

His daughter let out a whoop of sheer delight.

"But just this once."

"Oh, Dad, you're the greatest." Her arms locked around his waist, and she squeezed with all her might, her nose pressed against his flat stomach.

"Okay, okay, I get the idea you're pleased with my decision," Tanner said with a short laugh.

"Can we leave now?"

"Now?" Usually Nicole wanted to linger at the apartment until the last possible minute.

"Yes. Mrs. Parsons really did say I could help roll the meatballs, and you know what else?"

"What?"

"She's sewing me and Kristen identical costumes for the talent show."

Tanner paused—he hadn't known anything about his daughter needing a costume. "What talent show?"

"Oops." Nicole slapped her hand over her mouth. "I wasn't going to tell you because it's on Valentine's Day and I know you won't be able to come. I didn't want you to feel bad."

"Nicole, it's more important that you don't hide things from me."

"But you have to be in Seattle."

She was right. He'd hate missing the show, but he was scheduled to meet with the Foreign Trade Commission on the fourteenth regarding a large shipment of aluminum to Japan. "What talent do you and Kristen have?" he asked, diverting his disappointment for the moment.

"We're lip-synching a song from Heart. You know, the rock group?"

"That sounds cute. A fitting choice, too, for a Valentine's Day show. Perhaps you two can be persuaded to give me a preview before the grand performance."

Her blue eyes became even brighter in her excitement. "That's a great idea! Kristen and I can practice while you're away, and we'll show you when you come back."

It was an acceptable compromise.

Nicole dashed out of his bedroom and returned a couple of minutes later with her backpack. "I'm ready anytime you are," she announced.

Tanner couldn't help but notice that his daughter looked downright cheerful. More cheerful than any of the other times he'd been forced to leave her. Normally she put on a long face and moped around, making him feel guilty about abandoning her to the dreaded Mrs. Wagner.

By the time he picked up his briefcase and luggage, Nicole was waiting at the front door.

"Are you going to come in and say hello to Mrs. Parsons?" Nicole asked when Tanner eased his Mercedes into Kristen's driveway fifteen minutes later. Even in the fading late-afternoon light, he could see that the house was newly painted, white with green shutters at the windows. The lawn and flower beds seemed well maintained. He could almost picture rosebushes in full bloom. It certainly wasn't the type of place he'd associated with Kristen's loony mother.

"Are you coming in or not?" Nicole asked a second time, her voice impatient.

Tanner had to mull over the decision. He wasn't eager to meet that unfriendly woman who wore unzipped boots and flannel pajamas again.

"Dad!"

Before Tanner could answer, the door opened and Kristen came bowling out of the house at top speed. A gorgeous redhead followed sedately behind her. Tanner felt his jaw sag and his mouth drop open. No, it couldn't be! Tall, cool, sophisticated, this woman looked as though she'd walked out of the pages of a fashion magazine. It couldn't be Joanna Parsons—no way. A relative perhaps, but certainly not the woman he'd met in the grocery store that night.

Nicole had already climbed out of the car. She paused as though she'd forgotten something, then ran around to his side of the car. When Tanner rolled down his window, she leaned over and gave him one of her famous bear hugs, hurling her arms around his neck and squeezing enthusiastically. “Bye, Dad.”

“Bye, sweetheart. You’ve got the phone number of my hotel to give Mrs. Parsons?”

Nicole patted her jeans pocket. “It’s right here.”

“Be good.”

“I will.”

When Tanner looked up, he noted that Joanna was standing behind her daughter, her hands resting on Kristen’s shoulders. Cool, disapproving eyes surveyed him. Yup, it was the same woman all right. Joanna Parsons’s gaze could freeze watermelon at a Fourth of July picnic.

Three

"Would you like more spaghetti, Nicole?" Joanna asked for the second time.

"No, thanks, Mrs. Parsons."

"You asked her that already," Kristen commented, giving her mother a puzzled look. "After we've done the dishes, Nicole and I are going to practice our song."

Joanna nodded. "Good idea, but do your homework first."

Kristen exchanged a knowing look with her friend, and the two grinned at each other.

"I'm really glad you're letting me stay the night, Mrs. Parsons," Nicole said, as she carried her empty plate to the kitchen sink. "Dinner was great. Dad tries, but he isn't much of a cook. We get take-out food a lot." She wandered back to the table and fingered the blue quilted place mat. "Kristen told me you sewed these, too. They're pretty."

"Thank you. The pattern is really very simple."

"They have to be," Kristen added, stuffing the last slice of toasted French bread into her mouth. "Cause Mom let me do a couple of them."

"You made two of these?"

"Yeah," Kristen said, after she'd finished chewing. Pride beamed from her dark brown eyes. "We've made lots of things together since we bought the house. Do you have any idea how expensive curtains can be? Mom made the entire set in my room—that's why everything matches."

"The bedspread, too?"

"Naturally." Kristen made it sound like they'd whipped up the entire set over a weekend, when the project had actually taken the better part of two weeks.

"Wow."

From the way Nicole was staring at her, Joanna half expected the girl to fall to her knees in homage. She felt a stab of pity for Nicole, who seemed to crave a mother's presence. But she had to admit she was thrilled by her own daughter's pride in their joint accomplishments.

"Mom sews a lot of my clothes," Kristen added, licking the butter from her fingertips. "I thought you knew that."

"I… No, I didn't."

"She's teaching me, too. That's the best part. So I'll be able to make costumes for our next talent show." Kristen's gaze flew from Nicole to her mother then back to Nicole. "I bet my mom would teach you how to sew. Wouldn't you, Mom?"

"Ah…"

"Would you really, Mrs. Parsons?"

Not knowing what else to say, Joanna agreed with a quick nod of her head. "Why not? We'll have fun learning together." She gave an encouraging smile, but she wondered a bit anxiously if she was ready for a project like this.

"That would be great." Nicole slipped her arm around Kristen's shoulders. Her gaze dropped as she hesitated. "Dinner was really good, too," she said again.

"I told you what a great cook my mom is," Kristen boasted.

Nicole nodded, but kept her eyes trained to the floor. "Could I ask you something, Mrs. Parsons?"

"Of course."

"Like I said, Dad tries real hard, but he just isn't a very good cook. Would it be rude to ask you for the recipe for your spaghetti sauce?"

"Not at all. I'll write it out for you tonight."

"Gee, thanks. It's so nice over here. I wish Dad would let me stay here all the time. You and Kristen do such neat things, and you eat real good, too."

Joanna could well imagine the kind of meals Tanner Lund served his daughter. She already knew that he frequently ordered out, and the rest probably came from the frozen-food section of the local grocery. That was if he didn't have an array of willing females who did his cooking for him. Someone like this Becky person, the woman he was with now.

"Dad makes great tacos though," Nicole was saying. "They're his specialty. He said I might be able to have a slumber party for my birthday in March, and I want him to serve tacos then. But I might ask him to make spaghetti instead—if he gets the recipe right."

"You get to have a slumber party?" Kristen cried, her eyes widening. "That's great! My mom said I could have two friends over for the night on my birthday, but only two, because that's all she can mentally handle."

Joanna pretended an interest in her leftover salad, stirring her fork through the dressing that sat in the bottom of the bowl. It was true; there were limits to her mothering abilities. A house full of screaming eleven- and twelve-year-olds was more than she dared contemplate on a full stomach.

While Nicole finished clearing off the table, Kristen loaded the dishwasher. Working together, the two completed their tasks in only a few minutes.

"We're going to my room now. Okay, Mom?"

"Sure, honey, that's fine," Joanna said, placing the left-overs in the refrigerator. She paused, then decided to remind the pair a second time. "Homework before anything else."

"Of course," answered Kristen.

"Naturally," added Nicole.

Both vanished down the hallway that led to Kristen's bedroom. Watching them, Joanna grinned. The friendship with Nicole had been good for Kristen, and Joanna intended to shower love and attention on Nicole in the hope of compensating her for her unsettled home life.

Once Joanna had finished wiping down the kitchen counters, she made her way to Kristen's bedroom. Dutifully knocking—since her daughter made emphatic comments about privacy these days—she let herself in. Both girls were sitting cross-legged on the bed, spelling books open on their laps.

"Need any help?"

"No, thanks, Mom."

Still Joanna lingered, looking for an excuse to stay and chat. "I was placed third in the school spelling bee when I was your age."

Kristen glanced speculatively toward her friend. "That's great, Mom."

Warming to her subject, Joanna hurried to add, "I could outspell every boy in the class."

Kristen closed her textbook. "Mrs. Andrews, our new teacher, said the school wasn't going to have a spelling bee this year."

Joanna walked into the room and sat on the edge of the bed. "That's too bad, because I know you'd do well."

"I only got a B in spelling, Mom. I'm okay, but it's not my best subject."

A short uneasy silence followed while both girls studied Joanna, as though waiting for her to either leave or make a formal announcement.

"I thought we'd pop popcorn later," Joanna said, flashing a cheerful smile.

"Good." Kristen nodded and her gaze fell pointedly to her textbook. This was followed by another long moment of silence.

"Mom, I thought you said you wanted us to do our homework."

"I do."

"Well, we can't very well do it with you sitting here watching us."

"Oh." Joanna leapt off the bed. "Sorry."

"That's all right."

"Let me know when you're done."

"Why?" Kristen asked, looking perplexed.

Joanna shrugged. "I…I thought we might all sit around and chat. Girl talk, that sort of thing." Without being obvious about it, she'd hoped to offer Nicole maternal advice and some much needed affection. The thought of the little girl's father and what he was doing that very evening was so distasteful that Joanna had to force herself not to frown.

"Mom, Nicole and I are going to practice our song once we've finished our homework. Remember?"

"Oh, right. I forgot." Sheepishly, she started to walk away.

"I really appreciate your sewing my costume, Mrs. Parsons," Nicole added.

"It's no trouble, Nicole. I'm happy to do it."

"Speaking of the costumes," Kristen muttered, "didn't you say something about wanting to finish them before the weekend?"

"I did?" The look Kristen gave her suggested she must have. "Oh, right, now I remember."

The girls, especially her daughter, seemed relieved when Joanna left the bedroom. This wasn't going well. She'd planned on spending extra time with them, but it was clear they weren't keen on having her around. Taking a deep breath, Joanna headed for the living room, feeling a little piqued. Her ego should be strong enough to handle rejection from two eleven-year-old girls.

She settled in the kitchen and brought out her sewing machine again. The red costumes for the talent show were nearly finished. She ran her hand over the polished cotton and let her thoughts wander. She and Kristen had lived in the house only since September. For the six years following the divorce, Joanna had been forced to raise her daughter in a small apartment. Becoming a home owner had been a major step for her and she was proud of the time and care that had gone into choosing their small one-story house. It had required some repairs, but nothing major, and the sense of accomplishment she'd experienced when she signed her name to the mortgage papers had been well worth the years of scrimping. The house had only two bedrooms, but there was plenty of space in the backyard for a garden, something Joanna had insisted on. She thought that anyone studying her might be amused. On the one hand, she was a woman with basic traditional values, and on the other, a goal-setting businesswoman struggling to succeed in a male-dominated field. Her boss would have found it difficult to understand that the woman who'd set her sights on the position of senior loan officer liked the feel of wet dirt under her fingernails. And he would have been surprised to learn that she could take a simple piece of bright red cotton and turn it into a dazzling costume for a talent show.

An hour later, when Joanna was watching television and finishing up the hand stitching on the costumes, Kristen and Nicole rushed into the living room, looking pleased about something.

"You girls ready for popcorn?"

"Not me," Nicole said, placing her hands over her stomach. "I'm still full from dinner."

Joanna nodded. The girl obviously wasn't accustomed to eating nutritionally balanced meals.

"We want to do our song for you."

"Great." Joanna scooted close to the edge of the sofa, eagerly awaiting their performance. Kristen plugged in her ghetto blaster and snapped in the cassette, then hurried to her friend's side, striking a pose until the music started.

"I can tell already that you're going to be great," Joanna said, clapping her hands to the lively beat.

She was right. The two did astonishingly well, and when they'd finished Joanna applauded loudly.

"We did okay?"

"You were fabulous."

Kristen and Nicole positively glowed.

When they returned to Kristen's bedroom, Joanna followed them. Kristen turned around and seemed surprised to find her mother there.

"Mom," she hissed between clenched teeth, "what's with you tonight? You haven't been yourself since Nicole arrived."

"I haven't?"

"You keep following us around."

"I do?"

"Really, Mom, we like you and everything, but Nicole and I want to talk about boys and stuff, and we can't very well do that with you here."

"Oh, Mrs. Parsons, I forgot to tell you," Nicole inserted, obviously unaware of the whispered conversation going on between Kristen and her mother. "I told my dad about you making my costume for the talent show, and he said he wants to pay you for your time and expenses."

"You told your dad?" Kristen asked, and whirled around to face her friend. "I thought you weren't going to because he'd feel guilty. Oh, I get it! That's how you got him to let you spend the night. Great idea!"

Joanna frowned. "What exactly does that mean?"

The two girls exchanged meaningful glances and Nicole looked distinctly uncomfortable.

"What does what mean?" Kristen repeated the question in a slightly elevated voice Joanna recognized immediately. Her daughter was up to one of her schemes again.

Nicole stepped in front of her friend. "It's my fault, Mrs. Parsons. I wanted to spend the night here instead of with Mrs. Wagner, so I told Dad that Kristen had invited me."

"Mom, you've got to understand. Mrs. Wagner won't let Nicole watch anything but educational television, and you know there are special shows we like to watch."

"That's not the part I mean," Joanna said, dismissing their rushed explanation. "I want to know what you meant by not telling Mr. Lund about the talent show because he'd feel guilty."

"Oh...that part." The two girls glanced at each other, as though silently deciding which one would do the explaining.

Nicole raised her gaze to Joanna and sighed, her thin shoulders moving up and down expressively. "My dad won't be able to attend the talent show because he's got a business meeting in Seattle, and I knew he'd feel terrible about it. He really likes it when I do things like the show. It gives him something to tell my grandparents about, like I was going to be the next Madonna or something."

"He has to travel a lot to business meetings," Kristen added quickly.

"Business meetings?"

"Like tonight," Kristen went on to explain.

"Dad has to fly someplace with Mr. Becky. He owns half the company and Dad owns the other half. He said it had to do with getting a big order, but I never listen to stuff like that, although Dad likes to explain every little detail so I'll know where he's at and what he's doing."

Joanna felt a numbing sensation creeping slowly up her spine. "Your dad owns half a company?"

"Spokane Aluminum is the reason we moved here from West Virginia."

"Spokane Aluminum?" Joanna's voice rose half an octave. "Your dad owns half of Spokane Aluminum?" The company was one of the largest employers in the Northwest. A shockingly large percentage of their state's economy was directly or indirectly tied to this company. A sick feeling settled in Joanna's stomach. Not only was Nicole's father wealthy, he was socially prominent, and all the while she'd been thinking… Oh, dear heavens. "So your father's out of town tonight?" she asked, feeling the warmth invade her face.

"You knew that, Mom." Kristen gave her mother another one of those searching gazes that suggested Joanna might be losing her memory—due to advanced age, no doubt.

"I...I thought—" Abruptly she bit off what she'd been about to say. When Kristen had said something about Tanner being with Becky, she'd assumed it was a woman. But of course it was *John* Becky, whose name was familiar to everyone in that part of the country. Joanna remembered reading in the *Review* that Becky had taken on a partner, but she hadn't made the connection. Perhaps she'd misjudged Tanner Lund, she reluctantly conceded. Perhaps she'd been a bit too eager to view him in a bad light.

"Before we came to Spokane," Nicole was saying now, "Dad and I had a long talk about the changes the move would make in our lives. We made a list of the good things and a list of the bad things, and then we talked about them. One bad thing was that Dad would be gone a lot, until he can hire another manager. He doesn't feel good about leaving me with strangers, and we didn't know a single person in Spokane other than Mr. Becky and his wife, but they're real old—over forty, anyway. He even went and interviewed Mrs. Wagner before I spent the night there the first time."

The opinion Joanna had formed of Tanner Lund was crumbling at her feet. Evidently he wasn't the irresponsible parent she'd assumed.

"Nicole told me you met her dad in the grocery store when you bought the mix for the cupcakes." Kristen shook her head as if to say she was thoroughly disgusted with her mother for not taking her advice that night and curling her hair before she showed her face in public.

"I told my dad you don't dress that way all the time," Nicole added, then shifted her gaze to the other side of the room. "But I don't think he believed me until he dropped me off tonight."

Joanna began to edge her way toward the bedroom door.

"Your father and I seem to have started off on the wrong foot," she said weakly.

Nicole bit her lower lip. "I know. He wasn't real keen on me spending the night here, but I talked him into it."

"Mom?" Kristen asked, frowning. "What did you say to Mr. Lund when you met him at the store?"

"Nothing," she answered, taking a few more retreating steps.

"She asked my dad what I was doing up so late on a school night, and he told me later that he didn't like her attitude," Nicole explained. "I didn't get a chance to tell you that I'm normally in bed by nine-thirty, but that night was special because Dad had just come home from one of his trips. His plane was late and I didn't remember to tell him about the party stuff until after we got home from Mrs. Wagner's."

"I see," Joanna murmured, and swallowed uncomfortably.

"You'll get a chance to settle things with Mr. Lund when he picks up Nicole tomorrow night," Kristen stated, and it was obvious that she wanted her mother to make an effort to get along with her best friend's father.

"Right," Joanna muttered, dreading the confrontation. She never had been particularly fond of eating crow.

Four

Joanna was breading pork chops the following evening when Kristen barreled into the kitchen, leaving the door swinging in her wake. "Mr. Lund's here to pick up Nicole. I think you should invite him and Nicole to stay for dinner… and explain about, you know, the other night."

Oh, sure, Joanna mused. She often invited company owners and acting presidents over for an evening meal. Pork chops and mashed potatoes weren't likely to impress someone like Tanner Lund.

Before Kristen could launch into an argument, Joanna shook her head and offered the first excuse that came to mind. "There aren't enough pork chops to ask him tonight. Besides, Mr. Lund is probably tired from his trip and anxious to get home."

"I bet he's hungry, too," Kristen pressed. "And Nicole thinks you're a fabulous cook, and—"

A sharp look from her mother cut her off. "Another night, Kristen!"

Joanna brushed the bread crumbs off her fingertips and

untied her apron. Inhaling deeply, she paused long enough to run a hand through her hair and check her reflection in the window above the sink. No one was going to mistake her for Miss America, but her appearance was passable. Okay, it was time to hold her head high, spit the feathers out of her mouth and get ready to down some crow.

Joanna forced a welcoming smile onto her lips as she stepped into the living room. Tanner stood awkwardly just inside the front door, as though prepared to beat a hasty retreat if necessary. "How was your trip?" she ventured, straining to make the question sound cheerful.

"Fine. Thank you." His expression didn't change.

"Do you have time for a cup of coffee?" she asked next, doing her best to disguise her unease. She wondered quickly if she'd unpacked her china cups yet. After their shaky beginning, Joanna wasn't quite sure if she could undo the damage. But standing in the entryway wouldn't work. She needed to sit down for this.

He eyed her suspiciously. Joanna wasn't sure she should even try to explain things. In time he'd learn she wasn't a candidate for the loony bin—just as she'd stumbled over the fact that he wasn't a terrible father. Trying to tell him that she was an upstanding member of the community after he'd seen her dressed in a wool coat draped over pajamas, giving him looks that suggested he be reported to Children's Protective Services, wasn't exactly a task she relished.

Tanner glanced at his wristwatch and shook his head. "I haven't got time to visit tonight. Thanks for the invitation, though."

Joanna almost sighed aloud with relief.

"Did Nicole behave herself?"

Joanna nodded. "She wasn't the least bit of trouble. Nicole's a great kid."

A smile cracked the tight edges of his mouth. "Good."

Kristen and Nicole burst into the room. "Is Mr. Lund going to stay, Mom?"

"He can't tonight…"

"Another time…"

They spoke simultaneously, with an equal lack of enthusiasm.

"Oh." The girls looked at each other and frowned, their disappointment noticeable.

"Have you packed everything, Nicole?" Tanner asked, not hiding his eagerness to leave.

The eleven-year-old nodded reluctantly. "I think so."

"Don't you think you should check my room one more time?" Kristen suggested, grabbing her friend's hand and leading her back toward the hallway.

"Oh, right. I suppose I should." The two disappeared before either Joanna or Tanner could call them back.

The silence between them hummed so loudly Joanna swore she could have waltzed to it. But since the opportunity had presented itself, she decided to get the unpleasant task of explaining her behavior out of the way while she still had her nerve.

"I think I owe you an apology," she murmured, her face flushing.

"An apology?"

"I thought…you know… The night we met, I assumed you were an irresponsible parent because Nicole was up so late. She's now told me that you'd just returned from a trip."

"Yes, well, I admit I did feel the sting of your disapproval."

This wasn't easy. Joanna swallowed uncomfortably and laced her fingers together forcing herself to meet his eyes. "Nicole explained that your flight was delayed and she forgot to mention the party supplies when you picked her up at the babysitter's. She said she didn't remember until you got all the way home."

Tanner's mouth relaxed a bit more. "Since we're both being truthful here, I'll admit that I wasn't overly impressed with you that night, either."

Joanna dropped her gaze. "I can imagine. I hope you realize I don't usually dress like that."

"I gathered as much when I dropped Nicole off yesterday afternoon."

They both paused to share a brief smile and Joanna instantly felt better. It hadn't been easy to blurt all this out, but she was relieved that they'd finally cleared the air.

"Since Kristen and Nicole are such good friends, I thought, well, that I should set things right between us. From everything Nicole's said, you're doing an excellent job of parenting."

"From everything she's told me, the same must be true of you."

"Believe me, it isn't easy raising a preteen daughter," Joanna announced. She rubbed her palms together a couple of times, searching for something brilliant to add.

Tanner shook his head. "Isn't that the truth?"

They laughed then, and because they were still awkward with each other the sound was rusty.

"Now that you mention it, maybe I could spare a few minutes for a cup of coffee."

"Sure." Joanna led the way into the kitchen. While Tanner sat down at the table, she filled a mug from the pot keeping warm on the plate of the automatic coffeemaker and placed it carefully in front of him. Now that she knew him a bit better, she realized he'd prefer that to a dainty china cup. "How do you take it?"

"Just black, thanks."

She pulled out the chair across the table from him, still feeling a little ill at ease. Her mind was whirling. She didn't want to give Tanner a second wrong impression now that she'd managed to correct the first one. Her worry was that he might interpret her friendliness as a sign of romantic interest, which it wasn't. Building a new relationship was low on her priority list. Besides, they simply weren't on the same economic level. She worked for a savings-and-loan institution and he was half owner of the largest employer in the area. The last thing she wanted was for Tanner to think of her as a gold digger.

Joanna's thoughts were tumbling over themselves as she struggled to find a diplomatic way of telling him all this without sounding like some kind of man hater. And without sounding presumptuous.

"I'd like to pay you," Tanner said, cutting into her reflections. His checkbook was resting on the table, Cross pen poised above it.

Joanna blinked, not understanding. "For the coffee?"

He gave her an odd look. "For looking after Nicole."

"No, please." Joanna shook her head dismissively. "It wasn't the least bit of trouble for her to stay the night. Really."

"What about the costume for the talent show? Surely I owe you something for that."

"No." Once more she shook her head for emphasis. "I've had that material tucked away in a drawer for ages. If I hadn't used it for Nicole's costume, I'd probably have ended up giving it away later."

"But your time must be worth something."

"It was just as easy to sew up two as one. I was happy to do it. Anyway, there'll probably be a time in the future when I need a favor. I'm worthless when it comes to electrical outlets and even worse with plumbing."

Joanna couldn't believe she'd said that. Tanner Lund wasn't the type of man to do his own electrical repairs.

"Don't be afraid to ask," he told her. "If I can't fix it, I'll find someone who can."

"Thank you," she said, relaxing. Now that she was talking to Tanner, she decided he was both pleasant and forthright, not at all the coldly remote or self-important man his wealth might have led her to expect.

"Mom," Kristen cried as she charged into the kitchen, "did you ask Mr. Lund yet?"

"About what?"

"About coming over for dinner some time."

Joanna felt the heat shoot up her neck and face until it reached her hairline. Kristen had made the invitation sound like a romantic tryst the three of them had been planning the entire time Tanner was away.

Nicole, entering the room behind her friend, provided a timely interruption.

"Dad, Kristen and I want to do our song for you now."

"I'd like to see it. Do you mind, Joanna?"

"Of course not."

"Mom finished the costumes last night. We'll change and be back in a minute," Kristen said, her voice high with excitement. The two scurried off. The minute they were out of sight, Joanna stood up abruptly and refilled her cup. Actually she was looking for a way to speak frankly to Tanner, without embarrassing herself—or him. She thought ironically that anyone looking at her now would be hard put to believe she was a competent loan officer with a promising future.

"I think I should explain something," she began, her voice unsteady.

"Yes?" Tanner asked, his gaze following her movements around the kitchen.

Joanna couldn't seem to stand in one place for long. She moved from the coffeepot to the refrigerator, finally stopping in front of the stove. She linked her fingers behind her back and took a deep breath before she trusted herself to speak. "I thought it was important to clear up any misunderstanding between us, because the girls are such good friends. When Nicole's with Kristen and me, I want you to know she's in good hands."

Tanner gave her a polite nod. "I appreciate that."

"But I have a feeling that Kristen—and maybe Nicole, too—would like for us to get to know each other, er, better, if you know what I mean." Oh Lord, that sounded so stupid. Joanna felt herself grasping at straws. "I'm not interested in a romantic relationship, Tanner. I've got too much going on in my life to get involved, and I don't want you to feel threatened by the girls and their schemes. Forgive me for being so blunt, but I'd prefer to have this out in the open." She'd blurted it out so fast, she wondered if he'd understood. "This dinner invitation was Kristen's idea, not mine. I don't want you to think I had anything to do with it."

"An invitation to dinner isn't exactly a marriage proposal."

"True," Joanna threw back quickly. "But you might think…I don't know. I guess I don't want you to assume I'm interested in you—romantically, that is." She slumped back into the chair, pushed her hair away from her forehead and released a long sigh. "I'm only making matters worse, aren't I?"

"No. If I understand you correctly, you're saying you'd like to be friends and nothing more."

"Right." Pleased with his perceptiveness, Joanna straightened. Glad he could say in a few simple words what had left her breathless.

"The truth of the matter is, I feel much the same way," Tanner went on to explain. "I was married once and it was more than enough."

Joanna found herself nodding enthusiastically. "Exactly. I like my life the way it is. Kristen and I are very close. We just moved into this house and we've lots of plans for redecorating. My career is going nicely."

"Likewise. I'm too busy with this company to get involved in a relationship, either. The last thing I need right now is a woman to complicate my life."

"A man would only come between Kristen and me at this stage."

"How long have you been divorced?" Tanner asked, folding his hands around his coffee mug.

"Six years."

The information appeared to satisfy him, and he nodded slowly, as though to say he trusted what she was telling him. "It's been five for me."

She nodded, too. Like her, he hadn't immediately jumped into another relationship, nor was he looking for one. No doubt he had his reasons; Joanna knew she had hers.

"Friends?" Tanner asked, and extended his hand for her to shake.

"And nothing more," Joanna added, placing her hand in his.

They exchanged a smile.

"Since Mr. Lund can't be here for the talent show on Wednesday, he wants to take Nicole and me out for dinner next Saturday night," Kristen announced. "Nicole said to ask you if it was all right."

"That's fine," Joanna returned absently, scanning the front page of the Saturday evening newspaper. It had been more than a week since she'd spoken to Tanner. She felt good about the way things had gone that afternoon; they understood each other now, despite their rather uncertain start.

Kristen darted back into the kitchen, returning a minute later. "I think it would be best if you spoke to Mr. Lund yourself, Mom."

"Okay, honey." She'd finished reading Dear Abby and had just turned to the comics section, looking for Garfield, her favorite cat.

"Mom!" Kristen cried impatiently. "Mr. Lund's on the phone now. You can't keep him waiting like this. It's impolite."

Hurriedly Joanna set the paper aside. "For heaven's sake, why didn't you say so earlier?"

"I did. Honestly, Mom, I think you're losing it."

Whatever *it* was sounded serious. The minute Joanna was inside the kitchen, Kristen thrust the telephone receiver into her hand.

"This is Joanna," she said.

"This is Tanner," he answered right away. "Don't feel bad. Nicole claims I'm losing *it,* too."

"I'd take her more seriously if I knew what *it* was."

"Yeah, me too," Tanner said, and she could hear the laughter in his voice. "Listen, is dinner next Saturday evening all right with you?"

"I can't see a problem at this end."

"Great. The girls suggested that ice-cream parlor they're always talking about."

"The Pink Palace," Joanna said, and managed to swallow a chuckle. Tanner was really letting himself in for a crazy night with those two. Last year Kristen had talked Joanna into dinner there for her birthday. The hamburgers had been as expensive as T-bone steaks, and tough as rawhide. The music was so loud it had impaired Joanna's hearing for an entire week afterward. And the place was packed with teenagers. On the bright side, though, the ice cream was pretty good.

"By the way," Joanna said, "Nicole's welcome to stay here when you're away next week."

"Joanna, that's great. I didn't want to ask, but the kid's been at me ever since the last time. She was worried I was going to send her back to Mrs. Wagner."

"It'll work best for her to stay here, since that's the night of the talent show."

"Are you absolutely sure?"

"Absolutely. It's no trouble at all. Just drop her off—and don't worry."

"Right." He sounded relieved. "And don't wear anything fancy next Saturday night."

"Saturday night?" Joanna asked, lost for a moment.

"Yeah. Didn't you just tell me it was all right for the four of us to go to dinner?"

Five

"I really appreciate this, Joanna," Tanner said. Nicole stood at his side, overnight bag clenched in her hand, her eyes round and sad.

"It's no problem, Tanner. Really."

Tanner hugged his daughter tightly. He briefly closed his eyes and Joanna could feel his regret. He was as upset about missing his daughter's talent-show performance as Nicole was not to have him there.

"Be good, sweetheart."

"I will."

"And I want to hear all the details about tonight when I get back, okay?"

Nicole nodded and attempted a smile.

"I'd be there if I could."

"I know, Dad. Don't worry about it. There'll be plenty of other talent shows. Kristen and I were thinking that if we do really good, we might take our act on the road, the way Daisy Gilbert does."

"Daisy who?" Tanner asked, and raised questioning eyes to Joanna, as if he expected her to supply the answer.

"A singer," was the best Joanna could do. Kristen had as many cassette tapes as Joanna had runs in her tights. She found it impossible to keep her daughter's favorite rock stars straight. Apparently Tanner wasn't any more knowledgeable than she was.

"Not just *any* singer, Mom," Kristen corrected impatiently. "Daisy's special. She's only a little older than Nicole and me, and if she can be a rock star at fifteen, then so can we."

Although Joanna hated to squelch such optimism, she suspected that the girls might be missing one minor skill if they hoped to find fame and fortune as professional singers. "But you don't sing."

"Yeah, but we lip-synch real good."

"Come on, Nicole," Kristen said, reaching for her friend's overnight bag. "We've got to practice."

The two disappeared down the hallway and Joanna was left alone with Tanner.

"You have the telephone number for the hotel and the meeting place?" he asked.

"I'll call if there's a problem. Don't worry, Tanner, I'm sure everything's going to be fine."

He nodded, but a tight scowl darkened his face.

"For heaven's sake, stop looking so guilty."

His eyes widened in surprise. "It shows?"

"It might as well be flashing from a marquee."

Tanner grinned and rubbed the side of his jaw with his left hand. "There are only two meetings left that I'll have to deal with personally. Becky's promised to handle the others. You know, when I bought into the company and committed myself to these trips, I didn't think leaving Nicole would be this traumatic. We both hate it—at least, she did until she spent the night here with you and Kristen the last time."

"She's a special little girl."

"Thanks," Tanner said, looking suitably proud. It was obvious that he worked hard at being a good father, and Joanna felt a twinge of conscience for the assumptions she'd made about him earlier.

"Listen," she murmured, then took a deep breath, wondering how best to approach the subject of dinner. "About Saturday night..."

"What about it?"

"I thought, well, it would be best if it were just you and the girls."

Already he was shaking his head, his mouth set in firm lines of resolve. "It wouldn't be the same without you. I owe you, Joanna, and since you won't accept payment for keeping Nicole, then the least you can do is agree to dinner."

"But—"

"If you're worried about this seeming too much like a date—don't. We understand each other."

Her responding smile was decidedly weak. "Okay, if that's the way you want it. Kristen and I'll be ready Saturday at six."

"Good."

Joanna was putting the finishing touches to her makeup before the talent show when the telephone rang.

"I'll get it," Kristen yelled, racing down the hallway as if answering the phone before the second ring was a matter of life and death.

Joanna rolled her eyes toward the ceiling at the importance telephone conversations had recently assumed for Kristen. She half expected the call to be from Tanner, but then she heard Kristen exclaim, "Hi, Grandma!" Joanna smiled softly, pleased that her mother had remembered the talent show. Her parents were retired and lived in Colville, a town about sixty miles north of Spokane. She knew they would have attended the talent show themselves had road conditions been better. In winter, the families tended to keep in touch by phone because driving could be hazardous. No doubt her mother was calling now to wish Kristen luck.

Bits and pieces of the conversation drifted down the hallway as Kristen chatted excitedly about the show, Nicole's visit and their song.

"Mom, it's Grandma!" Kristen yelled. "She wants to talk to you."

Joanna finished blotting her lipstick and hurried to the phone. "Hi, Mom," she said cheerfully. "It's nice of you to call."

"What's this about you going out on a date Saturday night?"

"Who told you that?" Joanna demanded, groaning silently. Her mother had been telling her for years that she ought to remarry. Joanna felt like throttling Kristen for even mentioning Tanner's name. The last thing she needed was for her parents to start pressuring her about this relationship.

"Why, Kristen told me all about it, and sweetie, if you don't mind my saying so, this man sounds just perfect for you. You're both single parents. He has a daughter, you have a daughter, and the girls are best friends. The arrangement is ideal."

"Mother, please, I don't know what Kristen told you, but Tanner only wants to thank me for watching Nicole while he's away on business. Dinner on Saturday night is not a date!"

"He's taking you to dinner?"

"Me and Kristen and his daughter."

"What was his name again?"

"Tanner Lund," Joanna answered, desperate to change the subject. "Hasn't the weather been nasty this week? I'm really looking forward to spring. I was thinking about planting some annuals along the back fence."

"Tanner Lund," her mother repeated, slowly drawling out his name. "Now, that has a nice solid feel to it. What's he like, sweetie?"

"Oh, honestly, Mother, I don't know. He's a man. What more do you want me to say?"

Her mother seemed to approve that piece of information. "I find it interesting that that's the way you view him. I think he could be the one, Joanna."

"Mother, please, how many times do I have to tell you? I'm not going to remarry. Ever!"

A short pause followed her announcement. "We'll see, sweetie, we'll see."

"Aren't you going to wear a dress, Mom?" Kristen gave her another of those scathing glances intended to melt a mother's confidence into puddles of doubt. Joanna had deliberated for hours on what to wear for this evening out with Tanner and the girls. If she chose a dress, something simple and classic like the ones she wore to the office, she might look too formal for a casual outing. The only other dresses she owned were party dresses, and those were so outdated they were almost back in style.

Dark wool pants and a wheat-colored Irish cable-knit

sweater had seemed the perfect solution. Or so Joanna had thought until Kristen looked at her and frowned.

"Mom, tonight is important."

"We're going to the Pink Palace, not the Spokane House."

"I know, but Mr. Lund is so nice." Her daughter's gaze fell on the bouquet of pink roses on the dining-room table, and she reverently stroked a bloom. Tanner had arranged for the flowers to be delivered to Nicole and Kristen the night of the talent show. "You can't wear slacks to dinner with the man who sent me my first real flowers," she announced in tones of finality.

Joanna hesitated. "I'm sure this is what Mr. Lund expects," she said with far more confidence than she felt.

"You think so?"

She hoped so! She smiled, praying that her air of certainty would be enough to appease her skeptical daughter. Still, she had to agree with Kristen: Tanner *was* nice. More than nice—that was such a weak word. With every meeting, Joanna's estimation of the man grew. He'd called on Friday to thank her for minding Nicole, who'd gone straight home from school on Thursday afternoon since her father was back, and mentioned he was looking forward to Saturday. He was thoughtful, sensitive, personable and a wonderful father. Not to mention one of the best-looking men she'd ever met. It was unfortunate, really, that she wasn't looking for a husband, because Tanner Lund could easily be a prime candidate.

The word husband bounced in Joanna's mind like a ricocheting bullet. She blamed her mother for that. What she'd told her was true—Joanna was finished with marriage, finished with love. Davey had taught her how difficult it was for most men to remain faithful, and Joanna had no intention of repeating those painful lessons. Besides, if a man ever did become part of her life again, it would be someone on her own social and economic level. Not like Tanner Lund. But that didn't mean she was completely blind to male charms. On the contrary, she saw handsome men every day, worked with several, and had even dated a few. However, it was Tanner Lund she found herself thinking about lately, and that bothered Joanna. It bothered her a lot.

The best thing to do was nip this near relationship in the bud. She'd go to dinner with him this once, but only this once, and that would be the end of it.

"They're here!" The drape swished back into place as Kristen bolted away from the large picture window.

Calmly Joanna opened the hall closet and retrieved their winter coats. She might appear outwardly composed, but her fingers were shaking. The prospect of seeing Tanner left her trembling, and that fact drained away what little confidence she'd managed to accumulate over the past couple of days.

Both Tanner and Nicole came to the front door. Kristen held out her hands, and Nicole gripped them eagerly. Soon the two were jumping up and down like pogo sticks gone berserk.

"I can tell we're in for a fun evening," Tanner muttered under his breath.

He looked wonderful, Joanna admitted grudgingly. The kind of man every woman dreams about—well, almost every woman. Joanna longed to think of herself as immune to the handsome Mr. Lund. Unfortunately she wasn't.

Since their last meeting, she'd tried to figure out when her feelings for Tanner had changed. The roses had done it, she decided. Ordering them for Kristen and Nicole had been so thoughtful, and the girls had been ecstatic at the gesture.

When they'd finished lip-synching their song, they'd bowed before the auditorium full of appreciative parents. Then the school principal, Mr. Holliday, had stood at their side and presented them each with a beautiful bouquet of long-stemmed pink roses. Flowers Tanner had wired because he couldn't be there to watch their act.

"Are you ready?" Tanner asked, holding open the door for Joanna.

She nodded. "I think so."

Although it was early, a line had already begun to form outside the Pink Palace when they arrived. The minute they pulled into the parking lot, they were accosted by a loud, vibrating rock-and-roll song that might have been an old Jerry Lee Lewis number.

"It looks like we'll have to wait," Joanna commented. "That lineup's getting longer by the minute."

"I had my secretary make reservations," Tanner told her. "I heard this place really grooves on a Saturday night."

"Grooves!" Nicole repeated, smothering her giggles behind her cupped palm. Kristen laughed with her.

Tanner leaned his head close to Joanna's. "It's difficult to reason with a generation that grew up without Janis and Jimi!"

Janis Joplin and Jimi Hendrix were a bit before Joanna's time, too, but she knew what he meant.

The Pink Palace was exactly as Joanna remembered. The popular ice-cream parlor was decorated in a fifties theme, with old-fashioned circular booths and outdated jukeboxes. The waitresses wore billowing pink skirts with a French poodle design and roller-skated between tables, taking and delivering orders. Once inside, Joanna, Tanner and the girls were seated almost immediately and handed huge menus.

Neither girl bothered to read through the selections, having made their choices in the car. They'd both decided on cheeseburgers and banana splits.

By the time the waitress, chewing on a thick wad of bubble gum, skated to a stop at their table, Joanna had made her selection, too.

"A cheeseburger and a banana split," she said, grinning at the girls.

"Same here," Tanner said, "and coffee, please."

"I'll have a cup, too," Joanna added.

The teenager wrote down their order and glided toward the kitchen.

Joanna opened her purse and brought out a small wad of cotton wool.

"What's that for?" Tanner wanted to know when she pulled it apart into four fluffy balls and handed two of them to him, keeping the other pair for herself.

She pointed to her ears. "The last time I was here, I was haunted for days by a ringing in my ears that sounded suspiciously like an old Elvis tune."

Tanner chuckled and leaned across the table to shout, "It does get a bit loud, doesn't it?"

Kristen and Nicole looked from one parent to the other then shouted together, "If it's too loud, you're too old!"

Joanna raised her hand. "Guilty as charged."

Tanner nodded and shared a smile with Joanna. The smile did funny things to her stomach, and Joanna pressed her hands over her abdomen in a futile effort to quell her growing awareness of Tanner. A warning light flashed in her mind, spelling out danger.

Joanna wasn't sure what had come over her, but whatever it was, she didn't like it.

Their meal arrived, and for a while, at least, Joanna could direct her attention to that. The food was better than she remembered. The cheeseburgers were juicy and tender and the banana splits divine. She promised herself she'd eat cottage cheese and fruit every day at lunch for the next week to balance all the extra calories from this one meal.

While Joanna and Tanner exchanged only the occasional remark, the girls chattered happily throughout dinner. When the waitress skated away with the last of their empty plates, Tanner suggested a movie.

"Great idea!" Nicole cried, enthusiastically seconded by Kristen.

"What do you think, Joanna?" asked Tanner.

She started to say that the evening had been full enough—until she found two eager young faces looking hopefully at her. She couldn't finish her sentence; it just wasn't in her to dash their good time.

"Sure," she managed instead, trying to insert a bit of excitement into her voice.

"*Teen Massacre* is showing at the mall," Nicole said, shooting a glance in her father's direction. "Donny Rosenburg saw it and claims it scared him out of his wits, but then Donny doesn't have many."

Kristen laughed and nodded, apparently well-acquainted with the witless Donny.

Without the least bit of hesitation, Tanner shook his head. "No way, Nicole."

"Come on, Dad, everyone's seen it. The only reason it got an adult rating is because of the blood and gore, and I've seen that lots of times."

"Discussion is closed." He spoke without raising his voice, but the authority behind his words was enough to convince

Joanna she'd turn up the loser if she ever crossed Tanner Lund. Still, she knew she wouldn't hesitate if she felt he was wrong, but in this case she agreed with him completely.

Nicole's lower lip jutted out rebelliously, and for a minute Joanna thought the girl might try to argue her case. But she wasn't surprised when Nicole yielded without further argument.

Deciding which movie to see involved some real negotiating. The girls had definite ideas of what was acceptable, as did Tanner and Joanna. Like Tanner, Joanna wasn't about to allow her daughter to see a movie with an adult rating, even if it was "only because of the blood and gore."

They finally compromised on a comedy that starred a popular teen idol. The girls thought that would be "all right," but they made it clear that *Teen Massacre* was their first choice.

Half an hour later they were inside the theater, and Tanner asked, "Anyone for popcorn?"

"Me," Kristen said.

"Me, too, and could we both have a Coke and chocolate-covered raisins, too?" Nicole asked.

Tanner rolled his eyes and, grinning, glanced toward Joanna. "What about you?"

"Nothing." She didn't know where the girls were going to put all this food, but she knew where it would end up if she were to consume it. Her hips! She sometimes suspected that junk food didn't even pass through her stomach, but attached itself directly to her hip bones.

"You're sure?"

"Positive."

Tanner returned a moment later with three large boxes of popcorn and other assorted treats.

As soon as they'd emptied Tanner's arms of all but one box of popcorn, the girls started into the auditorium.

"Hey, you two, wait for us," Joanna called after them, bewildered by the way they'd hurried off without waiting for her and Tanner.

Kristen and Nicole stopped abruptly and turned around, a look of pure horror on their young faces.

"You're not going to sit with us, are you, Mom?" Kristen wailed. "You just can't!"

"Why not?" This was news to Joanna. Sure, it had been a while since she'd gone to a movie with her daughter, but Kristen had always sat with her in the past.

"Someone might see us," her daughter went on to explain, in tones of exaggerated patience. "No one sits with their parents anymore. Not even woosies."

"Woosies?"

"Sort of like nerds, only worse!" Kristen said.

"Sitting with us is obviously a social embarrassment to be avoided at all costs," Tanner muttered.

"Can we go now, Mom?" Kristen pleaded. "I don't want to miss the previews."

Joanna nodded, still a little stunned. She enjoyed going out to a movie now and again, usually accompanied by her daughter and often several of Kristen's friends. Until tonight, no one had openly objected to sitting in the same row with her. However, now that Joanna thought about it, Kristen hadn't been interested in going to the movies for the past couple of months.

"I guess this is what happens when they hit sixth grade," Tanner said, holding the auditorium door for Joanna.

She walked down the center aisle and paused by an empty row near the back, checking with Tanner before she entered.

Neither of them sat down, though, until they'd located the girls. Kristen and Nicole were three rows from the front and had slid down so far that their eyes were level with the seats ahead of them.

"Ah, the joys of fatherhood," Tanner commented, after they'd taken their places. "Not to mention motherhood."

Joanna still felt a little taken aback by what had happened. She thought she had a close relationship with Kristen, and yet her daughter had never said a word about not wanting to be anywhere near her in a movie theater. She knew this might sound like a trivial concern to some, but she couldn't help worrying that the solid foundation she'd spent a decade reinforcing had started to crumble.

"Joanna?"

She turned to Tanner and tried to smile, but the attempt was unconvincing.

"What's wrong?"

Joanna fluttered her hand weakly, unable to find her voice. "Nothing." That came out sounding as though she might burst into tears any second.

"Is it Kristen?"

She nodded wildly.

"Because she didn't want to sit with us?"

Her hair bounced against her shoulders as she nodded again.

"The girls wanting to be by themselves bothers you?"

"No…yes. I don't know what I'm feeling. She's growing up, Tanner, and I guess it just hit me right between the eyes."

"It happened to me last week," Tanner said thoughtfully. "I found Nicole wearing a pair of tights. Hell, I didn't even know they made them for girls her age."

"They do, believe it or not," Joanna informed him. "Kristen did the same thing."

He shook his head as though he couldn't quite grasp the concept. "But they're only eleven."

"Going on sixteen."

"Has Kristen tried pasting on those fake fingernails yet?" Tanner shuddered in exaggerated disgust.

Joanna covered her mouth with one hand to hold back an attack of giggles. "Those press-on things turned up every place imaginable for weeks afterward."

Tanner turned sideways in his seat. "What about makeup?" he asked urgently.

"I caught her trying to sneak out of the house one morning last month. She was wearing the brightest eye shadow I've ever seen in my life. Tanner, I swear if she'd been standing on a shore, she could have guided lost ships into port."

He smiled, then dropped his gaze, looking uncomfortable. "So you do let her wear makeup?"

"I'm holding off as long as I can," Joanna admitted. "At the very least, she'll have to wait until seventh grade. That was when my mother let me. I don't think it's so unreasonable to expect Kristen to wait until junior high."

Tanner relaxed against the back of his seat and nodded a couple of times. "I'm glad to hear that. Nicole's been after me to 'wake up and smell the coffee,' as she puts it, for the past six months. Hell, I didn't know who to ask about these things. It really isn't something I'm comfortable discussing with my secretary."

"What about her mother?"

His eyes hardened. "She only sees Nicole when it's convenient, and it hasn't been for the past three years."

"I...I didn't mean to pry."

"You weren't. Carmen and I didn't exactly part on the best of terms. She's got a new life now and apparently doesn't want any reminders of the past—not that I totally blame her. We made each other miserable. Frankly, Joanna, my feelings about getting married again are the same as yours. One failed marriage was enough for me."

The theater lights dimmed then, and the sound track started. Tanner leaned back and crossed his long legs, balancing one ankle on the opposite knee.

Joanna settled back, too, grateful that the movie they'd selected was a comedy. Her emotions were riding too close to the surface this evening. She could see herself bursting into tears at the slightest hint of sadness—for that matter, joy. Bambi traipsing through the woods would have done her in just then.

Joanna was so caught up in her thoughts that when Tanner and the others around her let out a boisterous laugh, she'd completely missed whatever had been so hilarious.

Without thinking, she reached over and grabbed a handful of Tanner's popcorn. She discovered that the crunchiness and the buttery, salty flavor suited her mood. Tanner held the box on the arm between them to make sharing easier.

The next time Joanna sent her fingers digging, they encountered Tanner's. "Sorry," she murmured, pulling her hand free.

"No problem," he answered, tilting the box her way.

Joanna munched steadily. Before she knew it, the popcorn was gone and her fingers were laced with Tanner's, her hand firmly clasped in his.

The minute he'd reached for her hand, Joanna lost track of what was happening on the screen. Holding hands seemed such an innocent gesture, something teenagers did. He certainly didn't mean anything by it, Joanna told herself. It was just that her emotions were so confused lately, and she wasn't even sure why.

She liked Tanner, Joanna realized anew, liked him very much. And she thoroughly enjoyed Nicole. For the first time since her divorce, she could imagine getting involved with another man, and the thought frightened her. All right, it terrified her. This man belonged to a different world. Besides, she wasn't ready. Good grief, six years should have given her ample time to heal, but she'd been too afraid to lift the bandage.

When the movie was over, Tanner drove them home. The girls were tired, but managed to carry on a lively backseat conversation. The front seat was a different story. Neither Tanner nor Joanna had much to say.

"Would you like to come in for coffee?" Joanna asked when Tanner pulled into her driveway, although she was silently wishing he'd decline. Her nerves continued to clamor from the hand-holding, and she wanted some time alone to organize her thoughts.

"Can we, Dad? Please?" Nicole begged. "Kristen and I want to watch the Saturday night videos together."

"You're sure?" Tanner looked at Joanna, his brow creased with concern.

She couldn't answer. She wasn't sure of anything just then. "Of course," she forced herself to say. "It'll only take a minute or two to brew a pot."

"All right, then," Tanner said, and the girls let out whoops of delight.

Occasionally Joanna wondered if their daughters would ever get tired of one another's company. Probably, although they hadn't shown any signs of it yet. As far as she knew, the two girls had never had a serious disagreement.

Kristen and Nicole disappeared as soon as they got into the house. Within seconds, the television could be heard blaring rock music, which had recently become a familiar sound in the small one-story house.

Tanner followed Joanna into the kitchen and stood leaning against the counter while she filled the automatic coffeemaker with water. Her movements were jerky and abrupt. She felt awkward, ungraceful—as though this was the first time she'd ever been alone with a man. And that was a ridiculous way to feel, especially since the girls were practically within sight.

"I enjoyed tonight," Tanner commented, as she removed two cups from the cupboard.

"I did, too." She tossed him a lazy smile over her shoulder. But Tanner's eyes held hers, and it was as if she was seeing him for the first time. She half turned toward him, suddenly aware of how tall and lean he was, how thick and soft his dark hair. With an effort, Joanna looked from those mesmerizing blue eyes and returned to the task of making coffee, although her fingers didn't seem willing to cooperate.

She stood waiting for the dark liquid to filter its way into the glass pot. Never had it seemed to take so long.

"Joanna."

Judging by the loudness of his voice, Tanner was standing directly behind her. A beat of silence followed before she turned around to face him.

Tanner's hands grasped her shoulders. "It's been a long time since I've sat in a movie and held a girl's hand."

She lowered her eyes and nodded. "Me, too."

"I felt like a kid again."

She'd been thinking much the same thing herself.

"I want to kiss you, Joanna."

She didn't need an analyst to inform her that kissing Tanner was something best avoided. She was about to tell him so when his hands gripped her waist and pulled her away from the support of the kitchen counter. A little taken aback, Joanna threw up her hands, as if to ward him off. But the minute they came into contact with the muscled hardness of his chest, they lost their purpose.

The moment Tanner's warm mouth claimed her lips, she felt an excitement that was almost shocking in its intensity. Her hands clutched the collar of his shirt as she eagerly gave herself up to the forgotten sensations. It had been so long since a man had kissed her like this.

The kiss was over much too soon. Far sooner than Joanna would have liked. The fire of his mouth had ignited a response in her she'd believed long dead. She was amazed at how readily it had sprung back to life. When Tanner dropped his arms and released her, Joanna felt suddenly weak, barely able to remain upright.

Her hand found her chest and she heaved a giant breath. "I...don't think that was a good idea."

Tanner's brows drew together, forming a ledge over his narrowed eyes. "I'm not sure I do, either, but it seemed right. I don't know what's happening between us, Joanna, and it's confusing the hell out of me."

"You? I'm the one who made it abundantly clear from the outset that I wasn't looking for a romantic involvement."

"I know, and I agree, but—"

"I'm more than pleased Kristen and Nicole are good friends, but I happen to like my life the way it is, thank you."

Tanner's frown grew darker, his expression both baffled

and annoyed. "I feel the same way. It was a kiss, not a suggestion we live in sin."

"I...really wish you hadn't done that, Tanner."

"I apologize. Trust me, it won't happen again," he muttered, and buried his hands deep inside his pockets. "In fact it would probably be best if we forgot the entire incident."

"I agree totally."

"Fine, then." He stalked out of the kitchen, but not before Joanna found herself wondering if she *could* forget it.

Six

A kiss was really such a minor thing, Joanna mused, slowly rotating her pencil between her palms. She'd made a criminal case out of nothing, and embarrassed both Tanner and herself.

"Joanna, have you had time to read over the Osborne loan application yet?" her boss, Robin Simpson asked, strolling up to her desk.

"Ah, no, not yet," Joanna said, her face flushing with guilt.

Robin frowned as he studied her. "What's been with you today? Every time I see you, you're gazing at the wall with a faraway look in your eye."

"Nothing's wrong." Blindly she reached toward her In basket and grabbed a file, although she hadn't a clue which one it was.

"If I didn't know better, I'd say you were daydreaming about a man."

Joanna managed a short, sarcastic laugh meant to deny everything. "Men are the last thing on my mind," she said flippantly. It was a half-truth. Men in the plural didn't interest her, but *man,* as in Tanner Lund, well, that was another matter.

Over the years Joanna had gone out of her way to avoid men she was attracted to—it was safer. She dated occasionally, but usually men who might be classified as pleasant, men for whom she could never feel anything beyond a mild friendship. Magnetism, charm and sex appeal were lost on her, thanks to a husband who'd possessed all three and systematically destroyed her faith in the possibility of a lasting relationship. At least, those qualities hadn't piqued her interest again, until she met Tanner. Okay, so her dating habits for the past few years had been a bit premeditated, but everyone deserved a night out now and again. It didn't seem fair to be denied the pleasure of a fun evening simply because she wasn't in the market for another husband. So she'd dated, not a lot, but some and nothing in the past six years had affected her as much as those few short hours with Nicole's father.

"Joanna!"

She jerked her head up to discover her boss still standing beside her desk. "Yes?"

"The Osborne file."

She briefly closed her eyes in a futile effort to clear her thoughts. "What about it?"

Robin glared at the ceiling and paused, as though pleading with the light fixture for patience. "Read it and get back to me before the end of the day—if that isn't too much to ask?"

"Sure," she grumbled, wondering what had put Robin in such a foul mood. She picked up the loan application and was halfway through it before she realized the name on it wasn't Osborne. Great! If her day continued like this, she could blame Tanner Lund for getting her fired.

When Joanna arrived home three hours later she was exhausted and short-tempered. She hadn't been herself all day, mainly because she'd been so preoccupied with thoughts of Tanner Lund and the way he'd kissed her. She was overreacting—she'd certainly been kissed before, so it shouldn't be such a big deal. But it was. Her behavior demonstrated all the maturity of someone Kristen's age, she chided herself. She'd simply forgotten how to act with men; it was too long since she'd been involved with one. The day wasn't a complete waste, however. She'd made a couple of important decisions in the last few hours, and she wanted to clear the air with her daughter before matters got completely out of hand.

"Hi, honey."

"Hi."

Kristen's gaze didn't waver from the television screen where a talk-show host was interviewing a man—at least Joanna thought it was a man—whose brilliant red hair was so short on top it stuck straight up and so long in front it fell over his face, obliterating his left eye and part of his nose.

"Who's that?"

Kristen gave a deep sigh of wonder and adolescent love. "You mean you don't know? I've been in love with Simply Red for a whole year and you don't even know the lead singer when you see him?"

"No, I can't say that I do."

"Oh, Mom, honestly, get with it."

There *it* was again. First she was losing *it* and now she was supposed to get with *it*. Joanna wished her daughter would decide which she wanted.

"We need to talk."

Kristen reluctantly dragged her eyes away from her idol. "Mom, this is important. Can't it wait?"

Frustrated, Joanna sighed and muttered, "I suppose."

"Good."

Kristen had already tuned her out. Joanna strolled into the kitchen and realized she hadn't taken the hamburger out of the freezer to thaw. Great. So much for the tacos she'd planned to make for dinner. She opened and closed cupboard doors, rummaging around for something interesting. A can of tuna fish wasn't likely to meet with Kristen's approval. One thing about her daughter that the approach of the teen years hadn't disrupted was her healthy appetite.

Joanna stuck her head around the corner. "How does tuna casserole sound for dinner?"

Kristen didn't even look in her direction, just held out her arm and jerked her thumb toward the carpet.

"Soup and sandwiches?"

Once more Kristen's thumb headed downward, and Joanna groaned.

"Bacon, lettuce and tomato on toast with chicken noodle soup," she tried. "And that's the best I can do. Take it or leave it."

Kristen sighed. "If that's the final offer, I'll take it. But I thought we were having tacos."

"We were. I forgot to take out the hamburger."

"All right, BLTs," Kristen muttered, reversing the direction of her thumb.

Joanna was frying the bacon when Kristen joined her, sitting on a stool while her mother worked. "You wanted to talk to me about something?"

"Yes." Joanna concentrated on spreading mayonnaise over slices of whole-wheat toast, as she made an effort to gather her scattered thoughts. She cast about for several moments, trying to come up with a way of saying what needed to be said without making more of it than necessary.

"It must be something big," Kristen commented. "Did my teacher phone you at work or something?"

"No, should she have?" She raised her eyes and scrutinized Kristen's face closely.

Kristen gave a quick denial with a shake of her head. "No way. I'm a star pupil this year. Nicole and I are both doing great. Just wait until report-card time, then you'll see."

"I believe you." Kristen had been getting top marks all year, and Joanna was proud of how well her daughter was doing. "What I have to say concerns Nicole and—" she hesitated, swallowing tightly "—her father."

"Mr. Lund sure is good-looking, isn't he?" Kristen said enthusiastically, watching for Joanna's reaction.

Reluctantly Joanna nodded, hoping to sound casual. "I suppose."

"Oh, come on, Mom, he's a hunk."

"All right," Joanna admitted slowly. "I'll grant you that Tanner has a certain amount of…appeal."

Kristen grinned, looking pleased with herself.

"Actually it was Mr. Lund I wanted to talk to you about," Joanna continued, placing a layer of tomato slices on the toast.

"Really?" The brown eyes opened even wider.

"Yes, well, I wanted to tell you that I…I don't think it would be a good idea for the four of us to go on doing things together."

Abruptly Kristen's face fell with surprise and disappointment. "Why not?"

"Well…because he and I are both really busy." Even to her own ears, the statement sounded illogical, but it was difficult to tell her own daughter that she was frightened of her attraction to the man. Difficult to explain why nothing could come of it.

"Because you're both busy? Come on, Mom, that doesn't make any sense."

"All right, I'll be honest." She wondered whether an eleven-year-old could grasp the complexities of adult relationships. "I don't want to give Nicole's dad the wrong idea," she said carefully.

Kristen leaned forward, setting her elbows on the kitchen counter and resting her face in both hands. Her gaze looked sharp enough to shatter diamonds. "The wrong idea about what?" she asked.

"Me," Joanna said, swallowing uncomfortably.

"You?" Kristen repeated thoughtfully, a frown creasing her smooth brow. She relaxed then and released a huge sigh. "Oh, I see. You think Mr. Lund might think you're in the marriage market."

Joanna pointed a fork at her daughter. "Bingo!"

"But, Mom, I think it would be great if you and Nicole's dad got together. In fact, Nicole and I were talking about it just today. Think about all the advantages. We could all be a real family, and you could have more babies… I don't know if I ever told you this, but I'd really like a baby brother, and so would Nicole. And if you married Mr. Lund we could take family vacations together. You wouldn't have to work, because… I don't know if you realize this, but Mr. Lund is pretty rich. You could stay home and bake cookies and sew and stuff."

Joanna was so surprised that it took her a minute to find her voice. Openmouthed, she waved the fork jerkily around. "No way, Kristen." Joanna's knees felt rubbery, and before she could slip to the floor, she slumped into a chair. All this time she'd assumed she was a good mother, giving her daughter everything she needed physically and emotionally, making up to Kristen as much as she could for her father's absence. But she apparently hadn't done enough. And Kristen and Nicole were scheming to get Joanna and Tanner together. As in married!

Something had to be done.

She decided to talk to Tanner, but an opportunity didn't present itself until much later that evening when Kristen was in bed, asleep. At least Joanna hoped her daughter was asleep. She dialed his number and prayed Nicole wouldn't answer.

Thankfully she didn't.

"Tanner, it's Joanna," she whispered, cupping her hand over the mouthpiece, taking no chance that Kristen could overhear their conversation.

"What's the matter? Have you got laryngitis?"

"No," she returned hoarsely, straining her voice. "I don't want Kristen to hear me talking to you."

"I see. Should I pretend you're someone else so Nicole won't tell on you?" he whispered back.

"Please." She didn't appreciate the humor in his voice. Obviously he had yet to realize the seriousness of the situation. "We need to talk."

"We do?"

"Trust me, Tanner. You have no idea what I just learned. The girls are planning on us getting married."

"Married?" he shouted.

That, Joanna had known, would get a reaction out of him.

"When do you want to meet?"

"As soon as possible." He still seemed to think she was

joking, but she couldn't blame him. If the situation were reversed, no doubt she would react the same way. "Kristen said something about the two of them swimming Wednesday night at the community pool. What if we meet at Denny's for coffee after you drop Nicole off?"

"What time?" He said it as though they were planning a reconnaissance mission deep into enemy territory.

"Seven-ten." That would give them both a few extra minutes to make it to the restaurant.

"Shall we synchronize our watches?"

"This isn't funny, Tanner."

"I'm not laughing."

But he was, and Joanna was furious with him. "I'll see you then."

"Seven-ten, Wednesday night at Denny's," he repeated. "I'll be there."

On the evening of their scheduled meeting, Joanna arrived at the restaurant before Tanner. She already regretted suggesting they meet at Denny's, but it was too late to change that now. There were bound to be other customers who would recognize either Tanner or her, and Joanna feared that word of their meeting could somehow filter back to the girls. She'd been guilty of underestimating them before; she wouldn't make the same mistake a second time. If Kristen and Nicole did hear about this private meeting, they'd consider it justification for further interference.

Tanner strolled into the restaurant and glanced around. He didn't seem to recognize Joanna, and she moved her sunglasses down her nose and gave him an abrupt wave.

He took one look at her, and even from the other side

of the room she could see he was struggling to hold in his laughter.

"What's with the scarf and sunglasses?"

"I'm afraid someone might recognize us and tell the girls." It made perfect sense to her, but obviously not to him. Joanna forgave him since he didn't know the extent of the difficulties facing them.

But all he said was, "I see." He inserted his hands in the pockets of his overcoat and walked lazily past her, whistling. "Should I sit here or would you prefer the next booth?"

"Don't be silly."

"I'm not going to comment on that."

"For heaven's sake," Joanna hissed, "sit down before someone notices you."

"Someone notices me? Lady, you're wearing sunglasses at night, in the dead of winter, and with that scarf tied around your chin you look like an immigrant fresh off the boat."

"Tanner," she said, "this is not the time to crack jokes."

A smile lifted his features as he slid into the booth opposite her. He reached for a menu. "Are you hungry?"

"No." His attitude was beginning to annoy her. "I'm just having coffee."

"Nicole cooked dinner tonight, and frankly I'm starving."

When the waitress appeared he ordered a complete dinner. Joanna asked for coffee.

"Okay, what's up, Sherlock?" he asked, once the coffee had been poured.

"To begin with I…I think Kristen and Nicole saw you kiss me the other night."

He made no comment, but his brow puckered slightly.

"It seems the two of them have been talking, and from what I gather they're interested in getting us, er, together."

"I see."

To Joanna's dismay, Tanner didn't seem to be the slightest bit concerned by her revelation.

"That troubles you?"

"Tanner," she said, leaning toward him, "to quote my daughter, 'Nicole and I have been talking and we thought it would be great if you and Mr. Lund got together. You could have more babies and we could go on vacations and be a real family and you could stay home and bake cookies and stuff.'" She waited for his reaction, but his face remained completely impassive.

"What kind of cookies?" he asked finally.

"Tanner, if you're going to turn this into a joke, I'm leaving." As far as Joanna was concerned, he deserved to be tormented by two dedicated eleven-year-old matchmakers! She started to slide out of the booth, but he stopped her with an upraised hand.

"All right, I'm sorry."

He didn't sound too contrite, and she gave a weak sigh of disgust. "You may consider this a joking matter, but I don't."

"Joanna, we're both mature adults," he stated calmly. "We aren't going to let a couple of eleven-year-old girls manipulate us!"

"Yes, but—"

"From the first, we've been honest with each other. That isn't going to change. You have no interest in remarriage—to me or anyone else—and I feel the same way. As long as we continue as we are now, the girls don't have a prayer."

"It's more than that," Joanna said vehemently. "We need to look past their schemes to the root of the problem."

"Which is?"

"Tanner, obviously we're doing something wrong as single parents."

He frowned. "What makes you say that?"

"Isn't it obvious? Kristen, and it seems equally true for Nicole, wants a complete family. What Kristen is really saying is that she longs for a father. Nicole is telling you she'd like a mother."

The humor drained out of Tanner's eyes, replaced with a look of real concern. "I see. And you think this all started because Kristen and Nicole saw us kissing?"

"I don't know," she murmured, shaking her head. "But I do know my daughter, and when she wants something, she goes after it with the force of a bulldog and won't let up. Once she's got it in her head that you and I are destined for each other, it's going to be pretty difficult for her to accept that all we'll ever be is friends."

"Nicole can get that way about certain things," he said thoughtfully.

The waitress delivered his roast beef sandwich and refilled Joanna's coffee cup.

Maybe she'd overreacted to the situation, but she couldn't help being worried. "I suppose you think I'm making more of a fuss about this than necessary," she said, flustered and a little embarrassed.

"About the girls manipulating us?"

"No, about the fact that we've both tried so hard to be good single parents, and obviously we're doing something wrong."

"I will admit that part concerns me."

"I don't mind telling you, Tanner, I've been in a panic all week, wondering where I've failed. We've got to come to terms with this. Make some important decisions."

"What do you suggest?"

"To start with, we've got to squelch any hint of personal involvement. I realize a certain amount of contact will be unavoidable with the girls being such close friends." She paused and chewed on her bottom lip. "I don't want to disrupt their relationship."

"I agree with you there. Being friends with Kristen has meant a good deal to Nicole."

"You and I went months without talking to each other," Joanna said, recalling that they'd only recently met. "There's no need for us to see each other now, is there?"

"That won't work."

"Why not?"

"Nicole will be spending the night with you again next Thursday—that is, unless you'd rather she didn't."

"Of course she can stay."

Tanner nodded, looking relieved. "To be honest, I don't think she'd go back to Mrs. Wagner's any more without raising a big fuss."

"Taking care of Nicole is one thing, but the four of us doing anything together is out of the question."

Once more he nodded, but he didn't look pleased with the suggestion. "I think that would be best, too."

"We can't give them any encouragement."

Pushing his plate aside, Tanner reached for his water glass, cupping it with both hands. "You know, Joanna, I think a lot of you." He paused, then gave her a teasing smile. "You have a habit of dressing a little oddly every now and then, but other than that I respect your judgment. I'd like to consider you a friend."

She decided to let his comment about her choice of clothing slide. "I'd like to be your friend, too," she told him softly.

He grinned, and his gaze held hers for a long uninterrupted moment before they both looked away. "I know you think that kiss the other night was a big mistake, and I suppose you're right, but I'm not sorry it happened." He hesitated, as though waiting for her to argue with him, and when she didn't, he continued. "It's been a lot of years since I held a woman's hand at a movie or kissed her the way I did you. It was good to feel that young and innocent again."

Joanna dropped her gaze to her half-filled cup. It had felt right for her, too. So right that she'd been frightened out of her wits ever since. She could easily fall in love with Tanner, and that would be the worst possible thing for her. She just wasn't ready to take those risks again. They came from different worlds, too, and she'd never fit comfortably in his. Yet every time she thought about that kiss, she started to shake from the inside out.

"In a strange sort of way we need each other," Tanner went on, his look thoughtful. "Nicole needs a strong loving woman to identify with, to fill a mother's role, and she thinks you're wonderful."

"And Kristen needs to see a man who can be a father, putting the needs of his family before his own."

"I think it's only natural for the two of them to try to get us together," Tanner added. "It's something we should be prepared to deal with in the future."

"You're right," Joanna agreed, understanding exactly what he meant. "We need each other to help provide what's lacking in our daughters' lives. But we can't get involved with each other." She didn't know any other way to say it but bluntly.

"I agree," he said, with enough conviction to lay aside any doubt Joanna might still hold.

They were silent for a long moment.

"Why?"

Strangely, Joanna knew immediately what he was asking. She had the same questions about what had happened between him and Nicole's mother.

"Davey was—is—the most charming personable man I've ever met. I was fresh out of college and so in love with him I didn't stop to think." She paused and glanced away, not daring to look at Tanner. Her voice had fallen so low it was almost a whisper. "We were engaged when my best friend, Carol, told me Davey had made a pass at her. Fool that I was, I didn't believe her. I thought she was jealous that Davey had chosen me to love and marry. I was sick that my friend would stoop to anything so underhand. I always knew Carol found him attractive—most women did—and I was devastated that she would lie that way. I trusted Davey so completely that I didn't even ask him about the incident. Later, after we were married, there were a lot of times when he said he was working late, a lot of unexplained absences, but I didn't question those, either. He was building his career in real estate, and if he had to put in extra hours, well, that was understandable. All those nights I sat alone, trusting him when he claimed he was working, believing with all my heart that he was doing his utmost to build a life for us…and then learning he'd been with some other woman."

"How'd you find out?"

"The first time?"

"You mean there was more than once?"

She nodded, hating to let Tanner know how many times she'd forgiven Davey, how many times she'd taken him back after he'd pleaded and begged and promised it would never happen again.

"I was blind to his wandering eye for the first couple of years. What they say about ignorance being bliss is true. When I found out, I was physically sick. When I realized how I'd fallen for his lies, it was even worse, and yet I stuck it out with him, trusting that everything would be better, everything would change…someday. I wanted so badly to believe him, to trust him, that I accepted anything he told me, no matter how implausible it sounded.

"The problem was that the more I forgave him, the lower my self-esteem dropped. I became convinced it was all my fault. I obviously lacked something, since he…felt a need to seek out other women."

"You know now that's not true, don't you?" His voice was so gentle, so caring, that Joanna battled down a rush of emotion.

"There'd never been a divorce in my family," she told him quietly. "My parents have been married nearly forty years, and my brothers all have happy marriages. I think that was one of the reasons I held on so long. I just didn't know how to let go. I'd be devastated and crushed when I learned about his latest affair, yet I kept coming back for more. I suppose I believed Davey would change. Something magical would happen and all our problems would disappear. Only it never did. One afternoon—I don't even know what prompted it…. All I knew was that I couldn't stay in the marriage any longer. I packed Kristen's and my things and walked out. I've never been back, never wanted to go back."

Tanner reached for her hand, and his fingers wrapped warmly around hers. A moment passed before he spoke, and when he did, his voice was tight with remembered pain. "I thought Carmen was the sweetest, gentlest woman in the world. As nonsensical as it sounds, I think I was in love with her before I even knew her name. She was a college cheerleader and a homecoming queen, and I felt like a nobody. By chance, we met several years after graduation when I'd just begun making a name for myself. I'd bought my first company, a small aluminum window manufacturer back in West Virginia. And I was working night and day to see it through those first rough weeks of transition.

"I was high on status," Tanner admitted, his voice filled with regret. "Small-town boy makes good—that kind of stuff. She'd been the most popular girl in my college year, and dating her was the fulfillment of a fantasy. She'd recently broken up with a guy she'd been involved with for two years and had something to prove herself, I suppose." He focused his gaze away from Joanna. "Things got out of hand and a couple of months later Carmen announced she was pregnant. To be honest, I was happy about it, thrilled. There was never any question whether I'd marry her. By then I was so in love with her I couldn't see straight. Eight months after the wedding, Nicole was born..." He hesitated, as though gathering his thoughts. "Some women are meant to be mothers, but not Carmen. She didn't even like to hold Nicole, didn't want anything to do with her. I'd come home at night and find that Carmen had neglected Nicole most of the day. But I made excuses for her, reasoned everything out in my own mind—the unexplained bruises on the baby, the fear I saw in Nicole's eyes whenever her mother was around. It got so bad that I started dropping Nicole off at my parents', just so I could be sure she was being looked after properly."

Joanna bit the corner of her lip at the raw pain she witnessed in Tanner's eyes. She was convinced he didn't speak of his marriage often, just as she rarely talked about Davey, but this was necessary if they were to understand each other.

"To be fair to Carmen, I wasn't much of a husband in those early months. Hell, I didn't have time to be. I was feeling like a big success when we met, but that didn't last long. Things started going wrong at work and I damn near lost my shirt.

"Later," he continued slowly, "I learned that the entire time I was struggling to hold the company together, Carmen was seeing her old boyfriend, Sam Dailey."

"Oh, Tanner."

"Nicole's my daughter, there was no doubting that. But Carmen had never really wanted children, and she felt trapped in the marriage. We separated when Nicole was less than three years old."

"I thought you said you'd only been divorced five years?"

"We have. It took Carmen a few years to get around to the legal aspect of things. I wasn't in any rush, since I had no intention of ever marrying again."

"What's happened to Carmen since? Did she remarry?"

"Eventually. She lived with Sam for several years, and the last thing I heard was they'd split up and she married a professional baseball player."

"Does Nicole ever see her mother?" Joanna remembered that he'd said his ex-wife saw Nicole only when it was convenient.

"She hasn't in the past three years. The thing I worry about most is having Carmen show up someday, demanding that Nicole come to live with her. Nicole doesn't remember anything about those early years—thank God—and she seems to have formed a rosy image of her mother. She keeps Carmen's picture in her bedroom and every once in a while I'll see her staring at it wistfully." He paused and glanced at his watch. "What time were we supposed to pick up the kids?"

"Eight."

"It's five after now."

"Oh, good grief." Joanna slung her bag over her shoulder as they slid out of the booth and hurried toward the cash register. Tanner insisted on paying for her coffee, and Joanna didn't want to waste time arguing.

They walked briskly toward their cars, parked beside each other in the lot. "Joanna," he called, as she fumbled with her keys. "I'll wait a couple of minutes so we don't both arrive at the same time. Otherwise the girls will probably guess we've been together."

She flashed him a grateful smile. "Good thinking."

"Joanna." She looked at him questioningly as he shortened the distance between them. "Don't misunderstand this," he said softly. He pulled her gently into the circle of his arms, holding her close for a lingering moment. "I'm sorry for what Davey did to you. The man's a fool." Tenderly he brushed his lips over her forehead, then turned and abruptly left her.

It took Joanna a full minute to recover enough to get into her car and drive away.

Seven

"Mom," Kristen screeched, "the phone's for you."

Joanna was surprised. A call for her on a school night was rare enough, but one that actually got through with Kristen and Nicole continually on the line was a special occasion.

"Who is it, honey?" No doubt someone interested in cleaning her carpets or selling her a cemetery plot.

"I don't know," Kristen said, holding the phone to her shoulder. She lowered her voice to whisper. "But whoever it is sounds weird."

"Hello." Joanna spoke into the receiver as Kristen wandered toward her bedroom.

"Can you talk?" The husky male voice was unmistakably Tanner's.

"Y-yes." Joanna looked toward Kristen's bedroom to be certain her daughter was out of earshot.

"Can you meet me tomorrow for lunch?"

"What time?"

"Noon at the Sea Galley."

"Should we synchronize our watches?" Joanna couldn't

resist asking. It had been a week since she'd last talked to Tanner. In the meantime she hadn't heard a word from Kristen about getting their two families together again. That in itself was suspicious, but Joanna had been too busy at work to think about it.

"Don't be cute, Joanna. I need help."

"Buy me lunch and I'm yours." She hadn't meant that quite the way it sounded and was grateful Tanner didn't comment on her slip of the tongue.

"I'll see you tomorrow, then."

"Right."

A smile tugged at the edges of her mouth as she replaced the telephone receiver. Her hand lingered there for a moment as an unexpected tide of happiness washed over her.

"Who was that, Mom?" Kristen asked, poking her head around her bedroom door.

"A…friend, calling to ask if I could meet…her for lunch."

"Oh." Kristen's young face was a study in skepticism. "For a minute there I thought it sounded like Mr. Lund trying to fake a woman's voice."

"Mr. Lund? That's silly," Joanna said with a forced little laugh, then deftly changed the subject. "Kristen, it's nine-thirty. Hit the hay, kiddo."

"Right, Mom. 'Night."

"'Night, sweetheart."

"Enjoy your lunch tomorrow."

"I will."

Joanna hadn't had a chance to walk away from the phone before it pealed a second time. She gave a guilty start and reached for it.

"Hello," she said hesitantly, half expecting to hear Tanner's voice again.

But it was her mother's crisp clear voice that rang over the wire. "Joanna, I hope this isn't too late to call."

"Of course not, Mom," Joanna answered quickly. "Is everything all right?"

Her mother ignored the question and asked one of her own instead. "What was the name of that young man you're dating again?"

"Mother," Joanna said with an exasperated sigh, "I'm not seeing anyone. I told you that."

"Tanner Lund, wasn't it?"

"We went out to dinner *once* with both our daughters, and that's the extent of our relationship. If Kristen let you assume anything else, it was just wishful thinking on her part. One dinner, I swear."

"But, Joanna, he sounds like such a nice young man. He's the same Tanner Lund who recently bought half of Spokane Aluminum, isn't he? I saw his name in the paper this morning and recognized it right away. Sweetie, your dad and I are so pleased you're dating such a famous successful man."

"Mother, please!" Joanna cried. "Tanner and I are friends. How many times do I have to tell you, we're not dating? Kristen and Tanner's daughter, Nicole, are best friends. I swear that's all there is to—"

"Joanna," her mother interrupted. "The first time you mentioned his name, I heard something in your voice that's been missing for a good long while. You may be able to fool yourself, but not me. You like this Tanner." Her voice softened perceptively.

"Mother, nothing could possibly come of it even if I was attracted to him—which I'm not." Okay, so that last part wasn't entirely true. But the rest of it certainly was.

"And why couldn't it?" her mother insisted.

"You said it yourself. He's famous, in addition to being wealthy. I'm out of his league."

"Nonsense," her mother responded in a huff.

Joanna knew better than to get into a war of words with her stubborn parent.

"Now, don't be silly. You like Tanner Lund, and I say it's about time you let down those walls you've built around yourself. Joanna, sweetie, you've been hiding behind them for six years now. Don't let what happened with Davey ruin your whole life."

"I'm not going to," Joanna promised.

There was a long pause before her mother sighed and answered, "Good. You deserve some happiness."

At precisely noon the following day, Joanna drove into the Sea Galley parking lot. Tanner was already there, waiting for her by the entrance.

"Hi," she said with a friendly grin, as he walked toward her.

"What, no disguises?"

Joanna laughed, embarrassed now by that silly scarf and sunglasses she'd worn when they met at Denny's. "Kristen doesn't know anyone who eats here."

"I'm grateful for that."

His smile was warm enough to tunnel through snowdrifts, and as much as Joanna had warned herself not to be affected by it, she was.

"It's good to see you," Tanner added, taking her arm to escort her into the restaurant.

"You, too." Although she hadn't seen him in almost a week, Tanner was never far from her thoughts. Nicole had stayed with her and Kristen when Tanner flew to New York for two days in the middle of the previous week. The Spokane area had been hit by a fierce snowstorm the evening he left. Joanna had felt nervous the entire time about his traveling in such inclement weather, yet she hadn't so much as asked him about his flight when he arrived to pick up Nicole. Their conversation had been brief and pleasantly casual, but her relief that he'd got home safely had kept her awake for hours. Later, she'd been furious with herself for caring so much.

The Sea Galley hostess seated them right away and handed them thick menus. Joanna ordered a shrimp salad and coffee. Tanner echoed her choice.

"Nicole's birthday is next week," he announced, studying her face carefully. "She's handing out the party invitations today at school."

Joanna smiled and nodded. But Tanner's eyes held hers, and she saw something unidentifiable flicker there.

"In a moment of weakness, I told her she could have a slumber party."

Joanna's smile faded. "As I recall, Nicole did mention something about this party," she said, trying to sound cheerful. The poor guy didn't know what he was in for. "You're obviously braver than I am."

"You think it was a bad move?"

Joanna made a show of closing her eyes and nodding vigorously.

"I was afraid of that," Tanner muttered, and he rearranged the silverware around his place setting a couple of times. "I know we agreed it probably wouldn't be a good idea for us to do things together. But I need some advice—from a friend."

"What can I do?"

"Joanna, I haven't the foggiest idea about entertaining

a whole troop of girls. I can handle contract negotiations and make split-second business decisions, but I panic at the thought of all those squealing little girls sequestered in my apartment for all those hours."

"How do you want me to help?"

"Would you consider…" He gave her a hopeful look, then shook his head regretfully. "No. I can't ask that of you. Besides, we don't want to give the girls any more ideas about the two of us. What I really need is some suggestions for keeping all these kids occupied. What do other parents do?"

"Other parents know better."

Tanner wiped a lock of dark brown hair from his brow and frowned. "I was afraid of that."

"What time are the girls supposed to arrive?"

"Six."

"Tanner, that's too early."

"I know, but Nicole insists I serve my special tacos, and she has some screwy idea about all the girls crowding into the kitchen to watch me."

Now it was Joanna's turn to frown. "That won't work. You'll end up with ten different pairs of hands trying to help. There'll be hamburger and cheese from one end of the place to the other."

"I thought as much. Good Lord, Joanna, how did I get myself into this mess?"

"Order pizza," she tossed out, tapping her index finger against her bottom lip. "Everyone loves that."

"Pizza. Okay. What about games?"

"A scavenger hunt always comes in handy when things get out of hand. Release the troops on your unsuspecting neighbors."

"So far we've got thirty minutes of the first fourteen hours filled."

"Movies," Joanna suggested next. "Lots of movies. You can phone early and reserve a couple of new releases and add an old favorite like *Pretty in Pink,* and the girls will be in seventh heaven."

His eyes brightened. "Good idea."

"And if you really feel adventurous, take them roller-skating."

"Roller-skating? You think they'd like that?"

"They'd love it, especially if word leaked out that they were going to be at the rink Friday night. That way, several of the boys from the sixth-grade class can just happen to be there, too."

Tanner nodded, and a smile quirked the corners of his mouth. "And you think that'll keep everyone happy?"

"I'm sure of it. Wear 'em out first, show a movie or two second, with the lights out, of course, and I guarantee you by midnight everyone will be sound asleep."

Their salads arrived and Tanner stuck his fork into a fat succulent shrimp, then paused. "Now what was it you said last night about buying you lunch and making you mine?"

"It was a slip of the tongue," she muttered, dropping her gaze to her salad.

"Just my luck."

They laughed, and it felt good. Joanna had never had a relationship like this with a man. She wasn't on her guard the way she normally was, fearing that her date would put too much stock in an evening or two out. Because their daughters were the same age, they had a lot in common. They were both single parents doing their damnedest to raise their daughters right. The normal dating rituals and practiced moves were unnecessary with him. Tanner was her friend, and it renewed Joanna's faith in the opposite sex to know there were still men like him left. Their friendship reassured her—but the undeniable attraction between them still frightened her.

"I really appreciate your suggestions," he said, after they'd both concentrated on their meals for several moments. "I've had this panicky feeling for the past three days. I suppose it wasn't a brilliant move on my part to call you at home, but I was getting desperate."

"You'll do fine. Just remember, it's important to keep the upper hand."

"I'll try."

"By the way, when *is* Hell Night?" She couldn't resist teasing him.

He gave a heartfelt sigh. "Next Friday."

Joanna slowly ate a shrimp. "I think Kristen figured out it was you on the phone last night."

"She did?"

"Yeah. She started asking questions the minute I hung up. She claimed my 'friend' sounded suspiciously like Mr. Lund faking a woman's voice."

Tanner cleared his throat and answered in a high falsetto. "That should tell you how desperate I was."

Joanna laughed and speared another shrimp. "That's what friends are for."

Eight

"Mom, hurry or we're going to be late." Kristen paced the hallway outside her mother's bedroom door while Joanna finished dressing.

"Have you got Nicole's gift?"

"Oh." Kristen dashed into her bedroom and returned with a gaily wrapped oblong box. They'd bought the birthday gift the night before, a popular board game, which Kristen happened to know Nicole really wanted.

"I think Mr. Lund is really nice to let Nicole have a slumber party, don't you?"

"Really brave is a more apt description. How many girls are coming?"

"Fifteen."

"Fifteen!" Joanna echoed in a shocked voice.

"Nicole originally invited twenty, but only fifteen could make it."

Joanna slowly shook her head. He'd had good reason to feel panicky. With all these squealing, giddy preadolescent girls, the poor man would be certifiable by the end of the night. Either that or a prime candidate for extensive counseling.

When they arrived, the parking area outside Tanner's apartment building looked like the scene of a rock concert. There were enough parents dropping off kids to cause a minor traffic jam.

"I can walk across the street if you want to let me out here," Kristen suggested, anxiously eyeing the group of girls gathering outside the building.

"I'm going to find a parking place," Joanna said, scanning the side streets for two adjacent spaces—so that she wouldn't need to struggle to parallel park.

"You're going to find a place to leave the car? Why?" Kristen wanted to know, her voice higher pitched and more excited than usual. "You don't have to come in, if you don't want. I thought you said you were going to refinish that old chair Grandpa gave us last summer."

"I was," Joanna murmured with a short sigh, "but I have the distinct impression that Nicole's father is going to need a helping hand."

"I'm sure he doesn't, Mom. Mr. Lund is a really organized person. I'm sure he's got everything under control."

Kristen's reaction surprised Joanna. She would have expected her daughter to encourage the idea of getting the two of them together.

She finally found a place to park and they hurried across the street, Kristen apparently deep in thought.

"Actually, Mom, I think helping Mr. Lund might be a good idea," she said after a long pause. "He'll probably be grateful."

Joanna wasn't nearly as confident by this time. "I have a feeling I'm going to regret this later."

"No, you won't." Joanna could tell Kristen was about to launch into another one of her little speeches about babies, vacations and homemade cookies. Thankfully she didn't get the chance, since they'd entered the building and encountered a group of Kristen's other friends.

Tanner was standing in the doorway of his apartment, already looking frazzled when Joanna arrived. Surprise flashed through his eyes when he saw her.

"I've come to help," she announced, peeling off her jacket and pushing up the sleeves of her thin sweater. "This group is more than one parent can reasonably be expected to control."

He looked for a moment as though he wanted to fall to the ground and kiss her feet. "Bless you."

"Believe me, Tanner, you owe me for this." She glanced around at the chaos that dominated the large apartment. The girls had already formed small groups and were arguing loudly with each other over some subject of earth-shattering importance—like Bruce Springsteen's age, or the real color of Billy Idol's hair.

"Is the pizza ready?" Joanna asked him, raising her voice in order to be heard over the din of squeals, shouts and rock music.

Tanner nodded. "It's in the kitchen. I ordered eight large ones. Do you think that'll be enough?"

Joanna rolled her eyes. "I suspect you're going to be eating leftover pizza for the next two weeks."

The girls proved her wrong. Never had Joanna seen a hungrier group. They were like school of piranha attacking a hapless victim, and within fifteen minutes everyone had eaten her fill. There were one or two slices left of four of the pizzas, but the others had vanished completely.

"It's time for a movie," Joanna decided, and while the

girls voted on which film to see first Tanner started dumping dirty paper plates and pop cans into a plastic garbage sack. When the movie was finished, Joanna calculated, it would be time to go skating.

Peace reigned once Tom Cruise appeared on the television screen and Joanna joined Tanner in the bright cheery kitchen.

He was sitting dejectedly at the round table, rubbing a hand across his forehead. "I feel a headache coming on."

"It's too late for that," she said with a soft smile. "Actually I think everything is going very well. Everyone seems to be having a good time, and Nicole is a wonderful hostess."

"You do? She is?" He gave her an astonished look. "I keep having nightmares about pillow fights and lost dental appliances."

"Hey, it isn't going to happen." Not while they maintained control. "Tanner, I meant what I said about the party going well. In fact, I'm surprised at how smoothly everything is falling into place. The kids really are having a good time, and as long as we keep them busy there shouldn't be any problems."

He grinned, looking relieved. "I don't know about you, but I could use a cup of coffee."

"I'll second that."

He poured coffee into two pottery mugs and carried them to the table. Joanna sat across from him, propping her feet on the opposite chair. Sighing, she leaned back and cradled the steaming mug.

"The pizza was a good idea." He reached for a piece and shoved the box in her direction.

Now that she had a chance to think about it, Joanna realized she'd been so busy earlier, serving the girls, she hadn't managed to eat any of the pizza herself. She straightened enough to reach for a napkin and a thick slice dotted with pepperoni and spicy Italian sausage.

"What made you decide to give up your evening to help me out?" Tanner asked, watching her closely. "Kristen told Nicole that you had a hot date tonight. You were the last person I expected to see."

Joanna wasn't sure what had changed her mind about tonight and staying to help Tanner. Pity, she suspected. "If the situation were reversed, you'd lend me a hand," she replied, more interested in eating than conversation at the moment.

Tanner frowned at his pizza. "You missed what I was really asking."

"I did?"

"I was trying to be subtle about asking if you had a date tonight."

Joanna found that question odd. "Obviously I didn't."

"It isn't so obvious to me. You're a single parent, so there aren't that many evenings you can count on being free of responsibility. I would have thought you'd use this time to go out with someone special, flap your wings and that sort of thing." His frown grew darker.

"I'm too old to flap my wings," she said with a soft chuckle. "Good grief, I'm over thirty."

"So you aren't dating anyone special?"

"Tanner, you know I'm not."

"I don't know anything of the sort." Although he didn't raise his voice, Joanna could sense his disquiet.

"All right, what's up?" She didn't like the looks he was giving her. Not one bit.

"Nicole."

"Nicole?" she repeated.

"She was telling me that the other day that you'd met someone recently. 'A real prince' is the phrase she used. Someone rich and handsome who was crazy about you—she claimed you were seeing a lot of this guy. Said you were falling madly in love."

Joanna dropped her feet to the floor with a loud thud and bolted upright so fast she nearly tumbled out of the chair. She was furiously chewing her pepperoni-and-sausage pizza, trying to swallow it as quickly as she could. All the while, her finger was pointing, first toward the living room where the girls were innocently watching *Top Gun* and then at Tanner who was staring at her in fascination.

"Hey, don't get angry with me," he said. "I'm only repeating what Kristen supposedly told Nicole and what Nicole told me."

She swallowed the piece of pizza in one huge lump. "They're plotting again, don't you see? I should have known something was up. It's been much too quiet lately. Kristen and Nicole are getting devious now, because the direct approach didn't work." Flustered, she started pacing the kitchen floor.

"Settle down, Joanna. We're smarter than a couple of schoolkids."

"That's easy for you to say." She pushed her hair away from her forehead and continued to pace. Little wonder Kristen hadn't been keen on the idea of her helping Tanner tonight. Joanna whirled around to face him. "Well, aren't you going to say something?" To her dismay, she discovered he was doing his best not to chuckle. "This isn't a laughing matter, Tanner Lund. I wish you'd take this seriously!"

"I am."

Joanna snorted softly. "You are not!"

"We're mature adults, Joanna. We aren't going to allow two children to dictate our actions."

"Is that a fact?" She braced both hands against her hips and glared at him. "I'm pleased to hear you're such a tower of strength, but I'll bet a week's pay that it wasn't your idea to have this slumber party. You probably rejected the whole thing the first time Nicole suggested it, but after having the subject of a birthday slumber party brought up thirty times in about thirty minutes you weakened, and that was when Nicole struck the fatal blow. If your daughter is anything like mine, she probably used every trick in the book to talk you into this party idea. Knowing how guilty you felt about all those business trips, I suppose Nicole brought them up ten or twelve times. And before you knew what hit you, there were fifteen little girls spending the night at your apartment."

Tanner paled.

"Am I right?" she insisted.

He shrugged and muttered disparagingly, "Close enough."

Slumping into the chair, Joanna pushed the pizza box aside and forcefully expelled her breath. "I don't mind telling you, I'm concerned about this. If Kristen and Nicole are plotting against us, then we've got to form some kind of plan of our own before they drive us out of our minds. We can't allow them to manipulate us like this."

"I think you may be right."

She eyed him hopefully. "Any suggestions?" If he was smart enough to manage a couple of thousand employees, surely he could figure out a way to keep two eleven-year-olds under control.

Slouched in his chair, his shoulders sagging, Tanner shook his head. "None. What about you?"

"Communication is the key."

"Right."

"We've got to keep in touch with each other and keep tabs on what's going on with these two. Don't believe a thing they say until we check it out with the other."

"We've got another problem, Joanna," Tanner said, looking in every direction but hers.

"What?"

"It worked."

"What worked?" she asked irritably. Why was he speaking in riddles?

"Nicole's telling me that you'd been swept off your feet by this rich guy."

"Yes?" He still wasn't making any sense.

"The purpose of that whole fabrication was to make me jealous—and it worked."

"It worked?" An icy numb feeling swept through her. Swallowing became difficult.

Tanner nodded. "I kept thinking about how much I liked you. How much I enjoyed talking to you. And then I decided that when this slumber party business was over, I was going to risk asking you out to dinner."

"But I've already told you I'm not interested in a romantic relationship. One marriage was more than enough for me."

"I don't think that's what bothered me."

"Then what did?"

It was obvious from the way his eyes darted around the room that he felt uncomfortable. "I kept thinking about another man kissing you, and frankly, Joanna, that's what bothered me most."

The kitchen suddenly went so quiet that Joanna was almost afraid to breathe. The only noise was the faint sound of the movie playing in the other room.

Joanna tried to put herself in Tanner's place, wondering how she'd feel if Kristen announced that he'd met a gorgeous blonde and was dating her. Instantly she felt her stomach muscles tighten. There wasn't the slightest doubt in Joanna's mind that the girls' trick would have worked on her, too. Just the thought of Tanner's kissing another woman produced a curious ache, a pain that couldn't be described—or denied.

"Kissing you that night was the worst thing I could have done," Tanner conceded reluctantly. "I know you don't want to talk about it. I don't blame you—"

"Tanner," she interjected in a low hesitant voice, which hardly resembled her own. "It would have worked with me, too."

His eyes were dark and piercing. "Are you certain?"

She nodded, feeling utterly defeated yet strangely excited. "I'm afraid so. What are we going to do now?"

The silence returned as they stared at one another.

"The first thing I think we should do is experiment a little," he suggested in a flat emotionless voice. Then he released a long sigh. "Almost three weeks have passed since the night we took the girls out, and we've both had plenty of time to let that kiss build in our minds. Right?"

"Right," Joanna agreed. She'd attempted to put that kiss completely out of her mind, but it hadn't worked, and there was no point in telling him otherwise.

"It seems to me," Tanner continued thoughtfully, "that we should kiss again, for the sake of research, and find out what we're dealing with here."

She didn't need him to kiss her again to know she was going to like it. The first time had been ample opportunity for her to recognize how strongly she was attracted to Tanner Lund, and she didn't need another kiss to remind her.

"Once we know, we can decide where to go from there. Agreed?"

"Okay," she said impulsively, ignoring the small voice that warned of danger.

He stood up and held out his hand. She stared at it for a moment, uncertain. "You want to kiss right now?"

"Do you know of a better time?"

She shook her head. Good grief, she couldn't believe she was doing this. Tanner stretched out his arms and she walked into them with all the finesse of tumbleweed. The way she fit so snugly, so comfortably into his embrace worried her already. And he hadn't even kissed her yet.

Tanner held her lightly, his eyes wide and curious as he stared down at her. First he cocked his head to the right, then abruptly changed his mind and moved it to the left.

Joanna's movements countered his until she was certain they looked like a pair of ostriches who couldn't make up their minds.

"Are you comfortable?" he asked, and his voice was slightly hoarse.

Joanna nodded. She wished he'd hurry up and do it before one of the girls came crashing into the kitchen and found them. With their luck, it would be either Kristen or Nicole. Or both.

"You ready?" he asked.

Joanna nodded again. He was looking at her almost anxiously as though they were waiting for an imminent explosion. And that was exactly the way it felt when Tanner's mouth settled on hers, even though the kiss was infinitely gentle, his lips sliding over hers like a soft summer rain, barely touching.

Thcy broke apart, momentarily stunned. Neither spoke,

and then Tanner kissed her again, moving his mouth over her parted lips in undisguised hunger. His hand clutched the thick hair at her nape as she raised her arms and tightened them around his neck, leaning into him, absorbing his strength.

Tanner groaned softly and deepened the kiss until it threatened to consume Joanna. She met his fierce urgency with her own, arching closer to him, holding on to him with everything that was in her.

An unabating desire flared to life between them as he kissed her again and again, until they were both breathless and shaking.

"Joanna," he groaned, and dragged in several deep breaths. After taking a long moment to compose himself, he asked, "What do you think?" The question was murmured into her hair.

Joanna's chest was heaving, as though she'd been running and was desperate for oxygen. "I…I don't know," she lied, silently calling herself a coward.

"I do."

"You do?"

"Good Lord, Joanna, you taste like heaven. We're in trouble here. Deep trouble."

Nine

The pop music at the roller-skating rink blared from huge speakers and vibrated around the room. A disc jockey announced the tunes from a glass-fronted booth and joked with the skaters as they circled the polished hardwood floor.

"I can't believe I let you talk me into this," Joanna muttered, sitting beside Tanner as she laced up her rented high-top white skates.

"I refuse to be the only one over thirty out there," he replied, but he was smiling, obviously pleased with his persuasive talents. No doubt he'd take equal pleasure in watching her fall flat on her face. It had been years since Joanna had worn a pair of roller skates. *Years.*

"It's like riding a bicycle," Tanner assured her with that maddening grin of his. "Once you know how, you never forget."

Joanna grumbled under her breath, but she was actually beginning to look forward to this. She'd always loved roller-skating as a kid, and there was something about being with

Tanner that brought out the little girl in her. *And the woman,* she thought, remembering their kiss.

Nicole's friends were already skating with an ease that made Joanna envious. Slowly, cautiously, she joined the crowd circling the rink.

"Hi, Mom." Kristen zoomed past at the speed of light.

"Hi, Mrs. Parsons," Nicole shouted, following her friend.

Staying safely near the side, within easy reach of the handrail, Joanna concentrated on making her feet work properly, wheeling them back and forth as smoothly as possible. But instead of the gliding motion achieved by the others, her movements were short and jerky. She didn't acknowledge the girls' greetings with anything more than a raised hand and was slightly disconcerted to see the other skaters giving her a wide berth. They obviously recognized danger when they saw it.

Tanner glided past her, whirled around and deftly skated backward, facing Joanna. She looked up and threw him a weak smile. She should have known Tanner would be as confident on skates as he seemed to be at everything else—except slumber parties for eleven-year-old girls. Looking at him, one would think he'd been skating every day for years, although he claimed it was twenty years since he'd been inside a rink. It was clear from the expert way he soared across the floor that he didn't need to relearn anything—unlike Joanna, who felt as awkward as a newborn foal attempting to stand for the first time.

"How's it going?" he asked, with a cocky grin.

"Great. Can't you tell?" Just then, her right foot jerked out from under her and she groped desperately for the rail, managing to get a grip on it seconds before she went crashing to the floor.

Tanner was by her side at once. “You okay?”

“About as okay as anyone who has stood on the edge and looked into the deep abyss,” she muttered.

“Come on, what you need is a strong hand to guide you.”

Joanna snorted. “Forget it, fellow. I’ll be fine in a few minutes, once I get my sea legs.”

“You’re sure?”

“Tanner, for heaven’s sake, at least leave me with my pride intact!” Keeping anything intact at the moment was difficult, with her feet flaying wildly as she tried to pull herself back into an upright position.

“Okay, if that’s what you want,” he said, shrugging, and sailed away from her with annoying ease.

Fifteen minutes later, Joanna felt steady enough to join the main part of the crowd circling the rink. Her movements looked a little less clumsy, a little less shaky, though she certainly wasn’t in complete control.

“Hey, you’re doing great,” Tanner said, slowing down enough to skate beside her.

“Thanks,” she said breathlessly, studying her feet in an effort to maintain her balance.

“You’ve got a gift for this,” he teased.

She looked up at him and laughed outright. “Isn’t that the truth! I wonder if I should consider a new career as a roller-skating waitress at the Pink Palace.”

Amusement lifted the edge of his sensuous mouth. “Has anyone ever told you that you have an odd sense of humor?”

Looking at Tanner distracted Joanna, and her feet floundered for an instant. “Kristen does at least once a day.”

Tanner chuckled. “I shouldn’t laugh. Nicole tells me the same thing.”

The disc jockey announced that the next song was for

couples only. Joanna gave a sigh of relief and aimed her body toward the nearest exit. She could use the break; her calf muscles were already protesting the unaccustomed exercise. She didn't need roller-skating to remind her she wasn't a kid.

"How about it, Joanna?" Tanner asked, skating around her.

"How about what?"

"Skating together for the couples' dance. You and me and fifty thousand preteens sharing center stage." He offered her his hand. The lights had dimmed and a mirrored ball hanging in the middle of the ceiling cast speckled shadows over the floor.

"No way, Tanner," she muttered, ignoring his hand.

"I thought not. Oh, well, I'll see if I can get Nicole to skate with her dear old dad." Effortlessly he glided toward the group of girls who stood against the wall flirtatiously challenging the boys on the other side with their eyes.

Once Joanna was safely off the rink, she found a place to sit and rest her weary bones. Within a couple of minutes, Tanner lowered himself into the chair beside her, looking chagrined.

"I got beat out by Tommy Spenser," he muttered.

Joanna couldn't help it—she was delighted. Now Tanner would understand how she'd felt when Kristen announced she didn't want her mother sitting with her at the movies. Tanner looked just as dejected as Joanna had felt then.

"It's hell when they insist on growing up, isn't it?" she said, doing her best not to smile, knowing he wouldn't appreciate it.

He heaved an expressive sigh and gave her a hopeful look before glancing out at the skating couples. "I don't suppose you'd reconsider?"

The floor was filled with kids, and Joanna knew the minute she moved onto the hardwood surface with Tanner, every eye in the place would be on them.

He seemed to read her mind, because he added, "Come on, Joanna. My ego has just suffered a near-mortal wound. I've been rejected by my own flesh and blood."

She swallowed down a comment and awkwardly rose to her feet, struggling to remain upright. "When my ego got shot to bits at the movie theater, all you did was share your popcorn with me."

He chuckled and reached for her hand. "Don't complain. This gives me an excuse to put my arm around you again." His right arm slipped around her waist, and she tucked her left hand in his as they moved side by side. She had to admit it felt incredibly good to be this close to him. Almost as good as it had felt being in his arms for those few moments in his kitchen.

Tanner must have been thinking the same thing, because he was unusually quiet as he directed her smoothly across the floor to the strains of a romantic ballad. They'd circled the rink a couple of times when Tanner abruptly switched position, skating backward and holding on to her as though they were dancing.

"Tanner," she said, surprise widening her eyes as he swept her into his arms. "The girls will start thinking…things if we skate like this."

"Let them."

His hands locked at the base of her spine and he pulled her close. Very close. Joanna drew a slow breath, savoring the feel of Tanner's body pressed so intimately against her own.

"Joanna, listen," he whispered. "I've been thinking."

So had she. Hard to do when she was around Tanner.

"Would it really be such a terrible thing if we were to start seeing more of each other? On a casual basis—it doesn't have to be anything serious. We're both mature adults. Neither of us is going to allow the girls to manipulate us into anything we don't want. And as far as the past is concerned, I'm not Davey and you're not Carmen."

Why, Joanna wondered, was the most important discussion she'd had in years taking place in a roller-skating rink with a top-forty hit blaring in one ear and Tanner whispering in the other? Deciding to ignore the thought, she said, "But the girls might start making assumptions, and I'm afraid we'd only end up disappointing them."

Tanner disagreed. "I feel our seeing each other might help more than it would hinder."

"How do you mean?" Joanna couldn't believe she was actually entertaining this suggestion. Entertaining was putting it mildly; her heart was doing somersaults at the prospect of seeing Tanner more often. She was thrilled, excited…and yet hesitant. The wounds Davey had inflicted went very deep.

"If we see each other more often we could include the girls, and that should lay to rest some of the fears we've had over their matchmaking efforts. And spending time with you will help satisfy Nicole's need for a strong mother figure. At the same time, I can help Kristen, by being a father figure."

"Yes, but—"

"The four of us together will give the girls a sense of belonging to a whole family," Tanner added confidently.

His arguments sounded so reasonable, so logical. Still, Joanna remained uncertain. "But I'm afraid the girls will think we're serious."

Tanner lifted his head enough to look into her eyes, and

Joanna couldn't remember a time they'd ever been bluer or more intense. "I am serious."

She pressed her forehead against his collarbone and willed her body to stop trembling. Their little kissing experiment had affected her far more than she dared let him know. Until tonight, they'd both tried to disguise or deny their attraction for each other, but the kiss had exposed everything.

"I haven't stopped thinking about you from the minute we first met," he whispered, and touched his lips to her temple. "If we were anyplace else right now, I'd show you how crazy I am about you."

If they'd been anyplace else, Joanna would have let him. She wanted him to kiss her, needed him to, but she was more frightened by her reaction to this one man than she'd been by anything else in a very long while. "Tanner, I'm afraid."

"Joanna, so am I, but I can't allow fear to rule my life." Gently he brushed the loose wisps of curls from the side of her face. His eyes studied her intently. "I didn't expect to feel this way again. I've guarded against letting this happen, but here we are, and Joanna, I don't mind telling you, I wouldn't change a thing."

Joanna closed her eyes and listened to the battle raging inside her head. She wanted so badly to give this feeling between them a chance to grow. But logic told her that if she agreed to his suggestion, she'd be making herself vulnerable again. Even worse, Tanner Lund wasn't just any man—he was wealthy and successful, the half owner of an important company. And she was just a loan officer at a small local bank.

"Joanna, at least tell me what you're feeling."

"I…I don't know," she hedged, still uncertain.

He gripped her hand and pressed it over his heart, holding it there. "Just feel what you do to me."

Her own heart seemed about to hammer its way out of her chest. "You do the same thing to me."

He smiled ever so gently. "I know."

The music came to an end and the lights brightened. Reluctantly Tanner and Joanna broke apart, but he still kept her close to his side, tucking his arm around her waist.

"You haven't answered me, Joanna. I'm not going to hurt you, you know. We'll take it nice and easy at first and see how things develop."

Joanna's throat felt constricted, and she couldn't answer him one way or the other, although it was clear that he was waiting for her to make a decision.

"We've got something good between us," he continued, "and I don't want to just throw it away. I think we should find out whether this can last."

He wouldn't hurt her intentionally, Joanna realized, but the probability of her walking away unscathed from a relationship with this man was remote.

"What do you think?" he pressed.

She couldn't refuse him. "Maybe we should give it a try," she said after a long pause.

Tanner gazed down on her, bathing her in the warmth of his smile. "Neither of us is going to be sorry."

Joanna wasn't nearly as confident. She glanced away and happened to notice Kristen and Nicole. "Uh-oh," she murmured.

"What's wrong?"

"I just saw Kristen zoom over to Nicole and whisper into her ear. Then they hugged each other like long-lost sisters."

"I can deal with it if you can," he said, squeezing her hand.

Tanner's certainty lent her courage. "Then so can I."

Ten

Joanna didn't sleep well that night, or the following two. Tanner had suggested they meet for dinner the next weekend. It seemed an eternity, but there were several problems at work that demanded his attention. She felt as disappointed as he sounded that their first real date wouldn't take place for a week.

Joanna wished he hadn't given her so much time to think about it. If they'd been able to casually go to a movie the afternoon following the slumber party, she wouldn't have been so nervous about it.

When she arrived at work Monday morning, her brain was so muddled she felt as though she were walking in a fog. Twice during the weekend she'd almost called Tanner to suggest they call the whole thing off.

"Morning," her boss murmured absently, hardly looking up from the newspaper. "How was your weekend?"

"Exciting," Joanna told Robin, tucking her purse into the bottom drawer of her desk. "I went roller-skating with fifteen eleven-year-old girls."

"Sounds adventurous," Robin said, his gaze never leaving the paper.

Joanna poured herself a cup of coffee and carried it to her desk to drink black. The way she was feeling, she knew she'd need something strong to clear her head.

"I don't suppose you've been following what's happening at Spokane Aluminum?" Robin asked, refilling his own coffee cup.

It was a good thing Joanna had set her mug down when she did, otherwise it would have tumbled from her fingers. "Spokane Aluminum?" she echoed.

"Yes." Robin sat on the edge of her desk, allowing one leg to dangle. "There's another news item in the paper this morning on Tanner Lund. Six months ago, he bought out half the company from John Becky. I'm sure you've heard of John Becky?"

"Of…course."

"Apparently Lund came into this company and breathed new life into its sagging foreign sales. He took over management himself and has completely changed the company's direction…all for the better. I've heard nothing but good about this guy. Every time I turn around, I'm either reading how great he is, or hearing people talk about him. Take my word, Tanner Lund is a man who's going places."

Joanna couldn't agree more. And she knew for a fact where he was going Saturday night. He was taking her to dinner.

"Mr. Lund's here," Kristen announced the following Saturday, opening Joanna's bedroom door. "And does he ever look handsome!"

A dinner date. A simple dinner date, and Joanna was more

nervous than a college graduate applying for her first job. She smoothed her hand down her red-and-white-flowered dress and held in her breath so long her lungs ached.

Kristen rolled her eyes. "You look fine, Mom."

"I do?"

"As nice as Mr. Lund."

For good measure, Joanna paused long enough to dab more cologne behind her ears, then she squared her shoulders and turned to face the long hallway that led to the living room. "Okay, I'm ready."

Kristen threw open the bedroom door as though she expected royalty to emerge. By the time Joanna had walked down the hallway to the living room where Tanner was waiting, her heart was pounding and her hands were shaking. Kristen was right. Tanner looked marvelous in a three-piece suit and silk tie. He smiled when she came into the room, and stood up, gazing at her with an expression of undisguised delight.

"Hi."

"Hi." Their eyes met, and everything else faded away. Just seeing him again made Joanna's pulse leap into overdrive. No week had ever dragged more.

"Sally's got the phone number of the restaurant, and her mother said it was fine if she stayed here late," Kristen said, standing between them and glancing from one adult to the other. "I don't have any plans myself, so you two feel free to stay out as long as you want."

"Sally?" Joanna forced herself to glance at the babysitter.

"Yes, Mrs. Parsons?"

"There's salad and leftover spaghetti in the refrigerator for dinner, and some microwave popcorn in the cupboard for later."

"Okay."

"I won't be too late."

"But, Mom," Kristen cut in, a slight whine in her voice, "I just got done telling you that it'd be fine if you stayed out till the wee hours of the morning."

"We'll be back before midnight," Joanna informed the babysitter, ignoring Kristen.

"Okay," the girl said, as Kristen sighed expressively. "Have a good time."

Tanner escorted Joanna out to the car, which was parked in front of the house, and opened the passenger door. He paused, his hand still resting on her shoulder. "I'd like to kiss you now, but we have an audience," he said, nodding toward the house.

Joanna chanced a look and discovered Kristen standing in the living-room window, holding aside the curtain and watching them intently. No doubt she was memorizing everything they said and did to report back to Nicole.

"I couldn't believe it when she agreed to let Sally come over. She's of the opinion lately that she's old enough to stay by herself."

"Nicole claims the same thing, but she didn't raise any objections about having a babysitter, either."

"I guess we should count our blessings."

Tanner drove to an expensive downtown restaurant overlooking the Spokane River, in the heart of the city.

Joanna's mouth was dry and her palms sweaty when the valet opened her door and helped her out. She'd never eaten at such a luxurious place in her life. She'd heard that their prices were outrageous. The amount Tanner intended to spend on one meal would probably outfit Kristen for an entire school year. Joanna felt faint at the very idea.

"Chez Michel is an exceptionally nice restaurant, Tanner, if you get my drift," she muttered under her breath after he handed the car keys to the valet. As a newcomer to town, he might not have been aware of just how expensive this place actually was.

"Yes, that's why I chose it," he said nonchalantly. "I was quite pleased with the food and the service when I was here a few weeks ago." He glanced at Joanna and her discomfort must have shown. "Consider it a small token of my appreciation for your help with Nicole's birthday party," he added, offering her one of his bone-melting smiles.

Joanna would have been more than content to eat at Denny's, and that thought reminded her again of how different they were.

She wished now that she'd worn something a little more elegant. The waiters seemed to be better dressed than she was. For that matter, so were the menus.

They were escorted to a table with an unobstructed view of the river. The maître d' held out Joanna's chair and seated her with flair. The first thing she noticed was the setting of silverware, with its bewildering array of forks, knives and spoons. After the maître d' left, she leaned forward and whispered to Tanner, "I've never eaten at a place that uses three teaspoons."

"Oh, quit complaining."

"I'm not, but if I embarrass you and use the wrong fork, don't blame me."

Unconcerned, Tanner chuckled and reached for the shiny gold menu.

Apparently Chez Michel believed in leisurely dining, because nearly two hours had passed by the time they were served their after-dinner coffee. The entire meal was everything Joanna could have hoped for, and more. The food was exceptional, but Joanna considered Tanner's company the best part of the evening. She'd never felt this much at ease with a man before. He made her smile, but he challenged her ideas, too. They talked about the girls and about the demands of being a parent. They discussed Joanna's career goals and Tanner's plans for his company. They covered a lot of different subjects, but didn't focus their conversation on any one.

Now that the meal was over, Joanna was reluctant to see the evening end. She lifted the delicate china cup, admiring its pattern, and took a sip of fragrant coffee. She paused, her cup raised halfway to her mouth, when she noticed Tanner staring at her. "What's wrong?" she asked, fearing part of her dessert was on her nose or something equally disastrous.

"Nothing."

"Then why are you looking at me like that?"

Tanner relaxed, leaned back in his chair, and grinned. "I'm sorry. I was just thinking how lovely you are, and how pleased I am that we met. It seems nothing's been the same since. I never thought a woman could make me feel the way you do, Joanna."

She looked quickly down, feeling a sudden shyness—and a wonderful warmth. Her life had changed, too, and she wasn't sure she could ever go back to the way things had been before. She was dreaming again, feeling again, trusting again, and it felt so good. And so frightening.

"I'm pleased, too," was her only comment.

"You know what the girls are thinking, don't you?"

Joanna could well imagine. No doubt those two would have them engaged after one dinner date. "They're probably expecting us to announce our marriage plans tomorrow morning," Joanna said, trying to make a joke of it.

"To be honest, I find some aspects of married life appealing."

Joanna smiled and narrowed her eyes suspiciously. "Come on, Tanner, just how much wine have you had?"

"Obviously too much, now that I think about it," he said, grinning. Then his face sobered. "All kidding aside, I want you to know how much I enjoy your company. Every time I'm with you, I come away feeling good about life—you make me laugh again."

"I'd make anyone laugh," she said, "especially if I'm wearing a pair of roller skates." She didn't know where their conversation was leading, but the fact that Tanner spoke so openly and honestly about the promise of their relationship completely unnerved her. She felt exactly the same things, but didn't have the courage to voice them.

"I'm glad you agreed we should start seeing each other," Tanner continued.

"Me, too." But she fervently hoped her mother wouldn't hear about it, although Kristen had probably phoned her grandmother the minute Joanna was out the door. Lowering her gaze, Joanna discovered that a bread crumb on the linen tablecloth had become utterly absorbing. She carefully brushed it onto the floor, an inch at a time. "It's worked out fine…so far. Us dating, I mean." It was more than fine. And now he was telling her how she'd brightened his life, as though *he* was the lucky one. That someone like Tanner Lund would ever want to date her still astonished Joanna.

She gazed up at him, her heart shining through her eyes, telling him without words what she was feeling.

Tanner briefly shut his eyes. "Joanna, for heaven's sake, don't look at me like that."

"Like what?"

"Like…that."

"I think you should kiss me," Joanna announced, once again staring down at the tablecloth. The instant the words slipped out she longed to take them back. She couldn't believe she'd said something like that to him.

"I beg your pardon?"

"Never mind," she said quickly, grateful he hadn't heard her.

He had. "Kiss you? Now? Here?"

Joanna shook her head, forcing a smile. "Forget I said that. It just slipped out. Sometimes my mouth disconnects itself from my brain."

Tanner didn't remove his gaze from hers as he raised his hand. Their waiter appeared almost immediately, and still looking at Joanna, he muttered, "Check, please."

"Right away, sir."

They were out of the restaurant so fast Joanna's head was spinning. Once they were seated in the car, Tanner paused, frowning, his hands clenched on the steering wheel.

"What's the matter?" Joanna asked anxiously.

"We goofed. We should have shared a babysitter."

The thought had fleetingly entered her mind earlier, but she'd discounted the idea because she didn't want to encourage the girls' scheming.

"I can't take you back to my place because Nicole will be all over us with questions, and it'll probably be the same story at your house with Kristen."

"You're right." Besides, her daughter would be sorely disappointed if they showed up this early. It wasn't even close to midnight.

"Just where am I supposed to kiss you, Joanna Parsons?"

Oh Lord, he'd taken her seriously. "Tanner…it was a joke."

He ignored her comment. "I don't know of a single lookout point in the city."

"Tanner, please." Her voice rose in embarrassment, and she could feel herself blushing.

Tanner leaned over and brushed his lips against her cheek. "I've got an idea for something we can do, but don't laugh."

"An idea? What?"

"You'll see soon enough." He eased his car onto the street and drove quickly through the city to the freeway on-ramp and didn't exit until they were well into the suburbs.

"Tanner?" Joanna said, looking around her at the unfamiliar streets. "What's out here?" Almost as soon as she'd spoken a huge white screen appeared in the distance. "A drive-in?" she whispered in disbelief.

"Have you got any better ideas?"

"Not a one." Joanna chuckled; she couldn't help it. He was taking her to a drive-in movie just so he could kiss her.

"I can't guarantee this movie. This is its opening weekend, and if I remember the ad correctly, they're showing something with lots of blood and gore."

"As long as it isn't *Teen Massacre.* Kristen would never forgive me if I saw it when she hadn't."

"If the truth be known, I don't plan to watch a whole lot of the movie." He darted an exaggerated leer in her direction and wiggled his eyebrows suggestively.

Joanna returned his look by demurely fluttering her lashes. "I don't know if my mother would approve of my going to a drive-in on a first date."

"With good reason," Tanner retorted. "Especially if she knew what I had in mind."

Although the weather had been mild and the sky was cloudless and clear, only a few cars were scattered across the wide lot.

Tanner parked as far away from the others as possible. He connected the speaker, but turned the volume so low it was almost inaudible. When he'd finished, he placed his arm around Joanna's shoulders, pulling her closer.

"Come here, woman."

Joanna leaned her head against his shoulder and pretended to be interested in the cartoon characters leaping across the large screen. Her stomach was playing jumping jacks with the dinner she'd just eaten.

"Joanna?" His voice was low and seductive.

She tilted her head to meet his gaze, and his eyes moved slowly over her upturned face, searing her with their intensity. The openness of his desire stole her breath away. Her heart was pounding, although he hadn't even kissed her yet. One hungry look from Tanner and she was melting at his feet.

Her first thought was to crack a joke. That had saved her in the past, but whatever she might have said or done was lost as Tanner lowered his mouth and tantalized the edges of her trembling lips, teasing her with soft, tempting nibbles, making her ache all the way to her toes for his kiss. Instinctively her fingers slid up his chest and around the back of his neck. Tanner created such an overwhelming need in her that she felt both humble and elated at the same time. When her hands tightened around his neck, his mouth hardened into firm possession.

Joanna thought she'd drown in the sensations that flooded

her. She hadn't felt this kind of longing in years, and she trembled with the wonder of it. Tanner had awakened the deep womanly part of her that had lain dormant for so long. And suddenly she felt all that time without love come rushing up at her, overtaking her. Years of regret, years of doubt, years of rejection all pressed so heavily on her heart that she could barely breathe.

A sob was ripped from her throat, and the sound of it broke them apart. Tears she couldn't explain flooded her eyes and ran unheeded down her face.

"Joanna, what's wrong? Did I hurt you?"

She tried to break away, but Tanner wouldn't let her go. He brushed the hair from her face and tilted her head to lift her eyes to his, but she resisted.

He must have felt the wetness on her face, because he paused and murmured, "You're crying," in a tone that sounded as shocked as she felt. "Dear Lord, what did I do?"

Wildly she shook her head, unable to speak even if she'd been able to find the words to explain.

"Joanna, tell me, please."

"J-just hold me." Even saying that much required all her reserves of strength.

He did as she asked, wrapping his arms completely around her, kissing the crown of her head as she buried herself in his strong, solid warmth.

Still, the tears refused to stop, no matter how hard she tried to make them. They flooded her face and seemed to come from the deepest part of her.

"I can't believe I'm doing this," she said between sobs. "Oh, Tanner, I feel like such a fool."

"Go ahead and cry, Joanna. I understand."

"You do? Good. You can explain it to me."

She could feel his smile as he kissed the corner of her eye. She moaned a little and he lowered his lips to her cheek, then her chin, and when she couldn't bear it any longer, she turned her face, her mouth seeking his. Tanner didn't disappoint her, kissing her gently again and again until she was certain her heart would stop beating if he ever stopped holding her and kissing her.

"Good Lord, Joanna," he whispered after a while, gently extricating himself from her arms and leaning against the car seat, his eyes closed. His face was a picture of desire struggling for restraint. He drew in several deep breaths.

Joanna's tears had long since dried on her face and now her cheeks flamed with confusion and remorse.

A heavy silence fell between them. Joanna searched frantically for something witty to say to break the terrible tension.

"Joanna, listen—"

"No, let me speak first," she broke in, then hesitated. Now that she had his attention, she didn't know what to say. "I'm sorry, Tanner, really sorry. I don't know what came over me, but you weren't the one responsible for my tears. Well, no, you were, but not the way you think."

"Joanna, please," he said and his hands bracketed her face. "Don't be embarrassed by the tears. Believe me when I say I'm feeling the same things you are, only they come out in different ways."

Joanna stared up at him, not sure he could possibly understand.

"It's been so long for you—it has for me, too," Tanner went on. "I feel like a teenager again. And the drive-in has nothing to do with it."

Her lips trembled with the effort to smile. Tanner leaned

his forehead against hers. "We need to take this slow. Very, very slow."

That was a fine thing for him to say, considering they'd been as hot as torches for each other a few minutes ago. If they continued at this rate, they'd end up in bed together by the first of the week.

"I've got a company party in a couple of weeks—I want you there with me. Will you do that?"

Joanna nodded.

Tanner drew her closer to his side and she tucked her head against his chest. His hand stroked her shoulder, as he kissed the top of her head.

"You're awfully quiet," he said after several minutes. "What are you thinking?"

Joanna sighed and snuggled closer, looping one arm around his middle. Her free hand was laced with his. "It just occurred to me that for the first time in my life I've met a real prince. Up until now, all I've done is make a few frogs happy."

Eleven

Kneeling on the polished linoleum floor of the kitchen, Joanna held her breath and tentatively poked her head inside the foam-covered oven. Sharp, lemon-scented fumes made her grimace as she dragged the wet sponge along the sides, peeling away a layer of blackened crust. She'd felt unusually ambitious for a Saturday and had worked in the yard earlier, planning her garden. When she'd finished that, she'd decided to tackle the oven, not questioning where this burst of energy had come from. Spring was in the air, but instead of turning her fancy to thoughts of love, it filled her mind with zucchini seeds and rows of tomato seedlings.

"I'm leaving now, Mom," Kristen called from behind her.

Joanna jerked her head free, gulped some fresh air and twisted toward her daughter. "What time will you be through at the library?" Kristen and Nicole were working together on a school project, and although they complained about having to do research, they'd come to enjoy it. Their biggest surprise was discovering all the cute junior-high boys who sometimes visited the library. In Kristen's words, it was an untapped gold mine.

"I don't know when we'll be through, but I'll call. And remember, Nicole is coming over afterwards."

"I remember."

Kristen hesitated, then asked, "When are you going out with Mr. Lund again?"

Joanna glanced over at the calendar. "Next weekend. We're attending a dinner party his company's sponsoring."

"Oh."

Joanna rubbed her forearm across her cheek, and glanced suspiciously at her daughter. "What does that mean?"

"What?"

"That little 'oh.'"

Kristen shrugged. "Nothing…. It's just that you're not seeing him as often as Nicole and I think you should. You like Mr. Lund, don't you?"

That was putting it mildly. "He's very nice," Joanna said cautiously. If she admitted to anything beyond a casual attraction, Kristen would assume much more. Joanna wanted her relationship with Tanner to progress slowly, one careful step at a time, not in giant leaps—though slow and careful didn't exactly describe what had happened so far!

"Nice?" Kristen exclaimed.

Her daughter's outburst caught Joanna by surprise.

"Is that all you can say about Mr. Lund?" Kristen asked, hands on her hips. "I've given the matter serious consideration and I think he's a whole lot more than just nice. Really, Mother."

Taking a deep breath, Joanna plunged her head back inside the oven, swiping her sponge furiously against the sides.

"Are you going to ignore me?" Kristen demanded.

Joanna emerged again, gasped and looked straight at her daughter. "Yes. Unless you want to volunteer to clean the oven yourself."

"I would, but I have to go to the library with Nicole."

Joanna noted the soft regret that filled her daughter's voice and gave her a derisive snort. The kid actually sounded sorry that she wouldn't be there to do her part. Kristen was a genius at getting out of work, and she always managed to give the impression of really wishing she could help her mother—if only she could fit it into her busy schedule.

A car horn beeped out front. "That's Mr. Lund," Kristen said, glancing toward the living room. "I'll give you a call when we're done."

"Okay, honey. Have a good time."

"I will."

With form an Olympic sprinter would envy, Kristen tore out of the kitchen. Two seconds later, the front door slammed. Joanna was only mildly disappointed that Tanner hadn't stopped in to chat. He'd phoned earlier and explained that after he dropped the girls off at the library, he was driving to the office for a couple of hours. An unexpected problem had arisen, and he needed to deal with it right away.

Actually Joanna had to admit she was more grateful than disappointed that Tanner hadn't stopped in. It didn't look as though she'd get a chance to see him before the company party. She needed this short separation to pull together her reserves. Following their dinner date and the drive-in movie afterward, Joanna felt dangerously close to falling in love with Tanner. Every time he came to mind, and that was practically every minute of every day, a rush of warmth and happiness followed. Without too much trouble, she could envision them finding a lifetime of happiness together. For the first time since her divorce she allowed herself the luxury of dreaming again, and although the prospect of remarriage excited and thrilled her, it also terrified her.

Fifteen minutes later, with perspiration beaded on her forehead and upper lip, Joanna heaved a sigh and sat back on her heels. The hair she'd so neatly tucked inside a scarf and tied at the back of her head, had fallen loose. She swiped a grimy hand at the auburn curls that hung limply over her eyes and ears. It was all worth it, though, since the gray-speckled sides of the oven, which had been encrusted with black grime, were now clearly visible and shining.

Joanna emptied the bucket of dirty water and hauled a fresh one back to wipe the oven one last time. She'd just knelt down when the doorbell chimed.

"Great," she muttered under her breath, casting a glance at herself. She looked like something that had crawled out of the bog in some horror movie. Pasting a smile on her face, she peeled off her rubber gloves and hurried to the door.

"Davey!" Finding her ex-husband standing on the porch was enough of a shock to knock the breath from Joanna's lungs.

"May I come in?"

"Of course." Flustered, she ran her hand through her hair and stepped aside to allow him to pass. He looked good—really good—but then Davey had never lacked in the looks department. From the expensive cut of his three-piece suit, she could tell that his real-estate business must be doing well, and of course that was precisely the impression he wanted her to have. She was pleased for him; she'd never wished him ill. They'd gone their separate ways, and although both the marriage and the divorce had devastated Joanna, she shared a beautiful child with this man. If he had come by to tell her how successful he was, well, she'd just smile and let him.

"It's good to see you, Joanna."

"You, too. What brings you to town?" She struggled to keep her voice even and controlled, hoping to hide her discomfort at being caught unawares.

"I'm attending a conference downtown. I apologize for dropping in unexpectedly like this, but since I was going to be in Spokane, I thought I'd stop in and see how you and Kristen are doing."

"I wish you'd phoned first. Kristen's at the library." Joanna wasn't fooled—Davey hadn't come to see their daughter, although he meant Joanna to think so. It was all part of the game he played with her, wanting her to believe that their divorce had hurt him badly. Not calling to let her know he planned to visit was an attempt to catch her off guard and completely unprepared—which, of course, she was. Joanna knew Davey, knew him well. He'd often tried to manipulate her this way.

"I should have called, but I didn't know if I'd have the time, and I didn't want to disappoint you if I found I couldn't slip away."

Joanna didn't believe that for a minute. It wouldn't have taken him much time or trouble to phone before he left the hotel. But she didn't mention the fact, couldn't see that it would have done any good.

"Come in and have some coffee." She led him into the kitchen and poured him a mug, automatically adding the sugar and cream she knew he used. She handed it to him and was rewarded with a dazzling smile. When he wanted, Davey Parsons could be charming, attentive and generous. The confusing thing about her ex-husband was that he wasn't all bad. He'd gravely wounded her with his unfaithfulness, but in his own way he'd loved her and Kristen—as much as he could possibly love anybody beyond himself. It had taken Joanna a good many years to distance herself enough to appreciate his good points and to forgive him for the pain he'd caused her.

"You've got a nice place here," he commented, casually glancing around the kitchen. "How long have you lived here now?"

"Seven months."

"How's Kristen?"

Joanna was relieved that the conversation had moved to the only subject they still had in common—their daughter. She talked for fifteen minutes nonstop, telling him about the talent show and the other activities Kristen had been involved in since the last time she'd seen her father.

Davey listened and laughed, and then his gaze softened as he studied Joanna. "You're looking wonderful."

She grinned ruefully. "Sure I am," she scoffed. "I've just finished working in the yard and cleaning the oven."

"I wondered about the lemon perfume you were wearing."

They both laughed. Davey started to tease her about their early years together and some of the experimental meals she'd cooked and expected him to eat and praise. Joanna let him and even enjoyed his comments, for Davey could be warm and funny when he chose. Kristen had inherited her friendly, easygoing confidence from her father.

The doorbell chimed and still chuckling, Joanna stood up. "It's probably one of the neighborhood kids. I'll just be a minute." She never ceased to be astonished at how easy it was to be with Davey. He'd ripped her heart in two, lied to her repeatedly, cheated on her and still she couldn't be around him and not laugh. It always took him a few minutes to conquer her reserve, but he never failed. She was mature enough to recognize her ex-husband's faults, yet appreciate his redeeming qualities.

For the second time that day, Joanna was surprised by the man who stood on her front porch. "Tanner."

"Hi," he said with a sheepish grin. "The girls got off okay and I thought I'd stop in for a cup of coffee before heading to the office." His eyes smiled softly into hers. "I heard you laughing from out here. Do you have company? Should I come back later?"

"N-no, come in," she said, her pulse beating as hard and loud as jungle drums. Lowering her eyes, she automatically moved aside. He walked into the living room and paused, then raised his hand and gently touched her cheek in a gesture so loving that Joanna longed to fall into his arms. Now that he was here, she found herself craving some time alone with him.

Tanner's gaze reached out to her, but Joanna had trouble meeting it. A frown started to form, and his eyes clouded. "This is a bad time, isn't it?"

"No…not really." When she turned around, Davey was standing in the kitchen doorway watching them. The smile she'd been wearing felt shaky as she stood between the two men and made the introductions. "Davey, this is Tanner Lund. Tanner, this is Davey—Kristen's father."

For a moment, the two men glared at each other like angry bears who had claimed territory and were prepared to do battle to protect what was theirs. When they stepped toward each other, Joanna held her breath for fear neither one would make the effort to be civil.

Stunned, she watched as they exchanged handshakes and enthusiastic greetings.

"Davey's in town for a real-estate conference and thought he'd stop in to see Kristen," Joanna explained, her words coming out in such a rush that they nearly stumbled over themselves.

"I came to see you, too, Joanna," Davey added in a low sultry voice that suggested he had more on his mind than a chat over a cup of coffee.

She flashed him a heated look before marching into the kitchen, closely followed by both men. She walked straight to the cupboard, bringing down another cup, then poured Tanner's coffee and delivered it to the table.

"Kristen and my daughter are at the library," Tanner announced in a perfectly friendly voice, but Joanna heard the undercurrents even if Davey didn't.

"Joanna told me," Davey returned.

The two men remained standing, smiling at each other. Tanner took a seat first, and Davey promptly did the same.

"What do you do?" her ex-husband asked.

"I own half of Spokane Aluminum."

It was apparent to Joanna that Davey hadn't even bothered to listen to Tanner's reply because he immediately fired back in an aggressive tone, "I recently opened my own real-estate brokerage and have plans to expand within the next couple of years." He announced his success with a cocky slant to his mouth.

Watching the change in Davey's features as Tanner's identity began to sink in was so comical that Joanna nearly laughed out loud. Davey's mouth sagged open, and his eyes flew from Joanna to Tanner and then back to Joanna.

"Spokane Aluminum," Davey repeated slowly, his face

unusually pale. "I seem to remember reading something about John Becky taking on a partner."

Joanna almost felt sorry for Davey. "Kristen and Tanner's daughter, Nicole, are best friends. They were in the Valentine's Day show together—the one I was telling you about...."

To his credit, Davey regrouped quickly. "She gets all that performing talent from you."

"Oh, hardly," Joanna countered, denying it with a vigorous shake of her head. Of the two of them, Davey was the entertainer—crowds had never intimidated him. He could walk into a room full of strangers, and anyone who didn't know better would end up thinking Davey Parsons was his best friend.

"With the girls being so close, it seemed only natural for Joanna and me to start dating," Tanner said, turning to smile warmly at Joanna.

"I see," Davey answered. He didn't appear to have recovered from Tanner's first announcement.

"I sincerely hope you do understand," Tanner returned, all pretence of friendliness dropped.

Joanna resisted rolling her eyes toward the ceiling. Both of them were behaving like immature children, battling with looks and words as if she were a prize to be awarded the victor.

"I suppose I'd better think about heading out," Davey said after several awkward moments had passed. He stood up, noticeably eager to make his escape.

As a polite hostess, Joanna stood when Davey did. "I'll walk you to the door."

He sent Tanner a wary smile. "That's not necessary."

"Of course it is," Joanna countered.

To her dismay, Tanner followed them and stood conspicuously in the background while Davey made arrangements to phone Kristen later that evening. The whole time Davey was speaking, Joanna could feel Tanner's eyes burning into her back. She didn't know why he'd insisted on following her to the door. It was like saying he couldn't trust her not to fall into Davey's arms the minute he was out of sight, and that irritated her no end.

Once her ex-husband had left, she closed the door and whirled around to face Tanner. The questions were jammed in her mind. They'd only gone out on one date, for heaven's sake, and here he was, acting as though…as though they were engaged.

"I thought he broke your heart," Tanner said, in a cutting voice.

Joanna debated whether or not to answer him, then decided it would be best to clear the air. "He did."

"I heard you laughing when I rang the doorbell. Do you often have such a good time with men you're supposed to hate?"

"I don't hate Davey."

"Believe me, I can tell."

"Tanner, what's wrong with you?" That was a silly question, and she regretted asking it immediately. She already knew what was troubling Tanner. He was jealous. And angry. And hurt.

"Wrong with me?" He tossed the words back at her. "Nothing's wrong with me. I happen to stumble upon the woman I'm involved with cozying up to her ex-husband, and I don't mind telling you I'm upset. But nothing's wrong with me. Not one damn thing. If there's something wrong with anyone, it's you, lady."

Joanna held tightly on to her patience. "Before we start arguing, let's sit down and talk this out." She led him back into the kitchen, then took Davey's empty coffee mug and placed it in the sink, removing all evidence of his brief visit. She searched for a way to reassure Tanner that Davey meant nothing to her anymore. But she had to explain that she and her ex-husband weren't enemies, either; they couldn't be for Kristen's sake.

"First of all," she said, as evenly as her pounding heart would allow, "I could never hate Davey the way you seem to think I should. As far as I'm concerned, that would only be counterproductive. The people who would end up suffering are Kristen and me. Davey is incapable of being faithful to one woman, but he'll always be Kristen's father, and if for no other reason than that, I prefer to remain on friendly terms with him."

"But he cheated on you…used you."

"Yes." She couldn't deny it. "But, Tanner, I lived a lot of years with Davey. He's not all bad—no one is—and scattered between all the bad times were a few good ones. We're divorced now. What good would it do to harbor ill will toward him? None that I can see."

"He let it be known from the moment I walked into this house that he could have you back anytime he wanted."

Joanna wasn't blind; she'd recognized the looks Davey had given Tanner, and the insinuations. "He'd like to believe that. It helps him deal with his ego."

"And you let him?"

"Not the way you're implying."

Tanner mulled that over for a few moments. "How often does he casually drop in unannounced like this?"

She hesitated, wondering whether she should answer his

question. His tone had softened, but he was obviously still angry. She could sympathize, but she didn't like having to defend herself or her attitude toward Davey. "I haven't seen him in over a year. This is the first time he's been to the house."

Tanner's hands gripped the coffee mug so tightly that Joanna was amazed it remained intact. "You still love him, don't you?"

The question hit her square between the eyes. Her mouth opened and closed several times as she struggled for the words to deny it. Then she realized she couldn't. Lying to Tanner about this would be simple enough and it would keep the peace, but it would wrong them both. "I suppose in a way I do," she began slowly. "He's the father of my child. He was my first love, Tanner. And the only lover I've ever had. Although I'd like to tell you I don't feel a thing for him, I can't do that and be completely honest. But please, try to understand—"

"You don't need to say anything more." He stood abruptly, his back stiff. "I appreciate the fact that you told me the truth. I won't waste any more of your time. I wish you and Kristen a good life." With that he stalked out of the room, headed for the door.

Joanna was shocked. "Tanner…you make it sound like I'll never see you again."

"I think that would be best for everyone concerned," he replied, without looking at her.

"But…that's silly. Nothing's changed." She snapped her mouth closed. If Tanner wanted to act so childishly and ruin everything, she wasn't about to argue with him. He was the one who insisted they had something special, something so good they shouldn't throw it away because of their fears.

And now he was acting like this! Fine. If that was the way he wanted it. It was better to find out how unreasonable he could be before anything serious developed between them. Better to discover now how quick-tempered he could be, how hurtful.

"I have no intention of becoming involved with a woman who's still in love with her loser of an ex-husband," he announced, his hands clenched at his sides. His voice was calm, but she recognized the tension in it. And the resolve.

Unable to restrain her anger any longer, Joanna marched across the room and threw open the front door. "Smart move, Tanner," she said, her words coated with sarcasm. "You made a terrible mistake getting involved with a woman who refuses to hate." Now that she had a better look at him, she decided he wasn't a prince after all, only another frog.

Tanner didn't say a word as he walked past her, his strides filled with purpose. She closed the door and leaned against it, needing the support. Tears burned in her eyes and clogged her throat, but she held her head high and hurried back into the kitchen, determined not to give in to the powerful emotions that racked her, body and soul.

She finished cleaning up the kitchen, and took a long hot shower afterward. Then she sat quietly at the table, waiting for Kristen to phone so she could pick up the two girls. The call came a half hour later, but by that time she'd already reached for the cookies, bent on self-destruction.

On the way home from the library, Joanna stopped off at McDonald's and bought the girls cheeseburgers and chocolate milk shakes to take home for dinner. Her mind was filled with doubts. In retrospect, she wished she'd done a better job of explaining things to Tanner. The thought of never seeing him again was almost too painful to endure.

"Aren't you going to order anything, Mom?" Kristen asked, surprised.

"Not tonight." Somewhere deep inside, Joanna found the energy to smile.

She managed to maintain a lighthearted facade while Kristen and Nicole ate their dinner and chattered about the boys they'd seen at the library and how they were going to shock Mrs. Andrews with their well-researched report.

"Are you feeling okay?" Kristen asked, pausing in mid-sentence.

"Sure," Joanna lied, looking for something to occupy her hands. She settled for briskly wiping down the kitchen counters. Actually, she felt sick to her stomach, but she couldn't blame Tanner; she'd done that to herself with all those stupid cookies.

It was when she was putting the girls' empty McDonald's containers in the garbage that the silly tears threatened to spill over. She did her best to hide them and quickly carried out the trash. Nicole went to get a cassette from Kristen's bedroom, but Kristen followed her mother outside.

"Mom, what's wrong?"

"Nothing, sweetheart."

"You have tears in your eyes."

"It's nothing."

"You never cry," Kristen insisted.

"Something must have got into my eye to make it tear like this," she said, shaking her head. The effort to smile was too much for her. She straightened and placed her hands on Kristen's shoulders, then took a deep breath. "I don't want you to be disappointed if I don't see Mr. Lund again."

"He did this?" Kristen demanded, in a high shocked voice.

"No," Joanna countered immediately. "I already told you, I got something in my eye."

Kristen studied her with a frown, and Joanna tried to meet her daughter's gaze. If she was fool enough to make herself vulnerable to a man again, then she deserved this pain. She'd known better than to get involved with Tanner, but her heart had refused to listen.

A couple of hours later, Tanner arrived to pick up Nicole. Joanna let Kristen answer the door and stayed in the kitchen, pretending to be occupied there.

When the door swung open, Joanna assumed it was her daughter and asked, "Did Nicole get off all right?"

"Not yet."

Joanna jerked away from the sink at the husky sound of Tanner's voice. "Where are the girls?"

"In Kristen's room. I want to talk to you."

"I can't see how that would do much good."

"I've reconsidered."

"Bravo for you. Unfortunately so have I. You're absolutely right about it being better all around if we don't see each other again."

Tanner dragged his fingers through his hair and stalked to the other side of the room. "Okay, I'll admit it. I was jealous as hell when I walked in and found you having coffee with Davey. I felt you were treating him like some conquering hero returned from the war."

"Oh, honestly, it wasn't anything like that."

"You were laughing and smiling."

"Grievous sins, I'm sure."

Tanner clamped down his jaw so hard that the sides of his face went white. "All I can do is apologize, Joanna. I've already made a fool of myself over one woman who loved someone else, and frankly that caused me enough grief. I'm not looking to repeat the mistake with you."

A strained silence fell between them.

"I thought I could walk away from you and not feel any regrets, but I was wrong," he continued a moment later. "I haven't stopped thinking about you all afternoon. Maybe I overreacted. Maybe I behaved like a jealous fool."

"Maybe?" Joanna challenged. "Maybe? You were unreasonable and hurtful and…and I ate a whole row of Oreo cookies over you."

"What?"

"You heard me. I stuffed down a dozen cookies and now I think I'm going to be sick and it was all because of you. I've come too far to be reduced to that. One argument with you and I was right back into the Oreos! If you think you're frightened—because of what happened with Carmen—it's nothing compared to the fears I've been facing since the day we met. I can't deal with your insecurities, Tanner. I've got too damn many of my own."

"Joanna, I've already apologized. If you can honestly tell me there isn't any chance that you'll ever get back together with Davey, I swear to you I'll drop the subject and never bring it up again. But I need to know that much. I'm sorry, but I've got to hear you say it."

"I had a nice quiet life before you paraded into it," she went on, as though she hadn't heard him.

"Joanna, I asked you a question." His intense gaze cut straight through her.

"You must be nuts! I'd be certifiably insane to ever take Davey back. Our marriage—our entire relationship—was over the day I filed for divorce, and probably a lot earlier than that."

Tanner relaxed visibly. "I wouldn't blame you if you decided you never wanted to see me again, but I'm hoping you'll be able to forget what happened this afternoon so we can go back to being…friends again."

Joanna struggled against the strong pull of his magnetism for as long as she could, then nodded, agreeing to place this quarrel behind them.

Tanner walked toward her and she met him halfway, slipping easily into his embrace. She felt as if she belonged here, as if he were the man she would always be content with. He'd once told her he wouldn't ever hurt her the way her ex-husband had, but caring about him, risking a relationship with him, left her vulnerable all over again. She'd realized that this afternoon, learned again what it was to give a man the power to hurt her.

"I reduced you to gorging yourself with Oreos?" Tanner whispered the question into her hair.

She nodded wildly. "You fiend. I didn't mean to eat that many, but I sat at the table with the Oreos package and a glass of milk and the more I thought about what happened, the angrier I became, and the faster I shoved those cookies into my mouth."

"Could this mean you care?" His voice was still a whisper.

She nodded a second time. "I hate fighting with you. My stomach was in knots all afternoon."

"Good Lord, Joanna," he said, dropping several swift kisses on her face. "I can't believe what fools we are."

"We?" She tilted back her head and glared up at him, but her mild indignation drained away the moment their eyes met. Tanner was looking down at her with such tenderness, such concern, that every negative emotion she'd experienced earlier that afternoon vanished like rain falling into a clear blue lake.

He kissed her then, with a thoroughness that left her in no doubt about the strength of his feelings. Joanna rested against this warmth, holding on to him with everything that was in her. When he raised his head, she looked up at him through tear-filled eyes and blinked furiously in a futile effort to keep them at bay.

"I'm glad you came back," she said, when she could find her voice.

"I am, too." He kissed her once more, lightly this time, sampling her lips, kissing the tears from her face. "I wasn't worth a damn all afternoon." Once more he lowered his mouth to hers, creating a delicious sensation that electrified Joanna and sent chills racing down her spine.

Tanner's arms tightened as loud voices suddenly erupted from the direction of the living room.

"I never want to see you again," Joanna heard Kristen declare vehemently.

"You couldn't possibly want to see me any less than I want to see you," Nicole returned with equal volume and fury.

"What's that all about?" Tanner asked, his eyes searching Joanna's.

"I don't know, but I think we'd better find out."

Tanner led the way into the living room. They discovered Kristen and Nicole standing face-to-face, glaring at each other in undisguised antagonism.

"Kristen, stop that right now," Joanna demanded. "Nicole is a guest in our home and I won't have you talking to her in that tone of voice."

Tanner moved to his daughter's side. "And you're Kristen's guest. I expect you to be on your best behavior whenever you're here."

Nicole crossed her arms over her chest and darted a venomous look in Kristen's direction. "I refuse to be friends with her ever again. And I don't think you should have anything more to do with Mrs. Parsons."

Joanna's eyes found Tanner's.

"I don't want my mother to have anything to do with Mr. Lund, either." Kristen spun around and glared at Tanner and Nicole.

"I think we'd best separate these two and find out what happened," Joanna suggested. She pointed toward Kristen's bedroom. "Come on, honey, let's talk."

Kristen averted her face. "I have nothing to say!" she declared melodramatically and stalked out of the room without a backward glance.

Joanna raised questioning eyes to Tanner, threw up her hands and followed her daughter.

Twelve

"Kristen, what's wrong?" Joanna sat on the end of her daughter's bed and patiently waited for the eleven-year-old to repeat the list of atrocities committed by Nicole Lund.

"Nothing."

Joanna had seen her daughter wear this affronted look often enough to recognize it readily, and she felt a weary sigh work its way through her. Hell hath no fury like a sixth-grader done wrong by her closest friend.

"I don't ever want to see Nicole again."

"But, sweetheart, she's your best friend."

"*Was* my best friend," Kristen announced theatrically. She crossed her arms over her chest with all the pomp of a queen who'd made her statement and expected unquestioning acquiescence.

With mounting frustration, Joanna folded her hands in her lap and waited, knowing better than to try to reason with Kristen when she was in this mood. Five minutes passed, but Kristen didn't utter another word. Joanna wasn't surprised.

"Does your argument have to do with something that

happened at school?" she asked as nonchalantly as possible, examining the fingernails on her right hand.

Kristen shook her head. She pinched her lips as if to suggest that nothing Joanna could say would force the information out of her.

"Does it involve a boy?" Joanna persisted.

Kristen's gaze widened. "Of course not."

"What about another friend?"

"Nope."

At the rate they were going, Joanna would soon run out of questions. "Can't you just tell me what happened?"

Kristen cast her a look that seemed to question her mother's intelligence. "No!"

"Does that mean we're going to sit here all night while I try to guess?"

Kristen twisted her head and tilted it at a lofty angle, then pantomimed locking her lips.

"All right," Joanna said with an exaggerated sigh, "I'll simply have to ask Nicole, who will, no doubt, be more than ready to tell all. Her version should be highly interesting."

"Mr. Lund made you cry!" Kristen mumbled, her eyes lowered.

Joanna blinked back her astonishment. "You mean to say this whole thing has to do with Tanner and me?"

Kristen nodded once.

"But—"

"Nicole claims that whatever happened was obviously your fault, and as far as I'm concerned that did it. From here on out, Nicole is no longer my friend and I don't think you should have anything to do with…with that man, either."

"That man?"

Kristen sent her a sour look. "You know very well who I mean."

Joanna shifted farther onto the bed, brought up her knees and rested her chin on them. She paused to carefully measure her words. "What if I told you I was beginning to grow fond of 'that man'?"

"Mom, no!" Her daughter's eyes widened with horror, and she cast her mother a look of sheer panic. "That would be the worst possible thing to happen. You might marry him and then Nicole and I would end up being sisters!"

Joanna made no attempt to conceal her surprise. "But, Kristen, from the not-so-subtle hints you and Nicole have been giving me and Mr. Lund, I thought that was exactly what you both wanted. What you'd planned."

"That was before."

"Before what?"

"Before…tonight, when Nicole said those things she said. I can't forgive her, Mom, I just can't."

Joanna stayed in the room a few more silent minutes, then left. Tanner and Nicole were talking in the living room, and from the frustrated look he gave her, she knew he hadn't been any more successful with his daughter than Joanna had been with hers.

When he saw Joanna, Tanner got to his feet and nodded toward the kitchen, mutely suggesting they talk privately and compare stories.

"What did you find out?" she asked the minute they were alone.

Tanner shrugged, then gestured defeat with his hands. "I don't understand it. She keeps saying she never wants to see Kristen again."

"Kristen says the same thing. Adamantly. She seems to think she's defending my honor. It seems this all has to do with our misunderstanding earlier this afternoon."

"Nicole seems to think it started when you didn't order

anything at McDonalds," Tanner said, his expression confused.

"What?" Joanna's question escaped on a short laugh.

"From what I can get out of Nicole, Kristen claims you didn't order a Big Mac, which is supposed to mean something. Then later, before I arrived, there was some mention of your emptying the garbage when it was only half-full?" He paused to wait for her to speak. When she simply nodded, he continued, "I understand that's unusual for you, as well?"

Once more Joanna nodded. She'd wanted to hide her tears from the girls, so taking out the garbage had been an excuse to escape for a couple of minutes while she composed herself.

Tanner wiped his hand across his brow in mock relief. "Whew! At least neither of them learned about the Oreos!"

Joanna ignored his joke and slumped against the kitchen counter with a long slow sigh of frustration. "Having the girls argue is a problem neither of us anticipated."

"Maybe I should talk to Kristen and you talk to Nicole?" Tanner suggested, all seriousness again.

Joanna shook her head. "Then we'd be guilty of interfering. We'd be doing the same thing they've done to us—and I don't think we'd be doing them any favors."

"What do you suggest then?" Tanner asked, looking more disgruntled by the minute.

Joanna shrugged. "I don't know."

"Come on, Joanna, we're intelligent adults. Surely we can come up with a way to handle a couple of preadolescent egos."

"Be my guest," Joanna said, and laughed aloud at the comical look that crossed Tanner's handsome face.

"Forget it."

Joanna brushed the hair away from her face. "I think our

best bet is to let them work this matter out between themselves."

Tanner's forehead creased in concern, then he nodded, his look reluctant. "I hope this doesn't mean you and I can't be friends." His tender gaze held hers.

Joanna was forced to lower her eyes so he couldn't see just how important his friendship had become to her. "Of course we can."

"Good." He walked across the room and gently pulled her into his arms. He kissed her until she was weak and breathless. When he raised his head, he said in a husky murmur, "I'll take Nicole home now and do as you suggest. We'll give these two a week to settle their differences. After that, you and I are taking over."

"A week?" Joanna wasn't sure that would be long enough, considering Kristen's attitude.

"A week!" Tanner repeated emphatically, kissing her again.

By the time he'd finished, Joanna would have agreed to almost anything. "All right," she managed. "A week."

"How was school today?" Joanna asked Kristen on Monday evening while they sat at the dinner table. She'd waited as long as she could before asking. If either girl was inclined to make a move toward reconciliation, it would be now, she reasoned. They'd both had ample time to think about what had happened and to determine the value of their friendship.

Kristen shrugged. "School was fine, I guess."

Joanna took her time eating her salad, focusing her attention on it instead of her daughter. "How'd you do on the math paper I helped you with?"

Kristen rolled her eyes. "You showed me wrong."

"Wrong!"

"The answers were all right, but Mrs. Andrews told me they don't figure out equations that way anymore."

"Oh. Sorry about that."

"You weren't the only parent who messed up."

That was good to hear.

"A bunch of other kids did it wrong. Including Nicole."

Joanna slipped her hand around her water glass. Kristen sounded far too pleased that her ex-friend had messed up the assignment. That wasn't encouraging. "So you saw Nicole today?"

"I couldn't very well not see her. Her desk is across the aisle from mine. But if you're thinking what I think you're thinking, you can forget it. I don't need a friend like Nicole Lund."

Joanna didn't comment on that, although she practically had to bite her tongue. She wondered how Tanner was doing. Staying out of this argument between the two girls was far more difficult than she'd imagined. It was obvious to Joanna that Kristen was miserable without her best friend, but saying as much would hurt her case more than help it. Kristen needed to recognize the fact herself.

The phone rang while Joanna was finishing up the last of the dinner dishes. Kristen was in the bath, so Joanna grabbed the receiver, holding it between her hunched shoulder and her ear while she squirted detergent into the hot running water.

"Hello?"

"Joanna? Good Lord, you sounded just like Kristen there. I was prepared to have the phone slammed in my ear," Tanner said. "How's it going?"

Her heart swelled with emotion. She hadn't talked to him since Saturday, and it felt as though months had passed since she'd heard his voice. It wrapped itself around her now, warm and comforting. "Things aren't going too well. How are they at your end?"

"Not much better. Did you know Kristen had the nerve to eat lunch with Nora this afternoon? In case you weren't aware of this, Nora is Nicole's sworn enemy."

"Nora?" Joanna could hardly believe her ears. "Kristen doesn't even like the girl." If anything, this war between Kristen and Nicole was heating up.

"I hear you bungled the math assignment," Tanner said softly, amused.

"Apparently you did, too."

He chuckled. "Yeah, this new math is beyond me." He paused, and when he spoke, Joanna could hear the frustration in his voice. "I wish the girls would hurry and patch things up. Frankly, Joanna, I miss you like crazy."

"It's only been two days." She should talk—the last forty-eight hours had seemed like an eternity.

"It feels like two years."

"I know," she agreed softly, closing her eyes and savoring Tanner's words. "But we don't usually see each other during the week anyway." At least not during the past couple of weeks.

"I've been thinking things over and I may have come up with an idea that will put us all out of our misery."

"What?" By now, Joanna was game for anything.

"How about a movie?" he asked unexpectedly, his voice eager.

"But, Tanner—"

"Tomorrow night. You can bring Kristen and I'll bring Nicole, and we could accidentally-on-purpose meet at the theater. Naturally there'll be a bit of acting on our part and some huffing and puffing on theirs, but if things work out the way I think they will, we won't have to do a thing. Nature will take its course."

Joanna wasn't convinced this scheme of his would work. The whole thing could blow up in their faces, but the thought of being with Tanner was too enticing to refuse. "All right," she agreed. "As long as you buy the popcorn and promise to hold my hand."

"You've got yourself a deal."

On Tuesday evening, Kristen was unusually quiet over dinner. Joanna had fixed one of her daughter's favorite meals—macaroni-and-cheese casserole—but Kristen barely touched it.

"Do you feel like going to a movie?" Joanna asked, her heart in her throat. Normally Kristen would leap at the idea, but this evening Joanna couldn't predict anything.

"It's a school night, and I don't think I'm in the mood to see a movie."

"But you said you didn't have any homework, and it sounds like a fun thing to do…and weren't you saying something about wanting to see Tom Cruise's latest film?" Kristen's eyes momentarily brightened, then faded. "And don't worry," Joanna added cheerfully, "you won't have to sit with me."

Kristen gave a huge sigh. "I don't have anyone else to sit with," she said, as though Joanna had suggested a trip to the dentist.

It wasn't until they were in the parking lot at the theater that Kristen spoke. "Nicole likes Tom Cruise, too."

Joanna made a noncommittal reply, wondering how easily the girls would see through her and Tanner's scheme.

"Mom," Kristen cried. "I see Nicole. She's with her dad. Oh, no, it looks like they're going to the same movie."

"Oh, no," Joanna echoed, her heart acting like a Ping-Pong ball in her chest. "Does this mean you want to skip the whole thing and go home?"

"Of course not," Kristen answered smugly. She practically bounded out of the car once Joanna turned off the engine, glancing anxiously at Joanna when she didn't walk across the parking lot fast enough to suit her.

They joined the line, about eight people behind Tanner and Nicole. Joanna was undecided about what to do next. She wasn't completely sure that Tanner had even seen her. If he had, he was playing his part perfectly, acting as though this whole thing had happened by coincidence.

Kristen couldn't seem to stand still. She peeked around the couple ahead of them several times, loudly humming the song of Heart's that she and Nicole had performed in the talent show.

Nicole whirled around, standing on her tiptoes and staring into the crowd behind her. She jerked on Tanner's sleeve and, when he bent down, whispered something in his ear. Then Tanner turned around, too, and pretended to be shocked when he saw Joanna and Kristen.

By the time they were inside the theater, Tanner and Nicole had disappeared. Kristen was craning her neck in every direction while Joanna stood at the refreshment counter.

"Do you want any popcorn?"

"No. Just some of those raisin things. Mom, you said I didn't have to sit with you. Did you really mean that?"

"Yes, honey, don't worry about it, I'll find a place by myself."

"You're sure?" Kristen looked only mildly concerned.

"No problem. You go sit by yourself."

"Okay." Kristen collected her candy and was gone before Joanna could say any more.

Since it was still several minutes before the movie was scheduled to start, the theater auditorium was well lit. Joanna found a seat toward the back and noted that Kristen was two rows from the front. Nicole sat in the row behind her.

"Is this seat taken?"

Joanna smiled up at Tanner as he claimed the seat next to her, and had they been anyplace else she was sure he would have kissed her. He handed her a bag of popcorn and a cold drink.

"I sure hope this works," he muttered under his breath, "because if Nicole sees me sitting with you, I could be hung as a traitor." Mischief brightened his eyes. "But the risk is worth it. Did anyone ever tell you how kissable your mouth looks?"

"Tanner," she whispered frantically and pointed toward the girls. "Look."

Kristen sat twisted around and Nicole leaned forward. Kristen shook a handful of her chocolate-covered raisins into Nicole's outstretched hand. Nicole offered Kristen some popcorn. After several of these exchanges, both girls stood up, moved from their seats to a different row entirely, sitting next to each other.

"That looks promising," Joanna whispered.

"It certainly does," Tanner agreed, slipping his arm around her shoulder.

They both watched as Kristen and Nicole tilted their heads toward each other and smiled at the sound of their combined giggles drifting to the back of the theater.

Thirteen

After their night at the movies, Joanna didn't give Tanner's invitation to the dinner party more than a passing thought until she read about the event on the society page of Wednesday's newspaper. The *Review* described the dinner, which was being sponsored by Spokane Aluminum, as the gala event of the year. Anyone who was anyone in the eastern half of Washington state would be attending. Until Joanna noticed the news article, she'd thought it was a small intimate party; that was the impression Tanner had given her.

From that moment on, Joanna started worrying, though she wasn't altogether sure why. As a loan officer, she'd attended her share of business-related social functions…but never anything of this scope. The problem, she decided, was one she'd been denying since the night of Nicole's slumber party. Tanner's social position and wealth far outdistanced her own. He was an important member of their community, and she was just a spoke in the wheel of everyday life.

Now, as she dressed for the event, her uneasiness grew, because she knew how important this evening was to Tanner—although he hadn't told her in so many words. The reception and dinner were all part of his becoming half owner of a major corporation and, according to the newspaper article, had been in the planning stages for several months after his arrival. All John Becky's way of introducing Tanner to the community leaders.

Within the first half hour of their arrival, Joanna recognized the mayor and a couple of members from the city council, plus several other people she didn't know, who nonetheless looked terribly important.

"Here," Tanner whispered, stepping to her side and handing her a glass of champagne.

Smiling up at him, she took the glass and held the dainty stem in a death grip, angry with herself for being so unnerved. It wasn't as though she'd never seen the mayor before—okay, only in pictures, but still… "I don't know if I dare have anything too potent," she admitted.

"Why not?"

"If you want the truth, I feel out of it at this affair. I'd prefer to fade into the background, mingle among the draperies, get acquainted with the wallpaper. That sort of thing."

Tanner's smile was encouraging. "No one would know it to look at you."

Joanna had trouble believing that. The smile she wore felt frozen on her lips, and her stomach protested the fact that she'd barely managed to eat all day. Tonight was important, and for Tanner's sake she'd do what she had to.

The man who owned the controlling interest in Columbia Basin Savings and Loan strolled past them and paused when he recognized her. Joanna nodded her recognition, and when he continued on she swallowed the entire glass of champagne in three giant gulps.

"I feel better," she announced.

"Good."

Tanner apparently hadn't noticed how quickly she'd downed the champagne, for which Joanna was grateful.

"Come over here. There are some people I want you to meet."

More people! Tanner had already introduced her to so many that the names were swimming around in her head like fish crowded in a small pond. She'd tried to keep them all straight, and it had been simple in the beginning when he'd started with his partner, John Becky, and John's wife, Jean, but from that point on her memory had deteriorated steadily.

Tanner pressed his hand to the middle of her spine and steered her across the room to where a small group had gathered.

Along the way, Joanna picked up another glass of champagne, just so she'd have something to do with her hands. The way she was feeling, she had no intention of drinking it.

The men and women paused in the middle of their conversation when Tanner approached. After a few words of greeting, introductions were made.

"Pleased to meet all of you," Joanna said, forcing some life into her fatigued smile. Everyone seemed to be looking at her, expecting something more. She nodded toward Tanner. "Our daughters are best friends."

The others smiled.

"I didn't know you had a daughter," a voluptuous blonde said, smiling sweetly up at Tanner.

"Nicole just turned twelve."

The blonde seemed fascinated with this information. "How very sweet. My niece is ten and I know she'd just love to meet Nicole. Perhaps we could get the two of them together. Soon."

"I'm sure Nicole would like that."

"It's a date then." She sidled as close to Tanner as she possibly could, practically draping her breast over his forearm.

Joanna narrowed her gaze and took a small sip of the champagne. The blonde, whose name was—she searched her mind—Blaise, couldn't have been any more obvious had she issued an invitation to her bed.

"Tanner, there's someone you must meet—that is, if I can drag you away from Joanna for just a little minute." The blonde cast a challenging look in Joanna's direction.

"Oh, sure." Joanna gestured with her hand as though to let Blaise know Tanner was free to do as he wished. She certainly didn't have any claims on him.

Tanner frowned. "Come with us," he suggested.

Joanna threw him what she hoped was a dazzling smile. "Go on. You'll only be gone a little minute," she said sweetly, purposely echoing Blaise's words.

The two left, Blaise clinging to Tanner's arm, and Joanna chatted with the others in the group for a few more minutes before fading into the background. Her stomach was twisted in knots. She didn't know why she'd sent Tanner off like that, when it so deeply upset her. Something in her refused to let him know that; it was difficult enough to admit even to herself.

Hoping she wasn't being obvious, her gaze followed Tanner and Blaise until she couldn't endure it any longer, and then she turned and made her way into the ladies' room. Joanna was grateful that the outer room was empty, and she slouched onto the sofa. Her heart was slamming painfully against her rib cage, and when she pressed her hands to her cheeks her face felt hot and feverish. Joanna would gladly have paid the entire three hundred and fifteen dollars in her savings account for a way to gracefully disappear.

It was then that she knew.

She was in love with Tanner Lund. Despite all the warnings she'd given herself. Despite the fact that they were worlds apart, financially and socially.

With the realization that she loved Tanner came another. The night had only begun—they hadn't even eaten yet. The ordeal of a formal dinner still lay before her.

"Hello again," Jean Becky said, strolling into the ladies' room. She stopped for a moment, watching Joanna, then sat down beside her.

"Oh, hi." Joanna managed the semblance of a smile to greet the likable older woman.

"I just saw Blaise Ferguson walk past clinging to Tanner. I hope you're not upset."

"Oh heavens, no," Joanna lied.

"Good. Blaise, er, has something of a reputation, and I didn't want you to worry. I'm sure Tanner's smart enough not to be taken in by someone that obvious."

"I'm sure he is, too."

"You're a sensible young woman," Jean said, looking pleased.

At the moment, Joanna didn't feel the least bit sensible. The one emotion she was experiencing was fear. She'd fallen in love again, and the first time had been so painful she had promised never to let it happen again. But it had. With Tanner Lund, yet. Why couldn't she have fallen for the mechanic who'd worked so hard repairing her car last winter, or someone at the office? Oh, no, she had to fall—and fall hard—for the most eligible man in town. The man every single woman in the party had her eye on this evening.

"It really has been a pleasure meeting you," Jean continued. "Tanner and Nicole talk about you and your daughter so often. We've been friends of Tanner's for several years now, and it gladdens our hearts to see him finally meet a good woman."

"Thank you." Joanna wasn't sure what to think about being classified as a "good woman." It made her wonder who Tanner had dated before he'd met her. She'd never asked him about his social life before he'd moved to Spokane—or even after. She wasn't sure she wanted to know. No doubt he'd made quite a splash when he came to town. Rich, handsome, available men were a rare commodity these days. It was a wonder he hadn't been snatched up long before now.

Five minutes later, Joanna had composed herself enough to rejoin the party. Tanner was at her side within a few seconds, noticeably irritable and short-tempered.

"I've been searching all over for you," he said, frowning heavily.

Joanna let that remark slide. "I thought you were otherwise occupied."

"Why'd you let that she-cat walk off with me like that?" His eyes were hot with fury. "Couldn't you tell I wanted out? Good Lord, woman, what do I have to do, flash flags?"

"No." A waiter walked past with a loaded tray, and Joanna deftly reached out and helped herself to another glass of champagne.

Just as smoothly, Tanner removed it from her fingers. "I think you've had enough."

Joanna took the glass back from him. She might not completely understand what was happening to her this evening, but she certainly didn't like his attitude. "Excuse me, Tanner, but I am perfectly capable of determining my own limit."

His frown darkened into a scowl. "It's taken me the last twenty minutes to extract myself from her claws. The least you could have done was stick around instead of doing a disappearing act."

"No way." Being married to Davey all those years had taught her more than one valuable lesson. If her ex-husband, Tanner, or any other man, for that matter, expected her to make a scene over another woman, it wouldn't work. Joanna was through with those kinds of destructive games.

"What do you mean by that?"

"I'm just not the jealous type. If you were to go home with Blaise, that'd be fine with me. In fact, you could leave with her right now. I'll grab a cab. I'm really not up to playing the role of a jealous girlfriend because another woman happens to show some interest in you. Nor am I willing to find a flimsy excuse to extract you from her clutches. You look more than capable of doing that yourself."

"You honestly want me to leave with Blaise?" His words were low and hard.

Joanna made a show of shrugging. "It's entirely up to you—you're free to do as you please. Actually you might be doing me a favor."

Joanna couldn't remember ever seeing a man more angry. His eyes seemed to spit fire at her. His jaws clamped together tightly, and he held himself with such an unnatural stiffness, it was surprising that something in his body didn't crack. She observed all this in some distant part of her mind, her concentration focused on preserving her facade of unconcern.

"I'm beginning to understand Davey," he said, his tone as cold as an arctic wind. "Has it ever occurred to you that your ex-husband turned to other women out of a desperate need to know you cared?"

Tanner's words hurt more than any physical blow could have. Joanna's breath caught in her throat, though she did her best to disguise the pain his remark had inflicted. When she was finally able to breathe, the words tumbled from her lips. "No. Funny, I never thought of that." She paused and searched the room. "Pick a woman, then, any woman will do, and I'll slug it out with her."

"Joanna, stop it," Tanner hissed.

"You mean you don't want me to fight?"

He closed his eyes as if seeking patience. "No."

Dramatically, Joanna placed her hand over her heart. "Thank goodness. I don't know how I'd ever explain a black eye to Kristen."

Dinner was about to be served, and, tucking his hand under her elbow, Tanner led Joanna into the banquet room, which was quickly filling up.

"I'm sorry, I didn't mean that about Davey," Tanner whispered as they strolled toward the dining room. "I realize you're nervous, but no one would ever know it—except me. We'll discuss this Blaise thing later."

Joanna nodded, feeling subdued now, accepting his apology. She realized that she'd panicked earlier, and not because this was an important social event, either. She'd attended enough business dinners in her career to know she hadn't made a fool of herself. What disturbed her so much was the knowledge that she'd fallen in love with Tanner.

To add to Joanna's dismay, she discovered that she was expected to sit at the head table between Tanner and John Becky. She trembled at the thought, but she wasn't about to let anyone see her nervousness.

"Don't worry," Tanner said, stroking her hand after they were seated. "Everyone who's met you has been impressed."

His statement was meant to lend her courage; unfortunately it had the opposite effect. What had she said or done to impress anyone?

When the evening was finally over, Tanner appeared to be as eager to escape as she was. With a minimum of fuss, they made their farewells and were gone.

Once in the car, Tanner didn't speak. But when he parked in front of the house, he turned off the car engine and said quietly, "Invite me in for coffee."

It was on the tip of Joanna's tongue to tell him she had a headache, which was fast becoming the truth, but delaying the inevitable wouldn't help either of them.

"Okay," she mumbled.

The house was quiet, and Sally was asleep on the sofa. Joanna paid her and waited on the front porch while the teenager ran across the street to her own house. Gathering her courage, she walked into the kitchen. Tanner had put the water and ground coffee into the machine and taken two cups down from the cupboard.

"Okay," he said, turning around to face her, "I want to know what's wrong."

The bewilderment in his eyes made Joanna raise her chin an extra notch. Then she remembered Kristen doing the same thing when she'd questioned her about her argument with Nicole, and the recollection wasn't comforting.

Joanna was actually surprised Tanner had guessed anything was wrong. She thought she'd done a brilliant job of disguising her distress. She'd done her best to say and do all the right things. When Tanner had stood up, after the meal, to give his talk, she'd whispered encouragement and smiled at him. Throughout the rest of the evening, she'd chatted easily with both Tanner and John Becky.

Now she had to try to explain something she barely understood herself.

"I don't think I ever realized what an important man you are," she said, struggling to find her voice. "I've always seen you as Nicole's father, the man who was crazy enough to agree to a slumber party for his daughter's birthday. The man who called and disguised his voice so Kristen wouldn't recognize it. That's the man I know, not the one tonight who stood before a filled banquet room and promised growth and prosperity for our city. Not the man who charts the destiny of an entire community."

Tanner glared at her. "What has that got to do with anything?"

"You play in the big league. I'm in the minors."

Tanner's gaze clouded with confusion. "I'm talking about our relationship and you're discussing baseball!"

Pulling out a kitchen chair, Joanna sat in it and took a deep breath. The best place to start, she decided, was the beginning. "You have to understand that I didn't come away from my marriage without a few quirks."

Tanner started pacing, clearly not in the mood to sit still. "Quirks? You call what happened with Blaise a quirk? I call it loony. Some woman I don't know from Adam comes up to me—"

"Eve," Joanna inserted, and when he stared at her, uncomprehending, she elaborated. "Since Blaise Ferguson's a woman, you don't know her from Eve."

"Whatever!"

"Well, it does make a difference." The coffee had finished filtering into the pot, so Joanna got up and poured them each a cup. Holding hers in both hands, she leaned against the counter and took a tentative sip.

"Some woman I don't know from Eve," Tanner tried again, "comes up to me, and you act as if you can't wait to get me out of your hair."

"*You* acted as if you expected me to come to your rescue. Honestly, Tanner, you're a big boy. I assumed you could take care of yourself."

"You looked more than happy to see me go with her."

"That's not true. I was content where I was." Joanna knew they were sidestepping the real issue, but this other business seemed to concern Tanner more.

"You were content to go into hiding."

"If you're looking for someone to fly into a jealous rage every time another woman winks at you, you'll need to look elsewhere."

Tanner did some more pacing, his steps growing longer and heavier with each circuit of the kitchen. "Explain what you meant when you said you didn't come away from your marriage without a few quirks."

"It's simply really," she said, making light of it. "Davey used to get a kick out of introducing me to his women friends. Everyone in the room knew what he was doing, except me. I was so stupid, so blind, that I just didn't know any better. Once the scales fell from my eyes, I was astonished at what a complete fool I'd been. But when I became wise to his ways, it was much worse. Every time he introduced me to a woman, I'd be filled with suspicion. Was Davey involved with her, or wasn't he? The only thing left for me to do was hold my head high and smile." Her voice was growing tighter with every word, cracking just as she finished.

Tanner walked toward her and reached out his hands as though to comfort her. "Joanna, listen—"

"No." She set her coffee aside and wrapped her arms around her middle. "I feel honored, Tanner, that you would ask me to attend this important dinner with you tonight. I think we both learned something valuable from the experience. At least, I know I did."

"Joanna—"

"No," she cut in again, "let me finish, please. Although it's difficult to say this, it needs to be said. We're not right for each other. We've been so caught up in everything we had in common and what good friends the girls are and how wonderful it felt to…be together, we didn't stop to notice that we live in different worlds." She paused and gathered her resolve before continuing. "Knowing you and becoming your friend has been wonderful, but anything beyond that just isn't going to work."

"The only thing I got carried away with was you, Joanna. The girls have nothing to do with it."

"I feel good that you would say that, I really do, but we both lost sight of the fact that neither one of us wants to become involved. That had never been our intention. Something happened, and I'm not sure when or why, but suddenly everything is so intense between us. It's got to stop before we end up really hurting each other."

Tanner seemed to mull over her words. "You're so frightened of giving another man the power to hurt you that you can't see anything else, can you?" His brooding, confused look was back. "I told you this once, but it didn't seem to sink into that head of yours—I'm never going to do the things Davey did. We're two entirely different men, and it's time you realized that."

"What you say may very well be true, Tanner, but I don't see what difference it's going to make. Because I have no intention of involving myself in another relationship."

"In case you hadn't noticed, Joanna, we're already involved."

"Roller-skating in the couples round doesn't qualify as being involved to me," she said, in a futile attempt at humor. It fell flat.

Tanner was the first to break the heavy silence that followed. "You've obviously got some thinking to do," he said wearily. "For that matter, so do I. Call me, Joanna, when you're in the mood to be reasonable."

Fourteen

"Hi, Mom," Kristen said, slumping down on the sofa beside Joanna. "I hope you know I'm bored out of my mind," she said, and sighed deeply.

Joanna was busy counting the stitches on her knitting needle and didn't pause to answer until she'd finished. "What about your homework?"

"Cute, Mom, real cute. It's spring break—I don't have any homework."

"Right. Phone Nicole, then. I bet she'll commiserate with you." And she might even give Kristen some information about Tanner. He'd walked out of her house, and although she'd thought her heart would break she'd let him go. Since then, she'd reconsidered. She was dying to hear something from Tanner. Anything. But she hadn't—not since the party more than a week earlier, and each passing day seemed like a lifetime.

"Calling Nicole is a nothing idea."

"I could suggest you clean your room."

"Funny, Mom, real funny."

"Gee, I'm funny and cute all in one evening. How'd I get so lucky?"

Not bothering to answer, Kristen reached for a magazine and idly thumbed through the pages, not finding a single picture or article worth more than a fleeting glance. She set it aside and reached for another. By the time she'd gone through the four magazines resting on top of the coffee table, Joanna was losing her patience.

"Call Nicole."

"I can't."

"Why not?"

"Because I can't."

That didn't make much sense to Joanna. And suggesting that Kristen phone Nicole was another sign of her willingness to settle this rift between her and Tanner. It had been so long since she'd last seen or heard from him. Ten interminable days, and with each one that passed she missed him more. She'd debated long and hard about calling him, wavering with indecision, battling with her pride. What she'd told him that night had been the truth—they did live in different worlds. But she'd overreacted at the dinner party, and now she felt guilty about how the evening had gone. When he'd left the house, Tanner had suggested she call him when she was ready to be reasonable. Well, she'd been ready the following morning, ready to acknowledge her fault. And her need. But pride held her back. And with each passing day, it became more difficult to swallow that pride.

"You know I can't call Nicole," Kristen whined.

"Why not? Did you have another argument?" Joanna asked without looking at her daughter. Her mind was preoccupied with counting stitches. She always knitted when she was frustrated with herself; it was a form of self-punishment, she suspected wryly.

"We never fight. Not anymore. Nicole's in West Virginia."

Joanna paused and carefully set the knitting needles down on her lap. "Oh? What's she doing there?"

"I think she went to visit her mother."

"Her mother?" It took some effort to keep her heart from exploding in her throat. According to Tanner, Nicole hadn't seen or heard from Carmen in three years. His biggest worry, he'd told her, was that someday his ex-wife would develop an interest in their daughter and steal her away from him. "Nicole is with her mother?" Joanna repeated, to be certain she'd heard Kristen correctly.

"You knew that."

"No, I didn't."

"Yes, you did. I told you she was leaving last Sunday. Remember?"

Vaguely, Joanna recalled the conversation—she'd been peeling potatoes at the sink—but for the last week, every time Kristen mentioned either Tanner or Nicole, Joanna had made an effort to tune her daughter out. Now she was hungry for information, starving for every tidbit Kristen was willing to feed her.

The eleven-year-old straightened and stared at her mother. "Didn't Mr. Lund mention Nicole was leaving?"

"Er, no."

Kristen sighed and threw herself against the back of the sofa. "You haven't been seeing much of him lately, have you?"

"Er, no."

Kristen picked up Joanna's hand and patted it gently. "You two had a fight?"

"Not exactly."

Her daughter's hand continued its soothing action. "Okay,

tell me all about it. Don't hold back a single thing—you need to talk this out. Bare your soul."

"Kristen!"

"Mom, you need this. Releasing your anger and frustration will help. You've got to work out all that inner agitation and responsive turbulence. It's disrupting your emotional poise. Seriously, Mom, have you ever considered Rolfing?"

"Emotional poise? Responsive turbulence? Where'd you hear about that? Where'd you hear about Rolfing?"

Kristen blinked and cocked her head to one side, doing her best to look concerned and sympathetic. "Oprah Winfrey."

"I see," Joanna muttered, and rolled her eyes.

"Are you or are you not going to tell me all about it?"

"No, I am not!"

Kristen released a deep sigh that expressed her keen disappointment. "I thought not. When it comes to Nicole's dad, you never want to talk about it. It's like a deep dark secret the two of you keep from Nicole and me. Well, that's all right—we're doing our best to understand. You don't want us to get our hopes up that you two might be interested in each other. I can accept that, although I consider it grossly unfair." She stood up and gazed at her mother with undisguised longing, then loudly slapped her hands against her sides. "I'm perfectly content to live the way we do…but it sure would be nice to have a baby sister to dress up. And you know how I've *always* wanted a brother."

"Kristen!"

"No, Mom." She held up her hand as though she were stopping a freight train. "Really, I do understand. You and I get along fine the way we are. I guess we don't need to complicate our lives with Nicole and her dad. That could even cause real problems."

For the first time, her daughter was making sense.

"Although heaven knows, I can't remember what it's like to be part of a *real* family."

"Kristen, that's enough," Joanna cried, shaking her head. Her daughter was invoking so much guilt that Joanna was beginning to hear violins in the background. "You and I *are* a real family."

"But, Mom, it could be so much better." Kristen sank down beside Joanna again and crossed her legs. Obviously her argument had long since been prepared, and without pausing to breathe between sentences, she proceeded to list the advantages of joining the two families.

"Kristen—"

Once more her daughter stopped her with an outstretched hand, as she started on her much shorter list of possible disadvantages. There was little Joanna could do to stem the rehearsed speech. Impatiently she waited for Kristen to finish.

"I don't want to talk about Tanner again," Joanna said in a no-nonsense tone of voice reserved for instances such as this. "Not a single word. Is that clearly understood?"

Kristen turned round sad eyes on her mother. The fun and laughter seemed to drain from her face as she glared back at Joanna. "Okay—if that's what you really want."

"It is, Kristen. Not a single word."

Banning his name from her daughter's lips and banning his name from her own mind were two entirely different things, Joanna decided an hour later. The fact that Nicole was visiting Carmen concerned her—not that she shared Tanner's worries. But knowing Tanner, he was probably beside himself worrying that Carmen would want their daughter to come and live with her.

It took another half hour for Joanna to build up enough courage to phone Tanner. He answered on the second ring.

"Hello, Tanner…it's Joanna." Even that was almost more than she could manage.

"Joanna." Just the way he said her name revealed his delight in hearing from her.

Joanna was grateful that he didn't immediately bring up the dinner party and the argument that had followed. "How have you been?"

"Good. How about you?"

"Just fine," she returned awkwardly. She leaned against the wall, crossing and uncrossing her ankles. "Listen, the reason I phoned is that Kristen told me Nicole was with her mother, and I thought you might be in need of a divorced-parent prep talk."

"What I really need is to see you. Lord, woman, it took you long enough. I thought you were going to make me wait forever. Ten days can be a very long time, Joanna. Ten whole days!"

"Tanner—"

"Can we meet someplace?"

"I'm not sure." Her mind struggled with a list of excuses, but she couldn't deny how lonely and miserable she'd been, how badly she wanted to feel his arms around her. "I'd have to find someone to sit with Kristen, and that could be difficult at the last minute like this."

"I'll come to you, then."

It was part question, part statement, and again, she hesitated. "All right," she finally whispered.

The line went oddly silent. When Tanner spoke again there was a wealth of emotion in his words, although his voice was quiet. "I'm glad you phoned, Joanna."

She closed her eyes, feeling weak and shaky. "I am, too," she said softly.

"I'll be there within half an hour."

"I'll have coffee ready."

When she replaced the receiver, her hand was trembling, and it was as though she were twenty-one again. Her heart was pounding out of control just from the sound of his voice, her head swimming with the knowledge that she'd be seeing him in a few minutes. How wrong she'd been to assume that if she put him out of her sight and mind she could keep him out of her heart, too. How foolish she'd been to deny her feelings. She loved this man, and it wouldn't matter if he owned the company or swept the floors.

Joanna barely had time to refresh her makeup and drag a brush through her hair. Kristen had been in her room for the past hour without a sound; Joanna sincerely hoped she was asleep.

She'd just poured water into the coffeemaker when the doorbell chimed.

The bedroom door flew open, and Kristen appeared in her pajamas, wide-awake. "I'll get it," she yelled.

Joanna started to call after her, but it was too late. With a resigned sigh, she stood in the background and waited for her daughter to admit Tanner.

Kristen turned to face her mother, wearing a grin as wide as the Mississippi River. "It's that man whose name I'm not supposed to mention ever again."

"Yes, I know."

"You know?"

Joanna nodded.

"Good. Talk it out with him, Mom. Relieve yourself of all that inner stuff. Get rid of that turmoil before it eats you alive."

Joanna cast a weak smile in Tanner's direction, then turned her attention to Kristen. "Isn't it your bedtime, young lady?"

"No."

Joanna's eyes narrowed. "Yes, it is."

"But, Mom, it's spring break, so I can sleep in tomorrow— Oh, I get it, you want me out of here."

"In your room reading or listening to a cassette should do nicely."

Kristen beamed her mother a broad smile. "'Night, Mom. 'Night…Nicole's dad."

"'Night."

With her arms swinging at her sides, Kristen strolled out of the living room. Tanner waited until they heard her bedroom door shut, then he started across the carpet toward Joanna. He stopped suddenly, frowning. "She wasn't supposed to say my name?"

Joanna gave a weak half shrug, her gaze holding his. No man had ever looked better. His eyes seemed to caress her with a tenderness and aching hunger that did crazy things to her equilibrium.

"It's so good to see you," she said, her voice unsteady. She took two steps toward him.

When Tanner reached for her, a heavy sigh broke from his lips and the tension left his muscles. "Dear Lord, woman, ten days you left me dangling." He said more, but his words were muffled in the curve of her neck as he crushed her against his chest.

Joanna soaked up his warmth, and when his lips found hers she surrendered with a soft sigh of joy. Being in Tanner's arms was like coming home after a long journey and discovering the comfort in all that's familiar. It was like walking in sunshine after a bad storm, like holding the first rose of summer in her hand.

Again and again his mouth sought hers in a series of passionate kisses, as though he couldn't get enough of the taste of her.

The creaky sound of a bedroom door opening caused Joanna to break away from him. "It's Kristen," she murmured, her voice little more than a whisper.

"I know, but I don't care." Tanner kept her close for a moment longer. "Okay," he breathed, and slowly stroked the top of her head with his chin. "We need to settle a few things. Let's talk."

Joanna led him into the kitchen, since they were afforded the most privacy there. She automatically took down two cups and poured them each some coffee. They sat at the small table, directly across from each other, but even that seemed much too far.

"First, tell me about Nicole," she said, her eyes meeting his. "Are you worried now that she's with Carmen?"

A sad smile touched the edges of Tanner's mouth. "Not particularly. Carmen, who prefers to be called Rama Sheba now, contacted my parents at the end of last week. According to my mother, the reason we haven't heard from her in the past three years is that Carmen's been on a long journey in India and Nepal. Apparently Carmen went halfway around the world searching for herself. I guess she found what she was looking for, because she's back in the United States and inquiring about Nicole."

"Oh, dear. Do you think she wants Nicole to come live with her?"

"Not a chance. Carmen, er, Rama Sheba, doesn't want a child complicating her life. She never did. Nicole wanted to see her mother and that's understandable, so I sent her back to West Virginia for a visit with my parents. While she's there, Carmen will spend an afternoon with her."

"What happened to…Rama Sheba and the baseball player?"

"Who knows? He may have joined her in her wanderings, for all I know. Or care. Carmen plays such a minor role in my life now that I haven't the energy to second-guess her. She's free to do as she likes, and I prefer it that way. If she wants to visit Nicole, fine. She can see her daughter—she has the right."

"Do you love her?" The question sounded abrupt and tactless, but Joanna needed to know.

"No," he said quickly, then grinned. "I suppose I feel much the same way about her as you do about Davey."

"Then, you don't hate her?" she asked next, not looking at him.

"No."

Joanna ran a fingertip along the rim of her cup and smiled. "Good."

"Why's that good?"

She lifted her eyes to meet his and smiled a little shyly. "Because if you did have strong feelings for her it would suggest some unresolved emotion."

Tanner nodded. "As illogical as it sounds, I don't feel anything for Carmen. Not love, not hate—nothing. If something bad were to happen to her, I suppose I'd feel sad, but I don't harbor any resentments toward her."

"That's what I was trying to explain to you the afternoon you dropped by when Davey was here. Other people have a hard time believing this, especially my parents, but I honestly wish him success in life. I want him to be happy, although I doubt he ever will be." Davey wasn't a man who would ever be content. He was always looking for something more, something better.

Tanner nodded.

Once more, Joanna dropped her gaze to the steaming coffee. "Calling you and asking about Nicole was only an excuse, you know."

"Yes. I just wish you'd come up with it a few days earlier. As far as I'm concerned, waiting for you to come to your senses took nine days too long."

"I—"

"I know, I know," Tanner said before she could list her excuses. "Okay, let's talk."

Joanna managed a smile. "Where do we start?"

"How about with what happened the night of the party?"

Instantly Joanna's stomach knotted. "Yes, well, I guess I should be honest and let you know I was intimidated by how important you are. It shook me, Tanner, really shook me. I'm not used to seeing you as chairman of the board. And then later, when you strolled off with Blaise, those old wounds from my marriage with Davey started to bleed."

"I suppose I did all the wrong things. Maybe I should have insisted you come with me when Blaise dragged me away, but—"

"No, that wouldn't have worked, either."

"I should have guessed how you'd feel after being married to Davey."

"You had no way of knowing." Now came the hard part. "Tanner," she began, and was shocked at how thin and weak her voice sounded, "I was so consumed with jealousy that I just about went crazy when Blaise wrapped her arms around you. It frightened me to have to deal with those negative emotions again. I know I acted like an idiot, hiding like that, and I'd like to apologize."

"Joanna, it isn't necessary."

She shook her head. "I don't mean this as an excuse, but you need to understand why I was driven to behave the way I did. I'd thought I was beyond that—years beyond acting like a jealous fool. I promised myself I'd never allow a man to do it to me again." In her own way, Joanna was trying to tell him how much she loved him, but the words weren't coming out right.

He frowned at that. "Jealous? You were jealous? Good Lord, woman, you could have fooled me. You handed me over to Blaise without so much as a hint of regret. From the way you were behaving, I thought you *wanted* to be rid of me."

The tightness in Joanna's throat made talking difficult. "I already explained why I did that."

"I know. The way I acted when I saw your ex here was the other kind of jealous reaction—the raging-bull kind. I think I see now where *your* kind of reaction came from. I'm not sure which one is worse, but I think mine is." He smiled ruefully, and a silence fell between them.

"Could this mean you have some strong feelings for me, Joanna Parsons?"

A smile quirked at the corners of her mouth. "You're the only man I've ever eaten Oreos over."

The laughter in Tanner's eyes slowly faded. "We could have the start of something very important here, Joanna. What do you think?"

"I…I think you may be right."

"Good." Tanner looked exceedingly pleased with this turn of events. "That's exactly what I wanted to hear."

Joanna thought—no, hoped—that he intended to lean over and kiss her. Instead his brows drew together darkly over brooding blue eyes. "Okay, where do we go from here?"

"Go?" Joanna repeated, feeling uncomfortable all of a sudden. "Why do we have to go anywhere?"

Tanner looked surprised. "Joanna, for heaven's sake, when a man and a woman feel about each other the way we do, they generally make plans."

"What do you mean 'feel about each other the way we do'?"

Tanner's frown darkened even more. "You love me."

Only a few moments before, Joanna would have willingly admitted it, but silly as it sounded, she wanted to hear Tanner say the words first. "I…I…"

"If you have to think about it, then I'd say you obviously don't know."

"But I do know," she said, lifting her chin a notch higher. "I'm just not sure this is the time to do anything about it. You may think my success is insignificant compared to yours, but I've worked damn hard to get where I am. I've got the house I saved for years to buy, and my career is starting to swing along nicely, and Robin—he's my boss—let me know that I was up for promotion. My goal of becoming the first female senior loan officer at the branch is within sight."

"And you don't want to complicate your life right now with a husband and second family?"

"I didn't say that."

"It sure sounded like it to me."

Joanna swallowed. The last thing in the world she wanted to do was argue with Tanner. Craziest of all, she wasn't even sure what they were arguing about. Thcy were in love with each other and both just too damn proud. "I don't think we're getting anywhere with this conversation."

Tanner braced his elbows on the table and folded his hands. "I'm beginning to agree with you. All week, I've been waiting for you to call me, convinced that once you did, everything between us would be settled. I wanted us to start building a life together, and all of a sudden you're Ms. Career Woman, and about as independent as they come."

"I haven't changed. You just didn't know me."

His lips tightened. "I guess you're right. I don't know you at all, do I?"

"Mom, Mom, come quick!"

Joanna's warm cozy dream was interrupted by Kristen's shrieks. She rolled over and glared at the digital readout on her clock radio. Five. In the morning. "Kristen?" She sat straight up in bed.

"Mom!"

The one word conveyed such panic that Joanna's heart rushed to her throat and she threw back her covers, running barefoot into the hallway. Almost immediately, her feet encountered ice-cold water.

"Something's wrong," Kristen cried, hopping up and down. "The water won't stop."

That was the understatement of the year. From the way the water was gushing out of the bathroom door and into the hallway, it looked as though a dam had burst.

"Grab some towels," Joanna cried, pointing toward the hallway linen closet. The hems of her long pajamas were already damp. She scooted around her daughter, who was standing in the doorway, still hopping up and down like a crazed kangaroo.

Further investigation showed that the water was escaping from the cabinet under the sink.

"Mom, Mom, here!" Dancing around, Kristen threw her

a stack of towels that separated in midair and landed in every direction.

"Kristen!" Joanna snapped, squatting down in front of the sink. She opened the cabinet and was immediately hit by a wall of foaming bubbles. The force of the flowing water had knocked over her container of expensive bubble bath and spilled its contents. "You were in my bubble bath!" Joanna cried.

"I… How'd you know?"

"The cap's off, and now it's everywhere!"

"I just used a little bit."

Three bars of Ivory soap, still in their wrappers, floated past Joanna's feet. Heaven only knew what else had been stored under the sink or where it was headed now.

"I'm sorry about the bubble bath," Kristen said defensively. "I figured you'd get mad if you found out, but a kid needs to know what luxury feels like, too, you know."

"It's all right, we can't worry about that now." Joanna waved her hands back and forth trying to disperse the bubbles enough to assess the damage. It didn't take long to determine that a pipe had burst. With her forehead pressing against the edge of the sink, Joanna groped inside the cabinet for the knob to turn off the water supply. Once she found it, she twisted it furiously until the flowing water dwindled to a mere trickle.

"Kristen!" Joanna shouted, looking over her shoulder. Naturally, when she needed her, her daughter disappeared. "Get me some more towels. Hurry, honey!"

A couple of minutes later, Kristen reappeared, her arms loaded with every towel and washcloth in the house. "Yuck," she muttered, screwing her face into a mask of sheer disgust. "What a mess!"

"Did any water get into the living room?"

Kristen nodded furiously. "But only as far as the front door."

"Great." Joanna mumbled under her breath. Now she'd need to phone someone about coming in to dry out the carpet.

On her hands and knees, sopping up as much water as she could, Joanna was already soaked to the skin herself.

"You need help," her daughter announced.

The child was a master of observation. "Change out of those wet things first, Kristen, before you catch your death of cold."

"What about you?"

"I'll dry off as soon as I get some of this water cleaned up."

"Mom—"

"Honey, just do as I ask. I'm not in any mood to argue with you."

Joanna couldn't remember ever seeing a bigger mess in her life. Her pajamas were soaked; bubbles were popping around her head—how on earth had they got into her hair? She sneezed violently, and reached for a tissue that quickly dissolved in her wet hands.

"Here, use this."

The male voice coming from behind her surprised Joanna so much that when she twisted around, she lost her footing and slid down into a puddle of the coldest water she'd ever felt.

"Tanner!" she cried, leaping to her feet. "What are you doing here?"

Fifteen

Dumbfounded, Joanna stared at Tanner, her mouth hanging open and her eyes wide.

"I got this frantic phone call from Kristen."

"Kristen?"

"The one and only. She suggested I hurry over here before something drastic happened." Tanner took one step toward her and lovingly brushed a wet tendril away from her face. "How's it going, Tugboat Annie?"

"A pipe under the sink broke. I've got it under control now—I think." Her pajamas hung limply at her ankles, dripping water onto her bare feet. Her hair fell in wet spongy curls around her face, and Joanna had never felt more like bursting into tears in her life.

"Kristen shouldn't have phoned you," she said, once she found her voicc.

"I'm glad she did. It's nice to know I can be useful every now and again." Heedless of her wet state, he wrapped his arms around Joanna and brought her close, gently pressing her damp head to his chest.

A chill went through her and she shuddered. Tanner felt so warm and vital, so concerned and loving. She'd let him think she was this strong independent woman, and normally she was, but when it came to broken pipes and floods and things like that, she crumbled into bite-sized pieces. When it came to Tanner Lund, well…

"You're soaked to the skin," he whispered, close to her ear.

"I know."

"Go change. I'll take over here."

The tears started then, silly ones that sprang from somewhere deep inside her and refused to be stopped. "I can't get dry," she sobbed, wiping furiously at the moisture that rained down her face. "There aren't any dry towels left in this entire house."

Tanner jerked his water-blotched tan leather jacket off and placed it around her shoulders. "Honey, don't cry. Please. Everything's going to be all right. It's just a broken pipe, and I can have it fixed for you before noon—possibly sooner."

"I can't help it," she bellowed, and to her horror, hiccuped. She threw a hand over her mouth and leaned her forehead against his strong chest. "It's five o'clock in the morning, my expensive Giorgio bubble bath is ruined, and I'm so much in love I can't think straight."

Tanner's hands gripped her shoulders and eased her away so he could look her in the eye. "What did you just say?"

Joanna hung her head as low as it would go, bracing her weight against Tanner's arms. "My Giorgio bubble bath is ruined." The words wobbled out of her mouth like a rubber ball tumbling down stairs.

"Not that. I want to hear the other part, about being so much in love."

Joanna sniffled. "What about it?"

"What about it? Good Lord, woman, I was here not more than eight hours ago wearing my heart on my sleeve like a schoolboy. You were so casual about everything, I thought you were going to open a discussion on stock options."

"*You* were the one who was so calm and collected about everything, as if what happened between us didn't really matter to you." She rubbed her hand under her nose and sniffled loudly. "Then you made everything sound like a forgone conclusion and—"

"I was nervous. Now, shall we give it another try? I want to marry you, Joanna Parsons. I want you to share my life, maybe have my babies. I want to love you until we're both old and gray. I've even had fantasies about us traveling around the country in a mobile home to visit our grandchildren!"

"You want grandkids?" Timidly, she raised her eyes to his, almost afraid to believe what he was telling her.

"I'd prefer to take this one step at a time. The first thing I want to do is marry you. I couldn't have made that plainer than I did a few hours ago."

"But—"

"Stop right now, before we get sidetracked. First things first. Are you and Kristen going to marry me and Nicole?"

"I think we should," the eleven-year-old said excitedly from the hallway, looking smugly pleased with the way things were going. "I mean, it's been obvious to Nicole and me for ages that you two were meant to be together." Kristen sighed and slouched against the wall, crossing her arms over her chest with the sophistication that befitted someone of superior intelligence. "There's only one flaw in this plan."

"Flaw?" Joanna echoed.

"Yup," Kristen said, nodding with unquestionable confidence. "Nicole is going to be mad as hops when she finds out she missed this."

Tanner frowned, and then he chuckled. "Oh, boy. I think Kristen could be right. We're going to have to stage a second proposal."

Feeling slightly piqued, Joanna straightened. "Listen, you two, I never said I was going to marry anybody—yet."

"Of course you're going to marry Mr. Lund," Kristen inserted smoothly. "Honestly, Mom, now isn't the time to play hard to get."

"Wh-what?" Stunned, Joanna stood there staring at her daughter. Her gaze flew from Kristen to Tanner and then back to Kristen.

"She's right, you know," said Tanner.

"I can't believe I'm hearing this." Joanna was standing in a sea of wet towels, while her daughter and the man she loved discussed her fate as though she was to play only a minor role in it.

"We've got to think of a way to include Nicole," Tanner said thoughtfully.

"I am going to change my clothes," Joanna murmured, eager to escape.

"Good idea," Tanner answered, without looking at her.

Joanna stomped off to her bedroom and slammed the door. She discarded her pajamas and, shivering, reached for a thick wool sweater and blue jeans.

Tanner and Kristen were still in the bathroom doorway, discussing details, when Joanna reappeared. She moved silently around them and into the kitchen, where she made a pot of coffee. Then she gathered up the wet towels, hauled them onto the back porch, threw them into the washer and started the machine. By the time she returned to the kitchen, Tanner had joined her there.

"Uh-oh. Trouble," he said, watching her abrupt angry movements. "Okay, tell me what's wrong now."

"I don't like the way you and my daughter are planning my life," she told him point-blank. "Honestly, Tanner, I haven't even agreed to marry you, and already you and Kristen have got the next ten years all figured out."

He stuck his hands in his pants pockets. "It's not that bad."

"Maybe not, but it's bad enough. I'm letting you know right now that I'm not about to let you stage a second proposal just so Nicole can hear it. To be honest, I'm not exactly thrilled about Kristen being part of this one. A marriage proposal is supposed to be private. And romantic, with flowers and music, not…not in front of a busted pipe with bath bubbles popping around my head and my family standing around applauding."

"Okay, what do you suggest?"

"I don't know yet."

Tanner looked disgruntled. "If you want the romance, Joanna, that's fine. I'd be more than happy to give it to you."

"Every woman wants romance."

Tanner walked toward her then and took her in his arms, and until that moment Joanna had no idea how much she did, indeed, want it.

Her eyes were drawn to his. Everything about Tanner Lund fascinated her, and she raised her hand to lightly caress the proud strong line of his jaw. She really did love this man. His eyes, blue and intense, met hers, and a tiny shiver of awareness went through her. His arms circled her waist, and then he lifted her off the ground so that her gaze was level with his own.

Joanna gasped a little at the unexpectedness of his action. Smiling, she looped her arms around his neck.

Tanner kissed her then, with a hunger that left her weak and clinging in its aftermath.

"How's that?" he asked, his voice husky.

"Better. Much better."

"I thought so." Once more his warm mouth made contact with hers. Joanna was startled and thrilled at the intensity of his touch. He kissed her again and again, until she thought that if he released her, she'd fall to the floor and melt at his feet. Every part of her body was heated to fever pitch.

"Joanna—"

She planted warm moist kisses across his face, not satisfied, wanting him until her heart felt as if it might explode. Tanner had awoken the sensual part of her nature, buried all the years since her divorce, and now that it had been stirred back to life, she felt starved for a man's love—this man's love.

"Yes," she breathed into his mouth. "Yes, yes, yes."

"Yes what?" he asked in a breathless murmur.

Joanna paused and smiled gently. "Yes, I'll marry you. Right now. Okay? This minute. We can fly somewhere…find a church… Oh, Tanner," she pleaded, "I want you so much."

"Joanna, we can't." His words came out in a groan, forced from deep inside him.

She heard him, but it didn't seem to matter. She kissed him and he kissed her. Their kiss continued as he lowered her to the floor, her body sliding intimately down his.

Suddenly Joanna realized what she'd just said, what she'd suggested. "We mustn't. Kristen—"

Tanner shushed her with another kiss, then said, "I know, love. This isn't the time or place, but I sure wish…"

Joanna straightened, and broke away. Shakily, she said, "So do I…and, uh, I think we should wait a while for the wedding. At least until Nicole gets back."

"Right."

"How long will that be?"

"The end of the week."

Joanna nodded and closed her eyes. It sounded like an eternity.

"What about your job?"

"I don't want to work forever, and when we decide to start a family I'll probably quit. But I want that promotion first." Joanna wasn't sure exactly why that was so important to her, but it was. She'd worked years for this achievement, and she had no intention of walking away until she'd become the first female senior loan officer.

Tanner kissed her again. "If it makes you happy keep your job as long as you want."

At that moment, however, all Joanna could think about were babies, family vacations and homemade cookies.

"That's her plane now," Tanner said to Kristen, pointing toward the Boeing jet that was approaching the long narrow landing strip at Spokane International.

"I get to tell her, okay?"

"I think Tanner should do it, sweetheart," Joanna suggested gently.

"But Nicole and I are best friends. You can't expect me to keep something like this from her, something we planned since that night we all went to the Pink Palace. If it weren't for us, you two wouldn't even know each other."

Kristen's eyes were round and pleading as she stared up at Tanner and Joanna.

"You two would have been cast adrift in a sea of loneliness if it hadn't been for me and Nicole," she added melodramatically.

"All right, all right," Tanner said with a sigh. "You can tell her."

Poised at the railing by the window of the terminal, Kristen eagerly studied each passenger who stepped inside. The minute Nicole appeared, Kristen flew into her friend's arms as though it had been years since they'd last seen each other instead of a week.

Joanna watched the unfolding scene with a quiet sense of happiness. Nicole let out a squeal of delight and gripped her friend around the shoulders, and the two jumped frantically up and down.

"From her reaction, I'd guess that she's happy about our decision," Tanner said to Joanna.

"Dad, Dad!" Nicole raced up to her father, and hugged him with all her might. "It's so good to be home. I missed you. I missed everyone," she said, looking at Joanna.

Tanner returned the hug. "It's good to have you home, cupcake."

"But everything exciting happened while I was away," she said, pouting a little. "Gee, if I'd known you were finally going to get rolling with Mrs. Parsons, I'd never have left."

Joanna smiled blandly at the group of people standing around them.

"Don't be mad," Kristen said. "It was a now-or-never situation, with Mom standing there in her pajamas and everything."

Now it was Tanner's turn to notice the interested group of onlookers.

"Yes, well, you needn't feel left out. I saved the best part for you," Tanner said, taking a beautiful solitaire diamond ring out of his pocket. "I wanted you to be here for this." He reached for Joanna's hand, looking into her eyes, as he slowly, reverently, slipped it onto her finger. "I love you, Joanna, and I'll be the happiest man alive if you marry me."

"I love you, Tanner," she said in a soft voice filled with joy.

"Does this mean we're going to be sisters from now on?" Kristen shrieked, clutching her best friend's hand.

"Yup," Nicole answered. "It's what we always wanted."

With their arms wrapped around one another's shoulders, the girls headed toward the baggage-claim area.

"Yours and mine," Joanna said, watching their two daughters.

Tanner slid his arm around her waist and smiled into her eyes.

* * * * *

Loved this book?

Visit Debbie Macomber's fantastic website at **www.debbiemacomber.com** for information about Debbie, her latest books, news, competitions, knitting tips, recipes, Debbie's blog and much more…

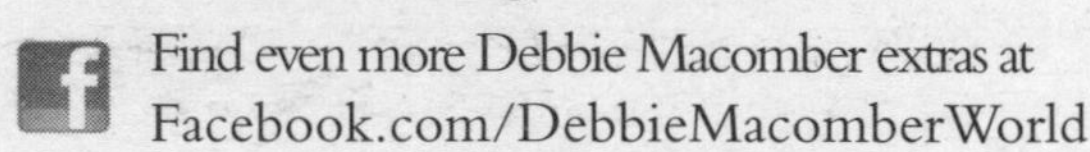

Find even more Debbie Macomber extras at Facebook.com/DebbieMacomberWorld

www.debbiemacomber.com